FINAL DUTY

Also by Paul Carson

Scalpel
Cold Steel

Final Duty

Paul Carson

WILLIAM HEINEMANN : LONDON

First published in the Republic of Ireland and the United Kingdom in 2000 by
William Heinemann

3 5 7 9 10 8 6 4

William Heinemann
The Random House Group Limited
20 Vauxhall Bridge Road, London SW1V 2SA

Random House Australia (Pty) Limited
20 Alfred Street, Milsons Point, Sydney, New South Wales 2061, Australia

Random House New Zealand Limited
18 Poland Road, Glenfield
Auckland 10, New Zealand

Random House (Pty) Limited
Endulini, 5a Jubilee Road, Parktown 2193, South Africa

The Random House Group Limited Reg. No. 954009

www.randomhouse.co.uk

A CIP catalogue record for this book is available from the British Library

Papers used by Random House are natural, recyclable products made from wood grown in sustainable forests. The manufacturing processes conform to the environmental regulations of the country of origin

Typeset by SX Composing DTP, Rayleigh, Essex
Printed and bound in the United Kingdom by
Clays Ltd, St. Ives plc, Bungay, Suffolk

ISBN 0 434 00845 1 (Ireland only)
ISBN 0 434 00815 X

To Jean, Emily and David.
Because they're worth it.

Acknowledgements

Chicago
Dr Sean Callan is a pychiatrist, playwright and columnist for the *Irish Medical Times*. He introduced me to his beautiful city and guided me through its highlights and midlights, and even the lowlights. Dr Callan explained the complexities of medical care as practised in North America and advised on technical details throughout. In truth this book would have been much more difficult and time-consuming to complete without his assistance.
Also: Dr Clair Callan, Vice-President for Science, American Medical Assn; Arnie Swerdlow, Chief of Surgery, North Chicago VA; Bruce Bergelson M.D., attending physician at the Rush North Shore Hospital, and the staff of its cardiac unit; John Barrett M.D., Director of Trauma Services at Cook County Hospital; Ed Donoghue M.D., Chief Medical Examiner for Cook County (one visit to his department on a gloomy October morning scared the hell out of me for life).

Dublin
Liam Mulligan, Chief Pilot with Airlink Airways, explained the intricacies of flying a Cessna 340; David Sheppard, Chief Pilot with Irish Air Transport, shared his experiences of flying within North America; Michael McGrath, manager, Knock Airport in Ireland.

To all I offer my thanks for their time, effort and experience shared so ungrudgingly.
Any mistakes within the text are mine and mine alone.

Paul Carson, August 2000
Dublin

1

Dr Jack Hunt was drafting his letter of resignation when the assassin entered the building.

A laminated nametag proclaimed her as Dr E. Berenski, a senior attending in Invasive Cardiology at Chicago's Carter Hospital. It was stuck crookedly to the breast pocket of her grimy white coat. The false identity and disguise had been supplied by an outsider; the bogus doctor's real name was Kate Hanzek, a thirty-two-year-old contract killer flown in from Denver to stalk and now kill her prey. She'd waited until an ambulance screeched into the Carter's emergency room bay, then shadowed the frenzied, blood-stained chase as a limp body was stretchered inside. Stethoscope swung around neck, navy scrubs under white coat, she looked the typical ER doctor.

'Out of the way, out of the goddamned way,' shouted one of the paramedics, 'the kid's bleeding to death.'

No one noticed Hanzek. No one was looking, all attention focused on the injuries to the young boy dragged from under the wheels of a stolen car crashed near one of the city's rundown projects.

'He's in shock. We couldn't even get an IV line,' another attendant cried as the heavy-duty wooden swing doors of the trauma room burst open. 'His chest's caved in.'

A surgical team swung into action. IV lines, drainage tubes and oxygen masks were pulled closer. 'Give him a litre of Crystalloid stat, we'll need bloods for group and cross-matching.' Fevered instructions filled the air as the medics struggled to stabilise the mutilated body.

Carter Hospital held the city's main paediatric trauma

department. Located on a corner site on W Harrison in the middle of Chicago's tight cluster of top medical facilities, the institution prided itself on its success statistics. But like every large organisation it had a constantly changing staff. Strange faces came and left almost as frequently as the ambulances ferrying the injured and wounded of the south and west inner city and suburbs, so Kate Hanzek soon merged with the hospital traffic on street level.

On the ninth floor, where the Heart Unit was based, Jack Hunt struggled to find the exact words. *Dear Professor Lewins, with some reluctance I voice my disquiet at certain practices within the Carter cardiology department.* The page was scrunched and trashed. First of all, Jack thought, he's not dear, and secondly, I don't think he gives a shit what's going on here.

He sat back in his chair and sighed, then reached for a fresh page. He glanced at the photo on his office desk, young wife and eight-year-old boy looking out, both laughing. It's for you guys, okay? If I have to quit this'll be the final move, I promise.

He started writing again. *Professor Lewins, it is with some regret that I inform you . . .'*

Hanzek reached the ground-floor elevators and squeezed in beside an elderly man in a wheelchair being pushed by an orderly. The attendant glanced at her briefly. 'What level?'

She didn't hesitate. 'Nine. Heart Unit.'

A nicotine-stained finger pressed six and nine, and two lights glowed.

She touched the handgun tucked inside an inner pocket, reassured by its hardness through the thin cloth against her skin. She had chosen a Heckler & Koch P7, a nine-millimetre pistol with a four-inch barrel and nickel finish. This was an expensive weapon, about a thousand dollars on the legitimate market and not the type used in most street crimes. It had served her well before. Hanzek moved her elbow to cover the bulge.

She rested her forehead on an open palm and kept the position until the doors opened at six. She even helped push the wheelchair outside and tucked the edge of the dressing gown under the old man's leg.

'Thanks doctor,' he mumbled before the doors shut across.

'No problem,' she returned, smiling slightly. Hanzek pressed the button again to be sure and felt the comforting jerk as the elevator shifted upwards. Apart from the smell of hospital disinfectant irritating her nostrils, everything was going to plan. She checked her watch: 1.15 exactly. On time, no glitches, no random security checks. No need to fall back on scheme two. The final agreed strategy was turning out just fine.

Since arriving here I have been frustrated and disappointed with apathy in the research department, indifferent medical standards and lack of leadership. I had expected more from a hospital with such a strong national reputation.

Jack Hunt paused, his pen hovering above the page. He searched for the words to emphasise his anger and disappointment. Another wasted year, maybe another career move looming.

Now aged thirty-nine, Jack had devoted his professional life to the study of heart disease in medical centres of excellence around the world. Sydney, London, Dublin, Philadelphia and, just before the move to Chicago, New York. In each facility he had collected extra qualifications and produced top-class research papers. He'd been approached five times with important job offers but had refused each one because the research programme wasn't sufficiently challenging. Equally he was well aware of the top spots for which he'd been passed over. He was no team player and cared little for the financial trappings of a lucrative private cardiology practice. He was an academic, research-driven and never more happy than when pondering the mysteries of medical science. Naïve, that's how one hospital chief had described him. And his restlessness had cost dearly. Compared to other professionals his age he was a pauper with less than $16K in savings and one car, a five-year-old Volvo estate with over fifty thousand miles on the clock. All other possessions could be fitted into six suitcases.

The Heart Unit at Chicago's Carter Hospital was one of the best in the world. It had promised much. But unfortunately for Jack it delivered little. Infuriated, he felt he had no choice but to start looking, yet again, for a suitable position. He was also now becoming desperate to find somewhere to settle and raise his family. His wife Beth was tired of their nomadic existence, the moving from hospital to hospital, country to country. She wanted another baby and somewhere finally to call home. And she was worried by the family's state of penury, her husband never staying long enough in one position to slide into an incremental salary.

His son Danny just wanted a local football team to support.

'This is the target.'

Earlier that morning in room 2852 of the Hyatt a six-by-eight black and white photograph was slipped across a small oak veneer table. The room had views of an adjoining office block and, behind that, a three-hundred-yard stretch of the Chicago river. In the early sun pleasure boats vied for space with tourist cruisers offering waterside views of the city's skyscrapers.

It was two minutes before ten, and outside the early summer morning was already hot and humid. Inside, Kate Hanzek wore cut-off denims and black tee-shirt, a stark contrast to the hospital-issue navy scrubs with the Carter Hospital logo that rested on the bed. The grimy white coat and false ID hung in a sliding-door wardrobe. Inside the right pouch was a stethoscope, the left bulging with an assortment of pens, scrunched-up paper and a dog-eared notebook held together with a rubber band. The usual debris most doctors carry. Next to the white coat was a long lightweight waterproof to cover the hospital garb as Hanzek left the hotel. A mousy brown wig lay on a shelf. The fully loaded Heckler & Koch rested snugly in its carry-case on the bed.

'He's one of the senior staff at the Heart Unit.'

The controller had given as much detail as he'd been instructed. Basic facts, nothing else. He was a small, bulky Korean with an East Coast accent, dressed neatly but unobtrusively in navy trousers and tee-shirt under a white linen jacket. He wore wrap-around shades even in the room.

Hanzek sat impassively at the desk beside the window, smoking a Marlboro. An air-conditioner struggled noisily in the background as she studied the photograph. Good face, she thought, even handsome. Good head of dark hair. She glanced at the eyes. Confident, self-assured. Pity he has to go, he looks cute.

'His name is Dr Jack Hunt.' The Korean was in a hurry to leave. Like the killers he'd hired he knew little about the target and cared even less. He was so far down the pecking order he was unaware who had really ordered and was paying for the hit. 'He's thirty-nine, Irish and around five eleven. I'd say he weighs in about one seventy. So no physical contact.'

The killer nodded. She was five six and kept herself lean and fit with regular workouts. But she was no streetfighter.

'Make it a clean hit – one to the head, one to the chest, then out. If you reach the Heart Unit on time the area should be quiet.' The Korean looked for reaction, but none came. 'Should be easy.'

Hanzek smiled slightly. Should be easy. What the fuck would he know what was or wasn't easy? She dabbed a handkerchief at her brow. The air-conditioner had given up its struggle and the room was becoming oppressively warm.

'The car's gonna be parked at the lower basement level. It'll be in the wrecker's yard within an hour, burnt to a shell.' The controller was almost finished. 'I'll tell the driver you'll meet him in the lobby at twelve. When it's over there'll be a different operator in a black Ford Thunderbird to take you to O'Hare.'

The elevator jerked to a halt at level nine of the Carter Hospital. Kate Hanzek's carefully prepared schedule was thrown into confusion the moment she stepped out and heard the shrill, urgent bleeping bouncing off the walls. Its sudden and strange pitch startled and almost deafened her. It certainly disorientated her. Hanzek looked to the right and saw the backs of three white-coated doctors rushing towards an open bay halfway along the corridor.

A black paramedic grabbed her sleeve, urging her on. 'Shift it. That alarm's been goin' for almost two minutes.'

Unknown to Hanzek, the cardiac arrest bell would continue to sound until a full crash team arrived at the patient's side. While it reverberated medical staff not involved in vital hospital routine had to drop everything and run to the alarm zone. But Hanzek didn't know where the intensive care unit was. Equally she knew nothing about cardiac resuscitation. For someone more familiar with stopping hearts using a well-directed bullet, this was alien territory.

'Move, for Christ's sake!' A young nurse in green scrubs and protective hair cap pushed past, concerned at the white-coated doctor apparently frozen to the spot. As she reached the open bay she glanced back. And Hanzek noticed the nurse's puzzlement change to a questioning look.

Still the klaxon sounded, making her ears ring, and she turned left, as the rehearsed scheme had directed, but was almost knocked over by two others. She abandoned the prepared plan and took the first corridor on the right, walking rapidly away from the action. Voices ahead forced her to switch again, now along a brightly lit atrium with open-plan offices and backs hunched at PC terminals. Non-medical personnel walked briskly around, paperwork in hands. Hanzek couldn't help but notice their doubting expressions. The emergency bell was still ringing. She began to hurry. She began to sweat.

'Can I help?' someone asked, but Hanzek waved a hand dismissively and changed direction. Her heart was racing as fast as her brain as she tried desperately to remember the floor's layout.

A disabled washroom to her left. With shaking hands and pounding heart she tried the handle. It turned and she locked the door behind her, then pressed her sweating brow against the cool tiles. Fuck it! Two thoughts crowded her mind. One, she was lost. Two, if she couldn't find Jack Hunt she'd take the driver out for getting her into such deep shit. She forced her hands steady, took deep, slow breaths to calm palpitations.

She glanced at her watch: 1.19. She was running out of time.

In addition, Professor Lewins, I am concerned that two of the senior attendings in this unit seem more preoccupied with baseball or the performance of their investment portfolios. That should put it up to him, Jack thought. He'll know bloody well who I mean. He's the professor, the main man. He's supposed to be driving this department, not sitting on his arse all day. *They show little enthusiasm in advancing the causes and treatments of heart disease and their relationship with the pharmaceutical industry seems unwise and potentially compromising.* After Sam Lewins, the professor of cardiology, there were, in addition to Jack, three other senior staff. The Irishman had made little attempt to hide his dismay at the clinical performances of the two longest-serving members.

Gradually he became aware of the shrill emergency alert.

The Heart Unit occupied most of the ninth level and was accessed by two elevators, one for gurneys only. It was divided into four separate but interlinked areas of management. The bulk of the department, the clinical division, was in the east wing and dealt exclusively with treatments. Here were the patient bays, intensive care, invasive cardiology and diagnostic radiology. The southern wing held the underfunded, understaffed and underused research laboratories. The west wing was reserved for administration, while the northern annexe was kept as offices for the professor and his immediate staff.

Jack Hunt was half out of his chair wondering whether he should answer the alarm. There were usually enough staff in the east wing, in the immediate treatment zone, to deal with emergencies and a full crash team could be beside the patient within three to four minutes. But the arrest bleep had been sounding for what seemed like ages. When it suddenly stopped, Jack relaxed. He returned to his letter of resignation.

Kate Hanzek knew she was way off track. At the Hyatt Regency the scheme had literally been drawn out, the areas colour-coded and numbered, each step measured. Get off at the elevator. Turn left, swing into the third corridor on the right, then immediately left. Walk about fifteen yards, then swing immediately right again. You are now in the office area for senior attendings. Room twenty-six is the tenth door ahead on the left. The door will be unlocked, maybe even partly open. Your target will be in there dictating reports until 1.30. He rarely hangs about. Get there a minute too late and he could be gone. Open the door and start shooting.

It had sounded so simple in the relative peace of the hotel room. But it was now a very different ball game. She was ruffled, lost and stuck in a disabled washroom. Her head was still spinning, her ears ringing. And it was 1.27. One half of her brain warned her to abort. But the stakes were high: two hundred thousand dollars for a successful hit. She decided to see it through.

When I was appointed to the Carter cardiology division there were certain guarantees offered about the unit's research commitments. You, in particular, were very aware of my published data on links between childhood infection and heart disease. Jack was working himself into a self-righteous lather.

He glanced at his watch: It was 1.29. Almost time to go.

Hanzek felt confident she was now on the right corridor. She had finally collected her wits, and slipped the washroom door lock and started walking briskly to the left. Her confident pace had returned and she no longer seemed out of place. 'The office zone for senior medical staff is painted the same throughout: sky blue walls, white ceilings.' The Korean had reinforced this during the briefing. A quick glance confirmed the description. 'All the doors are coloured navy blue. Each is clearly numbered.'

This time he was wrong, and Hanzek's nightmare suddenly intensified. The doors in this sector were all the same, but not navy blue. Here they were obviously brand new and unpainted, their natural beechwood retained. Worse still, not one was numbered.

I do not believe I can continue to work in this unit unless fundamental changes are agreed. Jack was hurrying to finish and get back to his patients. He was also concerned to find out what was going on in the cardiac arrest bay.

It was 1.32. Time for one more sentence.

Hanzek felt there was no option but to try each room in turn. She was uncertain coming at the target from an unknown approach, and the alarm still seemed shrill in her head. She was confused but determined. I'm nearly there; I'll finish him off one way or another. Her eyes darted nervously. At least I'm the only one around. That slit-eyed bastard at the Hyatt got something right.

She opened door after door, carefully so as not to alert anyone. Nothing. The whole division seemed abandoned. She gripped the Heckler & Koch firmly, her heart pounding again. This was the first time in her killing career she'd allowed herself to get into such a stupid situation. Every other hit had been uncomplicated. Plan where to strike, sight the target, shoot. Not this hide-and-seek she now found herself playing.

It was 1.35.

I may be forced to seek a new position and leave the Carter Hospital. Outside, Jack Hunt heard doors opening and shutting, hurried footsteps coming closer.

Hanzek was halfway down the corridor. She'd disturbed one young woman poring over textbooks. 'Sorry, wrong room.' She'd even forced a smile as she pulled the door closed. The gun felt unsteady and she paused only to wipe away sweat before gripping it firmly again. She hurried back to the start of the corridor and started counting, then stopped outside the tenth door on the left.

Inside she heard shuffling. Very gently she turned the handle.
It was 1.38.

Yours sincerely.
Jack scrawled his signature at the bottom of the page. He leaned forward in his chair and picked up the photo of his wife and child from the desk. I'm sorry, guys, but we could be off again. And that's going to cause one helluva row at home.

The killer had the door quarter-way open, her breath caught in anticipation. A finger squeezed gently on the trigger of the Heckler & Koch as she saw a head of jet-black hair and sensed someone sitting at a desk facing a window. The man started to turn and, for the first time ever, Kate Hanzek mumbled a sorry. Then she started shooting.
The digital clock on the office wall clicked over to 1.39.

2

The tall man counted the telephone rings. One, two, three, four, five, six. Stop. He focused on his watch until twenty seconds elapsed. The phone rang again. He counted another six rings before it cut out. Back to the timepiece. Twenty seconds. Ring. He snatched at the receiver. 'Well?'

In New York it was five in the afternoon of 14 June, one hour ahead of Chicago. Outside it was unpleasantly hot with temperatures in the mid-nineties. The streets steamed after a heavy downpour and pedestrians ducked and weaved on the sidewalks to avoid traffic splash. In the cool splendour of an exclusive downtown hotel the man's tall frame was squeezed into box three of a row of telephone booths. As someone who had access to every possible communication device known to the world, he rarely used public telephones. But for this call he needed a safe, clean and untraceable landline.

'What the fuck are you talking about?' Fortunately the doors of the cubicle were closed tightly so his increasingly agitated voice could not be overheard. 'I don't believe this. What do you mean Hunt's not dead?'

The news from his Korean agent was not good. It so distressed him he felt a migraine coming on and fumbled in his pockets for an Imigran spray. But no matter what gloss the contact tried to put on the day's events, disaster was probably the best description.

He tugged a handkerchief free and mopped at his brow. 'Tell me from the start,' he ordered, then pushed his back firmly against the doors, loosened his tie and listened. 'I don't believe I'm hearing this.' More babbling down the line. 'Fucking Jesus Christ,' he muttered as he took in the full implications. 'Stop, stop,' he finally pleaded. 'Let me get this straight. The bitch didn't just fail to take out Hunt, she took out somebody completely different?' His interpretation was confirmed. 'So who did she hit?' There was some hesitation before a name was offered.

The tall man slumped in the booth, bending at the waist and banging his forehead off the wall. He cursed silently. 'Sam Lewins? The professor?' Incredulous. 'She killed *that* Sam Lewins?'

The tall man was so stunned he didn't speak for almost a minute. Then he straightened up, flicked the top off the Imigran spray and sniffed the chemical deeply, squashing the handkerchief into his trouser pocket. Then he started talking, voice now firm and resolute.

'Okay, change of plan.' He coughed slightly, glanced outside to make sure no one was waiting to use the booth, then continued. 'The stuff we were going to plant on Hunt is to be switched to Lewins. Got that?' The Korean acknowledged. 'Everybody backs away from the Carter, and call off the surveillance.' He paused, thinking furiously, then, 'I want Hanzek and the driver taken out. If you want to stay upright on this earth and do business again you sort this fucking mess yourself. Got that?' The caller acknowledged and told him the killer and her driver were now back at the hotel. 'Make sure this happens out of town. I don't want any connection between the shooting and them being found in some dumpster.' Absolutely. 'This operation freezes until I think it out. Okay?' The Korean let it be known there was not the slightest doubt his orders were both understood and as good as done. 'Nobody talks to anyone until you hear from me.'

He slipped the receiver back on to its hook and adjusted his clothes. Before he left the cubicle he drew on the remaining dregs of his anti-migraine drug, then strode quickly towards the hotel exit, head pounding.

Three miles away, in his office on the top floor of a highrise between Whitehall and Battery Park, Stan Danker sat behind a large crescent-shaped cherrywood desk. He stared at the fax that had just been thrust under his nose: PROFESSOR SAM LEWINS SHOT DEAD IN HIS OFFICE ABOUT ONE HOUR AGO. THE HOSPITAL IS IN UPROAR AND I HAVE NO MORE DETAILS. YOU'LL HEAR AS SOON AS I DO.

Danker was poleaxed, almost unable to grasp the significance of the news. Professor Sam Lewins murdered? And in his office at the Carter Hospital? Jesus Christ, what is the world coming to?

Danker was the fifty-three-year-old North American director of Zemdon Pharmaceuticals, a Swiss giant rated the world's ninth largest drugs company and the second most profitable in Europe. It had a market capitalisation of around $90 billion and pro forma pharmaceutical sales of $14.5 billion annually. He was based at the company's swanky Manhattan offices with commanding views across the Hudson river and its ferries to Ellis Island. He had three pretty secretaries and a stunningly beautiful PA called Maria, employed as much for her looks as her scheduling skills.

He was a big man, six four and a little over one eighty pounds, no visible flab underneath his carefully tailored Brooks Brothers suits. Good head of steel-grey hair, granite face, deep blue eyes and straight, healthy-looking teeth. Big strong handshake, confident and self-assured. Except at that precise moment.

He buzzed the intercom. 'Maria, get me Zurich on the line immediately.'

Zemdon was planning a massive international product launch in early October. Passing through the firm's manufacturing plants at that moment was Cyclint, a cardiac wonderdrug they would claim reduced the incidence of heart attacks by twenty-eight per cent. It would, quite literally, be a life-saver for those with heart disease. And the Carter Hospital's Heart Unit in Chicago had been targeted as the focal point for the chemical's inauguration. The Midwest division had a hot reputation for excellence, and although that had faded somewhat in recent years, it was still considered one of the most prestigious cardiology facilities in the world. Any utterance from its chief was considered momentous, and his product recommendations, direct or indirect, guaranteed massive increases in sales. The Swiss pharmaceutical giant had pulled off a remarkable coup by recruiting Professor Sam Lewins. He had pledged to back Cyclint unconditionally and the corporation in turn had agreed to swell his bank account. This combined effort was scheduled to spring from Chicago and spread globally. But the campaign's success was inextricably linked to Lewins's ringing endorsements. And now he was dead.

The intercom crackled. 'Putting you through now.'

Danker took a deep breath and steeled his nerves.

3

Two days later Jack Hunt walked up the twenty concrete steps leading to the front entrance of the Carter Hospital. It was five minutes after eight in the morning and he was dressed in what he considered his best attire, a shabby and crumpled navy lightweight suit over a white open-necked shirt. He'd forced himself into the garb for a short hospital memorial service to be held later that day in honour of his late boss. The temperature was in the mid-eighties with strong sun and little cloud protection, and he was perspiring heavily as he pushed open the glass doors, sighing with relief as the air-conditioned coolness hit him.

The corridors along the Heart Unit on level nine were now being patrolled by a team of investigating law officers, blue-uniformed and peaked-capped cops conversing with plain-clothes detectives. Yellow crime-incident tape was strung along door handles, effectively sealing off the northern annexe and its offices where the assassin had prowled before striking. White-coated doctors and nurses in green scrubs were being stopped and interrogated, their heads shaking or nodding depending on the questions. But the general air of disbelief that such an appalling murder could happen in broad daylight in the sanctuary of a hospital was obvious. There were a lot of numbed expressions and robot-like movements, staff going through the motions.

Jack had been first on the scene when Sam Lewins was gunned down. He'd heard two shots echo along the outside corridor and sprinted to the door in time to see the tails of a white coat disappear round a corner. Bursting into Sam Lewins's room he found his boss lying on the floor in a pool of blood, paperwork ruffling in his spasming fingers. He'd cradled the wounded man in his arms, frantically trying to assess the situation, then called for a crash team. He'd lingered in the crowded and tense emergency room, still covered in gore, while the trauma squad fought to save Lewins's life. But despite IV lines, plasma expanders and drugs to reduce brain swelling, the professor heaved his last gasp and was pronounced dead. Within thirty minutes the whole facility was sealed off by security. One hour later the assassin's abandoned disguise was discovered in a washroom on street level.

Jack was making his way towards the chief administrator's office on the tenth floor, resignation letter tucked into a side pocket. Jesus, what a country. To think we thought New York was unsafe. Two attempted burglaries and one handbag snatching was as much as Beth could take. Chicago, I promised, would be different. Much safer. Where the hell else is there to go? Jack was well aware that medical research funding was mostly concentrated in North America, where the big players worked. Not Dublin or London or Sydney.

Wishing to avoid any confrontation with a hospital board still reeling from the brutal homicide, Jack left the white envelope with the administrator's secretary.

Next morning, 17 June, immediately after Jack flicked his 'in light' at hospital reception, he received a message that Steve Downes, the admin chief, wanted to see him.

'I've read your CV,' he explained as he ushered the Irish cardiologist into his office on the tenth floor.

The room was about thirty foot square with executive desk, thick pile carpet and the refreshing coolness of a working air-conditioner. The décor was subdued but in good taste with strategic lighting for maximum effect. There was a separate small boardroom with a private lavatory between both so that the administrator didn't have to bawl somebody out then stand next to him in a public urinal.

Downes was a stuffy, off-hand individual in his late fifties who usually wore double-breasted suits to conceal his spreading waistline. His hair was like strands of wire wool badly forced down. He had a turkey chin and seemed about three inches shorter than Jack, maybe five eight. That morning he was wearing an open-necked short-sleeved shirt and light slacks that did nothing to conceal his flab.

Jack was surprised to see his ring-bound file with maroon-coloured hardcover open on the desk. Inside its two-inch thickness was a record of career moves, qualifications and references. What the hell's this about?

'You've certainly been around.' Downes moved across the room and turned a page on the CV. His voice was deep baritone in stark contrast to Jack's Irish brogue, still strong after years away from home. 'Australia and Europe before Philadelphia and New York.' He glanced across the mahogany table separating both. 'Never thought of settling somewhere?'

Jack was caught off guard, uncertain where this was leading. The set-up puzzled him and he shrugged to avoid eye contact. 'I had my heart set on the Carter, Mr Downes.'

The administrator cut across him. 'Call me Steve. Let's dispense with formalities, I'm here to do business.'

Jack flicked at a non-existent piece of fluff on his sleeve. He'd still been in his working scrubs when Downes had called and hadn't bothered to change. 'Well, Steve, I was hoping Chicago would be the last stop. My wife and boy are more than a little fed up with all this moving. They'd like to settle down. We've been living out of rented accommodation for the past eight years.'

Downes turned another page. 'Maybe we can make you stay.'

Jack shifted uneasily in his chair. 'I'm not quite sure I understand. What exactly are you suggesting?'

Downes ignored the question, busy reading a list of the cardiologist's research papers. In the file they were numbered as well as alphabetically indexed, eighty-three in total and all published in prestigious medical annals. The *New England Journal of Medicine*; *British Medical Journal*; *Lancet*; *Journal of the American Medical Association*; *Medical Journal of Australia.* Editors who rejected as much as ninety per cent of offered research data had accepted Jack's material.

'Pretty impressive work.' Downes turned to another page with red highlighting along the margins. 'And the references speak highly of your commitment to academic research.' He quoted: 'Intelligent and thought-provoking style . . . obsessively careful in study design . . . excellent teacher.'

Jack grimaced in mock embarrassment. 'My life is medicine, Steve. I do nothing else. I don't golf or sail or skydive or climb mountains. What you see is what you get. I'm a full-time cardiologist.'

The administrator stared at him, then returned to the file. He tugged loose another button on his shirt and flapped the opening. 'You've been screened for HIV and hepatitis?'

Jack nodded. This was standard now in all US medical institutions. No test, no job.

Downes spun his chair from side to side, then reached for a remote control and adjusted the air-conditioning flow. 'What about checks for substance abuse?'

Jack pushed his chair forward and flicked at his CV until he found the page he wanted. 'It's all there. I've been tested more times than an Olympic athlete.'

Downes scanned the entries. 'That's good,' he murmured, 'we've had some bad luck with that recently.'

This was masterful understatement. Six months previously the hospital had suffered an embarrassing exposé by the *Chicago Sun-Times*. A journalist had trailed one of the hospital's senior physicians to a crack house near the Cabrini-Green housing projects and caught him on camera doing deals and smoking. After that it was open season on the staff in terms of random testing. Thirteen, so far all non-medical, had already been dismissed. The board put it up to everyone with a simple but stark message. Zero tolerance. One strike and you're out. One failed alcohol or proscribed drug sample and your career is over. Stay clean or else. Five others had left voluntarily within two months. Importantly, one was a junior doctor about whom rumours of instability had been surfacing.

'I see you're a family man.' Downes pored over another paragraph, then looked across. 'I like that. Family gives a man responsibilities, mortgages, hefty bank loans, commitments.' He forced a smile. 'Tends to keep a man in place.' The chair was spun again. 'Someplace anyway. Jesus, do you know how many doctors on the staff are in second or third marriages?'

Jack didn't respond; he sensed the administrator was off on a tangent and wouldn't be interrupted. He pretended to listen but he was furiously trying to decide what the conversation was all about.

Downes was now skipping towards the last pages of the CV. 'I often wonder how we'd get by without medics. Sure as hell it would make my life much easier.' He scrutinised Jack's registration with the Illinois Board of Medicine, his malpractice certificate. 'The hospital's currently facing three law suits for negligence. Medicaid's investigating one of our skin specialists for overutilisation.' This was a common euphemism for skimming off the top with unnecessary tests that inflated income. 'And last week two nurses in diagnostic imaging lodged formal complaints for sexual harassment against a radiologist there.' He finally looked across, and Jack offered a sympathetic shrug. 'You wouldn't give me that sort of trouble, would you?'

Jack held the other man's gaze. 'I'm still not with you, Steve. We're not on the same wavelength. What are you trying to tell me?'

Downes pushed his chair back and cradled both hands across his belly, eyes suddenly narrowing. 'I'm gonna say two things, both off the record.' Jack sat rock-still lest he miss a word. 'Sam Lewins was shot because he was an active paedophile.'

Jack's jaw dropped. He knew little of his late professor's personal life other than that he was separated from his wife and family and had recently taken to dyeing his hair. Downes's information hit him like a sledgehammer.

'The police found a ton of child porn in his apartment.' The administrator watched the other man's reaction. 'Real hard stuff is what I've been told. Then some freak rang the *Tribune* and claimed he took the dirty professor out. Warned he had a list as long as his arm to follow.' The hands were unclasped and rested on the table. 'Probably bullshit, but no doubt it'll hit the front page soon.'

Jack groaned loudly. Having a scandal in the cardiology division plastered across a Chicago broadsheet would be nothing short of hell. Everybody would suffer.

'The second point concerns you and it's also off the record.' Downes closed the file and pushed it to one side. 'We need someone with balls to take over the Heart Unit.' He hitched at his trousers. 'I think you're the right man at the right time for us.'

Jack was so shocked he didn't speak. His face muscles bunched, his eyelids flickered with the intensity of the situation. The letter of resignation had been turned into a job offer. And not just a run-of-the-mill prospect but Chief of Cardiology at one of the world's most prestigious heart units.

Before Jack could collect his thoughts, Downes introduced hospital attorney Forde Beck who presented him with a submission. Beck was of a similar breed to the administrator, sour-faced with a walrus moustache, thick-bellied, balding and grumpy with an upper Midwest nasal twang.

'Take this home with you,' he advised as he handed the detailed text over. 'Study it, then get back to us.' He stroked his moustache. 'Don't leave it too long.'

The covering letter outlined the pitch:

i. Assume position as Chief of Cardiology at the Carter Hospital, officially with effect from Monday, 28 June.
ii. Proposed annual salary $205,300.
iii. Pension and healthcare benefits as per page two.
iv. Responsibilities to the division as per pages three through ten.
v. Coordinate proposed drug launch for Zemdon Pharmaceuticals in October, page twelve.
vi. Termination of contract, page fourteen.

Please treat this offer with complete and total confidentiality.

This had all happened just before eleven that morning. A bemused, confused and elated Jack had taken the rest of the day off to go home and prepare his response. It was now twenty minutes after two in the afternoon and he was still struggling to come to terms with this dramatic reversal in his plans. He sat with his wife in the front room of their first-floor rented apartment on W Deming in the Lincoln Park district, the job proposal spread out on the floor, both scanning the sheets. Eight-year-old Danny, just back from a visit to the dentist, was outside in the garden practising penalty shooting.

'This is it, Hunt,' Beth enthused, eyes dancing with delight as she read the text for the hundredth time. A petite blonde Australian, she had a sunny disposition which balanced Jack's moods. 'The big one, the one you've always been working towards.' She hugged him tightly, planting a kiss on his lips.

But Jack drew back, face creased with concern. 'I don't know Beth. I think they believe I'm an easy option, a safe pair of hands.' He rested his back against a lounge chair and fanned his brow with one of the pages. 'They're facing a huge scandal and they know damned well it's going to crucify the hospital's reputation. So they're picking on the closest and cleanest.'

Beth looked across. 'Now what exactly does that mean?'

Jack focused on the ceiling. 'I've spent the past hour going over that contract and it stinks.' He ignored his wife's look of disbelief. 'They're looking for a politician, not a research doctor.' He jabbed a finger at items four and five. 'Responsibilities to the division: that's all standard copy, there's not one mention of investigation commitments. And look at the next section: Coordinate proposed drug launch for Zemdon Pharmaceuticals in October. They're expecting me to fawn to some chemical multinational and front up their latest blockbuster.'

'Now hold on Hunt,' Beth cut through. 'This isn't just your job we're dealing with here, it's our future. Our life together. Aren't you going to consider us in your calculations?' She ran a finger along the salary proposal. 'Two hundred and five thousand dollars. Now when did you ever collect that sort of pay-packet?'

Jack stood up and paced the floor. 'It's more than just the money, Beth. It's about being your own man and running your own show. Doing things my way, the way I know they should be done. It's about what I've seen and experienced elsewhere. The Carter has been living off its reputation for too long. Whoever takes over will have to move mountains to get that unit back to being a world-class one.'

'Then let it be you,' pleaded Beth. 'It's what I've been listening to for years. "I want to run my own division." How many times have I heard that before?'

Jack was now at his stubborn worst. 'If they really want me they'll have to offer a better package.' He punched at the sheets. 'I need more flesh on the bones of that proposal.'

Beth lost her cool. 'Will you stop being so selfish?' she shouted. The outburst was so out of character that Jack jumped, visibly startled. 'We need a home, a real house of our own.' She was now perched on a large armchair near a side window overlooking the communal plot, arms wrapped round her knees. Jack moved close beside, his back to the glass, and leaned on the sill. He was in denims and a short-sleeved shirt, his armpits streaked with sweat. 'Danny deserves better than rentals,' she added. Her brow was now creased with worry.

A cheer wafted over the hot and sticky air, followed by, 'Goal, goal!' Danny had hit the back of the net. Beth rapped on the window and waved encouragement while Jack gave a clenched-fist salute. The boy flailed his arms in delight when he spotted his dad. It was such an infrequent event.

Beth turned back. 'We've done all that. It's time you made *us* the priority.' She glared at her husband, eyes dancing with fire. Jack tried to outglare her but hadn't the heart. He knew she was right. And she was so beautiful he could rarely keep any disagreement going for long. Her ash-blonde hair, held in a clasp, had never lost its colour. She had long, dark eyelashes, brown eyes, high cheekbones and a generous mouth. She was five eight, a little below Jack's height, slim and graceful. She was wearing cream cotton shorts and a floppy blouse, white socks and Nike sneakers, and looked good enough to eat.

They'd met in Sydney while Jack worked at Parramatta General, the city's premier medical facility. They were peas from very different pods, the dark-haired Irishman with his nose in textbooks most of the time, the sun-kissed Aussie surfer who loved the outdoors. She'd told him early in their relationship she could never settle in Ireland, having read enough about the country to know that a good summer was when it only rained half the time.

But within weeks of her first visit she'd fallen in love with the rolling hills and valleys that fringed the white cottage where Jack grew up. On late summer evenings she would watch the sun roll along fields strewn with newly cut hay, shades of green rippling and changing. The lush pastures were a stark contrast to the dust bowls of her homeland and Beth had found herself pleading with her husband to stay longer. So Jack had returned to St Vincent's Hospital in Dublin for a six-month teaching post, bringing his family with him and delighting his older sister.

However an offer soon filtered through from Philadelphia: lecturer in cardiology with an option to switch to research. It would satisfy both Jack's ambitions and Beth's longing for blue skies and sunshine. They'd been in North America ever since.

'Take it,' Beth pleaded, holding Jack's hands tightly in her own. The grip was intense, her emotions raw. She searched his eyes for an answer. 'It's everything you've ever worked for, you'll be your own boss, running your own unit.' She forced him to look directly at her. '*Professor* Hunt. What more could you want?'

Jack pulled his hands away. 'A better deal. If they want a top-class candidate they're going to have to accept quite a few changes.'

Beth slumped backwards. Her shoulders sagged and she

covered her face with her hands. Jack tried to put his arms around her but was brushed away. 'I can't go on like this,' she said quietly. 'I'm not up to any more moves. I've had enough.' She wiped her eyes with the front of her blouse. 'And I don't think Danny could handle it either. He's made so many new friends here.' She tugged free her sweat-streaked hair, then re-fashioned it at the back. 'You keep looking,' she said finally. 'Maybe someday you'll find whatever it is that'll make you happy. But we may not be around to share it.'

An angry silence descended, and both turned to watch their son run up and down the garden.

The boy was their world – Beth's in particular. She'd been unable to work anywhere for any great length of time with all the moves, and Jack's involvement in medical projects absorbed most of his time. As a consequence her energies were largely channelled into bringing up Danny. And he was so active he demanded a lot of them. He was soccer mad, supporting teams in many countries: Chelsea in England, Real Madrid in Spain, Lazio in Italy. When he wasn't cheering for his squad he kicked anything remotely shaped like a ball and had broken more windows than his parents cared to remember. He was seven inches over four feet, dark-haired like his father with the same intense blue eyes. And he could be just as moody. When his temper was up he flushed bright red and trapped the tip of his tongue between his front teeth.

Neither spoke for almost five minutes, then Jack leaned down and kissed Beth's tears away. She tried to turn but he held her tightly, brushing his lips across her forehead. He took off his watch and pressed it firmly in her left hand. 'It's two forty-five. By five o'clock I'll have a deal.' Fresh tears welled in his wife's eyes. 'Take Danny to the park now and meet me here at five thirty.'

He straightened up, grim-faced and determined. He knew how hard it had been for Beth to say what she'd said. She didn't have a vindictive or malicious bone in her body. When she bared her heart, it was for real. He now wanted the professorship more than anything. But not at any price.

When Beth was about to leave with Danny, he went into the spare bedroom that doubled as a study and sat down at his PC. Outside, he heard the apartment door shut, then Beth shouting. He flicked on the computer and waited impatiently for the programs to kick in. The clock on the top left-hand corner of the monitor blinked 3.01. He had until five o'clock to save his marriage and career. He began drafting his first fax to Steve Downes.

Jack wasn't flattering himself. He knew why the administrator considered him an ideal candidate for the suddenly vacant position. Downes needed a quick solution to a series of long-standing problems that had suddenly, with Sam Lewins's death, become critical.

There were three other senior attendings attached to the Carter Heart Unit. Next in seniority to the late Sam Lewins was Harry Chan, a Hong Kong-born and Princeton-educated cardiologist. He was a small, edgy man with thick-lensed glasses, shaky hands and a nervous laugh. Harry had bad luck with women. He was in his third marriage and, according to in-house rumour, it wasn't too secure either. Harry also had bad luck with his other passion, gambling. He constantly moaned about lack of money and how he could improve his cash flow. His gambling debts and alimony payments overshadowed his life. Most felt Chan turned up at the Carter only to justify his salary.

Next was Martin Shreeve, who'd trained at the Cleveland Clinic. He was an overweight slob whose scrubs barely contained his flab. He had more hair on his face than his head, which at least helped disguise two double chins. Shreeve ate the wrong foods and drank more than was safe, smoked three packs of cigarettes a day and wouldn't walk five yards if he could drive. Gossip suggested he was heading for his own intensive care bay. He also had the unenviable reputation of daily being last in and first out of the unit.

The other senior doctor was Nat Parker, locally trained but originally from out west. Parker was a tall, gangly black man with restless limbs and a habit of shrugging his shoulders when irritated. He was known to be gentle and dependable, covering up for his colleagues more than was wise. Still, he was widely respected throughout the hospital, many openly commenting they wished he had the ambition and aggression to take over. But the division needed someone with juice at the helm. Someone clean. Someone free from scandal.

Someone like Jack Hunt.

At 3.35 he rang Downes and advised he was sending a detailed fax explaining his response to the offer. He added that he would like the final package agreed by five o'clock at the latest or his resignation would hold. The communication was five pages long and included specific requirements on revamping the research department and revitalising the clinical division. He also wanted an annual salary of $300,000. The pension and healthcare deal already on offer was acceptable.

He explained it to Downes. 'Four years ago the Carter was number two in the Top Ten Hospitals of North America.' This was a *US News & World Report* rating based on the facility's many world-class divisions. For example, the paediatric trauma unit attracted students and doctors from around the world who came to see and learn at first hand. 'The Heart Unit was the envy of the top East Coast institutions. But in the last listing we dropped to fifth position.' He heard Downes snort in disgust and pressed harder. 'And that's due to the decline in the cardiology section. You know that, and so do I.' The subsequent attack on the hospital's image through the media had alarmed many of the staff. 'You didn't hear the grumblings in the locker rooms, but I did. And it stuck in my craw.' There had been loud complaints that little was being done to reverse the trend. Sam Lewins had been the stumbling block to reform. With him out of the way, regardless of the horrific circumstances, pressure would fall on the board to revamp the division. 'If you advertise the post it will cause delays and real friction. Cut your losses and make a clean break,' he pushed. 'Go for an early appointment.' Then he hung up.

At 4.07 the phone rang.

'Jack, that you?' Hospital attorney Beck was on the line and sounding none too pleased. 'We don't take kindly to being pressurised into making big decisions like this. Chief of Cardiology at the Carter is a very highly regarded position throughout North America. If we advertise I imagine we'd get a lot of top-quality candidates responding.'

Jack held his nerve. 'Mr Beck, I'm not playing hardball. I don't enjoy mind games, they waste my time. You need a top cardiologist to lift that division. If you go for open competition the other three senior attendings working there will give you hell for snubbing them.' He paused to let that sink in. 'And I suspect any decent applicant looking at this outfit would give it a wide berth.'

He waited and listened. He couldn't hear Beck's breathing and decided this was a conference call.

'I'll get back.'

Beck sounded as if he was about to hang up so Jack cut across.

'I'm sending you an amended fax. Read it and let me know your answer. We've got less than an hour to work a deal.' Then he hung up.

The next communication detailed further failings at the Heart Unit about which Beck and Downes might not have been completely aware. The sloppy standards, the indiscipline and petty arrogances, the lack of formal teaching for in-training residents. He ended by increasing his salary bid to $310,000 to put this house in order. It wasn't the money, but he didn't want them to think he was anyone's fool. A puppet, easily bought and falling over himself to grab at the offer.

Jack fretted the time away bouncing a baseball against the study wall. He was drenched in sweat, his mouth dry. What was he doing? Were his principles once again going to deny him a decent career opportunity? He dreaded facing Beth and Danny with no job and a game plan that had backfired.

He raided the refrigerator and came away with a half-empty can of flat Coke. It disappeared in one gulp. Outside, the late-afternoon sun beat down, the air was still. Inside, even with the cooler on full, he perspired heavily. He checked his e-mails to distract his mind. There were three new messages, one from his server provider offering to enlist him in a draw for a free trip to Florida if he'd complete a quick questionnaire. He deleted it. The second was a circular from the American Heart Foundation. He didn't even bother to read that before erasing. The third stopped him in his tracks: JACK. I'VE JUST DISCOVERED I HAVE A BIG BROTHER. MAYBE YOU HAVE ONE? It was signed C.

Now what the hell did that mean?

Jack's pet project was a possible link between infection in childhood and the early development of heart disease. In short, if his hypothesis was correct, some relatively young individuals might have heart attacks because their arteries had been damaged by infection. To prove this he needed to study groups of patients with early-onset heart disease. But he had never stayed long enough in one place to follow this through. He had suggested the conjecture to colleagues worldwide via the Web and invited comment. He had received a lot of criticism and dismissive e-mails suggesting he was way off track and should concentrate on current knowledge. Except from one doctor: Carlotta Drunker in Sacramento, California.

All Jack knew about Carlotta was her age (forty-three), status (senior attending and research director) and marital status (single, no kids). Dr Drunker was also interested in the infection-to-heart disease link and the two began sharing information. She'd once mentioned there had been another doctor working along similar lines in Colorado but she'd lost contact with him.

At one stage Beth had suspected the flurry of correspondence reflected something more than just medical research and insisted on having every communication explained. She'd pouted for days afterwards, almost disappointed her husband wasn't interested in something other than medicine.

Recently, some of Carlotta's messages had seemed strange, even bizarre. Instead of the usual friendly and chatty banter there were one-liners, as today, that meant nothing to Jack. He'd even begun to wonder about his colleague's psychological health. But at that precise moment his own mental well-being was his main concern and it was shaky in the extreme. He deleted the e-mail.

Steve Downes finally called at 4.41. 'I'm pulling together our last offer.'

Jack nearly dropped the phone his palms were so wet. 'What's the delay?' He wiped the sweat on his denims and waited.

'It's a helluva lot of money you're asking,' complained Downes. 'I'm not sure the board would ratify this level of expenditure.'

Jack tried to imagine the administrator and his attorney sitting at a desk on the tenth floor poring over figures, doing the maths. Like every hospital-based doctor, Jack resented funds spent on non-medical personnel. And he'd done his homework. After the morning discussion he'd made a few discreet calls and soon learned Beck's salary was $190K, with Downes weighing in at more. These wages were a damned sight more than most of the doctors who worked in the same facility. That grated further. He decided to play his trump card: insider knowledge. And in medicine, more than any other profession, knowledge is power.

'Steve, let's cut to the chase. The Heart Unit's reputation will collapse when the *Tribune* carries the story about Lewins and his paedophile activities. You won't get a dog to even consider the position when it goes coast to coast.' He glanced at the computer screen. It was 4.43. Beth and Danny would be home soon. What was he doing? 'This is my final proposal. I'll take the job and revamp that unit provided there is more investment in research programmes. Not one useful publication has come out of the Carter in the past five years. You're worried about three recent law suits for negligence, but if the division continues like a rudderless ship you'll have a flood of malpractice claims.' He paused only to draw breath. 'Someone needs to make hard-hitting changes. It should be me. And I'll take personal responsibility for academic teaching and training in Invasive Cardiology.' This section especially had fallen behind badly, with one junior attending making a formal complaint about its poor academic schedules. 'I'm unhappy with the commitment to the Zemdon Pharmaceuticals launch and I think we should sideline that in the short term. There are much bigger issues demanding immediate attention.'

There was a moment's silence before the administrator came back. 'I could live with that. I could sell that deal.'

Jack slumped to the floor, drained by the effort. 'I need a yes or no by five o'clock. That's my deadline.' Then he pushed his luck. 'And my salary minimum has now risen to $320,000.'

He hung up before a string of oaths came down the line.

Jack paced the apartment. He turned the air-conditioning to maximum but it still felt oppressively sticky. His lips and mouth were dry. He counted his own pulse and was startled to find it racing at around a hundred a minute, thirty beats more than normal. His bladder was irritating him so much he was in and out of the bathroom just about every ten minues or so, as eager to pass a little water as a dog at a row of lamp-posts. By now the fridge was empty and he was left sucking ice cubes for relief.

Five o'clock came and went. His deadline had passed. What was going on? He checked at the front window to see if Beth and Danny were on their way home. Apart from a black cat sniffing at a spilled garbage bag and the occasional pedestrian, there was no sign.

At 5.15 he caved in and lifted the phone. *I could live with that. I could sell that deal.* Downes's parting words now haunted him. He started dialling. Why did you have to push so hard? $310K was more or less agreed. Goddamn it, why go to $320K and bust? But his fingers stopped at the last number. Hold in there. His stubborn resolve returned. Sit tight. He slid to the floor and willed the phone to ring.

*

They were in the room before he even heard their movements. Beth was soaked in sweat, her blouse clinging to her body. Danny was carrying his football under his left arm and a towel under his right, both legs covered in dirt. Neither spoke when they saw Jack on the floor, face racked with worry. But their expressions said it all. The boy looked as troubled as his mother, and it was clear he knew everything.

'I'm waiting for a call.'

Jack tried forcing a smile but Beth turned and walked out in disgust. 'Come on, Danny. Let's get an ice-cream.'

He'd never heard her so cold. He made to stand up but found himself weak. What am I going to say? I've blown it. I'm out of a job and back on the road. Scanning medical journals, sending out CVs, searching. Interviewing. This time I could be on my own. He glanced at his watch. It was now 5.48. That's it, you set the deadline. They've seen you down.

Beth's angry shouts about the empty fridge almost drowned out the ringing tones. He didn't snatch at the receiver, letting it run for almost thirty seconds.

'Jack Hunt.'

He was astounded how well he controlled his voice. He sensed Beth beside him and reached for her. She took his hand and squeezed it tightly. Danny was half in and out of the room, dancing from foot to foot, almost too frightened to listen.

'It's Forde Beck.'

Jack held his breath. Not Steve Downes. It could be a blast of rejection.

'There's a fax going down the line as we speak. I'll give you thirty minutes to read it through. Then let me know your response. If I haven't heard by six thirty I'll assume the offer doesn't interest and we'll start advertising.' This time Beck hung up before Jack could get the last word.

The communication was twelve pages long. Pages one to seven contained specific conditions relating to new and significant changes of responsibility in the Heart Unit. The onus to complete these revisions would lie with the new Chief of Cardiology and would be subject to regular audit. Pages eight to ten detailed various contractual obligations relating to academic standards and new funding for research. Page eleven was totally given over to disciplinary codes and dismissal clauses. In particular, it emphasised condition twenty-four relating to mandatory sampling for substance abuse. The last sheet, page twelve, contained the financial offer:

> This figure includes bonus payments as division professor and head of research with the extra teaching and training commitments as set out on pages 8–10. It also takes into account the anticipated share of profit from Invasive Cardiology and is based on an immediate commencement of duties. Allowing for these, but insisting on two-yearly reviews, the board has approved an annual salary of $325,000.

Jack re-read the last page, then passed it to Beth without a word. He looked over at Danny and gave him the thumbs up. The boy's face creased with relief and he skipped back into the front room and started kicking the hell out of a tennis ball.

Beth slipped to her knees and scanned the pages. She tore at the sheets, desperate not to find any nightmare codicil that might destroy the package. Finally satisfied, she smoothed out page twelve and devoured each word. Her eyes moved quickly as she checked over the three simple yet vital sentences. Jack could sense her taking in the full implications. The salary was beyond their wildest dreams. At last, a chance of a home of their own. A new car. Another baby.

She leapt on Jack, covering his face with kisses. 'You bastard, you hard-hearted Irish bastard. If I didn't love you so much I'd kill you.' She dragged him on to the bed, pushed the door quietly closed, then stood in front of her husband and took off her clothes. 'Don't even think of coming near me until you've accepted that offer.' She skipped into the bathroom and ran the shower.

As his wife showered, Jack rang to agree the full package.

'Welcome on board, professor,' laughed Beck. He sounded relieved, even elated. 'You struck a hard deal,' he congratulated, 'but nothing you didn't deserve. Come in tomorrow and sign the contract first thing. We're expecting big things of you.'

Jack couldn't stifle his sigh of relief. 'I can't say I enjoyed the bargaining but the hospital won't be disappointed with the choice.'

Beck coughed slightly. 'I hope not, professor. Sure as hell I wouldn't like to have to sack you after all this.'

Both laughed nervously.

4

Chicago in mid-summer. Hot. Temperatures often peak over the hundred mark, slowing walking to an oppressive crawl. Even breezes gusting through the highrises don't cool and most people take to the beaches, or the fountains or the comfort of an air-conditioner. Rollerbladers along the waterside esplanade cruise rather than force the pace while point-duty cops get irritable and snap at traffic violators. 'Shift it, for Chrissake. Don't even think of pulling over there.' Electrical utilities struggle to maintain the demand for the surge of cooling machines and cab drivers crow this isn't as bad as ninety-five when there were four hundred deaths from heat exhaustion inside two weeks. At the Cook County Medical Examiner's office giant refrigerated trucks are brought in to store bodies when the mortuary fills to capacity.

The heat didn't bother Hend de Mart; he was used to such conditions. He especially enjoyed the late-afternoon thunderstorms as they built in violent crescendos, sparking lightning shafts that danced along the skyscraper spires of Sears Tower and the Hancock Center in the downtown area. Often within as little as ten minutes the rumbling claps and zigzag bolts would peter out over Lake Michigan, leaving the city streets wet and steaming from the pursuing torrential cloudburst. In the rundown projects and Southside slums kids would splash in dirty potholes, kicking mud at one another with shrieks of delight. Even the drug dealers welcomed the downpours. Everyone was soaked to the skin, making them look less conspicuous.

Hend de Mart was thirty years old, two hundred and twenty pounds and six feet six inches of South African beef. Tough, mean and white, of Afrikaner extraction, he had sun-bleached blond hair swept back duck's-tail style, deep blue eyes, a prominent Adam's apple, rugged features and muscular frame. He was a natural bruiser. In his teens and early twenties he'd played rugby union for a Johannesburg divisional team where he'd earned the nickname 'Meat Cleaver'. De Mart knew only winning, victory at any cost. Bones were crunched, muscles torn, opponents hammered. His fearsome reputation and vicious ambition became assets when he joined the workforce of a local gold trading company. He was henchman as well as salesman, his physical bulk and mean streak often intimidating good customers into bigger deals. Wasters and debtors were pulped. The tough image became as effective in business as it had once been on the dusty playing fields.

De Mart now worked for Zemdon Pharmaceuticals. He'd been recruited in Johannesburg, briefed in Switzerland, then dispatched to New York under US director Stan Danker. The day after Jack Hunt was appointed Chief of Cardiology at the Carter Hospital, Danker signed the South African into his Manhattan racquet club and the two huddled together in the nook of a steam room out of earshot. It was a few minutes before eleven in the morning, when the facility was quiet.

'Hend, we're having some difficulties that need to be resolved urgently,' Danker began explaining as he wiped beads of sweat from his brow. 'And I want to outline how this industry works so you'll understand what I'm leading towards.' Both men were sat on wooden slats, bent at the waist, staring at the ground, warm mist clinging to their bodies. De Mart traced shapes with his large toes on the wet tiled floor. 'The basics are the same no matter how big or small the firm.' Danker ran the corner of a towel roughly through his hair. 'The ground troops are the men and women who call on hospitals or offices to promote our products. Over and above a sales pitch that interface is also an information-gathering exercise. Every doctor is noted for usefulness, prescribing patterns, personal habits. The reps then report to their immediate divisional superiors, who sieve and feed interesting or helpful snippets of intelligence to national headquarters.' He adjusted the steam flow. 'There are managing directors in every country and they report ultimately to Zurich. That's where the top brass are, the hub of the empire.' De Mart dragged his knees up and wrapped bear-like arms around them. He stared into the thickening mist – he'd heard this spiel before, in Switzerland. 'But we also run a number of discreet decision-making units.' Danker paused deliberately, and de Mart squinted at him quizzically through the gloom. 'Sometimes the wheels of profitability don't always run smoothly.' Danker went on. 'Sometimes it needs a gentle nudge.' He stood up and stretched, then looked around before squatting back on the slats.

De Mart's gaze never left him. 'What exactly does that mean?' The Afrikaner accent finally broke through.

Danker swung his arms from side to side, then twisted his neck so tightly it crunched. 'Lemme tell you a little bit more.' He rubbed both legs with the towel, then meticulously began drying each toe. The other man looked on impatiently. 'We produce pharmaceuticals. They have to get to the end user, the millions of patients around the world. Right?' De Mart nodded. 'Between us and them is the medical profession. They prescribe our products, we make a profit. They use somebody else's drug, we lose a sale. So we need them on our side. And the ones we need most are the opinion formers, the top men and women in medicine. Their comments or opinions can make or break a compound.' De Mart was in intense listening mode, okaying each point. 'Then there are the hostiles,' continued Danker, 'the shits who bad-mouth anything in our portfolio. We keep them under close scrutiny. One statement from anyone in that group and we counter-attack immediately.'

The South African interrupted. 'How?'

Danker glanced around; others had now entered the steam room and were too close. 'Let's have a swim.'

They moved to a large pool, tiled in turquoise with dolphin motifs. The water was warm and a gentle shimmer hung over the still surface. The area was deserted; the pre-lunch rush hadn't begun and they both dived in and began churning up the water.

Ten laps later, up on the side, Danker elaborated. 'We do it the gentle way first. The company has a lot of people in its pocket. Doctors, journalists, medical magazine editors. Media health programmers. Over the years we've cultivated contacts, spread a lot of money. Overseas junkets, lavish dinners and sponsorships, generous grants, equipment subsidies.' He slipped back into the comfort of the water and turned, elbows resting on the mosaic edge. 'So we call in a few favours. We know which editor will clear a page for a promotional piece, which doctor will write a slanted article, which journo will give us airtime.' He did a backstroke into deep water, then treaded gently. 'And if that isn't enough we take certain actions to ensure that a particular hostile doesn't bad-mouth us again.' He flipped to the bottom, touched the tiling, then kicked his heels to reverse. Gliding gently to the surface, he rubbed his eyes clear and looked up. 'Which is where you come in.'

De Mart grinned. 'I thought you'd never get to the point.'

'We've got the lowdown on almost every important medic.' Danker was back at the side of the pool. 'We know the wife-beaters, the drunks, the coke heads and the paedophiles. We even know the cross-dressers, the burnt out or just down and out. Sometimes a quiet word or a few photographs through the mail is all it takes to change someone's opinion. Or shut a mouth.' He dunked his head briefly, then shook the drops free. 'That way we keep the wheels of profitability running smoothly.'

The South African stood up and plunged into the deep end, churning the water with such force he almost raised the ambient temperature. He swam twenty laps, then vaulted out. Grabbing a towel, he swaggered around towards Danker, who was dragging his hair into shape.

'What do I have to do?'

Danker looked up. 'Hend, we want you to take control of Chicago. I'm not exaggerating when I say the company's future depends on this being successful.'

They were now sitting side by side on a ledge, Danker lean and taut, the other muscular and bull-necked. Contrasting accents, New York drawl and Afrikaner lilt. Twenty feet away a large window gave them a perfect view of a small work-out gym and inside some of Manhattan's top earners were trying desperately to sweat away expense-account dinners.

'You'll be paid handsomely, US dollars in a numbered Swiss bank account. No trail for the IRS. Your money can be withdrawn anywhere in the world at twelve hours' notice. If this goes to plan you'll be back in Johannesburg later this year a very wealthy man.'

De Mart looked deep into Danker's eyes, as if searching for a hidden agenda. 'I like what I'm hearing.' He was already dreaming of a fine-cut stone house along one of the better towns on the western Cape. Maybe Hout Bay with its spectacular sea views.

Enough money to buy a small fishing boat and idle away his hours lying in the sun, a line dangling in the deep blue waters.

'We have a worldwide product launch planned for early October,' Danker said. 'It's going to be high-profile and costly and was to be heavily endorsed by the Carter Hospital Heart Unit in Chicago. But four days ago our most important mouthpiece there was murdered and now we're left with an empty chair and no big chief to carry our promotion. We've put out feelers with all the other major US institutions but no one's interested. It's Chicago or nothing.'

'What's the problem?'

'The new professor. The hospital was in such a goddamned rush to get somebody on board they appointed an Irishman with no track record. He's a novice, an academic unused to the commercial side of medicine. Guy spends all his time wondering about the mysteries of the universe while the rest of us have to graft to make the profits that allow him to indulge his daydreams.'

'So what do we do?'

'The Carter administration is still keen to have the inauguration focused there. It'll bring prestige to the division and a much-needed cash injection. I've been in constant touch and know they're determined to run with it. But they're worried about this new man.'

De Mart looked puzzled. 'Do we really have a problem? If the hospital wants us as much as we need them, then where's the issue?'

Danker shook his head, droplets falling on to his shoulders. 'We can't take any chances, the stakes are too high. If the new chief won't play ball the inauguration could be a PR disaster. And we need that drug to succeed, there's no room for failure.'

There was a strained silence and de Mart began towelling his back and shoulders, muscles rippling with each movement.

'I want you to swamp this guy,' Danker said finally. 'Find out everything about him, what he likes to eat, where he shops for clothes, what his marriage is like. Does he drink a lot or take recreational drugs? If there's dirt, find it. But if there's not then woo him with whatever it takes to get him on board.' He stood up and grasped the other man's shoulder, holding his gaze firmly. 'We need that hospital.'

*

'To the new professor, my dad.' Eight-year-old Danny was holding a beaker of fizzy orange laced with a small amount of champagne. The dining table in the Hunt family's cramped apartment was draped with an Irish linen cloth edged with embroidered flowers; arranged on top were a selection of their Waterford crystal, three settings of fine bone china and shiny cutlery. To the side was a feast of barbecued steak and spicy ribs, mixed salad and fries with an open bottle of 1998 Sancerre and an empty half of Moët et Chandon.

It was the evening of Jack's first full day in his new position, and most of the previous ten hours had been spent in management conferences. But the weather was so inviting he'd slipped away as early as seemed decent to celebrate. Low clouds now blocked the oppressive heat leaving temperatures in the mid-eighties with mercifully low humidity.

Beth and Danny had dressed for the occasion, she in a simple long white cotton dress and canvas sneakers, hair pulled back and held in a butterfly clasp. The boy was in his best pants and tee-shirt. By contrast, Jack mooched about in denims and short sleeves as he cooked the food outside, then rushed in when the meat was ready. For a few minutes there was relative silence as each wolfed down the food and sipped their drinks. For husband and wife the occasion was unreal, dream-like. Something they'd fantasised about for years. Stability, a permanent salaried position. Without admitting it, Jack had woken up that morning half expecting a call from the Carter to say there'd been a dreadful mistake and the board was appointing an altogether different candidate to the top spot. But gradually the full implications sank in, and he began to lighten up.

'Hunt,' teased Beth, 'it's time you bought some decent clothes. You can't go to work dressed like a pauper. You've got to look like a professor as well as act like one.'

Danny piped in. 'Mum's right, the suit you wore the other day was the same I saw you in for that interview in New York.'

Jack put up his hands in mock surrender. 'Okay, I'll get a few shirts and ties if that keeps you happy.'

'And not in Filenes Basement,' warned Beth, 'try somewhere decent like Bloomingdales or one of those fancy boutiques along Oak Street.'

Jack put down his glass firmly and fixed his wife with a

reproachful eye. 'I wear scrubs when I'm in the hospital. I have no intention of spending a fortune on Armani suits that'll sit in my locker all day. I'll find something I feel comfortable with, and not too pricey.'

'I might do some shopping myself.' Beth had a twinkle in her eye. 'I think a girl deserves a little treat after all these years holding tight on the purse strings.'

Jack groaned loudly, but let the warning past.

'And can we start looking for a house to buy? This apartment is bursting at the seams. You've turned the only spare room into a study and we have to tiptoe round mountains of paperwork to get in and out.'

Jack was beginning to wonder whether his first month's salary would be spent before it was even deposited in his account. 'Let's take it one step at a time,' he cautioned. 'First I have to mould the division into shape and that's going to swallow a lot of effort. We may have to put some of your grand plans on hold until I get the basics right. Then we can go property hunting.' He tinkled his glass against Beth's and winked. 'Certainly we can get new clothes, maybe look at a car, then think of where we'd like to live.'

Danny knocked back his drink in one go and wiped his lips with a napkin. 'Don't take too long. There's a lot of windows at risk if I don't get a bigger garden to run around.' He jumped down from the table and grabbed his football from a box near the apartment door. Two minutes later he was kicking the hell out of the back plot.

Beth rested her elbows on the table and sipped contentedly on her wine. 'I like this one,' she said, inspecting the bottle. 'I could learn to live like this.'

Jack grinned and blew a kiss. 'It's all ahead of us. The contract's signed and there's no going back. Be patient, it's coming together at last.'

But his wife couldn't be contained. 'I'm just so excited,' she enthused.

'Me too.'

'So much to do. I'm itching to make real changes. Get out and enjoy life to the full. Find a home.'

Jack leaned across the table and they kissed, long and deep. 'That's exactly how I feel, but I can't afford to let it show. I walked the corridors today like I was used to being king of the castle. Even wore the Chief of Cardiology white coat. And boy did that make me feel good.'

Later, while Danny was fast asleep, they continued their celebrations in bed. When they were finally spent, an exhausted Beth rolled on to her side, stretching her body out fully for comfort. Soon there came an occasional twitch and murmuring, then gentle and relaxed breathing.

Jack stared at the ceiling, listening to his wife, feeling the closeness of her body. He couldn't ever remember being so contented.

5

One week after the brutal murder of Sam Lewins and just five days since he'd handed in his letter of resignation, Jack Hunt strode through the corridors of Carter Hospital Heart Unit. He was in a new summer outfit, bought that weekend: cream linen jacket over navy pants with blue shirt and red striped tie. He looked a million dollars. His jet-black hair was combed to order, his stubble neatly trimmed, and he walked with the air of a man on a mission. At 9.30 he spent half an hour checking the patient case load, then fielded a long-distance call from Zemdon Pharmaceuticals in New York. He promised he'd try to get back when he had time. Finally he made his way to his old office, now freed up by the police investigators, and sat down to collect his thoughts. There could be difficult times ahead, even controversial. But as he stared out at the distant highrises he knew he wouldn't be comfortable until he had turned round the division. First he wanted a few cosmetic changes.

'I'd like a corner suite big enough to conduct meetings and hold teaching seminars.' That was the initial request to hit administrator Steve Downes. 'And I'd like a decent-sized desk with PC networked to the rest of the zone.' Jack tried to imagine Downes sitting in his luxury rooms on the tenth floor, probably flicking at the air-conditioning unit with his remote control while the rest of the staff sweltered in the heat. He pressed ahead, relishing the challenge. 'I need a secretary, initially part-time, probably full-time later. It'll have to be someone with medical experience and computer skills.'

One level above, Downes crunched down on an antacid and chewed furiously. Then he loosened a button on his midriff to ease the strain. 'Anything else?' His sarcasm was wasted.

'Yeah. I'd like the office painted. You know, freshened up. New carpet, a few decent chairs. Some areas here look very shabby. That's not good for morale. I want everyone to know we're stepping out of the Dark Ages. The Heart Unit is going to look and perform like a showpiece of excellence.' Despite a weary sigh across the line, Jack struck again. 'And I'd like it ready by the end of the week.' There was a fit of coughing and spluttering.

'Jesus, that's really pushing things,' Downes complained.

'Not really,' the doctor came back. 'I spoke with the maintenance supervisor and he says he could pull a three-man crew up here immediately and have the work completed by Thursday at the latest.'

There was a sudden silence.

'You spoke with the maintenance supervisor?' Incredulity.

'Yeah, Steve. I know how busy you are and didn't want to wrap up your time with such detail. I want to start moving with some speed next week. I'd like the basics ready by then.'

Downes caved in and gave the necessary authorisation.

Sam Lewins had lost his long-serving assistant ten months earlier and had never bothered looking for a replacement. A call to a company specialising in medical recruitment produced quick results, and three girls were short-listed for the position as secretary to the new professor.

Jack interviewed them on the Friday, at the end of a hectic preparatory week during which his feet had barely made contact with the ground, in the freshly painted and newly carpeted corner office he'd been allocated. He'd chosen a grey-blue for the floor with soft cream walls. The desk and chairs were beech veneer and the overall effect looked good. The inner room, where he would work, overlooked W Harrison. In the near distance the giant grey monolith of Cook County Hospital dominated the streetscape, while below his window traffic snarled and weaved and the occasional ant-like pedestrian sheltered in the shade of nearby buildings. The temperatures had hovered around ninety all day, while inside the new professor's rooms a small fan did its best to relieve the stuffy atmosphere.

Jack had several times that week walked the area with a mixture of pride and disbelief, recalling the many cramped quarters he'd been forced to work in over the years. Sharing with other researchers, paperwork and tissue slides spilling on to the floors where they were usually stomped on. Chairs with stuffing hanging out, no telephone or computer communications. As he'd gazed around the splendour of the suite, he'd experienced a sense of disbelief. Professor Jack Hunt, Chief of Cardiology at the Carter Hospital, Chicago. Get used to it. You've chased positions like this for years and missed. Moved your family around the world. Now live up to the challenge.

'Hi, I'm Dr Hunt. Why don't you relax and tell me a little about yourself?' For the interviews he'd come straight from Invasive Cardiology where he'd been called to an urgent cardiac catheterisation. As happened so often, he was the only experienced senior attending available when many crises arose. 'I don't want to make this too formal and intimidating.'

Each girl was heard in turn. He flicked through the offered CVs, firing questions about past experience, present commitments and future plans. He had to fit the three meetings into his lunch hour and wasn't keen on stringing them out unnecessarily. Two of the applicants were dismissed almost immediately. They were bright, attractive and lively with good computing skills, but neither had sufficient nursing experience. The third was a twenty-eight-year-old black girl named Helen Bradley. She was petite and slim with a wide smile that brightened up the room.

'You look like a man in one helluva hurry.' She caught Jack off guard immediately. 'I can't remember when I last saw such chaos.' Her voice lifted and fell like a slow wave, accent distinctly Chicagoan. Her eyes drifted round the offices.

Jack looked across guiltily, then rested her curriculum vitae on the desk and leaned into his chair.

'Does it look that bad?'

'The phone outside hasn't stopped ringing since I came by, your PC isn't turned on.' She uncrossed her legs and leaned forward to look behind Jack's head. 'And you don't even know where the air-conditioning switch is.' She fixed a critical eye across the table. 'Professor, whether I get this job or not you better hire somebody fast cos you're barely treading water.'

Jack grinned, then scanned the girl's career record. 'Diploma in Intensive Care I see?'

Helen nodded, then slipped a large brown envelope across. 'Those are originals of my other certificates. I was an OR attendant for five years, then intensivist in the emergency room at Rush Presbyterian.'

'So why the career change?' In the outer office the telephone started up again.

'I've seen enough blood and guts to last me a lifetime. I'd like to work at something a little less demanding but still in medicine. And I can't handle the night duty with my kids.'

'How many children do you have?'

'Two, and they're both under five. They need their mom. My man doesn't get home most evenings till past nine and I can't leave them with a sitter that long.'

The persistent ringing outside stopped, then kicked in again within thirty seconds. Helen frowned and stood up. 'I'm finding it hard to concentrate with that noise. Can I answer it and get whoever it is off the line?'

Jack waved a hand, secretly delighting in the girl's casual confidence. 'I wish you would, the damned thing's beginning to jar on my nerves too.' While she was out of the room Jack scanned her references.

There was a muttered exchange at the front office, then Jack heard the telephone receiver being laid down. 'Zemdon Pharmaceuticals from New York. Could they have five minutes of your time?'

Jack groaned and pulled a face, but before he could reply Helen was back on the line, her words coming through clearly. 'I'm sorry, Professor Hunt is in the middle of interviews right now. Can I take your number and get him to return your call?' One minute later she was back in her seat. 'Now, where were we?'

Jack closed over the CV. This girl was dynamite, just what he needed. Brimming with confidence and full of initiative. 'When can you start?'

Helen glanced at her watch. 'I've got commitments later this afternoon.' She paused, forehead creased in thought. 'I guess you could sweet-talk me into staying a bit longer, but other than that, how does first thing Monday sound?'

Jack was on his feet and halfway out the door. 'Sounds great, but whatever you do,' he pleaded, 'don't leave in the next hour. I'm heading straight to admin to ratify your contract.'

He returned less than an hour later to find Helen had already hung his degrees and diplomas on the walls of the outer office.

When he walked in she was ordering headed 'Chief of Cardiology' notepaper and business cards. She'd already checked the telephone, fax and e-mail facilities were working. 'I think we'll get along just fine, Professor Hunt.' She flashed a winning smile. 'Oh, and two calls came in right now.' She flicked through scribbles on a legal pad. 'The *Chicago Tribune* was on the line. Their health columnist would like an interview. I gave him an hour between four and five this afternoon. Told him to be here sharp and get out sharp.'

Hunt's jaw dropped in astonishment. The *Tribune* was one of the most important and influential national broadsheets.

'Nothing like a good spread in this weekend's supplement to let the world know you've arrived.' Helen collected her handbag. 'And Zemdon Pharmaceuticals hounded me again for almost ten minutes to fix in a time slot next week. They sure are persistent.' She glanced around the offices, seeming satisfied with what she saw, then smiled at her new boss. 'See you Monday.'

At 6.30, after an overly long interview with the medical journalist, Jack held a short prearranged meeting with the other three senior attendings, Nat Parker, Harry Chan and Martin Shreeve. As Jack expected, Parker arrived first, all smiles and handshakes.

'Well Jack, you've certainly moved pretty fast since your appointment, and I can't see everyone being too pleased with the speed of it all.' His voice was rich and gravelly, his face mirroring his emotions. 'But I'm calling this straight now and up front.' He towered above Hunt by at least six inches, his gangly frame seeming to move of its own free will. Restless arms and legs, shoulders jumping, prematurely bald for his forty-six years. He wore a white coat over open-neck shirt and dark pants, official ID snapped to a lapel and stethoscope dangling loosely around his neck. 'I'm delighted you got the top spot.' He sat down and spread his long legs out, then glanced furtively at the open door. 'This place has been going to hell and somebody has to stop the rot.'

At least one on my side, thought Jack. Along the corridor footsteps and muffled noises could be heard approaching. Now how were the other two going to handle this? Jack had had nothing more than intimations so far.

Parker interrupted his musings. 'I was almost sorry about Sam Lewins until I read about that child porn stuff. I don't know what the old bastard was getting up to recently for he sure was acting real secretive. Didn't give a shit about the division.' The noises were now right outside the door. 'I'm backing you, Jack. Time we did some real work around here.'

Harry Chan and Martin Shreeve arrived together. Chan started his usual nervous laugh. 'Professor, many congratulations – officially!' The insincere grin and limp handshake irritated the hell out of Jack, the stupid chuckle he found grating. Chan was dressed in a lightweight navy suit over white shirt and bright yellow tie, the whole outfit too large for his slight frame. He pulled up a chair beside Parker and tried to start small talk, repeatedly fidgeting with his thick-lensed glasses. Finally he pushed them back on to the bridge of his nose so hard the skin indented.

Martin Shreeve was smoking a cigarette, and Jack caught a whiff of bourbon off his breath. 'Hi there,' he growled sourly, his whiskered double chins bobbling. He looked restless, oversized for his scrubs and with a disgruntled look suggesting he'd rather be a million miles away. 'Congratulations on the new position.' He edged to a corner and leaned against the wall, then looked around for an ashtray. Finding none, he tipped the embers into an open palm and held it there awkwardly. Finally, he stuffed the ash into a side pocket. There was a strict no-smoking policy throughout all levels of the Carter Hospital, and Jack knew Shreeve treated the by-law with open contempt. He sensed the first confrontation looming.

He went to the back office and returned with a bottle of champagne and four glasses. Shreeve's eyes brightened immediately the cork was popped and the glasses topped and handed round.

'I'm going to make this quick and to the point.' Jack insisted on tinkling everyone's glass, then raised his own and took a sip. The others followed suit. 'We're here to celebrate the division. Next week I'll outline the changes I'd like to introduce.' Chan and Shreeve exchanged nervous glances, but Nat Parker listened with an almost beatific smile and sipped more champagne. 'Until then all I want to say is that I hope we'll all get along just fine. We've known one another for some time and I think we recognise the Heart Unit is in need of restructuring.' He noticed the glum expressions on Chan and Shreeve deepen. It's coming boys, whether you like it or not. 'For today, let's celebrate and prepare for the future. We can deal with the new responsibilities next week.' He raised his glass. 'To the Carter Heart Unit.' Only Nat Parker returned the toast. The other two tried desperately to smile, but the end result didn't change their uneasy expressions.

As the group was breaking up, Jack tapped Shreeve on the shoulder and asked him to stay, waiting until the other two were out of earshot.

'Martin,' he said, voice as cold as ice. 'Make that the last cigarette you ever smoke on this level.'

Shreeve stared back, long and hard, then without a word he stepped outside and pulled the door closed.

'They're going to hate you.'

'I know.'

Beth and Jack were in bed, naked and damp with sweat after making love. It was just before midnight that same evening and he was relating the day's developments. He lay on his back, staring at the ceiling, Beth curled up beside him, her blonde tresses mussed and bedraggled.

She traced a finger along his chest. 'They'll say you're too squeaky clean.'

'Let them.'

'Maybe I should put them right.' She leaned over and ran her tongue along Jack's lips.

'Yeah?' He could just about make out the mischievous grin. 'And how?'

'Well,' she began provocatively, fingers now brushing along her husband's inner thighs. 'What about those girls in that Bangkok massage parlour? Four, wasn't it?'

'Three,' Jack immediately corrected. In fact it was closer to six, though he'd lost count at the end. He'd been en route to Australia and had stopped off at the Thai capital. Three days later he'd been put through the *Kama Sutra* from A to Z and was sore from the efforts. 'It was definitely three,' he lied. 'It's not the sort of thing you'd forget.'

This had all come out one night in Sydney after too many Fosters lagers, Beth trying to suss out his sexual history. They'd been dating for about two months when she discovered him in bed with a stunningly beautiful and dark-haired receptionist. That had caused a bust-up which lasted six weeks and threatened to destroy their relationship. She'd probed long and hard about his past life and he'd opened up too much.

'Look.' Jack decided to switch the conversation, sensing he was going to have all past misdemeanours re-examined. 'What happened years ago is over and done with. Okay, I got laid as often as I could. Sure I drank too much on occasions and I did smoke a little hash.' He levered himself on to one elbow. 'A man's gotta have some fun before he grows too old and forgets how. So squeaky clean I certainly am not.'

Beth tweaked his nose. 'I know that, but no one else does.'

They lay face to face, arms tightly around each other.

'What was it you once told me about doctors?' Beth asked. 'Some ten-year rule?'

Jack didn't speak for what seemed like ages and Beth nudged him in the ribs.

'Ten years out of med school and your graduation class has its pattern established. Many will have lost two or three patients through bad judgement or inexperience.'

'How many have you lost?' The words were whispered, the light-heartedness had disappeared.

'Three.'

Beth gasped. This was uncharted territory, even for her. 'How?'

They disentangled, and Jack returned his stare to the ceiling. 'The first one I gave a wrong injection. I was exhausted after being on duty for three days and nights in a row and mixed up the ampoules. He was very ill anyway and probably wouldn't have lasted much longer. My mistake certainly didn't help his prospects.' He ran a hand through his hair, then wiped at his brow with a corner of the bedsheet. 'The second I missed the diagnosis. Treated an elderly lady for what I thought was a heart attack and all the time she had this big blood clot in her lungs. The third was a little boy, about Danny's age.'

He heard another sharp intake of breath.

'Severe head injury I didn't move on quickly enough. Kid died from brain compression. He could have been saved, I just didn't read the vitals correctly.'

'Don't tell me any more.'

Jack leaned across and kissed Beth's forehead. 'I've had to learn to live with this. It's my career. You don't go through medicine without making mistakes. When they happen you keep going and learn from the experience.' He pulled his wife on top and held her as if there was no tomorrow. 'That's the life I chose.'

Neither spoke for a while, both wrapped in their own thoughts.

'What else does that ten-year rule say?'

'About five per cent of graduation class will be addicted to drink or drugs, some will be in their second or third marriage, others in therapy. A few will be involved in criminal activity such as insurance scams or drug dealing, and at least one will have committed suicide. Then, on rare occasions some homicidal nutcase will have surfaced.' He paused briefly. 'Apart from that the rest will be pretty normal.'

Beth arched her back to get a better look at her husband's face in the gloom. 'So what sort of freak show have you inherited at the Carter?'

Jack ran his hands slowly along her naked back. 'I've got a fifty-eight-year-old drunk and a fifty-five-year-old gambler. Nat Parker's the youngest, mid-forties, and steady as a rock. He's an excellent doctor. But the general unit morale is poor. It needs fresh blood.'

'Why do you have to rush at it? Can't the changes wait until things have settled down?' There was an air of pleading in Beth's voice. 'Don't make them hate you.'

Jack eased her higher on to his chest, curling his fingers through her hair. Through the thin walls they could hear Danny snoring. 'You know the way some people see an old building and just can't wait to restore its glory? Or a good, substantial company goes to seed because the boss is too goddamned lazy to move with the times? That's how I feel. If I don't make my presence felt from the start the division will only go from bad to worse.'

Beth rested her head on Jack's chest and listened to his heartbeat. She was a young mother in a strange city with an eight-year-old boy to rear and longing to have another baby. And her man wanted to change the world.

'Be careful, Hunt. Won't you?'

6

There is a cheap hotel in Chicago close to the River North Gallery District called Cloneys. It squats eight storeys high in a corner about half a mile from where the Kennedy Expressway melts into N Orleans. It's basically a dump, a pack-them-in and boot-them-out overnighter frequented by businessmen and tourists on low budgets. In the basement there is a dimly lit bar with cubicles along the walls and enough television sets so punters can catch any ball game no matter where they're sitting. Football, ice hockey, basketball, baseball. Out of season the bartenders record Australian rules matches and play them over and over. Even regular drinkers rarely notice the difference for it's always big, muscular men beating the pulp out of one another as they chase a ball. Cloneys' basement is for the serious boozer, the kind who prefers darkness and anonymity to bright sunshine or a walk in the park. The beer and bourbon chasers usually trying desperately to remember what they came in so long ago to forget. Even the cocktail waitresses look worn and tired, almost as desolate as the guzzlers they try so hard to serve.

Carter cardiologist Martin Shreeve was a regular at Cloneys. After work, sometimes before work, most weekends. His marriage was lifeless, his family grown up and long since departed to other states. His wife spent most of her time in Florida with a widowed sister. Shreeve was an alcoholic. He knew it and didn't give a damn; he was too far down the road to care. He'd done the maths and planned on retiring within the next two years. He reckoned he could eke out the remainder of his alcohol-hazed life between his apartment near City Hall, Cloneys and Wrigley Field, home of the Cubs. Shreeve was a big baseball fan. He didn't care whether his team was on a winning streak or a downer, he just soaked up the atmosphere. The clatter of trains on nearby tracks, the closeness of the seats, the spectators on the rooftops, the banter on the terraces. That was all he wanted from life. But he had another twenty-four months of cardiology to endure before he reached his goal. The late Professor Sam Lewins had been an unwitting ally. Equally indifferent and apathetic, he couldn't have given a damn whether the Carter Heart Unit was awash with booze. But now with Jack Hunt in charge, Shreeve's drink-sodden future seemed very insecure.

On the Sunday Shreeve sat on his own in Cloneys, squeezed into a cubicle at the back. It had just turned noon and outside the city was bustling with life and sun and tourists. In the gloom of the basement there was only a handful of sots, cigarettes burning in shaky hands, one or two mumbling to themselves. Shreeve had the weekend edition of the *Chicago Tribune* on the table in front of him, a two-page spread torn out and set aside for particular attention. He scanned the headline, CARTER'S NEW HEART MAN, then re-read the full piece, trying hard to ignore the accompanying photograph of a smiling and contented-looking Jack Hunt, 'Hotshot Professor' the byline.

'Don't read any more, it'll only make your blood pressure worse.'

Shreeve didn't look up as Harry Chan slid into the booth. Chan scanned the bar, waving away an approaching waitress, then gave one of his irritating laughs.

'How the hell can you see anything down here? This is gloomsville, man.'

Shreeve looked around, then shrugged dismissively. 'I can see, that's all that matters.' He pushed the newspaper across. 'Have you read this?'

Chan inspected the other man closely. 'Martin, some day you should shave and put on a few decent clean clothes.'

Shreeve was dressed in a long, oversized sweatshirt hanging loosely over equally oversized tracksuit bottoms. Stubble covered each chin. He ignored the comment and snarled, 'Did you see this?'

Chan lifted a page corner as if there was dog dirt on it. 'Yeah I read it.'

Shreeve squinted in the gloom. 'And?'

Chan leaned back and said nothing. Shreeve waited impatiently. 'And? What the fuck do you make of it?'

The other man raised both palms to calm Shreeve down. When he spoke it was slow and deliberate, his voice almost sounding solemn. 'We must tread carefully. Hunt will give us trouble if we let him.' Shreeve made to interrupt, but Chan continued. 'If we let him, Martin, only if we let him. I think Steve Downes believes he's going to be a walkover, putty in his hands.' He toyed with a beer mat. 'We don't know what changes he's planning, we don't know if they're workable anyway. Why don't we just wait? Go with it. If he strays too far he may find himself out on a limb. He's no team player, but he still needs us to run that division with him.'

Shreeve flagged a waitress and ordered another beer. When she was out of earshot he glowered across. 'I can't wait two fucking years. I couldn't put up with the Irish bastard that long. I know it's gonna be me or him.'

Harry Chan spun the news-spread around and scanned the text. 'The way it's shaping, Martin,' he said after three paragraphs, 'I wouldn't put big bucks on you.'

The *Tribune* article covered two full pages, allowing for advertising space. There was a potted history of the Heart Unit, much emphasis being devoted to its glory days and then analysis of the more recent decline. The health columnist had garnered many off-the-record quotes about low standards in high places. There were also a number of on-the-record statements from other department heads delighting in the new change of leadership. The unfortunate Sam Lewins was painted as the villain of the piece, his dramatic murder and the subsequent pornography discovery only reinforcing this distorted image.

'How could such an important division languish in mediocrity for so long?' pondered the journalist. He then went on to offer his own explanations: power play, personality clashes, lack of leadership et cetera. Without naming names he repeated in-house gossip on senior staff at the cardiology division. And the comments were none too flattering. Harry Chan had to grit his teeth as he skimmed the words. He couldn't bear to see himself identifiable through the thinly veiled camouflage. Most of the facility would know exactly whom the *Tribune* was hinting at with certain unflattering comments.

The interview with Jack Hunt occupied half a page. Career

history and list of medical publications. Lots of bullish quotes, including one from hospital administrator Steve Downes: 'An excellent candidate who was already working in the division, now with exciting plans to revamp the Heart Unit and return it to its rightful position as the premier Midwest cardiology site.' Head and shoulders picture of Downes taken when he was at least ten years younger and twenty pounds lighter. There was a separate head and shoulders, but much larger, of Hunt. As usual he was staring straight at the camera, earnest expression, determined. Combined with the accompanying fulsome profile the impression was that of a strong and resolute man being called in to save the day.

'Fucking prick,' was Chan's final comment as he scrunched up the paper. He flagged a waitress and ordered a couple of beers.

'And a bourbon chaser,' Shreeve growled as the bottles were set down.

The two sat in silence, Chan sipping thoughtfully, Shreeve slurping as if he'd heard the brewery had been bombed and rationing was on its way.

'I think it's all bluff,' Chan decided finally.

Shreeve stopped drinking long enough to give the matter his full attention. 'Whaddye mean?'

Chan was trying to make a pyramid with beer mats and it collapsed as he explained. 'I think Mr Big Shot Hunt has played his cards to get the top job but he's not going to rock the boat because he can't afford to make things worse than they already are. He has no managerial experience and is totally unused to the commercial realities of clinical medicine. He's been in academic research for too long. Those kind of guys are driven idealists.' He allowed a flicker of a smile, then raised his bottle and tinkled it off Shreeves's bourbon. 'You should relax, Martin. Lighten up. You and I have been here for years. That Irish bastard is a blow-in. We'll take him down a peg if we have to. Let's first see what he's going to throw at us. Then we'll decide if he's really worth worrying about.'

Martin Shreeve wiped sweat-stained palms along his tracksuit bottoms. He knocked the bourbon back in one go, then rinsed the dregs from his teeth with the remains of a beer. 'I'm gonna give him a couple of months' grace. But if he gives me any more lectures I'll lift his fucking head off at the shoulders.'

They shuffled outside, both squinting at the sunlight dancing off the glass from a nearby highrise, Shreeve drawing hungrily on his tenth cigarette of the day. They were two misfits full of Dutch courage, propping each other up over a gutter, each silently wondering what lay ahead.

Back in her apartment Beth Hunt was carefully slipping a full *Tribune* interview into a large envelope. Beside her Danny was holding on to six other packages. One copy was for Sinead, her husband's older sister in Dublin. Jack's parents had been dead for some years and he'd struggled to keep in contact with his remaining family. More often than not it was Beth who made the calls, wrote the letters, remembered the birthday and Christmas cards. Another was for Sydney, where Beth's parents and two brothers still lived. They communicated regularly and were always asking about job developments. They pined seriously after Danny and complained constantly about the distance between them all. Next there were three copies for close friends scattered around the world, and then one for Jack's former professor and mentor in New York. Finally came a much begrudged package for Dr Carlotta Drunker in Sacramento. Jack had insisted on this despite another bout of Beth's pouting. Clipped to the newspaper cutting was a single sheet on which he'd added a hasty scribble: 'Delighted you've found your big brother. Didn't even know you'd lost him! I've only got one sister, so no big brother.'

Beth read the three sentences about twenty times, determined she'd find a hidden meaning. She only gave up when her husband promised to take them all out for dinner.

7

At ten minutes after five on the morning of Monday, 28 June, Jack slipped out of bed. It had been a hot and oppressive night and he'd slept fitfully. He leaned across and dragged the single sheet up over Beth's shoulders where she lay curled up in her favourite corner, then sat rock-still as he watched her stir. Satisfied she hadn't woken, he kissed her gently on the forehead, then padded across the floor to the spare room. He booted his PC, yawning as he waited for the icons to appear. One minute later his fingers were dancing along the keyboard.

He started to read a file he'd been working on in snatches over the previous week. The text was separated into eleven sections and he began cutting and pasting, deleting and typing until he had reduced this to eight. Then he leaned back in his chair and studied the words. He was on overdrive.

Outside he could hear the early traffic rumbling along N Clark, a few hundred yards from the apartment. He checked his watch: 5.38. Back to the keyboard and more editing. He deliberated on the new arrangements. In the reflection of the monitor he could see his hair sticking up at all angles and tried to smooth it down. He rasped fingernails against the stubble on his chin. He re-read his work, frowning. Then a thought hit and he deleted more before adding two final lines.

'Hunt, what are you doing up so early?'

Beth's voice made him jump, and she laid a hand on his shoulder to reassure him.

'A few last-minute plans I have to polish,' he offered.

She was now leaning over his shoulder, reading from the screen. 'I hope you're not in one of your whirlwind modes today,' she fretted as she reached the end.

'No,' he denied, 'it's more a make-your-mind-up time.'

Beth groaned. She knew how her husband ticked. When something important was decided no amount of reasoning or persuading could sway his decision. Even in matters of love. Back in Sydney, when she'd been dating him for less than a few months, they'd had one of many blazing rows. She'd stormed away, leaving him fuming in a hospital car park in the middle of a mid-summer downpour. Two hours later, soaked and bedraggled, he'd turned up on her doorstep and proposed marriage. She'd refused, and kicked him out. So he'd padlocked her bike and sat beside it overnight until she finally appeared for work. There was another heated argument, followed by an even hotter hour in bed. Ten days later they married.

'Aren't you going to have some breakfast?' she called. Jack was already under the shower, humming contentedly. 'And keep that noise down, you'll wake Danny.'

But fifteen minutes later Jack was packing his briefcase while his wife looked on anxiously. 'I'll grab something in the canteen. This is kind of an important day and I want to be in the hospital as soon as possible.'

Beth kissed his cheek. 'Any idea what time you'll be home?'

The briefcase was snapped shut, the apartment door unlocked. 'I'll try and get back before Danny goes to bed. You two go ahead with dinner and keep me something I can heat up.'

Beth followed him out on to the stairwell, only a bath towel wrapped around her body for decency. 'Hunt, Hunt,' she whispered loudly.

Halfway down the steps her husband stopped and looked back up. 'It's a job, don't make it a nightmare.'

Her only response was a wave of a hand, then the front door of the apartment complex clunked shut.

The tornado hit the Heart Unit that evening.

'Hi, I think most of you know me.' Jack had summoned an after-hours conference for medical personnel only. 'But in case any of you don't, I'm your new professor. I'd like to tell you about a few changes we're going to make around here.'

As well as the three senior attendings, Parker, Chan and Shreeve, there were seven other medical staff gathered in an unoccupied bay in the Intensive Care Unit. Two young women and five young men dressed in scrubs, all looking tired and edgy. Jack had chosen to hold the meeting on familiar territory rather than amid the grandeur of his new offices, still not entirely at ease with them himself. And his new secretary, Helen Bradley, was working flat out to restore order to the management side of the division. He'd decided to give her some space.

'Let's begin with a simple and non-contentious issue.' He was perched on the edge of a vacant bed, all eyes fixed on him. 'I know how hard most of you work up here. I'm very aware you put in long hours and often only catnap when on duty.' A few heads nodded in agreement. 'So I'm going to suggest we start the division rounds one hour later than usual.'

The junior attendings couldn't believe what they were hearing; one even asked Jack to repeat what he'd just said. Nat Parker looked puzzled, while Martin Shreeve and Harry Chan exchanged relieved grins. Jack knew this wasn't what they were expecting and waited until he had their attention again. Then he drew a legal pad from a side pocket and traced a finger along notes he'd made.

'New York's Brooklyn Hospital has just been fined fourteen thousand dollars for overworking junior doctors,' he explained. 'And the New York University Medical Center was hit for sixteen thousand after inspectors discovered first-year cardiac residents working up to one hundred and thirty hours a week.' He balled the paper and tossed it into a nearby bin. 'I don't want investigators prowling this unit. We can't take more bad publicity. Of any kind.'

The almost palpable tension evaporated, and Jack watched as the group began loosening up. He hadn't dropped any bombshell, despite their expectations.

'I've also arranged for proper and substantial food in the division for those on-call. Over the past few months I've noticed we seem to live off Starbucks coffee and snack foods. There's no point lecturing our patients about lifestyle issues if we can't get our own acts together.' There were a few high fives and relieved grins among the junior attendings. Jack kept his head down, but noted every gesture out of the corner of an eye. He finally looked up. 'However there's a price some will have to pay for this.' The small group stiffened as the new professor fixed his gaze on his older colleagues. 'It's time we shouldered responsibility for the unit. The buck stops at the top, not with those in training. I'd like senior attendings *in* the hospital and on level nine ready for action on time every morning from now on.' He pretended to smooth a rumpled sheet on the bed. 'We've got into the habit of drifting in and out at our own leisure. That's got to stop. We now lead by example.'

He stood up, passed some paperwork to one of the juniors, and then scrutinised the full squad. 'That's all for today. We'll talk again mid-week.'

To those with an eye for such things it seemed as though Martin Shreeve would have a seizure there and then.

'Hi, I'm the new Chief of Cardiology.'

It was Tuesday, 29 June, 7.30 in the morning. Jack was in the coffee room of the operating theatres on the third floor. This was a basic unit, blue walls and white-tiled floor with a small table cluttered with medical magazines in the centre. There were five easy chairs, two with torn lining and one with stuffing hanging out. Here, six storeys beneath the Heart Unit, many cardiology patients were taken for operation. Damaged heart valve replacements, arterial bypass procedures, major blood vessel repairs. The two divisions were interdependent, the surgeons called in when the cardiac doctors believed operative intervention was the best option for their charges. Equally, the surgical team expected their cardiology colleagues to have the patients in as good a shape as possible. Heart surgery can exact a heavy toll on the body.

Jack shook hands with the three senior doctors, all male, then handed each a clipboard with four pages attached. 'Those are the new and revised guidelines I've drawn up for our mutual charges,' he explained. He allowed the trio a few minutes to skim the text, noticing eyebrows arch as they reached the end. Jeez, I'm the youngest one here, they'll think I'm straight out of med school.

Donovan, a small swarthy man in green fatigues, peered curiously at Jack over a pair of close-lens glasses. 'I'll have to go through this in some detail, but it looks pretty impressive.'

The other two, Pawlski and Reed, murmured their agreement as they too completed the last sheet. 'Not before time,' added Reed for good measure. He leaned back in one of the seats and inspected a bagel, and then obviously decided he didn't like the look of it. He was tall but with a prominent straining belly, as if he'd eaten more bread than was good for him. 'I wish you well with your plans. You'll be like a breath of fresh air upstairs.' He fixed the cardiologist with a warning eye. 'But I can't see everyone welcoming that wind of change.'

Jack forced a grin. 'They'll move with the times or find somewhere else to complain.'

He could see the heart surgeons were impressed but cautious. They knew the stakes and they knew the players.

On Wednesday Jack made his way to the bowels of the Carter Hospital and the pathology department. Here, six doctors and over twenty allied staff processed the many tissues sent from the divisions above. Blood, urine, sputum were analysed and reported. Organ specimens were dissected and microscopically inspected. Whole bodies were autopsied for cause of death or investigation of final disease progression. The most senior among the staff here was a Philadelphia-trained pathologist called Jay Neils. He was a good-humoured tall man with a quiet chuckle and a range of dirty jokes renowned throughout the house.

'So you're the new kid on the block?' he said. He was sitting behind a cluttered desk, inspecting Jack from head to toe as if sizing him up for one of his cutting tables. 'The dynamo from Dublin, the hustler with the stethoscope. Your reputation precedes you, professor.'

Jack grinned. He was getting used to the curious stares and whispered comments as he moved through the hospital. 'I thought I'd introduce myself,' he began, 'and see if we could work together on some research I'm keen to get moving.'

Neils laughed softly. 'I'm listening, professor, I'm all ears. If I look a little surprised it's only because we haven't seen anyone from the ninth floor in the last five years. Maybe the patients don't die up there. Maybe you guys are so crash hot you don't need our services.' He noticed Jack's questioning frown and dropped his voice an octave. 'Or maybe the last boss spent so much time looking at dirty pictures he forgot how to be a real doctor.'

Jack decided to ignore the jibes. Keep focused. This is an old team but with a new captain. No point going over the lost games. We're playing for the season ahead. 'Dr Neils, if you don't mind I'd prefer we talked about my research programme. I'm much more interested in those issues.'

Neils bowed his head, acknowledging he was out of line. 'Shoot.'

He lifted both feet awkwardly on to his desk, dislodging a mountain of paperwork, then disengaged the phone so as not to be disturbed.

'Okay,' Jack began. 'I'm going to ask your team to post anyone aged fifty-five and under who dies in our unit from a heart attack. I'd specifically like them to section the carotid, femoral and coronary arteries and check for evidence of previous infection.'

Neils interrupted. 'Infection?'

Jack nodded, and sat down in the only free chair; the other three in the pathologist's tiny office were blocked by textbooks or patient files. Somewhere a door slammed and a hint of formalin drifted by. 'That's the research strategy: can we prove early heart disease is caused by severe arterial thickening brought on by some microbial infection in early life.' He passed over a thick ring-bound file. 'That's the preliminary work I've pulled together so far.'

Neils felt the weight of the file. 'This is the *preliminary* work? How heavy is the main event going to be?'

Jack pressed ahead. 'I'd also like it if we could jointly collaborate with our paediatric colleagues. Arrange for any autopsies they request to include a study of the children's arterial tree for evidence of early disease. Then we could possibly do antibody titres for specific pathogenic bacteria I feel may be involved in this phenomenon.'

Neils didn't speak for a good minute, then slowly brought his legs down from the table and stood up. 'Looks like there's going to be some serious work done up in that division, professor. That'll be a change. I hope your buddies are just as fired up.' He skimmed through the ring-bound. 'This looks good, very interesting material. I hope we can do the business.' He slipped the phone back on to the hook. 'I'll talk with the head of trauma and the paediatric team. I don't see any immediate problems.'

Jack heaved a sigh of relief. This was the one meeting he'd been worrying about. For a division as stagnant as the Heart Unit had been he realised it would take some persuading to convince the rest of the hospital everything was about to change. And satisfy them that any joint effort would be useful and valid, not wasted. The research was critical. If his protocols were accepted by the pathologists, paediatricians and trauma team then the rehabilitation of the Heart Unit had truly begun. But its performance would be scrutinised with a more than critical eye. Not that that bothered him. He would welcome collaboration with other disciplines, relish any constructive criticism. He was confident each discussion would allow him to shine, reinforcing the impression of a revitalised cardiology department. And he could progress his vital research interest.

Wednesday was a good day.

Thursday was not.

Jack called another after-hours conference, this time in the new offices, chairs set around his desk in a circular fashion. Helen had suggested the format. 'Don't make any one of them feel less than the other,' she'd advised. 'You know how fragile doctors' egos are. Everybody wants to be the white shark, no one likes to think they're at the bottom of the food chain.' Before she'd gone home she'd left out freshly brewed coffee and enough savouries to take the edge off pre-dinner hunger.

They arrived in small groups, Jack watching the response as he greeted them one by one. The seven junior attendings huddled in one corner, gossiping and picking at the appetisers until they were almost all gone. Martin Shreeve declined a seat and glowered from the most distant corner of the room. Harry Chan fiddled with his spectacles, taking them off and shining the lenses, shoving them back on his nose, then repeating the whole procedure five minutes later. He seemed ill at ease. Nat Parker, by contrast, was relaxed. Even his restless limbs were at peace.

'I'm sorry to keep you back again, but there are a few more issues I want to clarify.' Jack inspected the range of expressions: bored, disinterested, tired, attentive, apprehensive, sullen and watchful. He walked from chair to chair, handing out a clutch of clipped legal pads. Their pages lifted as the breeze off a revolving fan passed. 'New guidelines,' he explained as each set was collected.

Martin Shreeve folded the sheets into a roll without looking. His scowl followed Jack around the room.

'Disciplinary matters, disputes, arguments. Everything to come through this office. I don't want any simmering grudges on the floor. If you've got something on your chest, then let me know. It's my responsibility to keep this show on the road.'

He allowed a few minutes for the group to study the text, noting Shreeve's dismissive pose.

'Turn to page six, please.' Paper rustled. 'I've been negotiating this morning with the ER division. All patients presenting with chest pains suspicious of myocardial infarction are to be moved immediately to the ninth floor rather than be kept down there for observation. I want a full quota of staff familiar and confident with cardiac catheterisation on call at all times. If the EKGs and enzymes confirm an evolving ischemic episode we're going to do emergency angiography and proceed to stenting or balloon dilatation. Our aim will be to preserve cardiac muscle and prevent damage rather than watch the injury evolve and only then treat the consequences.'

There was a collective groan, and Martin Shreeve suddenly pulled open his copy of the procedures. As he scanned the relevant page his face twisted in fury.

'Okay, I accept this means more work,' interrupted Jack, 'and it'll be both time-consuming and intensive. It'll shift the responsibility for acute heart conditions from the emergency room to the ninth floor. And that's going to mean more on-call for senior attendings.'

Shreeve finally lost it completely. 'Jesus Christ, this isn't a runner. I'm not hauling my ass round the division every fucking night of the week playing God.'

There was a stunned silence, the junior staff unsure where to look. Harry Chan slumped in his chair and rested his forehead on his hands while Nat Parker sat motionless, watching every move. Jack waited for the fury to abate.

'I'm delighted you've decided to use the complaints procedure so quickly and openly, Martin,' he said. 'And I'm listening to your understandable concerns.' He forced his voice to remain on an even keel, determined to allow no hint of irritation. 'But we're all in this together. The Heart Unit is going to move with the times. Anyone who feels they can't handle the changes had better reconsider their contract.' It was fighting talk, the first public and direct confrontation.

Shreeve stood up, and unclipped and dropped the pages on the floor one by one. 'I'm gonna see my lawyer.' He stormed out of the room, slamming the outer door.

Jack ignored the disruption. 'Now let's work through the rest of the programme and get home as soon as we can.'

It took another hour to discuss and absorb the other radical proposals he had drafted. When the meeting ended Jack sat for a long time staring out of his office window at the glittering lights of the distant downtown skyscrapers. The dissenters were being flushed out. Would they bend or leave? Would they conspire against him? Had the battle begun or was Shreeve's outburst no more than an expected skirmish, the feeble flailing of a man on the ropes?

The persistent ringing of the telephone in Helen's office interrupted his thoughts.

'Hunt, what time are you going to be home this evening?' It was Beth, and she sounded tired.

Jack glanced at his watch and cursed silently. It was 8.30. This would be the fourth night in a row he'd be home well past ten. Danny would be in bed and dinner would be cold.

'I'm on my way.'

He was on the street and flagging down a cab within ten minutes. Better get some flowers on the way. The city lights scorched past as he urged the cabbie on.

On Friday Jack managed the impossible. He persuaded the heads of four other divisions to come together over lunch. Heart surgeon Donovan from the cardiothoracic unit, Jay Neils from pathology, one Professor Ned Watson of paediatrics and the head of trauma, George Ver Barkmen. As so often happens in large medical institutions, these important doctors worked under the same roof but had never held joint meetings. They would be like ships in the night, passing each other in the corridors or staff car park, even occasionally being introduced at social gatherings. But relative strangers most of the time.

They gathered in the newly decorated professorial offices, exchanging brief pleasantries and keeping a close eye on their watches as Jack explained the rendezvous.

'This will only take fifteen minutes at the most,' he promised. The visitors heaved a joint sigh of relief. 'I've spoken with each of you individually and explained the changes I'm going to push through the Heart Unit.' He had everyone's undivided attention. 'In tandem I plan to stimulate the division with a research programme based on data I've been working on for some time.' Paperwork was distributed. 'That's the study protocol. It's based on material and statistics gleaned from my personal information base. In addition, on pages ten to fifteen you can read how I propose to audit and collate the facts we collect.'

None of the four was looking at the records; all were studying the young man sitting opposite. That he could move so fast, meet with so many and finally arrange such a gathering within his first weeks of tenure was extraordinary. Jack sensed they were impressed but wary.

'I want to lift the cardiology unit back to the top,' he added finally. 'Make it world class.'

The subsequent discussion ran for over seventy minutes. It was lively and invigorating, Jack saying little else, allowing the others to explore their responses. When they broke up he knew he'd won the day. He'd made an impression and now had the most important division heads behind him. The Heart Unit could only move forward.

If Jack was moving with great speed, his secretary Helen was no slouch either. She hounded her boss, forcing him to meet deadlines, double-checking his diary appointments. There were admin meetings to be squeezed in between grand rounds, change-of-staff interviews during lunch breaks, patient calls to be returned. Helen juggled each with determination. Her reputation soon became as strong as that of the man under whom she now served.

'The American Heart Foundation has invited you to speak at their November meeting. What'll I say?'

'I'll do it.'

Jack was in green scrubs, coffee in one hand, biscuit in the other. He was finding it increasingly difficult to follow his own divisional dietary rule changes. Helen was dressed in white uniform with red waistband, clipboard and pen at the ready.

'The Illinois Faculty of Cardiology would like you on their expert panel. It'll mean three meetings a year to discuss local issues.'

'Count me in.'

'The editor of JAMA would like you to read and comment on three research papers they're considering running.' Helen was coming to the end of her list, frowning as she watched Jack reach for another biscuit.

'Tell him I can only do one a month, and only if he has the references double-checked in-house.'

'Gotcha.' Helen was now smiling and she produced a long, slim brown envelope from behind the clipboard. 'Zemdon Pharmaceuticals are offering to fly you and Beth to Hawaii early December to speak at an international cardiology meeting they're hosting.' She waved the envelope provocatively under Jack's nose. 'Sounds very nice. It'll be cold here, might just be the break you need coming into a long Chicago winter.'

Jack noticed the card stapled to the envelope. Hend de Mart – Midwest Representative, Zemdon Pharmaceuticals. 'Send it back to him. I'm not interested.'

Helen shrugged. 'It's your call. Wish someone would invite me to Hawaii.'

Jack was halfway out the door and in a hurry. 'Anything else? I'd like to practise medicine for a while.'

He only half heard the shout that followed his flapping scrubs. 'You're a professor now, Jack Hunt. The simple doctoring days are over.'

Saturday, 3 July was the day the bomb finally exploded.

Jack summoned an early-morning conference for the full cardiology team. This included doctors, nurses and paramedics. There were twenty-four in total called to order in a small lecture theatre at street level. He'd insisted on one junior attending staying on the ninth floor to oversee patients. The girl he chose was soon to leave for a position in Washington, and he considered her presence at the meeting unnecessary.

In every medical institution Saturdays and Sundays are rest days. Apart from those on-call it's a forty-eight-hour battery recharger, a chance to experience some sort of normal life before the weekly grind kicks in again. An opportunity to shop, get laid, get drunk, go to a ball game, lie in the sun or dream of Caribbean cruises. Chill out and reacquaint yourself with the family who probably only see you in snatches. A definite and well-demarcated time for relaxation. It was completely unheard of, even throughout the rest of the hospital, to call a full division staff into the hospital early on a Saturday. But Jack did exactly that.

'Good morning,' he began. There was no response, just sullen faces staring, the occasional glance at watches. Most were in casuals, shorts and tee-shirts. Jack wore a white cotton V-neck, faded blue denims and sneakers. 'This will be a one-off, I promise. It's ruining my day as much as yours, so I want to get through the single agenda immediately and quickly. If we tried this mid-week there'd be too many interruptions and I consider the issue too important to rush through. It will be explained face-to-face, by me, not relayed second- or third-hand. I want no misunderstanding or different spin put on my words. What you'll hear is what I mean. Also, if anyone has any difficulties on this topic I'd like to know immediately. I especially don't want simmering dissent in the unit.'

There was little change in the glum expressions. Martin Shreeve and Harry Chan sat together at the very back of the hall, both apparently very interested in the wood grain of the benches. Nat Parker was in jeans and tee-shirt, squeezed between two nurses in a centre pew. He too seemed less than pleased to be there. The rest of the group was already showing signs of increased restlessness. Through a large window the bright sunshine of a mid-summer Chicago beckoned. Jack hit hard, fast and low.

'As from now all contacts with the pharmaceutical industry are banned.' He paused to let the opening salvo hit its target. 'I don't want to see a company representative in the Carter Heart Unit again. I don't care what happens throughout the rest of the hospital, that's none of my business. But cardiology is my responsibility. Anyone with stock options in pharmaceuticals should declare that interest.'

There was a stunned silence throughout the small audience. The glum expressions had changed to complete amazement. This was the most radical policy ever introduced.

'No attending should give selective public support for any chemical product. I don't want to see the usual cheap giveaways emblazoned with company logos lying around the division. That includes pens, paper, mugs, towels, calendars et cetera.' Jack held up a clutch of bulging plastic bags. 'This is what I removed from the corridors and offices late last night.' He left the lectern at which he was standing and began pacing. In his denims and V-neck he looked more like an IT lecturer than a professor of cardiology. 'In short, I don't want this department compromised in any way by outside generosity or inducements. Each and any drug we use must earn its place. None of us should take the sales pitch on anti-anginals, anti-hypertensives, lipid lowering agents et cetera without challenging the data.'

Chins dropped, mouths hung open. Jack had even engaged the interest of Shreeve and Chan.

‘I would also advise against accepting junket trips to exotic locations. I’m always suspicious of the motivation of companies involved in such practices. If their product is good, it’ll sell. If it isn’t, it won’t, and throwing money at it won’t change that.’ He paused only briefly. ‘In 1997 the chemical industry spent a billion dollars in direct product advertising compared to less than six hundred million the previous year. That’s a *Wall Street Journal* statistic. I don’t want any undue influence here, none of their products coming in by the back door.’

What Jack was demanding of his staff was little short of sensational. All had been wined or dined at some stage by pharmaceutical representatives. Many had been flown to conferences in far-flung destinations where the only obligation was to listen to a company lecture extolling their range of products. The rest of the time was usually spent at the poolside, or on shopping sprees. All had mugs or calendars, even ice-scrapers, product logos prominently displayed. Houses and apartments were often bursting at the seams with cheap giveaways. With some of the better freebies, such as expensive pens, it was occasionally possible to scrape off the company emblem and pretend your tastes extended to such luxury goods. No one was untainted by this apparently overwhelming generosity. Equally, no one was under any illusion that favours were expected in return – that was the unspoken trade-off. However, to lose such unsolicited and tax-free offerings was a bit like taking all the icing off a cake. Many, too, had stock options in pharmaceuticals. They insider-traded like Wall Street’s worst. To have to declare that interest, maybe even give up the investment, was dynamite.

Before anyone could respond, Jack made a call to arms. ‘The Carter Heart Unit has stagnated in recent years and its poor performance has tarnished the image of the rest of the hospital. That’s about to change. The days of sloppy standards and half-hearted effort are over. We’re here to earn our money and drive this division back to the top. I want to see important and ground-breaking research carried out so that in the future our treatments and techniques will pioneer and lift standards internationally.’ He stopped and faced his audience. ‘That’s all I have to say.’ He looked from tier to tier. ‘Any questions or difficulties with this?’

No one spoke, not a head turned. It was as if the group had frozen.

'Okay, let's get out of here and grab some sunshine.'

Maybe five miles away due north in Lincoln Park, Beth Hunt was playing frisbee with her son. All around families were enjoying a day out in the open air, barbecues were burning, beer was flowing, laughter was filling the air. Kids skateboarded or cycled, while other dads kicked balls or fielded throws. People were savouring life, squeezing every last moment out of the occasion. She knew the job demanded long hours from Jack, but it was hard on their son.

'Okay, Danny,' she shouted finally when she felt she could not run one more yard in the humid temperatures. 'Let's go home and see if the whirlwind has returned.'

They began the long trek back to W Deming.

8

'Ms Bradley, is Dr Hunt in his office right now?'

Three days after Jack Hunt's pharmaceutical embargo bombshell an enraged Steve Downes called his rooms. It was fifteen minutes before ten in the morning and thirty before Jack was due to conduct an invasive cardiology lecture. These were well attended and popular with junior staff, their boss coming across as a natural instructor.

'He's ploughing through a mountain of dictation. Would you like to speak with him?'

'I sure as hell do. Don't let him leave, I'm on my way there.'

Downes brushed gruffly past Helen without so much as a greeting. The door to the inner office was ajar and he stomped inside, then slammed it shut.

Jack was behind his desk, but barely visible. The table was cluttered with paperwork, patient files, stacks of medical journals and empty coffee cartons. One chair was submerged under textbooks, a wastepaper basket beside it surrounded by scrunched pages that had missed their target. He looked up when the door slammed to find a glowering face. Downes was tight up against the edge of the desk, his body half across, midriff straining beneath a striped shirt. His collar was open, tie pulled down loosely from the neck, face ashen and twitching. His wire-wool hair was in disarray. There were no opening civilities.

'What the hell's this about banning pharmaceuticals in the Heart Unit?'

Jack snapped the off button on his micro-cassette and motioned the other man into the only free chair available. Downes ignored the gesture and continued to stand.

'Simple rule, Steve.' Jack held the threatening stare. 'I want to make this a world-class outfit, untainted by commercial interests.'

'Goddamnit Hunt, we are committed to an international product launch in October. The Zemdon Corporation has pledged a half-million-dollar cash injection to revitalise this hospital. We need that money. You can sit up here in your academic ivory tower all fucking day and still not know what it takes to run an institution like this.'

'But what does Zemdon want in return?' Jack countered. He had eased himself into a better position, no longer looking straight up at his challenger.

'How the fuck should I know?' shouted Downes, spittle now gathering at the corners of his mouth. 'When you're being offered half a million just to use the facility's note paper you don't ask too many questions. That money could as easily go to one of the big East Coast institutions.'

Jack pulled himself closer to the desk, pushing aside paperwork to clear a space on the top. 'Let me tell you something about medicine, Steve.' He eyeballed the administrator. 'Money will not lift this Heart Unit to the top of the world rankings. People will. The doctors and nurses and paramedics who use their training and skills to turn patients' lives round. Those are our assets. I've worked in divisions awash with money and high technology but staffed by performing monkeys who didn't know one end of a stethoscope from the other.' He paused to take breath. 'If Zemdon buys into this division then any research paper we produce will be viewed as potentially unsound. I know this game, I've spent my working life in it. If I announce beta-blockers are the only sensible treatment for unstable angina, at the next cardiologists conference someone will sidle up to me and ask how much I was paid to endorse that range. The profession's full of cynics, and rightly so. Quality units work independently of direct commercial interest. And that's the way it's going to be here.' He glanced at his watch. It was coming up to 10.15.

'It's in your contract.' A smug smile flickered across Downes's face.

Jack leaned both elbows on the desk, stretched out his fingers and rested his chin on the tips. 'It's not, Steve. We sidelined that issue, remember? I didn't stand up in front of the whole division last Saturday without first checking our deal.' He reached into a drawer and pulled out his copy of the official agreement, turning until he reached page six. He quoted. 'Subsection 3A. Coordinate proposed drug launch for Zemdon Pharmaceuticals: to be reviewed within one calendar month of commencing duties.' He looked across. 'I'm reviewing it now. I want no part of that inauguration. Let them look somewhere else for a parrot.'

Downes's mouth opened and closed but nothing came out. Then he grabbed the vacant chair and pulled it forward. 'Don't fuck with me, Jack. This deal was agreed well before Sam Lewins was shot. He was totally cooperative and enthusiastic about the project. Said he felt it would give the division prestige and lift morale. The whole programme is in motion. There've already been promotional mail shots, advance advertisements, venues booked, staff lined up. This isn't something we can walk away from lightly. Can't you sacrifice your goddamned high principles for once in your life?'

Jack checked the time. He was already running late.

'I gotta go, Steve. Sorry. We'll have to talk this over another day. Right now it's well down on my list of things to do.'

He made to get up, but Downes was already on his feet and leaning across the desk again.

'You are obliged, professor.' His expression was rigid, face muscles bunching.

'Don't try and force anything, Steve. I don't like being backed into a corner.'

'I'm telling you the deal's done. It's your fucking duty to see it through.'

'Final duty, Steve. If this issue is pushed it could cause waves.'

Downes stood upright, breathing heavily. He reached into a side pocket for a handkerchief and dabbed at his forehead. 'We'll talk tomorrow.' He took a step back and then turned and left.

9

There are many sleazeballs in life and not all of them are lawyers. Dr Harry Chan was one.

Chan was fifty-five, in his third marriage and heavily in debt. He had two ex-wives and a bunch of kids to support. His current wife had expensive tastes in clothes and furniture and their relatively modest house in Chicago's Oak Park district had been redecorated four times in eight years, its furnishings replaced on each occasion. Recently she'd started to give off the same 'bored and what'll I do today' vibes.

Chan had another expensive mistress: the bookie near Union Station. He would bet on horses and dogs, ball games and big fights. In state and out of state. Even nags he had a feel for running on tracks in Hong Kong, England and Australia. Most of them were still looking for the finishing tape an hour after the winner was in his box and being driven home. Chan's gambling hunches were just as unlucky as his choice of women.

Desperate to keep solvent, three years before he'd set up a scam to provide extra income, working with a crooked stockbroker who had offices two blocks off Wall Street. Chan traded only in pharmaceuticals and scanned medical journals for hints of drug breakthroughs. He cultivated contacts with chemical companies assiduously and had sources in a number of research laboratories around the country. If some embryonic product was showing signs of being a winner, Harry bought stock. Equally, if a new compound looked certain to bomb he offloaded and passed the information to his broker, who advised preferred clients accordingly. Twice they'd conspired together and leaked selective information to the press before an official statement about one corporation's new drug treatments for epilepsy and schizophrenia. On each occasion both had made a small killing buying up stock ahead of the announcement. While it wasn't a big scam, and indeed barely covered Harry's betting debts at the time, he needed that cash flow to survive.

Now, Jack Hunt's new rules could break him completely. To Martin Shreeve the Irishman was nothing more than an open sore, a threat to his drunken lifestyle and retirement plans. But Harry Chan stood to lose a lot more.

'Dr Chan, could I have a few minutes to speak with you?'

Hend de Mart was waiting for the cardiologist in the Carter Hospital car park. It was four days after Hunt's Saturday conference and the whole division was still trying to come to terms with the radical changes being forced through. The diminutive Chan was so preoccupied he barely noticed the large shadow looming as he made to open the driver's side door. When he looked up, de Mart seemed to him like Sylvester Stallone on steroids. Dressed in light pants and a short-sleeved shirt the South African's physique reflected how well he had taken to the Midwest summer. He jogged daily in Lincoln Park, rollerbladed along the seafront, worked out in a small gym close to his apartment block. He was tanned and fit-looking, blond hair more bleached than usual, bulging with the kind of muscles Chan only saw in magazines.

The cardiologist squinted up through his thick-lensed glasses and laughed nervously. 'I'm sorry, I'm in a hurry to get home.' He was convinced he was about to be mugged.

De Mart flashed his company card and started talking.

That evening, outside the luxurious Four Seasons on E Delaware, a smartly dressed and intensely curious Chan paused at the hotel's street-level entrance. He inspected his shoes, adjusted his tie and polished his glasses. A quick glance at his reflection in the plate glass, a deep breath and he was inside looking for directions to the bar overlooking Michigan Avenue. Hend de Mart stood out in the early-evening crowd and he quickly guided his guest past the drinkers to the elevators.

'I'd like you to meet someone.'

On the twelfth floor a small but well-appointed private suite awaited. US director Stan Danker was waiting in a cocktail bar-cum-lounge with a floor-to-ceiling window showing off the outside sights. An open door connected to a dining room where two waiters hovered beside a table set for three, and in the mezzanine a long-legged blonde in a black uniform stood ready to serve refreshments.

'Dr Chan, how delighted I am we could meet.' Danker was at his charming best. He was in a beige lightweight suit over pale blue shirt with yellow bow tie. Grey hair gelled back. 'I've heard so much about you.' A big smile flashed, lots of teeth shown.

Chan shook hands limply and tried to smile back, but he was even more unsure of himself as he took in the scene.

Hend de Mart opened a button on his shirt and slipped off his tie. He was more formally dressed: slacks and jacket and now open-neck shirt exposing his prominent Adam's apple. Even though it was closing on eight o'clock the outside temperature was still high, but the efficiency of the hotel's air-conditioning relieved the oppressive warmth.

The blonde woman mixed cocktails and handed them out, then discreetly made her way to the dining room. For about ten minutes the three men sipped on their drinks and made small talk as they looked out at the street lights and traffic. People bustled along the sidewalks, clutching parcels, taking photos or checking restaurant menus. 'Wonderful town,' enthused Danker, and he and de Mart discussed the city, its good and bad sides. They paused to allow Chan to contribute, looking appropriately interested in his every word. They nodded gravely when he mentioned something unpleasant and smiled broadly when he suddenly thought of an upbeat angle to his hometown.

There was only one pre-dinner drink, then Danker led the way into the dining room where they were immediately fussed over. Courses were chosen, wines selected, iced water poured. Throughout the meal Danker continued his softly, softly approach. The conversation drifted from the weather to architecture then medical services throughout the Midwest region. Chan began to relax. The food, the wine, the casual conversation lulled him into a sense of security. He almost wished he'd brought his wife. A chance to show off. Hey, look at me, Dr Harry Chan being wined and dined by this top executive from New York. Sure I didn't get that professor's job (and how he'd had that rubbed in for days when the furniture freak at home found out), but I'm still an important man.

Coffee was served in the cocktail lounge, cigars offered but declined by all. Then the dining-room door was firmly closed. The blonde waitress offered final drinks but de Mart insisted none would be needed. Chan had had his hand half up, about to order a double helping of the best house brandy. He sensed the hospitality had finished, that the real business was about to begin.

Stan Danker stirred cream into his coffee and looked across at the cardiologist. He smiled slightly, but not as generously as when they'd first been introduced. 'I'm sure you're wondering why I wanted to meet with you.'

Chan laughed nervously but said nothing. His eyes flicked between the two men sitting opposite.

'I represent Zemdon Pharmaceuticals,' began Danker, 'one of the largest corporations in the world.' Chan blinked but kept his mouth firmly shut, except when sipping on his espresso. 'This October we will release the most exciting new product in the history of modern cardiology. It's a heart-attack preventer called Cyclint. I believe you know all about it.'

Advance announcements of Cyclint's release date and the preliminary data supporting its usefulness had already been circulated to every important cardiologist worldwide. Chan spoke for the first time. 'Yes, yes. I do. Big product. It could be a winner. Maybe I should buy some shares in your company?'

Danker smiled benignly and glanced at de Mart. The South African's expression didn't change; he sat stony-faced, listening and watching.

'Yes, we anticipate it will be a big product,' Danker continued. 'Indeed we've already put a lot of capital and resources into making sure it's a winner. And a considerable share of that money was going to be placed here locally, in Chicago.'

Chan suddenly straightened up. 'How so?'

Danker sighed deeply, his face betraying his disappointment. 'Our plan was to use the good offices of the Heart Unit at the Carter Hospital to get behind the product. We wanted the power and prestige of that division to promote Cyclint nationally and internationally.' He leaned across and fixed his gaze on Chan. 'This is off the record, but we had already engaged the services of Professor Lewins. He had agreed to be our opinion-former, our mouthpiece. Sam was going to lead the charge for Zemdon.'

'Now he's gone.' Harry Chan spoke the obvious.

'Yah,' de Mart finally opened up, 'he's gone. But Zemdon's still here and Cyclint will still be launched.'

'Which is where you come in.' Stan Danker was leaning back in his seat, studying the cardiologist closely.

Harry Chan looked genuinely confused. 'I'm sorry, I don't quite understand.'

'We need another opinion-former. We need someone now, today, not next week. We need someone with clout and from a high-profile heart unit to get behind Cyclint and speak openly and loudly about the product.'

'Enthusiastically,' interjected de Mart.

'We'd offer a very attractive financial package for the right man. A deal most doctors would find it hard to walk away from.'

De Mart continued the sales pitch. 'The money would be paid into a numbered Swiss bank account, away from the eyes of the IRS. There would be immediate access to it at any time once we have the arrangements agreed.' The South African had the terminology off pat. It had been used so effectively to land him.

Danker took over. 'There would be a heavy commitment at the outset, a lot of time and effort travelling and talking at medical conferences. We expect satellite-link international cardiology meetings, state and interstate seminars. Our man would be the vital linchpin to harness the interest in Cyclint and promote it aggressively. Hell, we'd expect him to say it's so good it should be put in the water supply.' They all laughed politely at that little joke.

Harry Chan set his coffee cup down on a small walnut table. His hands were visibly shaking as he took off his glasses and polished the lenses with a clean linen handkerchief he'd brought especially for the occasion. 'I don't know,' he worried, 'this is way out of my territory.'

Danker nodded towards de Mart and the big man went behind the cocktail bar, returning with a briefcase which he snapped open. Two legal pads were handed across to Chan; duplicates were set in front of Danker. The doctor studied the first page intently, eyes widening behind his thick lenses as he read. 'How did you get this?' The top sheet contained a summary of the cardiologist's financial status: his bank accounts, overdrafts, alimony commitments, betting debts, even his pharmaceutical-scam share dealings.

Stan Danker arched his hands and rested his chin on the tips of his fingers, lips pursed. 'Dr Chan,' he said gravely, 'Zemdon is an empire, a global corporation. We protect that federation with fierce determination. We don't just manufacture and sell chemicals. Like every multinational we gather information about people who can help us. And we like to know everything about them, their good sides and bad sides. Their business dealings, whether they're solvent or not.' The finger arch crumpled. 'We buy information when we need it. And we have a lot of outside sources.' He leaned forward. 'How we came by those figures isn't the issue here. Look at the second page, and then we'll talk some more.'

Page two detailed the financial package Zemdon was offering. At a stroke Chan's alimony commitments and gambling debts would be taken out. In addition, an initial deposit of half a million US dollars would be lodged into a secret account in Berne. If he cooperated fully with the proposed agenda surrounding Cyclint's launch, within six months another half a million dollars would find their way into the same account. Depending on sales and the enthusiasm with which the product was promoted, the cardiologist could reasonably expect a further similar but final payment. There was one overriding stipulation: Chan's crooked dealings in pharmaceuticals must cease immediately. The company couldn't risk making him their most high-profile promoter only to see him uncovered as a two-bit fraudster.

Chan studied the proposal carefully. Then he flicked back to the first page. Slower read. Turned to page two. Even slower read.

'Have you approached anyone else in the division with such an offer?' he said eventually.

Danker shook his head. 'No. We did consider everybody, even researched their lifestyles and finances as closely as yours. Your colleague Dr Shreeve is unstable. He drinks too much and couldn't carry himself like a spokesman. He has a serious image problem.'

'Yes,' agreed Chan quickly. 'He's been shooting his mouth off about talking to his lawyer. It's all bullshit. I think he's lost it.'

'So do we.'

'What about Parker?'

'Nat Parker's a fine doctor but he's too laid back and

undemanding. He doesn't have the hunger for the battle ahead.'

'And the new professor?' It was Chan's turn to fix his gaze on Danker. 'Have you considered him?'

'Dr Hunt is a bit of a wild cannon,' said Danker. 'He's committed himself to academic research for too long and has no commercial experience. He's not streetwise when it comes to business dealings. Dedicated, sure. Naïve, most definitely.' He spoke slowly, choosing his words carefully. 'We know about the new rules he's introduced at the unit.'

Chan cut across him. 'He has specifically stated he does not want anyone endorsing company products. He won't even allow representatives on to level nine. Jesus, I can't even use a simple ballpen if there's a corporation logo engraved on it.'

Danker let Chan's words hang in the air for a moment. 'We are very much aware of Dr Hunt's policies. We believe them to be ridiculous and petty, almost laughable if they weren't so irritating and inconvenient for our sales team.'

'How will you get around him? He could veto all this.'

Danker switched tack completely. 'Harry, how would you like to be professor of that division?' The Dr Chan bit was dropped. It was now first-name terms.

Chan looked confused again. 'I don't understand.'

'Let me put it like this. When Sam Lewins was murdered all of us at Zemdon felt certain you would be given the professorial post. You were the obvious choice. Very experienced cardiologist, long career with the Carter, highly regarded throughout the hospital and with your colleagues around the Midwest.' All of a sudden the gambling addiction, massive debts and share scam were forgotten. Now Chan was being painted a saint. 'I can tell you Jack Hunt didn't get that post by open competition. No sir, he pushed and scrambled all over the administration and forced their hand.'

Chan loosened his shirt collar and freed his tie. 'Go on.'

'Well, Harry, a guy who pushes that hard can sometimes fall right over the top.'

'What do you mean?'

Hend de Mart cut in. 'What Mr Danker is saying is that you shouldn't worry about Hunt. If you come on board Zemdon will protect you all the way. The Irishman will not be allowed to upset our plans. Indeed, the more of a nuisance he becomes the more we may have to disclose the irregularities in that appointment. If Hunt makes life difficult he'll have to go.'

Chan laughed nervously. 'What exactly do you mean?'

Stan Danker arched his fingers again. 'It's better you don't know everything, Harry. We're not talking violence. We don't work that way. But we have the lowdown on everyone, friend and foe. Hunt may come across as a reforming zealot, but we have different views.' His voice hardened. 'He will not be an obstacle, rest assured on that. And if he has to leave that division, for whatever reason, we'd like you to be prepared and ready to take over.' A smile flickered. 'Professor Harold Chan. Sounds good, doesn't it?'

Chan relaxed back into his leather seat. 'It sounds very good. Excellent, in fact.'

Hend de Mart started to close the briefcase. 'We'd like your answer by tomorrow at the latest. If Zemdon can't rely on the Carter Heart Unit then the money moves elsewhere.'

Chan suddenly leaned across and restrained the South African's hand. 'You can have my answer now. You look after Jack Hunt and I'm in. If I have to wear a billboard on the streets I'll make sure Cyclint's a winner.'

10

The annual cardiologists dinner was one of the most important social events in the Midwest medical calendar. Traditionally held in the Chicago Hilton overlooking Grant Park, it was an opportunity for eminent doctors throughout the state (and invited interstate guests) to meet and socialise away from the confines of their hospital bases. Heavyweights in cardiology, physicians and surgeons, came to swill at the same trough. It was a formal affair: tuxedos for the men and best dresses for the ladies.

The evening usually began with pre-dinner drinks to the pleasant strains of a string quartet. The assembled company would then retire to the main function room to wine and dine the night away. Before coffee and brandy there would be obligatory speeches and the transfer of the presidential seal. Then an open bar, gala ball with full orchestra and much gossiping. Long after the band had packed their instruments away the last reluctant stragglers would struggle to bed. The turnout was rarely below three hundred and the whole event was sponsored by the American Heart Foundation with a one-hundred-dollar contribution from each attending doctor. It was untainted by commercial interest with none of the usual vulgar pharmaceutical lobbying associated with many medical gatherings.

Three days before the event Jack was still refusing to go. 'Beth, I'm up to my neck in work. There's a second round of interviews for the junior attendings changeover, we have a nursing shortage with bed closures and high demand on who comes to level nine through ER. I've been fielding calls from agencies all week trying to get our staffing levels up. Everyone's under pressure. Sure I'd like a break this weekend, but not jammed into a room listening to boring speeches.'

This brought Beth's frustrations to a boil. 'I understand, but Hunt, do you know how long I sit in this apartment staring at the walls? With you off saving the world and turning that hospital upside down we don't seem to have much of a life together, let alone a social life.'

They were in bed, just before midnight, each as far away from the other as possible without actually falling on to the floor. Beth had the top sheet wrapped round her body, back turned to her husband, staring at the outside street lights.

'I know how much you want to change things.' Her voice was softer. 'And I know you won't be content until you have the Carter top of the cardiology hit parade. But try and factor Danny and me into your equations a little as well. I was looking forward to a night out.' She turned around and plumped up the pillows, then propped herself on her elbows. 'When was the last occasion I had something to dress up for? I haven't spent more than a hundred dollars on clothes for myself in the past year.'

Jack frowned into the gloom. One half of his brain was balancing his wife's criticisms, the other was back in the Heart Unit, making decisions, plotting moves. The division had stagnated for so long that getting things done was like poking at a slumbering giant. But he knew Beth was right: the workload *was* eating into family commitments excessively. He was home late and gone at the crack of dawn, goodnight kisses and rushed slices of shared toast each morning the only contact.

'I'd have to hire a tux, get new shoes, buy a dress shirt. And I haven't the time. That's the difficulty.'

'Can't you make the time, Hunt? Danny's complaining he never sees you, I almost have to make an appointment with Helen to get five minutes' uninterrupted conversation.'

'I know it's not good enough – believe it or not I am aware of the difficulties. But I'm under a lot of pressure. I've had a run-in with administration about a drug launch and the damned pharmaceutical company keeps pestering me with calls. I feel like I'm dodging them round corners.' Jack was now working himself into a lather of discontent. 'My research has gone to hell – I haven't progressed that programme one inch – and my mystery lover Carlotta Drunker has been filing e-mails with fresh research data almost twice a day.'

Beth shot back immediately. 'Tell her to clear off and study with somebody else. If you give me her number I'll soon put her right about stealing our time.'

Jack tried diversionary tactics. 'How about we take a weekend away, just the two of us?' He sure as hell didn't want his wife speaking with his research partner, not in her current mood. 'Maybe towards the end of next month when things should be lighter.'

Beth was unimpressed. 'You're stalling, Hunt. I've heard that line before. Can't you come up with something different?'

They lay in silence. Through the paper-thin walls came the gentle sound of Danny snoring. Finally, Beth uncurled herself and rolled over, in temptress mode, one hand drifting under the sheet. 'I'll look after things.' She nuzzled her lips along her husband's ear. 'You're too tense.' The hand drifted lower. 'You should learn to relax, take it easy. Don't bunch your muscles so tight.'

Jack eased himself down in the bed and turned round. In the gloom he watched his wife's body snake on top and he stroked her back. 'I'm sorry, honey. I just have so much on my mind.'

Beth's tongue danced along his lips provocatively. 'Then,' she whispered, 'I'll have to make you think of something else.'

Twenty minutes later: 'I guess we're going to the ball?'

'Damned sure we are,' murmured Beth. 'That sort of fun doesn't come without a price.'

Beth shopped for the event with determination, walking Chicago's Magnificent Mile from end to end. Up escalators, down stairs, highrise after highrise. Bloomingdales and Henri Bendel at 900 N Michigan, Saks Fifth Avenue in Chicago Place, designer boutiques along Oak St. Big-dollar stores, places where credit cards heat up even as you walk through the doors. She finally tracked down a complete outfit – dress, shoes and accessories – at Neiman Marcus on N Michigan. And didn't dare tell her husband how much it had cost. The sales assistant described the dress as simple but eye-catching, and she wasn't exaggerating. It was an above-the-knee little number in black silk with provocatively low neckline, tiny shoulder straps and just enough at the back to be decent. Matching shoes and clutch bag. The girl then suggested Beth hire a fake diamond choker with combination earrings and bracelet for the night, even made an appointment with a nearby jeweller.

Before they left that Saturday evening Beth was fussing over her hair. Jack was in new shoes and dress shirt (chosen and bought by his wife) with a tuxedo Beth had plucked from a rack and measured against one of his old jackets. For once there was no evening shadow along his beard line and he looked quite dashing in the outfit. While he waited he read Danny his bedtime story. The babysitter had arrived and was settling in.

'Come on Hunt, what do you think?'

Father and son exchanged weary glances. This was the fifth call from the master bedroom. 'I'll be there in a moment.' He turned the storybook page and continued while Danny snuggled closer, savouring a rare moment of intimacy with his dad.

'We don't have a moment, the taxi will be here soon.' Beth sounded desperate.

Jack kissed his son's forehead and tucked the sheets higher.

'If you don't go,' Danny whispered, 'mum'll murder you.'

Jack grimaced and made a slit-the-throat sign. 'Then cut me up into little pieces and feed me to the piggies?'

Danny raised his eyes to heaven. He hated it when his father used baby talk. 'Come on dad, get a life.' He pulled himself up on to a pillow. 'If she's gonna ice you she'll use some hitman from out of town.'

Jack stopped in his tracks and turned round. 'I don't know what TV programmes you're watching, young man, but I'm not sure I approve of that sort of talk.'

Danny grinned from ear to ear. His dark hair was tousled, his usually bright blue eyes leaden with tiredness despite the humour. 'You wouldn't even know if we had a TV.'

Jack was caught out on that and knew it. He pulled a face at his son, who pulled an even more gruesome one back.

'Better go check mum,' advised Danny as he curled beneath the sheets. 'I'd like you guys home sometime before Christmas.'

Now, with the cab driver ringing at the apartment bell, Beth was ready. The final touch was her hair pulled back, bouncing gently along the nape of her neck. Jack wanted to rip off every stitch and relive some of his Bangkok moments. Beth noticed the glint in his eye and waved him away. 'Take a cold shower, I only wanted you to tell me how I look.'

He came as close as she'd allow, his eyes drifting along the vision in front. The exposed cleavage seemed so inviting. He leaned across and kissed her very gently on the lips, tasting the gloss. 'You are absolutely stunning. I've never seen you so beautiful.' She gave him a cynical glance. 'No, seriously,' he protested, 'this is for real. You'll steal the show.' His eyes drifted to the long tanned legs revealed by a hemline was at least three inches above knee level. He whistled softly and pounded his chest. 'Don't stray too far,' he warned, 'I want everyone to know you're mine.'

Beth picked up her clutch bag and inspected the final result in the mirror. Front, back, side to side. Pouted to make sure her lipstick wasn't smudged.

'Mind you, I'd still prefer stockings and suspenders.'

A lipstick flew past his head.

Jack held Beth's elbow as they steered themselves from registration towards the gathering crowd. He wore his identification badge with pride. Professor J. Hunt, Carter Hospital, Chicago. May as well make the best of this. He glanced around the throng, hoping to catch a familiar face. As they moved between drinkers he noticed many doing double-takes. Yeah, I'm the Irishman who got the Lewins job. I'm the one who's causing all the ripples in the Carter. What were you expecting, a hunch back with an eye in the centre of his head? Then he realised it wasn't him but his wife who was the centre of attention. He chided himself for being so full of self-importance.

'Professor Hunt?' A portly man with flushed face and bulbous nose stuck out a hand. 'I'm Con Willams from the American Heart Foundation. If you don't mind we're going to separate you from your lovely lady. There's a seat reserved at table eight.'

Jack frowned, but before he had a chance to respond he watched his wife being steered in the opposite direction by a block of a man in a waiter's uniform. She was whizzed between guests – 'Table fourteen, lady' – and finally seated between a crew-cut in a tuxedo and an attractive brunette in a red dress.

'Hi, I'm Lisa,' announced the brunette. 'Delighted to meet you. I've heard so much about your husband.'

The crew-cut to her right leaned across and shook hands. 'I'm Peter Kowlski. How do you do?' He flagged a passing waiter. 'Can I offer you champagne?' Before Beth had a chance to decide Kowlski had ordered a bottle of Krug. 'Your husband's the hottest ticket in town, Mrs Hunt, and you're the closest I'm going to get to him.'

By now the table had filled, hands being shaken, introductions made, name tags inspected. There did seem to be a deliberate effort to split couples, so Beth relaxed. Soon she was enjoying herself, her glass topped up almost any time she took a sip. She began to feel warm and bubbly, her usual reserve slipping.

'I read the *Tribune* piece,' Kowlski said as he buttered a bread roll. 'You must be delighted with your husband's new position.'

Beth's face glowed with pride. 'We're both over the moon. We've been on the move for years looking for a suitable appointment. Jack's thrilled of course, but it's almost more important for me. Now I can actually buy a house, a new car, some decent clothes.' The list stopped as Beth considered the question again. 'No more living out of suitcases,' she said finally, her eyes misting as she recognised the truth in every word.

The listeners smiled warmly at her obvious happiness. A second bottle of champagne was offered, and Kowlski inspected then nodded his approval. He turned round again. 'And the professor's got some big research programme in the pipeline.'

The main course was being served, giving Beth enough space to collect her wits. She felt embarrassed at baring her soul to total strangers. 'Yes, he's trying to link up childhood infection and early-onset heart disease.' Boy, that came out easy. How many times have I heard Hunt use that line? Too many, obviously. 'It's something he's been working on for years.'

'Oh.' Kowlski was brushing crumbs on to a side plate. 'And are there others following this same study?' Lisa was smiling politely but Beth felt a bit guilty for not talking about something more interesting. 'I believe there's someone in Colorado, and there's certainly a female researcher in Sacramento.' Beth giggled slightly, the champagne kicking in. 'She's been sending so many e-mails I thought Jack was actually having an affair.' She giggled again and Lisa joined in.

'And is he?' the brunette asked mischievously.

Beth forked vegetables into her mouth and began crunching on them. 'Not unless they're having it off behind the scanner in the angiography department.' They all laughed loudly.

Kowlski now turned in his chair so he had Beth in full view. 'So who is this mystery lady?' His eyes were dancing, teasing.

Beth declined more champagne this time and asked for iced water. 'I've never met her,' she confessed, 'but she seems just another boring doctor who thinks of nothing but work.'

'I know most of the department in Sacramento,' said Lisa. She was pushing the food around her plate, showing little interest in the fare. She hadn't touched her champagne. 'Do you have a name?'

'Carlotta Drunker.' Beth searched the other girl's face for a response. 'Know her?' Lisa's brow furrowed. 'No, can't say I do. Must work in a different section.'

At the same time Jack was sitting rather forlornly on his own, straining to make conversation with the portly Con Williams. There was an empty seat to his left; a card on a side plate claimed it was reserved for Monique Casselte, Vendine Placements, New York.

'That was a helluva shock about Sam Lewins,' Williams mumbled in between mouthfuls of roast beef. 'Strangest carry-on I've ever heard. Never met the man myself but from all accounts he was a fairly regular sort.'

Jack decided this was not the place to indulge in personal opinions on his late boss. 'Real shame,' he offered with no great enthusiasm. 'It certainly shook our division. The staff were on edge for days after the shooting.'

'Hell, I bet they were. Hospitals are supposed to be sanctuaries from street violence. This damned city's becoming gun crazy. Drive-by shootings, turf wars over crack territory. I don't think the cops are pulling their weight.' Williams was working himself into a righteous indignation. 'There's not enough officers on the beat. Too many sitting in squad cars when they should be on the streets and visible.'

Jack wished he was a million miles away. He dreaded another two hours in this boring man's company. He forced a smile and pretended to listen.

The chair beside was suddenly pulled backwards and Jack turned to find the darkest blue eyes he'd seen in years.

'I'm sorry I'm late.' A slender hand reached out. 'Monique Casselte. How do you do?'

Jack stood up and edged to one side. 'Please,' he pulled out the empty seat, 'make yourself comfortable.' He flagged a passing waiter and asked for the dinner menu. 'You've missed the main course, you must be starving.'

The late arrival was in a long cream tubular dress that clung to her body. Slender neck, high-gloss lips and the merest hint of mascara on her eyelashes. High cheekbones with a beauty spot to the left of her forehead. Her dark hair was tied back and held in place by a glittering clasp. The seductive aroma of Chanel flared Jack's nostrils, and without caring how rude it appeared he turned his back on the portly Con Williams.

'Thank you.' Monique directed an obvious glance at Jack's nametag. 'Professor Hunt.'

'Call me Jack. We can't spend all night like stuffed turkeys.'

'Well, Jack, I'm really not that hungry. I try not to rely on the meal at these events. You can never be sure how the food's going to turn out.'

Jack had dined handsomely and drunk nearly half a bottle of Robert Mondavi Cabernet Sauvignon. 'I can't complain about the fare,' he said. 'For such a large turnout the chefs have hit it just right.'

Monique poured herself iced water and sipped, eyes taking in the room. 'Quite an important gathering.'

Jack looked around, trying to spot Beth. About twenty feet away he could see her joined in animated conversation with fellow diners, head to head and laughing. Good, at least she's enjoying herself. That'll take the heat off me next week. Better make the best of the evening. He dabbed at his lips with a napkin and leaned into his chair.

'What line of business are you in, Monique?'

'Medical recruitments. We track career moves and place doctors and nurses when vacancies arise.' The voice was heavily accented – French, Jack decided. 'And we advise on career choices within the profession.'

Jack was immediately interested. 'That so?' He looked at the place card again. Vendine Placements, New York. How come you weren't around when I was on the move and looking for work? 'And where do you recruit?'

'Big med schools along the East Coast for junior staff. Britain, Europe, Australia and New Zealand for more experienced positions. We have a team in the Philippines right now trying to bring in five hundred trained nurses. The demand is constant and ever-changing.'

'That I can believe,' said Jack. He leaned out of the way as a waiter removed his plate. 'Right now we're experiencing staff shortages in the Carter Heart Unit.'

Monique edged a fraction closer. 'You must be a very busy man, then?'

Jack shrugged. 'Goes with the job. I only took over the division recently and there's a lot of restructuring taking place.'

'And I suspect you hate that side of your responsibilities?' A wine waiter hovered behind, but Monique refused. 'Most doctors do, they're not trained in management.'

'Exactly,' agreed Jack. 'I've spent all my working life in hospitals and laboratories. I like dealing with patients and I'm challenged by the mysteries of medicine. But I get bored witless with committee meetings, staff interviews, personality clashes, keeping the peace while getting on with the work.'

'Time-consuming?'

'Very. I'm in a bit of trouble at home for not putting in enough appearances.'

They discussed doctors' lives and doctors' wives and doctors' workloads. Dessert was served, but again Monique declined. Jack wolfed down a chocolate pudding with layers of fresh cream while his partner looked on, an amused smile flickering on her face.

'Don't you get fed at home?' she teased.

'Not with as many calories. My wife keeps a close eye on our diet so this is a real treat.' He moved closer, conspiratorially. 'And she's sitting about ten tables away so won't know a thing.' He suddenly looked up in mock horror. 'Unless you tell her.'

Monique giggled, and Jack laughed. He accepted another glass of wine and glanced round to make sure Con Williams wasn't put out at being ignored. The big man was now engrossed in conversation with a retired heart surgeon.

'So, Monique, do you think you could help with our staff shortages?'

'I wish I could say yes, but I deal only with senior positions.'

'Administrative or medical?'

'Medical only. We track movements at the top. Hospitals, research institutions, academic houses. For example, I know all about your recent promotion.'

Jack inspected his conversation partner more closely. 'But what use could I be to your group?'

Monique smiled. 'Since you were elevated to the professorial position you are now considered a potential employee. Changes in status often create opportunities for others. We follow the players. Something might arise in the future to tempt your interest.'

Jack laughed. 'It'd have to be pretty exciting. I fought tooth and nail for this job.'

Monique poured more iced water. 'You're very young to be taking over such an influential post. Will you keep things the same as your old boss?

'God, no.' Jack almost flinched. 'There have been a number of sweeping changes already. My main agenda is to stimulate the research department and jolt it back to life.'

Monique rested her chin on an upturned palm and offered her full attention. 'Tell me more.'

One hour later Jack had his arms around his wife's waist as they danced to the strains of a Johnny Mathis classic.

'Who was that lush I saw you chatting up?'

Jack drew back slightly and looked at Beth. 'That was no lush, Miss Jealous. And I was not chatting her up. She was someone like myself, obliged to turn up for functions like this and trying to make the best of the evening.' He guided her past a couple threatening to lurch off the highly polished floor. 'You seemed to be enjoying yourself no end, so you can't complain. What was all the laughing about?'

Beth pulled her man tighter and planted a wet kiss on one cheek. 'I told them about the affair you're having with that researcher from Sacramento.'

Jack groaned. 'I hope you're joking. I really hope you're joking.'

But Beth just danced and giggled until dawn.

Five days later, on Thursday, 15 July, Jack Hunt walked into his offices on level nine to find Monique Casselte waiting. Helen was on the phone and obviously very busy, her desk threatening to disappear under a mountain of paperwork and patient files. She motioned towards the visitor with one hand while her other waved in the air as she negotiated with a downtown nursing agency.

'Monique.' Jack's surprise was obvious. 'What are you doing here?' Then a hopeful thought struck him. 'Don't tell me, you've pulled off some deal to relieve our staff shortages.'

Monique stood up and shook the offered hand. She was dressed in a lightweight skirt and matching blazer with open-neck blouse. Bare legs, navy high heels. 'Sorry, that's really not my territory.' She glanced towards Helen, noting that her attention was totally consumed by her work. 'I'd like five minutes of your time in private.' She held up a burgundy leather valise. 'This is company business.'

Jack steered her into a chair in his office, removing his own clutter to make space, then closed the door. He glanced at his watch. 'It'll have to be five minutes and no more. I'm due to start grand rounds right now.'

Monique sat upright in her seat, valise on lap. The casual intimacy of their first meeting at the cardiologists dinner was gone.

'Professor Hunt, my agency has been asked to approach you with a job offer.'

Jack's mouth gaped in surprise. 'What?'

'As I mentioned when we spoke, I work with Vendine Placements in New York. And as I mentioned my responsibility is top medical personnel only.' Jack nodded. 'A multinational pharmaceutical group has retained our services to make a formal approach to you.'

'To do what?'

'Head up their research division in cardiology.'

'Where?'

'London, England. That would be much closer to your home in Ireland.'

Jack studied his visitor closely. The difference between the siren who'd engaged him in conversation for most of the evening five days before and the businesswoman now in front of him was remarkable. The long dress and high-gloss lips, the aroma of perfume, the fluttering eyelashes were gone.

'Monique, I don't want to sound ungracious, and I certainly can't say I'm not flattered, but this is a non-starter.'

'You haven't heard the package.' It was obvious Monique wasn't going to give up easily, and Jack deliberately looked at his watch. The gesture was ignored. 'My clients will offer an attractive financial deal to include transfer of your family and short-term settlement in one of their luxury penthouses in Knightsbridge.'

Jack's eyebrows arched. Knightsbridge. Very fashionable. Very expensive. 'Am I allowed to know who your clients are?'

Monique smiled for the first time. 'No deal, no name. I'm sorry, but those are my instructions.'

'And why me? Why not one of the East Coast hotshots?'

'I am advised this company knows all about you. They are aware of your track record in research and your interests in cardiology. They've familiarised themselves with all your publications and experience in other countries.' She patted the valise. 'They are prepared to offer higher than your current salary.'

Jack stared straight ahead, trying not to let his surprise show. 'That does sound tempting.'

'I have here details of the full financial package with guarantees on family transfer commitments and relocation. My instructions are to leave the proposal with you and contact you within one week for an answer.' She started to unzip the valise. 'The multinational is not identified by name; as I said, that will be revealed if you wish to pursue this further.'

'Monique,' Jack cut in, 'you're a busy woman and I'm up to my neck in work so let's not waste each other's time. I can give you my answer this minute. I'm not interested, full stop. I don't care what package has been strung together, or what fancy location your clients have lined up.'

'Shouldn't you at least read the offer?'

Jack was on his feet and had the door open. 'No,' he said firmly. 'An emphatic no. I'm here to stay and no amount of persuading is going to change my mind. Now, if you don't mind I'd like to get back to practising medicine.'

Monique swept past him to the outer office, then stopped briefly. She reached into the top pocket of her jacket and offered a business card. 'In case you change your mind. The offer stands for one week. You can reach me at the New York office.'

As Jack rushed along the corridors he was already fifteen minutes late. His students and junior staff would be kicking their heels, noting the time and no doubt complaining. Jeez, I make this big issue about standards and can't even keep them myself. But Monique Casselte's words still echoed in his brain.

My clients will offer an attractive financial deal to include transfer of your family and short-term settlement in one of their luxury penthouses in Knightsbridge . . . they are prepared to offer higher than your current salary.

Bloody job offers are like buses. You wait for one for years then two come along within four weeks.

11

'London?' Beth couldn't believe the job offer. 'You mean London in England? Like the river Thames, Houses of Parliament, Big Ben? That London?'

'You've got it in one,' confirmed Jack over a very late dinner that same evening. 'Trafalgar Square, King's Road, Kensington. All that stuff.' He twirled a fork around spaghetti, then caught some of the meat. One eye was on the food, the other darting at an in-house proposal on department meetings. Beth reached across the table and snatched the paperwork away. 'Hey,' Jack protested, one hand grasping at thin air. 'I need to respond to that circular by tomorrow. Gimme it back.' But the sheets were already scattered to the far corner of the room where Jack eyed them nervously. 'I hope those pages are numbered.'

Beth gritted her teeth. 'Forget the hospital work, tell me what this woman said.' She was already dressed for bed in a white cotton nightie held on her shoulders by thin loops.

Jack rolled the end of a bread roll around the plate and popped it in his mouth. He took a long drink of iced water, then leaned back in his chair, hunger now satisfied. He had discarded his day wear and was in shorts and tee-shirt. 'That was very tasty.'

Beth's impatience burst through. 'Hunt, if you drag this out one more minute you can sleep on your own for the rest of the week.'

Jack grinned. 'Okay, this very attractive woman called Monique—'

'I don't need the attractive bit, I know all that. I saw the two of you together over dinner last Saturday. I don't want to hear how smooth her skin was, how radiant her smile. I don't need her bra size. I want to know what she offered you today.' She paused, then quickly added, 'And I'm talking business. If she proposed anything else I'll find out from Helen. She kept an eye on proceedings.'

'How do you know that?'

'She and I have become close friends, Mister Cardiologist.' Beth gave one of her clever smiles. 'We have quite a few telephone conversations about you when you're patrolling those hospital corridors. I hear every snippet of gossip, so nothing escapes my attention. Now get on with the story.'

Jack pushed his chair back from the table and stretched out his legs. 'The deal wasn't outlined completely because I cut her short. But the thrust of it was a top research position in cardiology with some multinational pharmaceutical. We'd be located to London, all expenses paid. Put up in one of their fancy apartments in Knightsbridge and paid a better salary.'

Beth leaned across the table and dabbed the tip of a finger in the remains of the Bolognese sauce. 'Which company?'

'That wasn't disclosed.'

'So what'd you say?'

'No go. Not interested. I'm exactly where I want to be and damned if I'm moving.'

'Good.' Beth's eyes were teasing. 'We're making our home here in Chicago. If you'd said yes you'd have gone on your own.' She studied her husband carefully. 'Now, do you want those pages back?'

Jack glanced to where the sheets lay. One was on top of the lounge chair, another underneath, while four more kept one another company along the passageway leading to the bedrooms. The apartment was tight and compact. Small kitchen overlooking the back plot, then a dining-cum-sitting area with lounge chairs. A corridor ran from this relatively large room to the three bedrooms, none of them large.

'Am I allowed?' he asked.

'Only when you agree to set aside a day to go house hunting.'

Jack groaned. More commitments. 'How about sometime next week?' he offered hopefully. 'There's a heap of work building up and I have another meeting with the pathologists. They want me to go through the autopsy requirements. The head of trauma faxed me some interesting data he's collating and I'm going to have to squeeze a meeting with him. Then—'

Beth shook her head. 'I don't want to hear one more word about that Heart Unit tonight. We need a home, somewhere we can settle. God knows we can afford it now after all those years of scrimping and saving.' She began collecting the dinner plates, rattling them briskly. 'Starting tomorrow I'm contacting realtors' offices to find what's on offer. I will not spend this winter in this apartment. It's too small and cramped. We need space, and if you can't clear a slot to go looking then you can live with any decisions I make.' She marched to the kitchen.

Jack weighed up the situation. Beth was right (as usual). But he was consumed with the spilling over of responsibilities from the Carter Heart Unit. There was a lot more to do than just be the chief and lead by example. There was administration, committee meetings, peer review audits. And outside demands. Earlier that afternoon Helen had sidelined him beside one of the intensive care bays.

'Decisions, professor. I've been chasing you all day and these can't wait.'

Jack was in green scrubs at the time, two stethoscopes around his neck, pager bleeping intermittently. He leaned against the wall and signed off drug regimes for six patients under his care, then handed a clipboard to one of the junior attendings with instructions on moving yet another acute heart attack victim up from ER.

'Shoot.'

'Cardiology residents would like one extra lecture a week on diagnostic imaging interpretations.'

'Can we fit it in?'

'Only at lunchtime. Either that or a seven o'clock start on Thursdays.'

Jack thought this over quickly. Lunch was his only chance to catch up with reports. In between sandwiches and coffee he dictated letters to referring doctors and summarised patient discharge notes. 'Make it seven on Thursdays.' One hour less in bed, but he could get through the traffic quicker at that hour. He still hadn't bought himself a car, preferring to grab a CTA bus along N Clark into the downtown area, then connecting with another to W Harrison. It was quick and undemanding, and he could get through forty minutes' uninterrupted work.

'Request from *The Cardiologist*.' This was a trade publication delivered free to practising physicians throughout North America. 'They'd like to reprint your papers on infection to heart disease theory and want you to submit an editorial for that edition.'

Jack made a snap decision. 'They can run the reprints but I can't write the editorial. Tell them how honoured I am—'

Helen interrupted. 'I know, I know. I'll make it sound like you're on crutches and can barely move a muscle.'

'Whatever it takes,' agreed Jack, grinning. His pager bleeped again and he noted the telephone extension. 'More?'

'Yes. A Mr Hend de Mart of Zemdon Pharmaceuticals has been sitting in my office for two hours staring me in the face. Says he would like two minutes of your time to ask one simple but important question.'

Jack's eyes rolled to heaven. 'Jeez, these guys just won't let up. What part of the word "no" don't they understand?'

Helen doodled with a pen on one of the pages. 'It's your call, professor. But give me an answer one way or the other. I'd like the big gorilla out of my field of vision asap.'

Jack rested the back of his head on the wall behind. 'Tell him I'm sorry but the new guidelines on drug company reps on this level stand firm. He can sit there all night for all I care but I'm not discussing anything with him.'

'Gotcha.' Helen slipped the paperwork under an arm. 'Now,' she continued, fixing a questioning look on her boss, 'Dr Carlotta Drunker. Have you been in contact with this lady before?'

'Yes. She's one of the top researchers in California. We've shared data for some time, mutual interests.'

'Well,' said Helen carefully, 'I have taken three calls from her today.'

'Looking for me?'

'Yessir, looking for you, and won't take no for an answer.' Her face creased in concern. 'She really sounds weird, kind of overwrought. I mean she demanded to speak with you. Demanded.' The word was exaggerated. 'Once while you were in ER, again while you were on division rounds, and finally one hour ago. I tried to reach you but you didn't answer.'

Jack thought quickly. 'I was setting up a central line. Left my coat and pager outside the bay.' He glanced at his watch. Running behind as usual. 'Did she leave a message?'

'Check your e-mails. That's all. Check your e-mails.'

Which is what Jack did before he went to bed. While Beth conditioned and moisturised in front of the mirror at her dressing table he flicked through the messages on his PC. There were six, the first five from Carlotta Drunker.

JACK. DID YOUR RESEARCH INCLUDE SUBJECTS IN NORTH AMERICA? I NEED TO KNOW URGENTLY.
REGARDS C.

JACK. RUBENSTEIN IN COLORADO HASN'T BEEN IN TOUCH WITH ME FOR SIX WEEKS NOW. DID HE EVER COMMUNICATE WITH YOU? C.

DON'T SEND ANYTHING IMPORTANT BY E-MAIL OR POST.

JACK. CHECK YOUR RELATIVES. C.

LEUCOCYTE TRANSMIGRATION IN DAMAGED MYOCARDIAL MUSCLE PREDICTIVE OF ULTIMATE PROGNOSTIC OUTCOME. C.

Jack studied the last message for almost five minutes trying to make sense of its content. Leucocyte means white cell, that I can understand. Transmigration? On the move? Moving? From where to where? Damaged myocardial muscle. Damaged heart muscle, okay? Predictive of ultimate outcome? What the hell is she getting at? Helen's right, she is weird. And getting worse. He re-read the messages. Don't send anything important by e-mail or post . . . check your relatives. Seriously weird.

Then he had a sudden pang of guilt. With all the changes in his personal and professional life his research programme had suffered. He knew he was deliberately avoiding responding to Carlotta, embarrassed to admit he was stalled. Still, he *did* have so much on his plate. He had a wife and boy; she was single and probably more focused without the distractions of family. She'd just have to wait until he got his act together and had something fresh to offer.

He opened the final message, frowning as he recognised it was from the cardiology professor's office in the Carter Hospital.

JACK.
YOUR LOVELY WIFE BETH ASKED ME TO SEND THIS. SHE SAYS IT'S THE ONLY WAY SHE CAN GET THROUGH TO HER BUSY CARDIOLOGIST HUSBAND. SHE'S GOING HOUSE HUNTING WHETHER YOU LIKE IT OR NOT. SORT IT OUT YOURSELVES, THIS ISN'T IN MY JOB DESCRIPTION!
HELEN.

Jack started to laugh. He was still laughing five minutes later as Beth protested her innocence and ignorance of the whole affair.

In California, Dr Carlotta Drunker wasn't laughing. Separated from Chicago by fifteen hundred miles and a three-hour time lapse, the researcher sat in the front room of her second-floor apartment, a pair of binoculars trained on all movement outside.

Carlotta lived within a gated community, a development of brick and terracotta roofed medium-rise blocks and single-storey dwellings in an exclusive suburb north of Sacramento. Here there was a communal swimming pool and tennis court, manicured lawns and walkways. The project was discreetly surrounded by razor-wire-topped chain-link fencing which in turn was camouflaged between carefully planted and fast-growing shrubs. The only way in and out was through a single entrance to the east where two armed security guards vetted callers and delivery vans. Even long-term residents had to show their IDs. Any stranger was first cleared by telephone link with the living quarters they intended to visit. No one was allowed past the boom without permission.

The forty-three-year-old researcher was five ten, of slim build with blue eyes, dark lashes and a high forehead. She had long jet-black hair usually swept back in tresses over one shoulder. Petite pug nose and narrow chin.

At seven minutes past eight that evening, West Coast time, she was dressed in denim overalls with a heavy-duty red-on-blue tartan shirt, shoulder pads and three thick sweaters underneath for bulk. Her hair was pulled up and stuck firmly underneath a yellow baseball cap. Despite the air-conditioner running at full tilt she sweated profusely. She checked her watch: 8.10. The binoculars were now fixed on the security gate. There was no movement apart from the shadow of one of the guards inside the booth. She bit at her lower lip nervously. Behind her the television was turned on at maximum volume, the apartment walls shaking to the sound of a Christian revival meeting. A determined agnostic, Carlotta loathed all forms of religious broadcasts. But that evening the hymns and prayers and hallelujahs suited her purpose and she gritted her teeth and endured the torment.

At 8.15 the intercom from security to her apartment sounded and she closed the living-room door to answer. The prayer groups now continued their exertions unheard.

'Gentleman here to see you, Miss Drunker.'

Carlotta focused the binoculars through a side window. The evening was still bright with an orange glowing sunset, its colours dancing off car roofs in the parking lot. She quickly picked up a vehicle waiting at the boom, a battered-looking '91 Acura Integra. At the wheel she could just about make out the driver, a burly-looking male in a red-on-blue tartan shirt and yellow baseball cap.

'Let him in, he's expected.' She strained to keep the tension out of her voice.

'Sure thing.'

The Integra pulled up beside her residential block and the driver got out. He appeared to be in no obvious hurry and spent some time fiddling in the boot, repeatedly removing the yellow cap to wipe at his brow. In the bright sunlight Carlotta identified the caller clearly. He had a big nose, low-set forehead and thick lips. The visitor eventually closed the car doors and slowly made his way inside the complex.

He was greeted by Carlotta who shushed him silent immediately, then made him crouch down in the hallway. First she produced five hundred dollars in twenties. The visitor, an underemployed actor who freelanced at anything coming his way, counted and pocketed the bills. Then a legal pad with felt-tip writing was held up for him to read. LEAVE THE TV CHANNEL AS IT IS. OKAY? He acknowledged with a nod of his head. Then another directive. THERE'S A CAB BOOKED TO COLLECT YOU AT NINE. I'VE ALREADY CLEARED THIS WITH SECURITY. OKAY? The visitor gave a thumbs-up sign. Finally, the last message. *PLEASE* DON'T LEAVE THE APARTMENT UNTIL THE CAB COLLECTS. OKAY? Another nod.

The visitor let himself into the living room, took one look at the television and pulled a most unpleasant face. Carlotta offered a rueful smile and rubbed her finger and thumb together, letting her employee know who was calling the shots. He grimaced and sat down in an easy chair, pulled a novel from a side pocket and settled down to read.

Twelve minutes later Carlotta let herself out of the apartment. As casually as she could she strolled to the Integra and three minutes later was past security heading due south. As she drove she checked continuously in the rear-vision mirror. After two sudden diversions on to slip roads and a short stop in a crowded supermarket car park, she decided she was safe.

12

By 19 July Hend de Mart decided to speed up developments in Chicago. He made contact with his mole in the Carter Hospital, an informer called Caleb Rossi. Rossi was a wiry and edgy-looking youth who worked in the biochemistry department. De Mart had first met him two weeks earlier in a small bar on the Westside, TV blaring in the background with the latest ball game, pool table at the rear. Rossi spoke in a low-pitched mewl, drawing hungrily on one cigarette after another.

'I can tell you anything you want to know about the place,' he crowed. 'I know who's knocking whose wife off, who's shooting up in the toilets and then faking their urine samples. I can tell you who's skimming off in the stores and selling the stuff on the streets.' Rossi ordered another beer and gulped at it. 'You pay and I'll bounce anything you need.' De Mart gave him three single hundred-dollar bills immediately, then a list of further requirements. Rossi's eyes widened. 'Want some dope? Mebbe score an ounce of crack? You name it man, I'll get it.'

The South African leaned right into his face. 'Just do what I ask. No questions, keep everything we talk about to yourself, okay?' Rossi nodded warily. Beside his puny frame the other man looked like an angry bear. 'And don't try and sell me any crap. I'm here to do a job, then I want to get the fuck away as soon as possible.'

Rossi held up both hands. 'Okay man. You're the boss.'

De Mart dropped a false business card on the table. 'If you need me in a hurry call that number. It's an answering service. They can't contact me; I call them for messages. Ask for Mr Hend. Never use any other name.' He eased himself out of a side door into the sun, leaving an anxious-looking Rossi staring at his broad back.

With the launch of Cyclint ever closer, the South African was already planning the return to his homeland. He'd even searched the Internet for properties along the Cape peninsula and had his eye on a split-level bungalow set back from the harbour on Hout Bay. Every day he dreamed of the beach and the sea and a fishing line cast off the end of a pier.

Cook County was boring him, he found the flat Midwest plains dull and uninteresting. He fled its highways to the back roads where the franchises had yet to arrive. Fat Boy's Garage, Hank & Wilma's Good Eating Joint, Crazy Gord's Crazy Golf. It nearly made him throw up.

'I need a young thug.'

De Mart sat on a grassy patch surrounding a highrise opposite Sears Tower. Tour buses disgorged their passenger loads into harsh sunlight and queues built up as visitors scrambled to see the city's sights from the world's second tallest building. It was an ideal spot for clandestine meetings, people coming and going, constant movement. No one was interested in anyone else.

Rossi had agreed to meet him there during his lunch break. He was chain-smoking and edgy and hid behind wraparound shades, obviously uncomfortable in the other man's company. He wore denims, a short-sleeved shirt and scuffed trainers and sweated profusely in the noon heat. For three days in a row temperatures had hovered around the one-hundred-degree mark and most stayed indoors or kept their journeys short. As the two men spoke a fire engine scorched past, its klaxon drowning out their words. Rossi waited until it swung off into the distance.

'What sort of a young thug? I know lots who fit that description. How young do you want? I ain't got no five-year-old crack dealers, if that's what you mean.' He tried to laugh at his own joke but only ended up in a fit of coughing. Finally he cleared his throat and spat out a lump of tar-stained phlegm. Two elderly tourists looked at him with disgust and de Mart moved to the recesses of the highrise where there were fewer hanging about.

'Some kid about eight or nine. Tough and fast.'

The Carter tech thought this over, checking his mental database. 'No sweat. Got any number like that where I live.' He flicked the ash off his cigarette then stubbed the butt underfoot. 'What's he gotta do?'

*

The youngster was called Luther and he offered no second name. De Mart collected him at ten the following morning and he sat in the back seat of the South African's black Toyota Camry, sullen and silent.

He was about five six, lean and hungry-looking. Shaven head and face showing the scars of previous encounters. A row of rings in both ears, one stud in the nose. Rossi had said he was no more than nine years old but to de Mart he looked older, maybe eleven. He was wearing a muscle shirt at least a size too big for his frame, denims with holes on both knees, the back pockets torn off. No socks, Nike trainers. He chewed gum angrily, staring out the side windows at the passing streets.

He'd been picked up on a road running alongside one of the Southside slums. Derelict buildings, rundown projects, crack houses. De Mart had circled the same prearranged patch four times before Luther came out from the shadows. The kid had walked around the Toyota, inspecting it suspiciously from every angle, then opened the boot. Satisfied, he yanked open the back door and climbed inside, immediately checking all directions for hostile activity.

'Shift it man, I don't want the fucking cops crawling all over me.'

He had the voice of a youth but the attitude of a hardened delinquent. He slid so far down in the seat only his eyes upwards were visible.

'Half now, half when I finish.'

De Mart handed over a hundred-dollar bill. Luther held it against the light, then squeezed the note into a side pocket.

'Let's go.'

They drove along side and back streets, keeping well away from the main roads. One minute they were in a fashionable district with expensive highrises and chic boutiques, two turns later they were in Seedsville: rundown shops, cheap liquor stores, porno houses. De Mart kept the air-conditioning on full blast against the rising outside temperatures. At Oz Park he swung right on to W Webster, then left down N Clark. He drove slowly and carefully, anxious not to cross a red light or switch lanes unnecessarily. Again, good shops cheek by jowl with trash house stores. Restaurants, pawn brokers, McDonald's, pizza-to-go. The few people on the streets hugged the shaded areas for relief from the stifling heat.

By 11.30 the Toyota had cruised to the small school near W Deming where Danny Hunt had made so many friends and was now top scorer in the junior league soccer team. The official teaching semesters were over: it was now summer camp with activities confined to mornings only. Luther scanned the street. It was a quiet tree-lined avenue, occasional traffic and few pedestrians. The junior college was a single-storey cluster of red-brick blocks behind a small chain-link fence. There was an entrance about fifty yards further along with one bored-looking security guard resting in the shade of a large elm tree.

'When the kids come out for their break, make your move.'

Luther nodded. He stuck his gum on the headrest of the driver's seat, then tore the wrapper off a fresh strip and slid it slowly along his tongue. 'See that big white house behind, where those guys are pulling at the walls?'

De Mart scanned the road. About fifty yards further back three workmen in shorts were chipping away at a crumbling boundary division. Rubble lay scattered beside them. Against the sun each of the brickies wore caps with long neck protectors. They were intent on the wall and oblivious to anything else. 'I got it.'

Luther inspected the older man's face. 'Fifteen minutes. Then I'll be running along that side of the road and past the house. I don't wanna hit the end of the street on my own.' He scowled, and de Mart scowled back.

'Listen kid, don't fuck with me and I won't fuck with you.' The strange accent unsettled Luther, and he turned away.

'I'll be ready as soon as you hit the tarmac.'

De Mart started the engine and slowly eased the car past the school entrance. The security guard didn't offer a second glance. When they reached an intersection, Luther jumped out and vaulted the chain-link. De Mart fixed the time on his watch, parked and waited.

At 11.45 the blocks opened and children screamed out from the teaching units, all high as kites. Most carried some sort of snack: chocolate bars, cookies or crisps and a fruit drink. They scuffled and pushed among themselves, while others peeled off for an impromptu soccer scramble. A few of the quieter ones huddled together to trade cards of their favourite baseball or football stars. Most of the girls skipped or gossiped.

On full attendance there would be sixty under-twelves working off steam. The yard was supervised by a teacher, that day a young woman wearing a broad-rimmed straw hat and white cotton dress. The air was so oppressive she moved to a dark corner underneath a window awning and unscrewed the top of a bottle of cold water. She checked how her charges were behaving, then began sipping. The soccer kids were whooping with delight. They'd split into two teams and already Danny's side had scored a goal. He was running around, hands pumping the air, brow soaked in sweat. He stood out from the rest with his jet-black hair, most of the rest sun-bleached blonds.

Luther skulked around the side of the buildings until he found a vantage point, then slumped down and waited behind a row of bicycles chained in a bay. He spotted Danny soon enough. The boy was exactly as described. He gave it five minutes by his stolen watch, then darted from the shadows towards the shrill shouts. The children were in their summer uniforms: khaki shorts and short-sleeved grey cotton shirts with the school logo on the breast pocket. White ankle socks and trainers.

It was one of the girls who first noticed him. He was tall and mean-looking and certainly not in summer-camp clothes. She nudged to the others and they backed away, apprehensive. Two ran for the teacher on yard duty.

Luther noticed them out of the corner of an eye, his main attention focused on the dark-haired boy trying to dribble a soccer ball. He moved stealthily but fast, as only a street hoodlum knows how. Then in like a bullet. Luther had a good ten-inch advantage in height, was leaner and tougher and an experienced brawler. His shaven head bobbed as he came from behind. The first blow caught Danny on the back of the neck and he started to turn, the shock momentarily stunning him. As he spun round Luther smashed a fist into his face, following with an uppercut to the chin. The smaller boy started to crumple, blood pouring from his nose and mouth.

The yard was now in pandemonium with kids screaming hysterically and running for the safety of a teacher or an open door. Anything. Luther kept pounding; body punches, head hits, back thumps. As his victim slumped to the ground, he managed to land three solid kicks to legs and groin.

The school had a quota of three other teachers and one ancillary helper. As the confused and disturbed cries from the playground intensified they ran outside to discover their young colleague on her knees, cotton dress covered in blood. She was distraught and sobbing as she cradled the lolling head of a dark-haired boy lying limp on the scuffed and patchy grass.

The boy didn't move or cry. He didn't even whimper. He was unconscious.

'I need you immediately.'

Jack's secretary had sidled up to him in the middle of a divisional conference. He was in hospital fatigues and discussing the management of congestive heart failure with three junior attendings. He looked across, obviously annoyed. 'Sure this can't wait?'

Helen grabbed his right arm, her grip biting deeply. 'No, it goddamned can't wait.'

When they were out of earshot she spun him round. 'Your boy's down in the ER. Beth's with him. There's been some kind of incident at school.'

Jack stared at her, confused and uncertain. 'Danny? My Danny? In this ER?'

They were standing beside the elevators, Helen punching buttons. Mercifully the doors opened immediately and she pushed him inside and slammed the palm of her hand on to the console for street level. As the doors closed she watched Jack's bewildered expression.

'What happened?'

Danny was barely recognisable. He was stripped naked and lying on his back on a gurney inside a trauma bay. He was moaning. His blood-, sweat- and dirt-stained clothes were bagged and at his feet. Beth was at his side, ashen-faced, clutching his hand and whispering loudly, 'It's okay, Danny, everything's going to be okay. Mum's here and now dad's here too. Come on, Danny, come on. Wake up. Dad's come all the way from that big office upstairs to see you.' Her son's face was swollen and bruised, both eyes closed over, blood traces clinging to both nostrils. His chest wall was scratched and bruised, his genitals swollen and discoloured. There were scratch and bruise marks on both legs, then the unmistakable tread marks of a trainer where he'd been stomped on aggressively.

Jack's first emotion was simple and typically doctorish. His son's chest was rising and falling – he's alive.

The curtains surrounding the bay were suddenly pulled back and one of the trauma doctors, a young man in scrubs with N. Munten on the nametag, pushed past with a clutch of X-rays. 'You Professor Hunt?' Jack nodded weakly, momentarily speechless. 'Everything looks good. Pupils equal and reacting, good response to stimuli. Can move all limbs. He was mumbling when he arrived and that's a healthy sign. Prelim films show no breakages. I've asked the radiologists to confirm that.' He glanced towards his patient, who was now stirring restlessly. 'Facial bones are damned hard to call so I do need that second opinion. Chest and limb shots are clear. Definitely no breakages.' He slipped a hand on to Danny's abdomen and gently moved his fingers along. 'No sign of any internal bleeding.' He glanced towards Beth, then back to Jack. 'A helluva beating, but nothing he won't recover from.'

Jack's mouth dropped and he grabbed Beth by the shoulders and turned her anguished face to him. 'Beating? Did somebody do this deliberately? What the hell happened?' But Beth could barely say a word. She gripped her husband's fatigues, her body swaying and buckling. Her eyes glazed and began to roll in her head. Jack quickly caught her under the arms and set her down gently on a chair.

On the gurney Danny was now trying to sit up, his arms slipping off the cloth edges. He moaned loudly, then his strength failed and he fell back on to the pillow. Munten was beside him, watching every move, assessing the level of consciousness.

'Mum? Mum?' The words were barely audible through the parched, swollen and blood-stained lips. 'Mum, where are you?'

Munten forced a smile. 'Good sign, Mrs Hunt. He's beginning to come round.'

But Beth was oblivious to the encouragement. The ER was becoming overly warm, the bay seemed to be darkening. She slid to the floor, leaving a flustered trauma doctor scrambling for a nurse attendant and an extra gurney.

FLASH! FLASH! FLASH!

'Okay, turn him round.'

FLASH! FLASH! FLASH!

'Can that be enough?' Beth was pleading. 'I don't think he's up to any more.'

The duty officer looked at his photographer colleague and shrugged. 'Ya got enough?' The photographer was already putting the lens cap on. He nodded and left.

It was four in the afternoon of the following day and the Hunt family was at the Lincoln Park PD, the closest division to where Danny had been attacked. The boy had spent the previous night in the paediatric division of the Carter Hospital. 'Just for observation,' the trauma team had advised when all X-rays had been cleared. He'd finally been allowed home when the duty paediatrician recognised Jack and decided the boy couldn't get any better supervision. 'Anything you're concerned about, ring me immediately.'

However, Danny was stable. Sore as hell and bruised beyond recognition, but able to walk and talk and eat. When Jack eventually learned of the state in which Beth had found him he offered a silent prayer of thanks. It sounded so bad he found it hard to believe his son had escaped serious injury.

The school principal had called, he too in a state of shock. And totally perplexed. 'Mrs Hunt, the staff are stunned. We have never, and I do really mean never, had an incident like this before. I just can't get my head round this.'

Nor could the duty officer at the Lincoln Park station. The episode had been reported immediately and a squad car and paramedic team promptly dispatched. Statements were taken, descriptions noted, clues searched for. The assailant had never been seen in the school or area before. No one saw him creep in and no one spotted him running like hell to escape. But those kids who had seen the attack and could recall it (when they were calmed down) were convinced of one thing: the attacker was looking for Danny and nobody else. He could have grabbed any child (and there were smaller and closer targets), but he made for Danny, did the business and fled the scene.

Now, in a back room of the police building, Danny was naked again as his injuries were recorded. That ordeal over, Beth helped him dress while her husband gave as much background information as he felt helpful to the duty officer, a large man called Nelson. He had crew-cut hair and a bushy moustache, which he stroked as he listened to the story. The three sat in hard chairs around a scratched and scored table. Danny was left in the company of a female detective in a separate room.

'Now why don't ya all just try and get yar thoughts together.' Nelson's accent was untainted upstate country. 'Ya don't know why yar boy's been singled out for such a hiding?' The officer had his hands twined together over his paunch. His uniform collar was open at the neck, his booted legs stretched out in front. His eyes were like slits and for all the world he seemed as if he might fall asleep. But his questions probed. 'And ya, Mrs Hunt, ya've never known Danny to get into arguments with other kids?'

No, definitely not.

'Not even silly little quarrels? Like whose team's better, that sort of stuff?'

Another emphatic no.

'Ya ever find anything strange or unusual in the boy's room, school locker?'

No.

'Either of ya had a serious disagreement with one of the other parents?'

No.

'What about yar relatives?'

None in this country.

'How long ya all been here anyway?'

Close on a year. Before that we spent six months in Philadelphia and New York.

'That all?' Nelson stroked his moustache even more aggressively, as if the timescale had given him new insights. 'Not such a long time to make enemies.'

At this Jack exploded. 'What goddamned enemies? The school principal said this thug has never been seen before. They think it's a random scrap.'

'Could be, Dr Hunt, could be.' Nelson started to twiddle his thumbs. He shifted one booted leg over the other. 'But that's a good school. It's not some rundown inner-city slum where the kids have to duck every time there's a shooting over crack territory.'

'What are you getting at?' Jack was trying to control his anger.

Nelson stood up and hitched at his belt, then shook a leg to restore the circulation. 'I just can't figure this out either, Dr Hunt. It's a real puzzle. I've been in the division close on eight years and never had to deal with anything similar.' He pushed his chair tight to the table. 'Happened all the time when my call included some of the tough projects. But not since I was moved out here. This is a good area with nice people. Kids just don't give each other that sort of a beating.'

The policeman's words troubled Beth for the rest of the day. *Kids just don't give each other that sort of a beating.* They sure as hell do, and my son's appearance is walking proof. *This is a good area with nice people.* That comment, far from reassuring, unsettled her more. Why Danny? And why such a violent assault? Those in the school circle she'd spoken to and who'd come to sympathise were genuinely bewildered by the aggressive nature of the assault. It was so out of character, so out of place in their lives and the school they'd chosen. A few did react peculiarly, though. Beth noticed that especially.

Back home she began to torment her son with questions.

'Have you been fighting with other kids?'

'Are you mixing with anyone we don't know about?'

'Has anyone ever threatened you before?'

'Has anyone offered you drugs?'

'What about beer or stuff like that?'

'Are you sure you don't know who that boy was? Don't worry about telling me, he won't be allowed to get near you again. But I need to know if you do know him. I need a name.'

Danny finally lost his cool and screamed, 'No, no, no. I don't know anything and I don't know who he is!' His face blazed red, his tongue trapped so tight between his teeth it started to bleed. He went to his room and slammed the door. After a few minutes his mother heard him sobbing.

'We need to get out of here.'

Beth was upright on the bed, legs curled underneath her body Yoga-style, still dressed despite the hour. It was five minutes after two, and in the adjoining room Danny had finally fallen into an exhausted sleep. Jack was stretched out beside her and staring at the ceiling. He knew every crack in its plasterwork, every shadow in its paint. They'd been like that for almost an hour, conversing in half sentences and unanswered questions for the most part.

He looked over. His wife's usually beautiful features were now taut and strained, tears welling in her eyes.

'There's no way we're staying in this area after what happened.'

Beth shook her head from side to side, then dabbed at her eyes with the corner of the sheet. 'I thought New York was bad, but this is another world.' Her voice rose in anger. 'And that policeman didn't seem remotely concerned.'

'Ah come on, Beth,' Jack tried reasoning. 'The man did his job and called it as he saw it. Everyone's shocked with this, even the school principal.' He stretched across to comfort his wife but was angrily brushed aside. 'It's one of those freak incidents that can happen anywhere. You read about it every day in the papers.'

'Don't try feeding me that line, Hunt. We've been all over the world and never been harmed. First there were the burglaries and the bag-snatching in New York, now my son gets beaten up. This is no country in which to raise kids.'

Jack returned his stare to the ceiling, at a loss as to what to say. The incident with Danny had shaken him as much as Beth. It had shaken his confidence in the police and in American society, and made him feel impotent. He was a man unable to protect his wife and boy in the face of an unprovoked attack.

Beth uncurled her legs and stood up. She began pacing the room restlessly. 'Maybe you should contact that woman again and see if you can still get that job in London.' She turned towards Jack, eyes red-rimmed, face streaked with mascara. 'Wasn't there a cardiology position in Sydney you said you were interested in? Couldn't you make a few enquiries and see if it's still open?'

She sounded desperate and Jack grabbed her, holding her trembling body close. 'Shush, shush. It's okay, Beth. Relax. We have to get over this. We're not going running round the world again, we're staying here. No thug is going to frighten us away. I fought hard for this job and it's exactly what I want, what *we* want.' Beth sobbed into his chest. 'We'll start looking for a house immediately, I promise.' He held his wife's face in both hands and tried to kiss away her tears, her pain tearing him apart. 'You get the brochures and I promise I'll set aside the time to look. We'll get out of here and start our lives in a new area.'

Jack didn't sleep that night. He eventually persuaded Beth to lie down and watched as she twitched into a disturbed doze, but he counted the hours through until dawn. Beth cried out twice and he held her close, whispering and soothing and comforting. You'd better get your act together, this is no way to lead your life. You've got the job, you've got the money, now get off your arse and get a home. But where will I get the time? *Make it, Hunt.* He could almost hear Beth's rebuke. *You'd make time if there was some project you wanted to see through.*

He was in the shower at 5.30 and dressed by six. Beth and Danny were still asleep as he let himself out of the apartment into another warm Chicago morning. Time. He grabbed the first CTA bus that came along and slumped into the back seat. The deck was almost deserted, only a few early risers like himself yawning and squinting at the beams of sunlight flashing between the highrises. He started dictating. 'Helen, can you clear a space in my diary next week. Say a full half day on Wednesday afternoon or Thursday morning.' He pressed the stop button. Thursday mornings were already booked for lectures. He pressed start. 'Helen, let's try for Tuesday morning or Wednesday afternoon.'

13

Dr Gert Crozer was Operations Executive for Zemdon Pharmaceuticals. On Wednesday, 21 July he was waiting impatiently on the top floor of the company's New York headquarters.

'Herr Danker is delayed?'

Crozer had flown in from Zurich that morning for an urgent conference with his North American director, and the afternoon meeting was already five minutes late. Maria, Danker's PA, fretted as she tried to put the visitor at ease. She'd already produced a ream of faxes that had clicked in overnight and was now struggling to prepare a pot of his special-blend coffee.

'Should be here any moment, Dr Crozer. Maybe you'd prefer to wait in his office?'

Crozer frowned his displeasure. The Zemdon executive was a sixty-one-year-old Swiss national, tall and long-limbed with short grey hair parted severely to one side. He preferred to dress formally, usually well-cut cashmere and wool suits and starched white shirt with company tie. He was slightly stooped, his demeanour that of a man constantly preoccupied. He wore thin wire reading glasses that helped soften his hawk-like face and conceal his eyes. Despite the heat he was dressed in a sombre charcoal suit with faint blue stripe, white shirt and an uninspiring blue-spotted tie with the Zemdon ZDN logo. He was in New York on business and did not plan on staying longer than necessary. He did not enjoy travelling, despising foreigners and feeling out of place and discontented when away from home.

'Would you like a sandwich? I can get chef to fix anything you'd like.' Maria was doing her best. The North American division occupied the upper twenty levels of the Manhattan highrise and had a canteen with four part-time cooks.

She was dressed demurely in a high-neck beige blouse with matching skirt. There was no cleavage and very little of her long legs exposed. Her hair was tied in a bun at the back, her left wrist encircled by a single gold bracelet. There were no rings on her fingers. Usually Maria stalked the HQ in tight-fitting, slinky little black numbers guaranteed to set pulses racing. She would drip gold: necklinks, bracelets, rings. But that day, on Stan Danker's orders, she had toned everything down. Danker had even warned her against wearing anything higher than quarter-inch heels.

Crozer was sitting in a wooden high-back with curved side rests, studying paperwork. He slipped off his wire-frame glasses and massaged his temples, then sighed deeply. 'I do not wish anything else. Just coffee and hand towels.' His accent became more pronounced when he spoke forced English. He lifted another page and scanned the message. 'Where *is* Herr Danker?'

Maria opened the door to the inner suite. 'I'll go check.'

Crozer allowed himself a hint of a smile, relishing the effect his presence had on others, more often a mixture of fear and apprehension. Most people fled his company at the first opportunity.

'Dr Crozer, how nice to see you again.' Stan Danker bustled into his office all smiles, flashing teeth and waving hands. 'Did Maria attend to you?' He was in a beige jacket and dark blue shirt over navy slacks. 'Anything else we can get?'

Crozer ignored the greeting and lifted the corner of a face towel. 'These are all I need. Hot cloths and fresh coffee.' The brew had been dispatched from Zurich forty-eight hours earlier. It was mixed locally, ground, snap frozen, then packaged off. No one else ever touched it.

Danker moved to the other side of his crescent-shaped cherry-wood desk and sat down. To his left was a computer terminal flashing Zemdon's current North American sales performances, to his right a bank of telephone and fax machines. He pressed an intercom. 'Maria, hold all calls for the next hour.' Then he slipped off his jacket and draped it over the back of his chair. 'You want to know about Chicago?'

Gert Crozer leaned back in his chair, crossed his legs and waited. His wire-frame glasses now rested on the table in front.

'I have to tell you, Dr Crozer, we have a problem. As you know,

Sam Lewins had agreed to head up the Cyclint launch, had managed to get the administration on side and was preening himself for the main event. After the shooting the hospital board panicked, rushed into promoting the first clean face they could lay their hands on. Contacts I know say the chief administrator is regretting the decision. He's putting up a brave front but cursing his luck. Now the problem is this Dr Jack Hunt—'

'I know everything about this man.' Crozer cut in icily. 'I know his background, his career posts, his academic papers. I possibly know more about Dr Hunt than he does himself.'

Danker was caught off guard. He coughed to hide his discomfiture and collect his thoughts. What the hell was Crozer doing in New York looking for a briefing on Chicago if he knew the whole set-up already? And who was passing the information? 'Then perhaps you're already aware of the difficulties we're experiencing with him?'

Crozer started polishing his glasses on the end of his tie. 'Some details have reached Zurich. That is why I felt it wise to speak with you directly rather than learn of this second-hand.'

Danker cleared his throat noisily. At least the bastard doesn't know everything. 'Hunt has refused to become involved with the Cyclint launch.'

'Have you offered him any inducements? Surely he can be bought? He *is* a doctor.'

Crozer's doctorate was in pharmacology and he was known to make disparaging comments about the medical profession at every opportunity. However, Stan Danker couldn't find any humour in the remark. He'd been breaking his balls trying to snake Hunt. 'He's no walkover. We've had him profiled and there's no obvious chink in his armour. He's not into drink or drugs. Stable marriage, good-looking wife. No track record on taking bribes from us or any other company. He's never fronted any commercial product and shuns links with pharmaceuticals.'

'I believe he has forbidden promotional contacts in the corridors of the Heart Unit.'

'Yeah.' Where did he learn that? 'He sure as hell is making life difficult for everyone.'

'But our company in particular.'

Danker was anxious to let Crozer know he wasn't sitting around all day wringing his hands. 'I've moved one of my troubleshooters over there. He's working to resolve the situation.'

'And are we close to a successful outcome?'

Danker slumped back in his chair. The short answer was no, but he couldn't admit that. 'Let's just say we're working very hard behind the scenes to make this happen. We still have the chief administrator on board and I know he's using his good office to exert pressure on Hunt. Reminding him of his obligations and making sure he understands the implications of non-cooperation.'

'And do you have a back-up strategy?'

'We've approached one of the other cardiologists in the division. Standard overtures, good financial package and guarantees. He'll swing in behind us if the problem isn't resolved.'

Crozer stared ahead, momentarily engrossed in his own thoughts. Danker watched him closely out of the corner of an eye. He knew the Cyclint launch was proceeding apace in other countries with high-profile cardiac units and mouthpieces engaged through Zemdon's pockets. But the linchpin, the hub of that universal inauguration in Chicago, was still uncertain. Daily briefings from Hend de Mart suggested Jack Hunt would not fall. The Irishman was stubborn, every standard approach failing miserably. Telephone calls, faxes, mail drops, holiday offers – Hunt hadn't responded to any. Danker knew de Mart would pursue his own agenda if pushed, but he still wasn't convinced any strategy would sway the Irishman. The bastard was so full of high principles he could run for pope and get white smoke on the first count. Why me? he bleated silently. Why couldn't Zurich have planned this in London or Berlin or Paris or Hong Kong? But he knew the answer. North America was the largest and most prestigious international market for all pharmaceuticals. Success there guaranteed healthy profits, and often helped strengthen weaker zones.

'I don't think I have to remind you that Chicago is vital to Cyclint's success.' Crozer interrupted Danker's thoughts. 'We have put too much effort into that hospital, there can be no turning back.' He stood up and walked to the large plate-glass window with its views over the Hudson river. A thin mist was coiled around nearby skyscrapers; below, ant-like pedestrians scurried along the busy streets. 'And Cyclint is vital to Zemdon's future, Herr Danker. Without it we could go bankrupt. There are law suits arriving by the day.'

Danker nodded. He knew the scene only too well. The company was in deep trouble after their allergy compound, Allattack, had gone belly up. Billions of dollars had been lavished developing and promoting the product, but within a year it had to be withdrawn after causing one hundred and eighty-four deaths. Zemdon's R&D division was now at the centre of an international investigation with independent medical scrutineers challenging the data the corporation had submitted to support the drug's release. Lawyers were circling the Swiss giant like vultures.

'If we fail with Cyclint,' Crozer continued, 'we fail as a company. We do not have the reserves for continuous litigation. We need Cyclint. And we need Chicago.' He stepped back from the window and pressed the intercom. 'Order me a taxi, please.' Then he turned back to his North American director. 'Whatever tactics you are using seem not to be working, Herr Danker. Perhaps you should consider a fresh approach.' He dabbed at his forehead with the edge of a face towel. 'I suggest you implement your back-up strategy. And soon.'

14

'I like Luther. He did a good job.'

Hend de Mart sat in an air-conditioned coach in one of Chicago's rapid transit trains. Better known as the El, the carriages ran overground, underground and somewhere in between, depending on destination.

On Friday, 23 July, he bought two tickets for a city tour. Joining him was Carter Hospital lab tech Caleb Rossi. They grabbed the most secluded seats available, close to the end. Rossi sat opposite, staring out the window and chewing on his nails so tightly they threatened to disappear. He was in his usual tatty denims and stained tee-shirt. His hair looked as if it had been cut by a barber with one eye and a bad attack of the shakes. Outside, the sky was a mixture of sun and fluffy cloud, the temperature around eighty-seven degrees and humid. Inside, the coach was cool, and Rossi pulled his arms together for warmth.

They boarded an Orange Line at Clark and said little between there and State as some loud-mouthed Texan insisted on standing close by while he shot rolls of film, catching the outside sights from the elevated tracks. He finally disembarked to inspect the cast-iron façade of the Page Brothers Building. The train then swung south and ran above Wabash. Clickety-clack, clickety-clack on the old rails.

Rossi opened up, his usual harsh tones softened for discretion. 'The way I heard it called, the professor's kid was pulped. They had him in the ER for most of that afternoon, all sorts of doctors coming in to give opinions.' He snorted in disgust. 'You wouldn't get that attention even if you were on life support.'

A large woman carrying so many bags she was barely visible

shuffled along the aisle and sat close by. The conversation stopped dead. Soon, the train left the Loop and they were over the Levee District, a once notorious area populated by prostitutes, gamblers and hoodlums. It had all been cleaned up since the twenties.

'What's the gossip about Hunt?'

The carriage swayed as it entered Roosevelt where the tracks split. Here the parcel lady exited.

'He ain't so fucking bullish since his boy took that hit. Calmed down quite a bit.'

Neither spoke for the next five minutes, both staring out at the buildings and streets, each engrossed in his own thoughts. De Mart was delighted to learn that Jack Hunt was subdued. He had grown fed up with chasing the doctor, making appointments that were cancelled or ignored. Letters, faxes and telephone calls were equally dismissed. Back in Johannesburg, if someone had tried this de Mart would have pummelled him. Put manners on him. Initially under directions from Stan Danker to solicit the cardiologist, de Mart was on a different course now. The courtship had gone on long enough.

'I want the kid for another job. Luther.'

Rossi looked over sharply. 'What's it gonna be this time? Knock the fucking professor's head off? Give his wife a big one?' He now had an ugly grin. 'That's one classy broad. If you want someone to give her a big one, I'll do it for free.'

De Mart turned away, the very thought disgusting him.

The train had climbed to its highest point, affording the best view of the city skyline from anywhere on the El system. Outside, the traffic edged slowly forward while pedestrians clung to the shade; in the distance, glass-fronted highrises glimmered. It was a good day to be in an air-conditioned carriage enjoying the sights.

Except Rossi wasn't relishing the trip. He knew Chicago. Its good sides, bad sides, high sides and low sides. Especially the low sides. So an hour on the El wasn't exactly his idea of fun. And he was still unsure of the mean-looking man sitting opposite and staring into his face. Bleached-blond hair swept back, rippling muscles, deep and penetrating blue eyes. Bulging Adam's apple. It unnerved him. On the other hand, he'd been paid up front and in cash. Good money too, enough to clear his bar tab and keep a few dollars over. And Luther had clipped two hundred bucks just for beating the shit out of some kid. He did that regularly down in the projects and nobody had ever given him a dime. So there was something to be said for this big bastard.

'I'll need a heavier cut.' Rossi's voice was nervous, and he sat on his hands to stop them shaking. 'Luther will want more too. I know how he works. Two hundred for the first hit, then—'

De Mart leaned across so he was only inches away. 'Don't fuck with me. Okay? You're doing just fine. Don't ruin it for both of us.'

Rossi tried to outstare him but felt too intimidated. That weird accent. Scary. He rammed a stick of gum in his mouth and began chewing furiously. 'Hundred more for both of us,' he asserted, pushing his luck. 'That's the going rate.'

They got off separately at Western, switched tracks and took the next return train downtown. This time they sat in different carriages. Rossi fled at Library while de Mart stayed on until Clark. From there he flagged a cab. He glanced at his watch. It was 1.33 and he had two hours to kill before he collected Luther. And he had a pounding headache.

Beth Hunt was not a nervous woman by nature. She'd travelled the world trailing her husband's career moves and had seen most sights, pleasant and unpleasant. She reckoned she could handle herself in challenging situations. But her boy was a different matter. He was only a kid, eight years old and still naïve enough to believe in Santa Claus. Sure he was tough on the soccer pitch, where he didn't hold back in tackles. And he mixed well with other children in the many schools he'd visited; generally he was popular and gregarious. He could handle change: new faces, strange teachers, foreign countries. He was usually a self-assured, well-adjusted, bright and cheerful youngster. But he'd found it very difficult to cope with the assault. It was unprovoked, out of the blue and still a mystery. And so violent. Nobody could place the assailant and Danny hadn't seen him long enough to remember what he looked like. The most difficult part of his recovery was the loss of confidence. For days he refused to leave the apartment, staying in his bedroom, playing computer games or slouching in front of the television watching *I Love Lucy* re-runs. He frowned constantly, as though some dark secret was haunting him. His facial swelling was almost healed, the bruises fading, the aches and pains easing and the simple analgesics working, but the boy's mind was troubled.

'Okay Danny, shift it. You're not spending another afternoon stuck in front of that glowing monster.' Beth was emphatic. She towered over Danny, hands on hips, determined expression.

'Ah mum,' the boy started to protest as he was dragged to a half-standing position.

'No "ah mums",' retorted Beth, 'we're going out. It's a beautiful day and it's time you shook yourself down and got back into life. I'm going to buy a baseball bat, helmet, ball and mitt and we'll play down in the park.'

That sounded good to Danny. His dad had once taken him to Comiskey Park to watch the White Sox and the game had caught his interest. Soccer was his passion, but he was willing to try a new adventure.

Luther emerged from the shadows of a rundown pawnshop in Chinatown. De Mart parked the Toyota about three hundred yards further ahead, got out and pretended to check the bargains in a cheap electrical store. The kid ambled along the street as if he was out for a stroll. He wore denim shorts, frayed at the ends, sweatshirt with Coca-Cola logo and what looked like canvas beach shoes. The shirt was cut off at one shoulder exposing a tattoo of a dagger through a heart, and against the glare he wore a baseball cap. In his left hand he clutched a cheap sports bag.

He'd spotted the Toyota and waited until he had clearly identified de Mart. Not that anyone would easily miss the shape behind the steering wheel; the South African almost swamped the front-seat space.

Luther opened the passenger door and got in, immediately rolling down the window and squashing the bag between his feet. He flicked on the radio and turned up the volume. Right arm outside, he tapped his fingers to the music.

De Mart started the engine, checked his lane was clear and eased into the traffic. 'Where'd you get the fancy timepiece?' Dangling loosely off Luther's left wrist was a gold watch, its strap too big for the kid's thin arm.

'A big fat dude driving a big fat car made a big fat mistake.'

They were cruising along South State, stuck behind a furniture van threatening to pitch off the road, its wheels were so misaligned.

'He just gave it to you?' The van jerked to one side, allowing the

Toyota to surge past.

Luther kept staring ahead. 'Dude knew what was good for him.'

The tough talker with the young voice pushed both feet on to the dash then slipped the seat back as far as it would shift. De Mart noticed scars on the bare legs. Some were irregular and superficial, others were sharp and straight and deep, like from a knife or razor. But by now the story had intrigued him.

'This dude makes some mistake and all of a sudden decides to give you his watch?' He tried imitating the youngster's accent, and Luther looked at him sourly.

'The dude' – now the words were exaggerated, as if he was lecturing a moron – 'was in the wrong territory. The dude was trying to pull kids. The dude was looking for back-shirt boys and thought he could throw a few dollars around then shoot his wad.'

'So what happened?'

Luther spat out the window, then turned slowly towards de Mart. 'He got me. And I ain't no back-shirt boy. I threatened to cut his dick off.' He returned his gaze to the traffic ahead. 'Dude kindly offered his watch just to get me out of the car.'

They were now in the downtown area and heading north. 'And did you?'

Luther drummed his fingers on the rooftop. 'Did I what man?'

'Did you get out of the car?' For the first time since he'd met the boy, de Mart noticed his sullen expression lighten.

'Sure I got outa the fucking car. And when I did I had his watch in this hand.' He shook his wrist, then grinned. 'And his dick in my other hand.'

The Toyota lurched to the left, almost clipping an oncoming yellow cab. The driver, sallow-skinned with a Muslim hat, gesticulated angrily from behind the wheel. De Mart swore as he corrected the swerve. 'Luther,' he eventually muttered, 'you're one mean little bastard.'

The kid laughed all the way to the W Fullerton intersection. 'Sure am, Mr Hend. Sure am.'

At the corner of N Clark and W Newport in the immediate northern Chicago suburbs was a giant sports superstore. Every ball game catered for. Soccer, baseball, basketball, football, tennis, golf et cetera. If it was a ball and it could be hit and there was a target, they had it. Rows and rows of club shirts, tracksuits, footwear, caps, hats and protective helmets. Sports videos, sports posters, sporting hero photographs. Card size, page size, life size.

Danny had been promised a baseball mitt, helmet and ball and his mother walked the galleries while he looked at colours and sizes.

'What about a White Sox shirt?' He was chancing his arm and knew it.

'No.'

He tried to frown but it wouldn't come, so he pouted instead. They switched to a different aisle where there were junior league helmets from floor to ceiling. No team logos and only two shades, blue and black. The assistant, an elderly man who wheezed and puffed with every move, did his best to help. He did a double-take when he saw Danny's bruising. 'You been in an accident, son?' Fortunately, the question passed unanswered.

The first helmet chinstrap was too tight, the next too loose, then another was too wide. Eventually one that fitted and didn't bite into the skin was selected. The salesman matched it to a blue helmet with visor. Danny stood in the middle of the row, a grin running the full length of the strap. Beth wanted to swoop him up in her arms and hug him to death. This was the first time she'd seen him happy in days.

'Seems to be content with that anyway,' the assistant grunted. He'd been up and down ladders for ten minutes and was exhausted. 'Now let's get a mitt and ball. Shouldn't take long to sort.'

'Two hundred dollars up front. Rest when the job's done.'

De Mart had followed Beth's Volvo estate all the way from W Deming. He'd planned for Luther to make his move outside the apartment, but this was hastily rearranged when the arrival coincided with the targets leaving. He hadn't been sure how far their jaunt was going to take them; nonetheless, he'd trailed the Volvo along N Clark, keeping at least four cars behind.

'Get down, get down,' he'd snapped at his passenger. 'I don't want anyone seeing you.' A scowling Luther had scrambled into the back seats where he squeezed himself into a corner and out of sight.

When the Volvo had stopped near the superstore, waiting for a break in traffic, indicators blinking, de Mart had slipped past on the outside and had watched all movement in the rear-vision mirror. Then he'd doubled back and parked along a side street.

They were waiting now. There were few pedestrians and even fewer vehicles passing by, and after five minutes the South African decided to act. The main roads were busy; the side streets relatively quiet. He'd checked his *Chicago Guide* and worked out a quick getaway. A few glances around confirmed the location.

'Go for it.'

Luther lifted his head to eye level, then reached an open palm across the seats. He didn't budge until two crisp one-hundred-dollar bills were handed over.

'Okay son.' The sales assistant was coaching Danny on how to hold his new junior league bat. They had an aisle to themselves, Danny squatting behind him like he'd seen the big boys do on the television. Helmet in place, mitt on and Beth throwing. In between rows of White Sox and Cubs merchandising a make-believe game of baseball took place.

Luther reached into his sports bag and removed a thin-bladed knife. On to the fingers of his left hand he slipped a knuckle-duster, too big really, but it stayed in place when he closed his fist. 'Ten minutes from now.' He tugged his new gold watch round so he could study its dial. 'You have this door open and the engine running.'

De Mart stared ahead. He heard the back door slam shut, felt the Toyota rock gently. He turned on the motor, then edged the air-conditioner to full, drilling his fingers on the steering wheel. A quick glance around reassured him that there was no one on the street likely to offer trouble.

'Now lady, if junior here wants to change that helmet you'll have to hold on to the receipt and bring it back in its original box.' Beth and Danny were at the checkout, waiting for credit card clearance.

Luther was on his knees at the back tyres of the Volvo. The knife slipped past the worn treads with ease and air quickly escaped. Now he was at the right front tyre. Within seconds it too began to deflate violently. Smash! One front headlight felt the force of the knuckle-duster. Luther moved to the other side of the car, glancing between the windows to make sure he wasn't going to be interrupted. About five cars away someone was pulling on to the road, waiting for a break in traffic. Luther hung on, then smash. Another headlight shattered.

'You a fan of the Sox?' Danny nodded, unsure whether this was a good thing or not. The salesman wheezed his surprise. 'And Wrigley Field only a few miles up the road. Son, you're missing the best team in town.' He turned to Beth. 'Lady, you take this boy to a Cubs game. He'll see a real team in action.' They laughed together, each satisfied with the contact.

Beth took Danny's hand to leave. He skipped beside his mother, baseball mitt on, happy as a sandboy and holding his new helmet, ball and junior league bat inside their packaging.

Now Luther's description had been read to Danny countless times. His height and lean frame, shaven head. Earrings, nose stud. Tough and mean face with possibly old scars. A photokit outline had been drawn up and finally agreed by those kids at summer school who could remember the blurred image. This had been copied and hung on the school noticeboard.

But when Danny walked out of the sports store the first thing to grab his attention was the estate. It was low on the ground. Then he noticed the windscreen wipers had been snapped off, the headlights smashed. But what really rang the alarm bells was the menacing face that looked up, held his gaze for a terrifying minute and then disappeared among the other vehicles.

'Yar sure it was the same kid?' Officer Nelson of the Lincoln Park PD was perplexed, and showed it.

'Of course we are.' The frightened and exasperated mother was trying to steel her composure. Through gritted teeth Beth recounted the incident while Danny sat on a bench close to the reception counter. He was ashen and shaking, close to tears. 'My boy knows his description backwards.'

Nelson stroked his moustache. 'There's always tough-looking kids hanging around the streets. Easy to get confused.'

Beth lost it completely. 'We are not confused, officer!' she screamed.

Her anger echoed along the corridors and heads poked out from distant rooms. Another policeman sidled up to the front but was waved away. 'S'okay. Lady's just letting off a little steam.'

Nelson waited until they were alone again, then produced an incident report. 'Any other car vandalised apart from the Volvo?'

'No.' Sullen.

'Any other car even touched?'

'No.' Snappy.

'Anybody else see this kid?'

'Not that I'm aware of.'

'Did ya see where he went?'

'No, I ran back into the store for help. When one of the staff checked outside he'd gone.' Weary. The accent was beginning to grate, the 'yars' had lost its regional charm. Nelson was now no more than a redneck showing little interest in the Hunt family plight. A hot tear escaped Beth's eye and she brushed at the wetness with the corner of a sleeve. Nelson reached beneath the counter and came up with a box of tissues. He slid it across without looking.

'Thanks,' Beth mumbled. She snagged one out and dabbed at her eyes. 'You okay, Danny?' The boy nodded. He was still shaking.

'I'll cruise a squad car, see if we can spot this kid.'

'Is that all?' Beth snapped. 'Can't you put his description in the local papers and television and things?' She was desperate for a more aggressive response. 'Somebody must know who he is.'

Nelson stroked his moustache, then leaned across the counter. 'Ma'am, I recognise how distressing this is becoming for ya. But beating up yar son and then taking lumps out of yar car doesn't put this kid among the FBI's ten most wanted criminals.' He shuffled the paperwork in front of him. 'I'm gonna have a word with some of the guys in the division, see what they can come up with.' He was in dismissive mode. 'But this sure is the strangest carry-on I've come up against in some time.'

Danny was inconsolable. On the way back to the apartment, after the tyres had been replaced, he shook and sobbed so much Beth could take it no longer and pulled off the road to comfort him. She cradled the boy's head against her chest. 'It's okay, Danny, it's okay. I'm here beside you. I'm just as upset as you, but we're fine. Nobody got hurt.' She brushed her own tears against her son's sweat-streaked hair. 'I know that policeman will find out who this kid is. We'll get to the bottom of the whole affair. And then your dad will give him such a hiding.'

Danny pulled back angrily. 'My dad's never around. My dad spends all his time at work and you know it.' Beth was stunned at the intensity of the boy's rage. 'So don't tell me my dad will stick up for me when I get into trouble for I know he'd be a million miles away.' Danny dissolved into tears again, leaving his mother staring out of the window at the broken screen wipers.

On the street people were walking about, shopping and eating and sipping drinks. They seemed content, enjoying the sunshine. But inside the vandalised Volvo there was no peace. Just a broken-hearted mother and her terror-stricken son.

Click. Whirrrrrrr. Click. Whirrrrrrr.

The argument went on late into the night. Beth and Jack shouting at each other, frustrated and angry, confused and frightened.

'This bloody city has the highest homicide rate in the country,' Beth wept. 'I don't know why that scumbag is picking on us but I'm warning you, Hunt. If anything like this happens again I'm leaving. And taking Danny. We're gone, and that's definite.'

Click. Whirrrrrr. Click. Whirrrrr.

About one hundred yards from the residence two men sat in a black Mercedes M340 with tinted windows, listening to the furious exchanges.

'I've arranged with Helen to clear time and go house hunting.'

'I don't want to look at houses, I want out of here. I've had enough. Danny is terrified to poke his nose out of the door. That's no life for a boy. Living in fear of being beaten up or . . . or . . . attacked in some way.' Beth's words tumbled out between sobs.

'Listen, I've been asking around and a couple of the surgeons suggested we check out the North Shore districts. They say they're safe and beautiful with great amenities and schools. Evanston or Wilmette or Highland Park. Maybe even Lake Forest. We could start looking pretty much immediately.'

'Hunt, I'm so fed up with your empty promises.' Beth's fury echoed round the apartment. 'Leave it to me, I'll work things out,' she mimicked. 'How many times have I heard those bloody words? Well I've had just about as much of this as I can take. You should have heard Danny today.' She poured acid on to Jack's misery. 'My dad's never around. My dad spends all his time at work and you know it.' She walked into the bedroom and slammed the door shut. Through the walls Jack heard her final stinging rebuke. 'You'll come home one day and find you've lost us both.'

Jack slumped into the lounge chair and stared at the silent TV. My God, what's happening? I was convinced this job would solve all our problems. Financially secure at last, staying in one place and not forever wondering where the next move would lead. But it's turned out exactly the opposite, we're at each other's throats. Where did it all go wrong? Danny's words had cut him to the soul and he had to choke back his own emotion.

Then the rational doctor took over and he analysed the situation as he saw it. We have no money worries (at last). The Carter position is exactly what I want, it's challenging but demanding but that's what I thrive on. And my reforms are shaking up the division – it *will* be turned into a world-class unit again. So where's the problem?

He looked around. Right here, in this apartment. My family life is crumbling. He pondered every angle on the thug who seemed to be stalking them and the thought crossed his mind that Martin Shreeve had arranged some sort of revenge for his changes at the Heart Unit. But the idea was ridiculous. Shreeve was a drunk, nothing more. He didn't have the cunning to set up such a plot. The more he reasoned the more bizarre the circumstances seemed. It had to be a mindless vandal prowling the neighbourhood.

He glanced at his watch and groaned. On the road again in five hours. Better get some sleep. Don't let it be another night staring at the ceiling.

15

It got hotter. For five days in a row temperatures in the Midwest topped ninety degrees with almost one hundred per cent humidity. American Electric had three million customers in seven of the affected states and pleaded for restraint in power use. The utility was struggling from the strain of keeping air-conditioners running at full tilt. It was more comfortable in the northern Plains and much of the Ohio Valley where afternoon highs barely made the eighties. Along the East Coast they also sweltered, New York creeping past ninety for close on a week. Thirty-three heat-related deaths were recorded, twelve in Missouri, eleven in Illinois, eight in Ohio and two in North Carolina. Most of the fatalities happened in urban areas.

'When you're in a country home, you can just open the windows,' said a spokeswoman for the Illinois Department of Health. 'But when you're in downtown Chicago, there's not much cool air to stir.' Local radio and television stations called in the advice experts. The mayor held regular press briefings and passed on his own words of wisdom on surviving the weather. He ordered the beaches to be kept open and patrolled at night to allow Chicagoans to cool down. However, Tom Skilling, chief meteorologist at WGN-TV, warned there was no immediate respite in sight. There could be heavy thunderstorms, but no drop in temperatures.

And it got hotter on the Southside. Frustrated by the lack of good leads in a series of slayings attributed to four killers, the FBI offered $20K for information leading to the arrests of the murderers. The need for help from the community was keen. Police announced that the number of victims linked by DNA tracing had risen to twelve. The latest casualty was a young woman found in the basement stairwell of an abandoned building.

It was no easier for Jack Hunt.

'How much time do I have?' He was in the outer office of the professorial suite signing letters, issuing directives and frantically trying to reschedule an admin meeting.

Helen looked on, an amused smile on her face. She checked her watch. 'It's ten thirty. Beth's already called in to confirm the bank appointment at eleven sharp. If I were you, professor, I'd show up promptly.'

Jack's pager bleeped and he noted the extension, picked up a telephone, dialled and waited, then listened. 'What type of arrhythmia?' He was assessing a cardiac crisis from information fed by a paramedic in an ambulance screaming its way towards the Carter. 'What have you given so far?' More details were offered. 'Call out the vitals and any other medical conditions.' He scribbled the data on the back of his hand with a ballpoint. 'Okay,' he decided immediately. 'Give Adenosine three milligrams in a rapid IV bolus.' Right. 'If the tachycardia continues after two minutes give a second bolus. How far are you from the ER?' Coming along W Harrison. 'Go straight there and I'll have one of our team waiting.' He killed the call, then dialled seven digits. While he waited he scrawled his signature along a row of correspondence Helen had laid on the desk. The phone was picked up at the other end. 'Bob, get down to ER. There's a fifty-three-year-old female coming in by ambulance with an unspecified supra ventricular arrhythmia. Paramedic says she's not looking good.' He hung up, then redialled. 'It's Jack Hunt from the Heart Unit. Paramedics are bringing in a critical cardiac; I've sent one of our team down. The patient will probably need urgent transfer to level nine.' He dropped the phone, glanced at his watch, then lifted a sheaf of paperwork. 'I'll work through this on the way and call in before you leave this evening. Okay?'

Helen shook her head as she watched the controlled chaos unfolding. 'You've got about twenty minutes. Better hurry.' Jack started for the door but was called to order. 'Are you going to front up to the bank manager in green fatigues?'

He swore silently, then rushed into the inner office, dragging the scrubs over his head. Three minutes later he was on his way out again, the tail of his shirt flapping and his zip undone. As he fled along the corridors he ignored the amused looks and slid to a halt at the elevators, punching at the buttons. The lift opened and Jack practically fell on to Harry Chan as he made his way out. The diminutive cardiologist was deeply engrossed in a discussion with a tall, broad-shouldered, bleached-blond man. Chan iced the conversation immediately.

'Jack, how are things?' Jack thought Chan was smiling harder than ever. 'You seem in a terrible rush. Don't let me detain you.'

Jack made to say something but the lift doors were closing. As he watched them glide shut the tall man seemed to be staring intently at him.

Two minutes later he was on the forecourt of the Carter desperately scanning the road for a cab. About half a dozen people were gathered in a makeshift line on the sidewalk in front also looking for transport, so Jack dashed to the other side of the road, dodging through the traffic, ignoring the blaring horns. He clutched the jumble of pages to his chest as he vaulted the last five feet and reached the safety of the walkway. He was sweating profusely in the heat, that side of W Harrison offering no protective shade.

'Come on, come on.'

There was a bumper-to-bumper tailback and no yellow taxis. Suddenly he spotted one moving very slowly towards the queue on the other side and he was out on the road again, more hooters sounding, more snaking through tight gaps. The cab was closing in on the line, but stopped as the stream slowed to a halt. Jack noticed an elderly lady flagging furiously and he put on a sharp spurt, practically throwing himself on the bonnet just as the driver started to cut in. 'North Clark,' he shouted as he scrambled into the back, his papers tumbling all over the seat. 'And as fast as you can or I'm going to lose a wife.' The cabby inspected his dishevelled fare in the rear mirror and shrugged. Then he edged his car into a break in traffic and headed east. Jack kept his head well down and ignored the angry shouts from the waiting throng as they cruised past.

He mopped at his brow with the sleeve of his shirt and pushed his face into the cooling draught coming from the front air-conditioner, then started sifting through the workload. It was all committee meetings, staff conferences, financial control and outside directives. Dull as dishwater. There were two telephone messages from Carlotta Drunker but Jack ignored them, guiltily slipping both into a side pocket. He'd tried calling her twice but each time was diverted to an answering machine. He also noticed a letter from Steve Downes, and scanned it quickly: 'Dear Professor Hunt, I trust you have had time to reconsider your decision regarding the drug launch for the Zemdon Corporation. As I emphasised during our brief conversation your support for this event will direct much-needed funds to the hospital and raise its profile in a positive light. The company would like an answer as soon as possible. Perhaps we should speak once more before you reach a final conclusion?' Bugger off Downes, I've made my call.

He decided he couldn't face ploughing through the rest, and set them aside and tried forcing himself to relax. His heart was still racing from the exertion, his armpits and neck streaked with perspiration. He checked the time: 10.50. What a way to meet a bank manager. *Hunt, couldn't you at least have had a shower or freshened yourself up in some way?* He dreaded another lashing from Beth. He'd finally been able to calm her down after the attack on the Volvo, making her see some kind of reason. 'We don't have to leave the city, we just have to find a decent home in a decent area that's safe and secure and where you won't feel under siege.' This was during yet another late-night discussion while Danny was asleep. 'I'm as upset as you are. Don't think I'm not tossing and turning every night wondering what the hell's going on. But threatening to pull out and go is crazy talk. We're not quitters, Beth, we're fighters. We've come too far to walk away from this opportunity. We're here to stay.'

Officer Nelson of the Lincoln Park PD hadn't offered Jack much comfort when he'd made discreet enquiries about progress in the hunt for their tormentor. He'd sensed the policeman felt they were overreacting, that they'd become paranoid from the fright. 'Yar all going to have to wait till we get a sighting. He'll turn up somewhere. His sort always does.' The policeman had confirmed there were more patrols around the streets near the apartment complex, and Jack consoled himself with that. But he hadn't been able to bring himself to tell Beth about the police's seeming indifference to their plight.

The taxi had now left the downtown area and was speeding towards the northern suburbs. Lincoln Park on the right, where Jack had had snowball fights with Beth and Danny during the last snows of the previous winter. The zoo, where they'd watched and laughed at the frolics of the sea lions. It seemed a lifetime ago. So much had happened since, and not all for the better.

He noticed a tall, bulky man jogging along the green hillocks, and a thought suddenly struck him. Who was that in the elevator with Harry Chan? He certainly was big. He remembered Helen's words about the representative from the Zemdon Corporation stalking her office. A big gorilla, that's how she'd described him. A sense of concern fleetingly darkened his features. That wouldn't make sense; Harry's a changed man. He checks into the hospital on time, he's taking up the slack in patient caseload and applying more effort. Even prowls the ER when anyone with chest pains turns up. Martin Shreeve isn't exactly smiling, but he's a lot less surly. He's not smoking and doesn't smell of booze. Maybe he's resigned to his lot. And I know Nat Parker's delighted with the changes. He and I carried the can for that division for far too long.

'Where'd you say this bank was?' the cabby blurted out. He was a small tubby man in a sweat-stained tee-shirt.

'Corner of Clark and Roslyn.'

The taxi slowed to a crawl and two heads craned out at the buildings to the right. It was just after eleven. 'No bank here.' The driver turned in his seat. 'I think there's one about a mile further on. Want me to keep going?'

Jack cursed. He'd been in such a hurry that morning he hadn't really been listening to Beth's shouted instructions. 'Go for it.' He slumped back in his seat, wiped at his forehead, then straightened his tie and tucked in his shirt. Jeez, I'm a wreck. And I'm late, and sure as hell in trouble again.

The manageress of the local branch at Associated Bank Chicago was a middle-aged black woman in cotton blouse and tight navy skirt. Short hair with fringe and wispy tail along the neckline, deep husky voice. Her office was a twenty-foot-square cubicle in an open-plan suite with street views. It was functional rather than elaborate with desk, chairs and a small filing cabinet. She almost wept when Jack outlined the family finances, explaining how he preferred to live off income and not borrow unnecessarily.

'I'm a cautious man,' he offered, noting the look of incredulity from the other side of the desk. To his left Beth sat in her best summer dress, watching and listening. 'My father almost went bankrupt speculating on property and stock markets. When things crashed it was his family who bailed him out. I accept that experience has made me careful with money. Seeing him go cap in hand for help scarred me for ever. I could never let anything like that happen to my wife and boy.'

The manageress smiled. 'I understand. Such an experience would make you think twice about overspending. But I feel you're being unduly conservative. Perhaps it's time to stretch the reserves a little. After all, this *is* America and here credit rules.' She opened a drawer and pulled out a folder. The pages were blank and a sharp pencil now hovered over the pristine whiteness. 'Can you give me a ballpark guide to your salary at the Carter?'

Jack cleared his throat, then looked sheepishly at Beth. She turned away. 'Three hundred and twenty-five thousand dollars a year.'

The point of the pencil snapped.

'It really hit home when you called out that figure.' Beth and Jack were sipping on iced coffee in a nearby Starbucks. She reached across and tugged his shirt collar into better shape. 'And did you see the look on her face?'

Jack squirmed with embarrassment. The manageress had written down his salary details, repeated them twice to confirm their accuracy, then leaned forward, her face creased in wonder. 'That's a decent paycheque. Can I ask why you're still renting?' Jack hadn't been able to offer a credible explanation.

'I told you so,' crowed Beth. 'Here we are with more money than we've ever had in our lives and we're still driving the same battered car, living in the same cramped quarters and wearing the same worn clothes. Whether you like it or not we *are* going to lighten up. You're in one of the top positions in Chicago, the bank lady said so.'

Jack couldn't suppress a smile of satisfaction. '*Professor* Hunt,' the manageress had said with more than a little relish. 'We don't get too many professors in this branch. In fact I have to admit you're the only one. We'd better take good care of you.'

Jack drained his coffee, tipped the container into a bin and stood up. He took Beth's hand and led her into the sunlight. 'I know this is the biggest thing to happen to us. And I know we haven't had time to enjoy it because I've been swamped with work. Why don't we take the rest of the day off? Go shopping and spend a little.'

Beth wrapped her arms around her husband's neck and covered him with kisses. 'Now you're talking my kind of language.'

So they claimed the afternoon for themselves and mooched around car yards. With Danny in tow they looked at a Ford Explorer, a Plymouth Neon and a Cadillac Deville. In the end they ignored all three and opted for a metallic silver Chevrolet Suburban 4×4 with beige trim, a five-door estate with sleek lines and plenty of room inside. 'It's a good all-year-rounder,' the dealer had said.'In the winter it'll just glide through snow and ice.' Beth, safety always her number one priority, had forced the sale. While Jack and Danny kicked a softball around the lot, she'd got to test-drive the latest model. Jack couldn't help but notice the delight on his boy's face while they waited. He couldn't remember the last time they'd had a few minutes to themselves, just messing and gossiping and being close.

'Done,' Beth had said emphatically after cruising N Lake Shore Drive. She'd scooted along E Elm and past the brownstone townhouse survivors of the Great Fire, then hit the highway near Oak Street beach, its sands teeming with citizens trying to cool down in the waves of Lake Michigan. Switching lanes, she'd kept to the waterside. In the blue shimmering distance yachts and pleasure boats cruised off the shoreline. She'd finally pulled off near Diversey Harbor, returning along Stockton Drive.

Back at the yard she'd stepped out from the vehicle and given it her endorsement. 'Let's go for it.' Danny had given his mother the thumbs up; he'd approved the choice from the beginning. 'Hunt, it's time you got one of your own too.'

Jack had only scowled at his wife in reply. He hated driving, loathed traffic snarls and preferred to work on papers even with one hand clinging to the safety rail of a bus. Cabs were quick to flag if he was stuck. 'Let's take one thing at a time. Anyway, this is a family day. I say we head to the beach as soon as we've sorted the finances here.' Danny had given a whoop of delight and jumped in the air with unrestrained glee. 'Then we'll find somewhere decent to eat and let our hair down.'

The dealer had never made a quicker sale.

From the third-floor window of a steak and chophouse off

Michigan Avenue they admired their first major purchase since Jack's appointment. Outside, the metallic paintwork of the Chevrolet gleamed in the early-evening sunlight squeezing between the skyscrapers. After each course they sipped and chatted happily, each quietly content with the day they'd spent together. For Beth and Danny the new car was the first tangible sign of their rise to prosperity. For Jack it marked a small but important milestone in restoring his wife's sanity, reassuring her that the position at the Carter did mean a fresh beginning. There would be no more scares, he secretly promised. Car first, then a house. The bank had offered all sorts of attractive financial packages to help secure the right property, and his salary would allow them move to a safe and stable neighbourhood. He realised the fight for a better deal at the beginning had now taken on an extra significance. He glanced again at the Chevy, noting passers-by also admiring its shiny newness. This job means the world to us. Stability, security, financial independence. He poured a final glass of wine and sniffed the bouquet, then savoured a mouthful.

Here's to you, professor. You're here to stay.

'We had a wonderful afternoon.' In the outer room of his office suite, Jack was recounting the previous day's activities to Helen. 'Drove the Chevy out of the yard, collected our beachwear, then headed to the lake.' He was elated, delighting in the stolen hours well spent with his family. 'It was so hot along the front we didn't stay too long. Swam for maybe an hour, then played ball. I had a few beers in the shade and then Beth cruised us along the northern suburbs before heading back downtown before the traffic rush.'

Helen was moving a thick pile of fresh typing on to the desk, and Jack pulled a face as he noticed them surface. 'Sorry, professor, but it just keeps building up. You take one day off and there's two days' work waiting when you return.'

Jack dragged a chair up tight and started at the top. 'Let's see how much we can get through before my next appointment.' He started reading and sorting: immediate attention, not so immediate and downright waste of time. He'd blocked all incoming messages unrelated to division business. He'd already noticed four PLEASE RETURN messages from Zemdon Pharmaceuticals in New York and immediately tore them up.

'How's Beth feeling?' Helen asked in between telephone calls.

'Much better. She's getting all excited about looking for a new house and I think she's finally been able to put that young thug out of her mind. I haven't seen her looking so relaxed in ages.'

Another call came through and Helen redirected it. 'That's good. She was so worked up any time she rang in here I was beginning to get worried myself.'

'Well she's back to her usual self. Telling me off for not dressing properly, warning me to be home at a reasonable hour, checking my e-mails in case my secret lover in Sacramento has forwarded something cryptic.' He was reading a telephone message from Carlotta, as bizarre as usual: 'Don't call me at home. Use the hospital line.' He shook his head, bewildered by the mystery.

Helen suddenly stopped what she was doing, a frown on her face. 'Did you shift the hard disk in your office yesterday?' she asked.

Jack continued writing. 'No.' Then he slowly looked up. 'Why do you ask that?'

Helen collected a bundle of letters and started slipping them into envelopes. 'That new carpet in your office shows up every dip. It's got quite a thick pile. When I was sorting through files there this morning I noticed the hard disk had been moved. The dent in the carpet was very obvious. Usually the frame covers its own impression.'

Jack pushed the paperwork to one side, thinking furiously. The hard disk contained his study data and the next research project protocol. No one else had a key to the inner office except Helen.

'I was right here at this desk all day apart from an hour at lunch,' his secretary added.

Jack felt a frisson of anxiety but played down the situation. He didn't want Helen becoming as suspicious as he was. Luckily he did back everything up on to separate diskettes. He had duplicate data on the hospital and home computers. Any material on one PC was added to the other so he could continue his work whether he was in W Harrison or W Deming. 'Probably the cleaners,' he muttered. But he decided to keep his office locked for the time being and to spend the next half an hour checking his files.

'Here's another bunch.' Jack stifled a groan while Danny scuttled into the back garden with a ball, hoping to escape. 'Yah wanna get outa here then yah gotta look,' Beth said, trying out her best

Mafioso impression. Her husband looked at her as if she'd lost her reason but she ignored him and dropped a selection of realtors' offerings on to his knees.

It was Saturday, a rest day. The temperatures had dropped by ten degrees; the humidity was less sapping. The city was cushioned within a hazy cloud cover. Ideal park or beach conditions. But within an hour the trio was in the new metallic silver 4×4, northbound along Sheridan to the outer suburbs. In the back Danny flicked through photographs of houses while in the passenger seat Jack acted as navigator. Yet another excuse he'd dreamed up to avoid driving.

Evanston had Northwestern University and too many co-eds, Beth decided after about twenty minutes combing the territory. An hour later and Highland Park and Lake Forest were declared too far out for comfortable commuting. But Wilmette looked very interesting. She scrutinised the area closely, her attention to detail beginning to wear Danny's patience. 'Ah mum,' he complained repeatedly as street after street was cruised. He could see kids kicking balls around on green plots or having water fights or just chasing one another. Having fun – certainly not cooped up in a car looking at boring houses.

But Beth was determined. If this was going to be her home she wanted to be damn sure she picked the right neighbourhood. She'd seen enough hospital residences, eaten in too many cafeterias, spent too many hours staring out of grimy windows at clinic traffic. She wanted a decent-sized dwelling on a decent-sized plot with a decent view. She wanted a school close by so her boy could go back and forth safely and mix with other kids. She wanted a garden big enough for football practice, and where she could grow flowers and plant shrubs. And she wanted a nursery for the next baby.

After much bickering all finally agreed on Wilmette. It was a prosperous district with brick-paved streets, Victorian and vintage homes on good-sized plots, family cars in driveways. Children ran about freely; bikes and trikes lay around as if the owners knew they'd still be there later. And there were green open spaces, perfect for soccer.

They explored it with Paul Ridge, senior realtor at Suburban Properties, an agency close to the town centre. Ridge had showered them with attention and more glossy brochures. 'We'll find the right development for you, Mrs Hunt,' he'd boomed from behind his desk. He seemed too old for the job with his straggling grey hair and shaky hand movements, scrawny in an oversized crumpled linen suit and red bow tie. His face was deeply wrinkled; his rheumy eyes squinted over half-moon glasses. But his voice made up for any perceived weakness. Ridge shouted rather than spoke, so much so that his prospective clients pushed their chairs back from the front of his desk rather than cover their ears. Danny had been left outside in the car, engine and air-conditioner running, consoling himself with an extra large ice-cream.

The elderly realtor had taken an immediate shine to the new arrivals, especially when he learned their budget. His eyes had lit up and he'd offloaded a bunch of prospectuses he was sifting through. 'I think we'll go for the luxury end of the market, don't you?' He'd winked at Beth. 'You seem like a lady who'd appreciate something special.'

Ridge took them on a tour of the locale, pointing out schools, speciality shops and the railway station. Jack spent ten minutes studying train timetables. It looked good. If they chose a residence nearby each morning he could ride the Metra to NorthWestern station in downtown Chicago, leaving a few minutes after six in the morning, arriving 6.45. A brisk walk or cab drive and he'd be at his desk at seven, maybe 7.15 at the latest. Later in the day he could catch a train in the city and be in Wilmette station around 6.30. There would be no journeys in angry traffic jams to shoot up his blood pressure.

'Some of these homes were built a century ago,' Ridge said when they returned to his office. He was searching through a filing cabinet. 'Most of the traditional stuccos are from the twenties.' He dragged out more prospectuses and pushed the drawer shut so firmly the cabinet shook. 'I've got a couple of million-dollar properties near the lake, a few around eight hundred thousand closer in.' He squinted at Beth over his glasses. 'I don't believe Mrs Hunt wants to look at anything beneath that.' Jack raised his eyebrows.

Two hours later Beth had narrowed her choices to three fine-looking houses within a five-mile radius. While driving to inspect one, a brick, steel and glass modern wonder, Jack spotted a completely different property on Shimna Avenue, a tree-lined street three blocks from the Baha'i Temple on Linden.

They parked outside and walked the front plot. A large red on blue For Sale sign was stuck firmly into the overgrown lawn. The house, built in the late 1800s, had a high, narrow-angled slate roof with wood-framed windows. Through their glass Jack could just about make out an old-fashioned kitchen with appliances and fixtures that looked straight out of the fifties. The general décor suggested it hadn't been changed for years. It reminded Jack of his parents' home near Dublin.

'I thought you wanted to see the one in the brochure.' Beth pointed to the prospectus she was holding.

But Jack was not going to be rushed. His eyes widened as he took in the setting. It wasn't as brash and in your face as the one they'd been heading towards, and had an old-world charm and shabbiness he found appealing. 'I kind of like this one,' he announced finally. 'It's full of character rather than flashy. We should check it out.' Beth immediately added it to her list of 'must sees'. Jack noticed her delighting in the situation. Searching for a home at last.

'Has it got a number or name?' she asked as she watched her husband wander the front plot. The grass was long with brown patches, the area obviously not watered for some time.

Jack peered at an ivy-covered sign to the left of the entrance door. 'The letters are very badly worn.' He rubbed the palm of his hand against the dirt and stood back to inspect. 'Joliet,' he announced finally, then closed in for a better examination. 'Definitely Joliet.'

Beth inspected the front of the building, squinting against the strong sun. 'That's an unusual name.' Her brow creased in thought as she studied the plot of land. 'But I could learn to like it.' She scribbled some notes on the realtor's circular and started for the car. 'Hurry, we've got two more to look over.'

But Jack was now stomping the back plot, mostly grass with edges of neglected shrubbery. It was big. Plenty of space for a soccer-mad eight-year-old and room for improvement in the garden. Beth would get it into shape in no time.

Before they drove away Jack took one last glance at the house. It was a fine building. Close to the city and in a safe and family-orientated neighbourhood, larger than the others they'd seen. He scanned the advertisement until he found the price. Eight hundred thousand dollars. Jeez, that's an awful lot of money. The excitement he'd felt cooled a little, but he continued to look back at it, noticing the narrow roofs with their well-worn shingles. It could certainly be a fine home.

On Monday morning Jack was feeling bullish and optimistic. Things were looking up. After division rounds and an impromptu teaching session with two of his brighter med students he made his way to his office, lingering by Helen's desk to sort through post and trade newspapers. A headline on page three of American Medicine stopped him in his tracks, RESEARCH CARDIOLOGIST KILLED IN HIT-AND-RUN INCIDENT. He scanned the report, feeling sick as he recognised the victim's name.

> Sacramento: Friday
> Local police here believe cardiology academic Dr Carlotta Drunker was killed in a hit-and-run accident. Two days ago the forty-three-year-old researcher was discovered lying on the roadside near the gated community where she lived. Preliminary investigation revealed she had sustained fatal injuries consistent with vehicle impact. 'At this stage we have had no sightings of the vehicle involved,' said a Sacramento PD spokesperson. 'We appeal to anyone who was in the area between the hours of six and ten o'clock on the evening of Wednesday, 28 July, to come forward.'

Jack was stunned.

'Anything wrong?' Helen had noticed his shocked expression. They were sitting in the outer office of the professorial suite, twenty minutes after the division rounds had been completed.

Jack read the brief report again, then crumpled the paper. His shoulders sagged and he felt suddenly weary and dejected. Why didn't I return her messages? She was trying to contact me that day we were at the beach. Maybe she was mentally unhinged, depressed or something. Threw herself in front of an oncoming car. God knows how often that happens with psychiatric patients. One call might have made all the difference.

'My Californian research colleague,' he offered finally. 'The one that Beth made such a fuss about. Sent me a lot of e-mails.'

'I remember her.' Helen began flicking through back pages of her daybook. 'The one who sent those weird messages.'

'That's her. And I didn't get back.'

He smoothed out the news page and turned it towards Helen. She skimmed the text, head shaking as she reached the end. 'What a waste of life.'

Jack leaned his elbows on the desk. 'I think she was unstable. The e-mails I picked up at home were becoming more and more bizarre. And none of the calls to this office made much sense either. To be honest I was avoiding talking to her. I'd slipped behind in my research and had nothing new to offer.'

Helen glanced at her watch, then flicked through the unit diary. 'Time to get back to work, professor. The show must go on here.'

Jack sighed and slowly stood up, rocked by the news of Carlotta's death. 'What's happening?' That day's page was inspected. 'Okay, I'll be in the cath lab if you need me.'

Helen waited until he was out of sight, then cut out the news report. She read it again, then leaned back into her chair, deep in thought. Finally she shook her head as if trying to dislodge some silly idea, turned to her PC and began typing. There was an hour's dictation to get through.

Jack made his way to the invasive cardiology theatre. This was a standard operating room with a regular op table underneath adjustable halogen lights. In addition there were two thirty-inch-square high-tech X-ray imaging scanners linked to TV monitors. Waiting for him on the op table was patient Dan Horton, a forty-eight-year-old white male. He was underneath green drapes, lightly sedated and only vaguely aware of his surroundings. A nurse in blue scrubs and face mask sat beside him. She squeezed her charge's hand for reassurance. All activity in the theatre was visible through thick plate glass in an adjacent room. Inside that same antechamber a twenty-inch TV monitor was networked so that images offered inside could be shared.

It was demonstration and lecture time, and that day Jack had an audience of five junior attendings and three med students. He introduced himself before scrubbing up, then quickly gowned and masked before slipping on a pair of latex gloves. Stretching his fingers, he clasped and unclasped both hands until the fit was comfortable. He nodded, and the waiting nurse flicked the switch on a small stainless-steel speaker hanging just above the patient. Now every word Jack spoke could be heard in the viewing chamber.

'Okay team,' he began. 'Mr Horton has been experiencing indigestion and heartburn for the past six months. He thought this was due to bad diet but became aware of the same symptoms last week when he tried to jog along the beach near 57th Street. Then he felt pain in the chest going up into the jaw line.'

On the op table, Dan Horton barely heard a word. His glazed eyes rolled from the nurse to the masked face of the man standing over him.

'If you read the printout of his personal history,' Jack continued, 'you'll see our patient is a heavy smoker, and moderate drinker with a positive family history for ischemic heart disease.'

In the outside viewing room the listeners exchanged copies of medical notes. Fingers pointed to important and relevant factors in the unfolding story.

'He takes only occasional exercise and has raised serum lipids. Physical examination was unremarkable. However, an EKG taken yesterday showed sinus bradycardia with changes in leads three and AVF. There was non-specific flattening of the apical leads.' Jack shifted slightly to stop a leg cramping, then went on. 'This combination of symptoms and cardiographic changes was significant and so we proceeded to angiography. Injection of the left main stem revealed it to be rather small, as was the whole left coronary system. The left circumflex system was also narrowed. There was evidence of retrograde filling of the acute marginal branch of the right coronary artery via collaterals from the left coronary system. Injection of the right coronary artery revealed it to be large and dominant. There was a critical lesion at the right mid-heart border level but with TIMI grade three flow to the distant dominant vessel.'

The jargon went straight over the patient's head, but the trainees understood fully what Jack was describing. Dan Horton had a dangerous stricture of one of the major arteries along his heart muscle. If that vessel closed fully he would experience a severe and possibly fatal heart attack. That he was lying on the op table reflected well on the Carter Heart Unit's new regime. He'd been identified as at risk, investigated, and was now about to be treated, all within two days of showing up at ER.

'Today,' Jack concluded, 'we're going to proceed with angioplasty and stenting of his mid-right coronary lesion.'

A stent was a small and carefully designed piece of steel used to dilate and hold apart thickened arteries, allowing a normal blood flow again. The technique, 'stenting', was a skilled procedure, learned after many hours observing others at work. The first solo runs were always carried out under senior guidance, but Jack had performed so many the operation was now routine, though not without risk. Any sudden or jerky movement could damage the blood vessel or dislodge a clot, which in turn would precipitate a massive stroke. Experienced and steady hands were vital for safety. And no interruptions.

'I'm now making an incision in Mr Horton's right femoral artery. He's had a local anaesthetic and shouldn't feel a thing.' Jack glanced down at his patient who now had his eyes closed. 'He's had aspirin and heparin to minimise clotting.'

The theatre went quiet. The halogen lights bore down, whitening many blues and greens. Outside, the listeners could hear only their instructor's breathing.

Fifteen minutes later. 'The stent I'm using is attached to this slender introducer' – he held up a long flexible strip for all to see – 'and it enters the arterial system through the incised vessel.' Jack inserted the tip of the introducer into the blood stream and began threading it northwards. With skill and experience, it was further twisted and turned in the correct direction. 'If you look at the screen you should now see the steel tip enter the coronary arterial tree.'

In the antechamber heads craned towards the monitor. Dan Horton's heart could be seen beating and an audio transmitted the lub-dub sound of chamber valves opening and closing as blood rushed in to be pumped elsewhere. The stent glided slowly along the blood vessels until it reached the stricture. Critical position. The trainees could almost feel their own pulses racing as they looked on.

The stent now had to be teased into the blockage and expanded to open the vessel wall and allow the easier through-flow of blood.

'We're there,' came a triumphant announcement.

The celebration was suddenly cut short by a sharp rapping on the viewing glass. Standing watching was hospital administrator Steve Downes. He caught Jack's attention and beckoned him over.

On the TV monitors the proof of the cardiologist's skill could be clearly seen. The flow of blood past the stricture had improved dramatically, the narrowing now wider. Mission accomplished certainly, but there was still touchdown to negotiate. However, Steve Downes's body language clearly suggested he wasn't prepared to hang about. He summoned Jack again. Jack finished up and went over.

'I want a blood and urine sample.'

Jack was livid. 'Jesus Christ, I don't believe this.' He'd had to rush to finish the stenting and unduly hurry to repair his patient's entry incision. He was convinced the administrator had something important to say, like the Heart Unit was on fire or they'd been awarded the Nobel Prize for medicine. Not that he'd been selected for random substance abuse testing. 'Couldn't this have waited until some other time?' he snapped as he rolled up a sleeve and exposed the crook of his elbow. 'What the hell do you think I was doing in there? Painting the goddamned cabinets? Why didn't you give me some sort of notice?' The outburst was stupid, and he immediately regretted losing his temper, especially in front of the trainees. He noticed them turn away to avoid the embarrassing confrontation.

Downes glared angrily. 'That's why it's called random sampling. We don't give notice.'

The two backed off from further unnecessary conflict, but both still simmered.

Then Jack couldn't produce a urine sample for over twenty minutes. Trying to pee on demand with someone looking over your shoulder to ensure you don't adulterate the specimen isn't easy at the best of times. He found it extremely difficult on this occasion, and later watched Downes leave the Heart Unit looking more than a little disturbed.

The news of the new cardiology professor's public outburst filtered through the division. As each one told the story embellishments were made, just to spice it up. By the end of that day Jack was being made out to be brash, arrogant and bad-tempered. Typically Irish. All that was missing was a head of red hair to match his fiery temper. Only his secretary stood up for him, fiercely defending Jack against the criticism, dismissive of what was just gossip and the usual hospital bad-mouthing.

16

The request from Steve Downes was simple and to the point: 'Professor Hunt, I'd like it if we could meet at lunchtime today to try and clear up one or two issues that have surfaced on level nine.'

To Jack the message was bothersome but acceptable. He was still chasing his tail with the pressure of work in the Heart Unit. The nursing shortage was ongoing, the patient load just as onerous. Even though he hated doing it, Jack had been forced to involve Downes in some of the troubleshooting. He'd drafted a submission outlining the difficulties, highlighting the pressure points, and suggesting a number of changes, including roster restructuring. The full strategy was teased out with Helen, Jack relying heavily on her local knowledge of the nursing situation, before a final text was delivered to the tenth floor. So the request for a formal meeting didn't really come as a surprise.

'Jack, good to see you again.' The administrator was dressed in a light grey double-breasted suit with white shirt and navy bow tie. The shirt was so tight around the neck that Downes's turkey chin wobbled more than usual as he spoke. His wire hair for once was combed to order. He gripped Jack's shoulder as he ushered him in. 'We've got important business to get through and not much time, so let's get started right away.' Downes seemed too saccharine-sweet for Jack's liking, especially after their unpleasant encounter less than forty-eight hours previously. 'Take a seat and I'll order coffee.'

Jack was still in green scrubs, two stethoscopes around his neck, pager clipped to his waistband. He sat well back from the executive desk, noting the scattering of material covering its surface. Zemdon Pharmaceutical logos everywhere.

Before he had a chance to collect his thoughts, Downes was at the other side, slipping his jacket off, loosening the top button of his shirt. He pushed the Zemdon promotions to one side and pressed an intercom. 'Ask Mr Danker to come through.' Then he looked across at Jack. 'There's only one item on the agenda and that's your difficulties in the Heart Unit. I'd like this gentleman to listen in on our discussion as he may be able to contribute something positive.' A remote control was pointed at the air-conditioner and a gentle hum immediately kicked in.

Stan Danker was in the room almost before Jack knew it. The thick-pile carpet muffled footsteps, the door had obviously been left ajar. He sized up the new arrival. Tall and lean, granite face and slate-grey eyes. Immaculately tailored single-breast navy suit, pale blue shirt and bright yellow tie.

'Delighted we could meet, Dr Hunt.' There was a show of teeth and a false smile. 'Mr Downes has been very accommodating to arrange this engagement.' The handshake almost cracked Jack's knuckles. 'I know you're busy so I won't interrupt until asked.' He moved smartly to the only other vacant chair and sat down. Out of the corner of his eye Jack noticed him staring intently in his direction.

'I read through your summary.' Downes was waving the five pages Helen had prepared. 'Things certainly are tight. Nursing shortages, delays in diagnostic imaging facilities, pressure from the cardiothoracic team to clear the backlog of bypass procedures.'

There were currently two hundred and ten on the cardiac surgery waiting list. The surgeons had a full complement of staff and were chomping at the bit to trim the queue, but pressure within the Heart Unit meant delays in screening patients. One group was ready and eager, the other swamped and ill-prepared. There was the potential for inter-divisional friction.

'I've spoken with all the downtown medic agencies and I'm afraid we're not getting any positive vibes. Recruitments are down twenty per cent on last year and most on their books live in the outer suburbs and are voting with their feet to work locally. So I can't see an immediate resolution to that particular difficulty in the near future.' Downes turned the pages and ran a finger along the text until he reached the next detail he was searching for. 'Diagnostic imaging. Radiology informs me they cannot allocate more time to cardiology. The ER squad have first call on emergency screening and they've been so busy nearly every other division has been forced to cut back. You're not the only one pressing for quicker access. I'm afraid it's a supply-and-demand stand-off, with demand far outstripping supply.'

Jack cut in. 'What you're telling me is nothing is likely to change in the Heart Unit.'

Downes shrugged his shoulders. 'Not through the usual channels anyway.' He glanced towards Stan Danker and Jack followed the movement. The other man now had his head down, apparently inspecting his fingernails. He didn't look up.

'Is that it?' Jack was half out of his chair, but Downes immediately waved him back.

'That's not it,' he snapped. 'You've got a problem – actually, a *list* of problems. You asked me for advice on resolving them and I've had to look at a number of different angles to see if I can come up with any solutions.'

Jack sensed the other man's annoyance. If this had been a one-to-one discussion he could have relaxed and talked over the issues. But he had a feel for Stan Danker's presence. It was most unusual for an outsider to be allowed to listen in on hospital business.

'I'm not going to bore you with the finer details of every conversation I've had, but there is nothing I can usefully offer that will help with the Heart Unit's difficulties. There are other divisions just as stretched and I'm trying to pull strings for them as well. But your situation is unique in that there is an outside source of supply we can tap.'

Jack noticed Stan Danker sit more upright in his seat. Here it comes, the shakedown.

'Perhaps I should explain.' Danker had now turned fully towards Jack. His East Coast accent was as smooth and polished as the shoes he wore. 'I represent Zemdon Pharmaceuticals. Our company is prepared to look at the difficulties you're experiencing and offer very practical and immediate assistance.'

Jack eyeballed him. 'Your company, Mr Danker, has been flooding my office with telephone calls and faxes. Despite specific instructions to the contrary one of your representatives has practically pitched tent in my secretary's office. I've taken to using the emergency stairwell to avoid him.' His voice was hard, his stare fixed.

'Get off your high horse for Christ's sake.' Steve Downes sliced through Jack's diatribe. 'Mr Danker flew in from New York first thing to make this meeting.' He slammed a fist on his desk, the blow so forceful that paperwork fluttered to the floor. 'You might at least give him the courtesy of a hearing.'

Jack ignored the administrator's outburst and looked at his watch. It was 1.40. 'I have a conference scheduled for two o'clock with the paediatric team. It can't be switched or delayed.' He faced the Zemdon director. 'You flew in from New York to meet me without my knowing. If that turns out to be a wasted journey that's your affair.' He gestured towards Downes. 'My position on undue pharmaceutical influence in high-profile units is well known and on record.'

If Stan Danker was put out being painted as a pariah, he didn't show it. 'Let me cut to the chase, Dr Hunt.' He shifted in his chair. 'You need nurses and technology and I can provide both. The Zemdon Corporation is prepared to fund three cardiac nursing positions for the next two years. The girls will be fully trained and experienced in all aspects of intensive coronary care. They can take over preps for catheterisation and monitor acute coronary and post-op observations for your surgical cases. My feeling is that could impact significantly on the surgical waiting list.'

Downes added his tuppenceworth. 'I can't get that sort of staff. He can. I can't *pay* for that sort of staff. He can.'

'I listened to your difficulties with access to diagnostic technology,' Stan Danker continued. 'Zemdon can put the Carter Heart Unit in pole position throughout North America by being the first cardiology division to take possession of the GE Innova 2000 imager.' Jack stopped himself from interrupting. Did he say GE Innova 2000? 'As you know,' Danker continued, 'this system is the latest in cardiac diagnostic technology. It allows remarkable clarity in visualising obscured blood vessels and pinpoints procedural devices like catheters and guide wires. I'm told it is especially useful in emergencies when investigation and treatments can be fast-forwarded by accuracy and speed of detail.'

'We're talking an eighty-thousand-dollar investment here, Jack.' Steve Downes was swinging from side to side in his swivel chair, watching his latest professor's reaction. 'There's also a separate budget of nine thousand dollars for annual maintenance.'

'We'll take care of that,' added Danker.

This was no cheap pharmaceutical giveaway, and Jack knew it.

At a stroke the nursing shortages could be resolved, his backlog of cases cleared. And the GE 2000 was cutting-edge technology. It would carry the Carter Heart Unit to the top in cardiology league tables throughout North America.

'This is a very generous offer,' he said. 'Indeed I'm astounded by the gesture.' He studied Danker's face. The pharmaceutical director was as wound up as a coiled spring. 'But what would Zemdon want in return?'

Danker leaned forward in his chair and rested his chin on an upturned palm. Jack thought he was studying him like a beast inspects its prey. 'We are launching a new cardiology compound in October. It's called Cyclint, a heart-attack preventer.'

Jack said, 'I know all about it, I've studied the advance data. On face value this could be a big commercial success.'

Danker's features slackened. 'We're certainly hoping so, Dr Hunt. Indeed we're planning to make it a blockbuster, bigger than Viagra.'

Jack knew many chemical firms compared new product performances against the stunning success of the male impotence drug. So when Stan Danker talked of a blockbuster he realised the firm was calculating annual sales of up to a billion dollars a year.

'The programme is at an advanced stage.' The New York executive was now in full flow. He'd relaxed his large body into the chair, crossed one leg over the other. The spring was gently uncoiling. 'Advance orders look very healthy, the drug is already packed and waiting for shipment around the world. We're getting positive feedback from many eminent cardiologists, all anxious to start their patients on therapy.'

'So what do you expect me to do?' Jack was pretending to fiddle with his pager, anything to distract attention. He was feverishly trying to decide his approach. Run with what was going to unravel and bite the bullet on his openly declared distaste for pharmaceutical alliances, or say no and risk carrying the Heart Unit into a winter of discontent?

'We'd like you to front our promotion here in Chicago.' Danker finally got straight to the point. 'We had engaged your late professor for this role, and he was very enthusiastic. Sam Lewins felt the event would lift the profile of the division. Now, if you agree to this deal Zemdon will also back the Carter with an unconditional grant of half a million dollars to be used in whatever way the administration feels appropriate.' He pulled his jacket open further and tugged at his tie. 'It's a substantial package, Dr Hunt. I can tell you no other pharmaceutical company has ever put forward such an arrangement.'

As Danker finished his sales pitch, Jack noticed him exchange a satisfied glance with Downes. He decided to switch tactics.

'Mr Danker, what guarantees do I have that the data submitted on behalf of Cyclint are not going to be called into question?'

Danker allowed a slight smile. 'I can assure you, Dr Hunt, the research and study trials have been scrutinised minutely by all international licensing agencies including the FDA in Washington. Cyclint has been given the green light worldwide.'

'So was your allergy compound, Allattack,' Jack said quietly. 'And I remember the hype surrounding that product release. How many people died after being prescribed it? Was it one hundred or two hundred? Or was it three hundred?'

Stan Danker's features darkened, and when he spoke again it was through gritted teeth. 'The exact number is one hundred and eighty-four.' His eyes had narrowed to angry slits. 'And we're defending Allattack's record aggressively. The data submitted to support that compound were exactly as they should have been. Accurate and laboriously screened.'

'Yet it's been withdrawn,' Jack countered. He glanced over at Steve Downes, noting the other man's murderous look. 'And the word on the grapevine is your firm is on the ropes and struggling to defend the legal challenges coming down the tracks.' His pager bleeped and he noted the telephone extension. 'And you want me to support your new product against this background? Isn't that the real reason you're throwing in the fancy imagers and financial sweeteners?'

Downes made to interrupt, but Jack waved a hand to silence him.

'Well I can give you my answer right this minute, Mr Danker. It's a firm no.' Jack stood up and pushed his pager along his waistband. 'And let me tell you why.' He thought Stan Danker was about to leap up and throttle him there and then, his face was so twisted with rage. 'Those gestures you offered are very generous and would make my life and that of all my staff a lot easier. But we'd be forever in your debt. This year it's a product launch, but who's to know what might be requested next year? Attend an international conference and speak in praise only of your cardiac products? Will my whole team be under obligation to prescribe Cyclint based on your gifts? Will our clinical judgements be clouded by commercial pressures?' He was halfway out of the door. 'You'll have to look elsewhere for someone to front this campaign because he certainly won't come from within my division.'

His pager sounded again and he rushed to get away, almost knocking over Downes's secretary as she carried in a tray of coffee.

17

Sunday afternoon, 22 August and the city of Chicago was under the cosh of a series of electrical squalls sweeping in from the western plains. Zigzag lightning flashes bolted along the steel spires of the downtown skyscrapers, thunderclaps snapping at their tails. Angry winds blew the hot and humid air across Lake Michigan, delivering relief to both citizens and power utilities. Air-conditioning units were turned down, walking was less stifling and rollerbladers returned in droves to the seafront. Following hard on the heels of the tempest came the deluge, torrential showers drilling at rooftops and streets, sheets of water overflowing storm drains and flooding sidewalks. But Cook County sighed with relief, washed clean and freshened up.

In bed in their W Deming apartment, Jack and Beth listened to the cloudburst. First the peals of thunder, then the pounding hailstones, finally the steady drone of heavy rain. The sullen clouds had spread a gloom and through the drawn bedroom curtains sudden beams of light tore through the darkness.

It was baby-making time.

Outside in the living room Danny was watching his favourite video, *Jaws*, his shrieks and howls following each shark attack. The movie would run for almost two hours, allowing the boy time out and his parents some privacy. Which increasingly meant hectic love-making as both strove for that much-wanted second child. It was sex for results more than pleasure. Ball-busting strain. And today Jack couldn't perform. After twenty minutes writhing and heaving he slumped back on the bed, exhausted and frustrated. He dragged at a sheet corner and wiped his sweating body.

'I can't do it, I just can't.'

They lay in silence, staring at the ceiling, trying not to let their bodies touch. Finally Beth turned round. 'What's wrong?'

Jack avoided the probing stare. 'There's nothing wrong. I'm not a machine; I can't function like this. We used to be so hot together, now it's almost an ordeal.' His voice sounded as stressed as his exertions.

Beth wrapped the top sheet around her body. Fresh thunder-claps rattled the window, followed seconds later by more darting light. A howling wind vented its fury. Soon the rain would start up again. From the lounge came the familiar music of an impending sharp-toothed attack, then Danny's yells of delight. The first time he'd seen the movie he'd been scared stiff. Now, probably into his tenth viewing, he greeted each appearance of the great white shark with hilarity.

Beth propped herself on one elbow; with the other hand she forced her husband's face towards her. 'Jack, I know you better than you think. If I can't spin your wheels it means there's some-thing on your mind. Tell me, what's bothering you?'

'Nothing,' he lied.

But there were a number of issues worrying Jack. On the positive side the young thug who'd attacked Danny and vanda-lised their Volvo seemed to have melted away like the snows of a Midwest winter. That, at least, gave peace of mind. But there was simmering disagreement about the property in Wilmette.

Two days previously they'd gone back to inspect the rambling Victorian home and Jack had regressed into his cautious financial mode. The elderly owners, their children now grown up and departed, had long since fled to Florida leaving 'Joliet' unattended and on the market. Six months later there hadn't even been one serious offer. And Jack wasn't surprised.

Despite its attractive exterior of red brick and tall narrow roof with moss-covered tiles, the interior oozed neglect and smelled musty. The carpets were threadbare, the remaining curtains tatty and too old to be of any use. The general décor was jaded and outdated. Shabby pastels on the ground floor, scruffy blues and greens upstairs. The stairs creaked, the railings wobbled. Many of the wood-framed windows showed signs of rot and needed to be replaced. But at the top of the house the attic conversion was a dream, bright sunshine spilling into a large and airy space. There were two skylights, high wooden beams and a big enough spread for sleep and play. Danny had claimed it immediately. 'I could put up my soccer posters here.' He'd wandered around, pointing and directing. 'And I could have the bed in that corner, then store my football gear and baseball bat and things over there.' Beth had already discovered a small door leading to rafters that had been sheeted with plywood for storage. 'This is brilliant,' she'd enthused. 'Look at all the extra space for your toys.' Danny had immediately investigated.

After an hour's further exploring Jack had noticed that Beth kept returning to one room on the second level that overlooked the back garden. That day the sun was high in the sky, throwing shafts of yellow light inside. The area was about twenty foot square with a separate closet for shower and wash basin, the walls faded pink. Cobwebs clung to the ceiling corners. 'This could be the nursery,' she'd murmured when she and Jack were alone. Danny was still exploring the rafters upstairs.

'It's going to take a fortune to put this place right,' Jack had replied. 'Eight hundred thousand and at least another fifty thousand to make it habitable.'

'But this will be our home for ever,' Beth had said, in exasperation. 'The end, final choice. No more searching. It's a decent neighbourhood with good schools and it's safe. What more could you ask for?' Jack had thought she sounded like a mouthpiece for a real estate agency at that point. Since they'd begun house-hunting he'd wondered on occasion whether he really knew his wife. They'd been together close on ten years and this was the first time she'd shown any hunger for affluence. It wasn't his style.

'We don't have to be so lavish,' he'd tried arguing. 'There are other houses in other areas that are just as good and don't need so much work.'

Beth had pulled the window open and was looking outside. To her right and across the road was a large open green with kids running about, their whoops of delight carrying in the still air. 'For God's sake, Hunt, get a life,' she'd said. 'Do you want to settle for second best and regret it? And what about the safety factor? We agreed to get out of the city centre.'

She'd then slammed the window so forcefully the frame rattled and dust lifted. Then she'd stomped out of the room. 'Danny, let's shift it. Your father's penny-pinching again.'

Jack had bitten his tongue, trying hard not to start another argument, but the disharmony had concerned him. So too had the confrontation with Steve Downes and the Zemdon executive. Downes knew his position. He'd already warned the administrator he would not front the Cyclint launch. And using the Heart Unit's difficulties as a pawn in the corporation's power play really irritated him. What worried him most was the sure knowledge that that particular show was far from over.

However, something else had surfaced, something that unsettled him even more.

'Special post delivery,' his secretary Helen had announced on Friday afternoon, just as they were finishing up. 'You have to sign and only you can accept.' A courier in uniform had been waiting in the outer office, bored and repeatedly checking his watch. Jack had scrawled his name on the official documentation, noting that the small padded bag had a California postmark. Inside his own room he'd opened it to find a computer diskette and a letter from a Sacramento attorney. The lawyer represented 'the late Dr Carlotta Drunker' and was now completing the instructions of her will. 'Dr Drunker stated clearly that in the event of her death this disk should be sent to you by special delivery.'

Jack had immediately felt awash with guilt. He'd re-read the letter, then pocketed it, mentally making a note to reply. But what'll I say? Thanks, but I'm not sure why Carlotta chose me? I was no real friend, just an unreliable cyber-acquaintance who couldn't even make one call when she was obviously in so much distress? The remorse had persisted until curiosity took over and he'd finally slipped the disk into the office PC and opened the file.

'Bye. Don't hang about here too long or you'll be in trouble with Beth.'

Jack had been so engrossed in the material he was scrolling through that Helen's parting words hadn't registered. At 6.30 he'd suddenly realised he'd be home late yet again and had quickly packed his briefcase and rushed for the streets, making sure to take the diskette.

'What are you reading?' Beth had asked later. Jack had practically ignored her and Danny throughout dinner, struggling to make light conversation, itching to get back to the PC.

At ten o'clock Danny had hugged him goodnight. At eleven Beth had run a bath and invited him to join her. For once he'd declined and she'd retired on her own, complaining loudly of being neglected and spurned. Jack had paid no attention.

By three o'clock the next morning he'd finished reading. Carlotta's material had confirmed many of the conclusions of his own personal medical investigations. However, their allied data now allowed him to take a quantum leap towards concluding the study. The two academics had been plodding along independently while all the time their combined work had had the potential to unlock the burden of proof. But instead of being delighted Jack had found the new information unsettling, and as he lay in bed that Sunday afternoon listening to the cloudburst he was determined not to share his worries with Beth.

'I can't understand it.' He decided to offer something in response to his wife's concern, but it was more to distract than enlighten. 'Steve Downes pulled me over for another random drugs test.' He ran a hand through his straggling hair and found it damp with perspiration. 'On Thursday I was in the middle of division rounds when he marched in with a white-coated assistant. "You gotta pee again for me, professor." I couldn't believe it.'

'Why?' Beth pulled a pillow under her arm and settled back to listen. 'He's entitled to check. Isn't that part of the contract?'

'Sure it is,' agreed Jack. 'But I gave him samples only three weeks ago.'

'Oh.' It was a reflective 'oh'. As in, I see what you're getting at. 'Did you ask why he was giving you so much attention?'

'Yeah. Claimed I was overreacting. "We had one girl down in haematology had to produce the goods five times in eight weeks," he told me.' Jack was mimicking the hospital administrator's high-pitched accent. '"It's just the way the dice rolls."' Beth giggled, and he relaxed slightly. 'But then he had this assistant guy follow me into the toilet. He was practically looking over my shoulder until I urinated. Back off, I said. I get nervous when another man stands too close to me in the toilet.'

He didn't add that Downes had been extremely precise and fussy during the testing. 'Professor Hunt,' Downes had reminded Jack unnecessarily, 'this is a tamper-free receptacle.' The blood was drawn. 'I'd like you to initial here and here that this specimen was taken from you today and transferred directly to the laboratory.'

Beth's giggling eventually died down, and the two of them lay quietly on their beds for a while, until Beth broke the silence.

'Have you noticed a black Mercedes on the street recently? It looks like one of those big four-wheel-drives only it's got tinted windows so you can't see who's inside.'

Now Jack leaned up on one elbow, surprised at the switch in conversation. 'What are you talking about?'

His wife sighed deeply, as if about to confess some troubled secret. 'Maybe it's my imagination running riot. I've become so scared since that kid attacked Danny.' She turned around. 'I've scrutinised every car and van, delivery truck and garbage utility, and a black Mercedes with tinted windows has definitely been parked along the road for weeks. I've asked about it and nobody seems to own it.'

This was news to Jack. He'd been so preoccupied with events at work and home he usually walked the neighbourhood in a semi-trance, oblivious to traffic. But he knew Beth was very tuned in to her surroundings. She escorted Danny to and from school or summer camp, or on longer trips to Lincoln Park when he was bored and needed wide open spaces in which to let off steam. W Deming and district was her territory; nobody moved without her noting it.

'I've never seen anyone driving or leaving. It's rarely parked in the same spot. Once I looked out at three in the morning and some guy was stomping up and down. I could see a cigarette tip glowing as he circled.'

Jack lay back on the bed deep in thought. Then he shook himself. These are the sort of crazy ideas I used to hear in psychiatric divisions, he reminded himself. If Beth goes on like this she'll crack. She's worried about some unseen enemy and I'm caught up in hospital intrigue. This has got to stop.

He glanced at his watch on the bedside locker. In thirty minutes time *Jaws* would end, then Danny would come bursting into the bedroom wanting to recall every move. And they'd react like they'd never heard the story before.

He sat forward on the bed, knees drawn up, then turned so that he had Beth's full attention. She stared back, her face creased with concern.

'Why don't we drop this persecution complex? I can't allow two drug tests to drag me into a witch-hunt. You can't check every vehicle in Chicago. Who would want to keep tabs on us? We're just ordinary folks leading ordinary lives.' He slipped a hand under the sheets, stroking and caressing. 'Why don't we go back to doing what we know best?' His mouth found hers and they kissed, deeply and passionately. 'Let's try for that baby again.'

This time he succeeded, but at the back of his mind the worries lingered.

Three hours later Jack opened the front door of the apartment complex and ushered his wife and son outside. They chased Danny as he sprinted to their Chevy. The heavy rains had left wet roads and deep puddles, steam rising from nearby roofs. Danny stopped only to splash in a blocked storm drain, Beth screeching with giggles as she tried to duck out of the way. After much hooting and shouting, they finally drove off to Pitchers restaurant near Oz Park. It specialised in steaks with French fries and was child-friendly.

'One Texas special with fries, one chargrilled T-bone with fries, one small sirloin with fries.'

Throughout the meal Jack made small talk with Beth and joked with Danny. He watched his wife and boy interact. Like many busy and self-centred men he didn't often get a sense of the other side of his life. Family. That evening he caught the sparkle in a mother's eye each time she spoke with her child, felt deeply the innocence and vulnerability of an eight-year-old boy.

'I was thinking again about the house in Wilmette. You know, Joliet.'

Beth looked up from a large chocolate éclair smothered in cream. 'And?' Her voice sounded suspicious.

'I've been doing some calculations.' Jack pulled out an envelope and turned it so he could see his own scribbles on the back. 'Okay, it's old and rundown and shabby. But it's structurally sound.'

Beth put down her spoon and listened. Danny kept shovelling ice-cream into his mouth.

'Associated Bank Chicago will give us a one hundred per cent mortgage. We have to pay the deposit, but they'll deal with the rest. I rang the manageress after we'd finished looking over it the other day and she told me not to worry about renovations and decorating. The lady said go for it.'

'So money isn't an object any longer?' Beth asked, and Jack noted the doubting tone.

'Forget about the money, *I'm* the real problem. I'm addled, Beth, and that's the truth. Work has me so ground down I can't think straight. Then I'm humming and hawing about what this and that is going to cost and whether we'll plunge ourselves into debt.'

Beth reached across and took her husband's hand. 'It's got great potential, Hunt. I know you're not interested in any of those new homes we saw. You were taken with Joliet the first time we stopped by. It's your cautious "don't bankrupt me" attitude that's tormenting.'

'There's still a lot of work to put it right,' Jack cautioned.

'So? I've already decided on a colour scheme. Give me three months and I'll have it licked into shape. I'm not going to touch the downstairs, just the upper levels. Once we choose a kitchen there'll be so much work going on I think it'd be better to hire professionals and finish it off properly.' She was now bubbling over with enthusiasm, her nails digging into Jack's skin. 'But I do want to tackle the nursery myself.'

'Nursery?' Danny interrupted. His face was covered in ice-cream. 'What do you mean? Are we going to have a baby?'

Jack grinned and ruffled his son's hair. 'No, we're just thinking ahead, that's all. But don't you think it's time you had space to kick a ball?'

'If I get the attic for myself you got a deal.'

Jack gave his son a high five. 'Sold to the man in the corner wearing the short trousers.' He winked at Beth. 'Guess we're in for it. Can't back down now, not after junior here has claimed his territory.'

'We're in this together,' Beth said emphatically. 'No more moves, no more interviewing, no more hospital food. We're here to stay.' She hugged Danny despite his protests. People at the adjoining table were watching, amused grins on their faces. Beth was now bubbling over with delight. 'Let's go home and celebrate.' She blew a kiss in her husband's direction and he caught it. 'You're back to your old bullish self, Hunt. And we're going to buy the house of our dreams. I think a bottle of bubbly is in order.' She glanced at her watch. 'If we hurry I know where there's a liquor store still open.'

They argued over the champagne for ten minutes. Beth, feeling a little tipsy from the wine but drunk with the idea of finally owning her own home, wanted only the best. Dom Perignon. Jack wanted to show some country loyalty and held out for an Australian bubbly. Danny was tired and becoming fretful and wanted to get away. He tugged at his dad's trouser pocket. In the end Dom Perignon won.

They drank most of the bottle between them, Beth becoming more giggly and elated with each glass. Danny was allowed three mouthfuls ('Hey, I like that stuff') before he was ushered to bed. Then husband and wife cuddled on the living room sofa, discussing the new house and what changes they would make. Before long they were asleep in each other's arms.

18

The days rushed past. At the Carter Hospital Jack's revolution took shape. Anxious to consolidate and progress his research agenda he arranged further meetings with the major division heads. Some had been having second thoughts about their involvement. The paediatricians wanted more background data, the pathologists insisted on formal autopsy guidelines while the surgeons expressed the desire to opt out as they weren't totally convinced about the time frame. A whole afternoon was set aside to sell the package again to each faction.

Yet another morning was occupied outlining new protocols from administration. An experimental three-month schedule was being introduced throughout the hospital where in-house senior pharmacists would oversee prescribing patterns. And doctors just hate having their judgements scrutinised.

More irritatingly, an audit of drug selection and dosages would be conducted in intensive care units. The bottom line for each medic was extra work and the cardiology team's responses reflected the general disquiet. Ill-tempered pouts and disgruntled asides. Unusually, Nat Parker was the only senior to protest.

'Hell, Jack, this place is weighed down with bureaucracy.' His limbs seemed more restless than usual, shoulders shrugging with irritation. 'All this is going to do is create more paperwork.'

Jack agreed, but could do little about the situation. 'Admin has the stats to back this up,' he explained. 'In one study preventable adverse drug events were reduced by sixty-six per cent when a pharmacist checked prescribing habits. Hard to argue with that.'

The sour expressions remained unchanged. However, the new professor was more unnerved by the lack of dissent shown by the two other senior cardiologists. Harry Chan and Martin Shreeve appeared indifferent to his announcement, Shreeve in particular wearing a lazy smile throughout the debate. While he didn't contribute a word, his body language shouted.

'Some of the errors uncovered,' Jack summed up, keeping one eye fixed on Shreeve, 'include wrong dose, wrong frequency, inappropriate choice and duplicate therapy.' Then he decided to drive the pace. 'What do you think about that, Martin?'

Shreeve shrugged his shoulders. 'You're the professor, you call the tune. If the men in suits say jump I guess we better start limbering up.' There were nervous giggles among the juniors. Shreeve's attitude was so out of character even Nat Parker craned his head to make sure he knew where the words were coming from.

'Indeed.' Jack hadn't the energy to continue the discussion. 'Let's call it a day and maybe we'll get a chance to talk it over again at a later date.' As he watched his team in their white coats and green scrubs disperse to clinical duties he was left feeling unhappy with the confusing reactions.

Jack knew that events at home were overshadowing work, and he was concerned he might be losing touch with the unit. Anxious for feedback, he sidelined Harry Chan. 'Everything okay? Any problems I should know about?'

Chan's irritating laugh made him wish he'd never opened his mouth. 'Like a dream. Everything's going along just fine.' There was more self-satisfied smirking. 'In fact, boss, I can't recall when things looked so good.'

Jack couldn't decide what annoyed him more, the grating laughs and smug grins or being called boss. No one had used the term before and he resented it deeply, having taken great care to ensure the cardiology squad understood that recognition and results came from team effort rather than individual initiative.

He returned to his office and closed the door firmly, warning Helen not to disturb him. He sat behind his desk, feet on the table, brow furrowed as he considered the situation. Harry Chan seems remarkably upbeat. That's reassuring anyway, there can't be anything lurking in the shadows. But what the hell's going on with Martin Shreeve? For someone threatening legal retribution he's too bloody passive for my liking. Then he chided himself for not taking comfort from some of the more positive changes. Lighten up, things are moving ahead. You can't keep looking over your shoulder. Shift it, there's work to be done.

Ten minutes later he was out along the corridors, overseeing patients, checking prescribing, talking with the ER team. This is how it should be. Busy doctoring, being in charge and making your presence felt. Lifting the division by example. He began to relax.

On Thursday, 2 September, Jack and Beth put down the deposit on their dream house.

Driving north out of the city of Chicago on Sheridan Road, you know you are in Wilmette when the road curves. On the right is a majestic view of Lake Michigan, on the left a large and imposing temple constructed of lacework masonry that looks as if it was transported direct from India. This curious structure is the Baha'i Temple, one of fifteen houses of worship in the locale. Hugging the waterside, Wilmette is on the southern tip of a string of suburbs that make up the affluent North Shore district. Most million-dollar-plus properties abut the lake, while towards the village there is little for sale below two hundred thousand.

In his wildest dreams Jack would never have contemplated living somewhere so well-heeled. If asked, he would have said it wasn't his, or Beth's, style. But getting his family out of the city was the only way he could persuade Beth to stay in Chicago. From the passenger seat he watched her as she drove their new Chevy towards the offices of Suburban Properties, obviously excited about the move to the prestigious location. I'm learning something new about this woman every day, he mused.

'If I may say so, Mrs Hunt, this is a fine home,' boomed Paul Ridge, the senior realtor at Suburban Properties.

Beth and Jack shuffled their chairs back from his desk. Danny, reflecting the honest discourtesy of children, put both hands over his ears and grimaced. Fortunately, Ridge missed the gesture, his head buried in a mound of paperwork. Beth flashed a severe warning in the boy's direction and Danny shrugged with mock innocence. Across the table wrinkled and gnarled fingers sifted through pages of legal text. That day Ridge was in a more formal dark suit with white shirt and bow tie. By contrast, his latest recruits wore shorts and sweats. Against the heat Beth had tied up her blonde tresses. The air was humid again, but temperatures were mercifully only in the low eighties with high cloud filtering the sun.

'We can settle the sale today with a deposit of one hundred and sixty thousand dollars – that's twenty per cent of the agreed figure of eight hundred thousand dollars.'

Jack started writing out a cheque. Associated Bank Chicago had cleared the finances, with Jack putting up ten thousand dollars' earnest money.

'I'll need the balance' – Ridge's rheumy eyes peered at the figures he'd scribbled on a legal pad – 'of six hundred and forty thousand dollars' – he paused to let the figure sink in – 'by the last day of this month if you're to take possession as arranged. There'll be the usual extras, such as recording and title fees, points, transfer taxes et cetera.'

Eight hundred thousand dollars. As the final agreed figure was spoken Beth looked across at her husband, her eyes now serious and determined. She'd dreamed of this day for years, fantasising about it in many grubby hospital accommodations. Staring at peeling paint, tired wallpapers and threadbare carpeting, she'd wondered whether she would ever own a home of her own.

In one residence the conditions had been so bad she'd insisted on moving out. Roaches in the bathroom and utility, mould along the ceiling, damp creeping from ill-fitting window frames. Danny was only a baby at the time, less than one year old, and like every first-time mother Beth fretted over the child constantly. 'I'm going to nominate you as founder, treasurer and sole member of the Slightly Anxious Society,' Jack had teased. Certainly, Beth could see dangers where none could reasonably have existed. If her new baby crawled on dirty floors (despite her scrubbing them twice daily), she was convinced he would pick up germs. If Danny sneezed, she blamed the faulty air-conditioning or the poor heating or inadequate ventilation. If the temperatures rose a degree, the baby was stripped to his cotton vest. If the heat dropped, he was wrapped in heavy woollens. Beth tried to out-guess the weather, sure it was conspiring against her. But although she had no control over the elements, she did have some say when it came to her living quarters. So on that occasion she'd marched out and spent ten days in a budget hotel while Jack scrambled for a rental. In the end they were fortunate to locate an apartment within walking distance of his work. There,

Beth and Danny eked out another six months of depressing existence while Jack clocked up more points on his swelling CV.

That had been the pattern of their lifestyles. Always on the move, from one higher training position to the next. Sydney, London, Dublin, Philadelphia, New York. Some better than others, but all less than adequate for a young mother and growing boy. As Danny passed the toddler stage, evolving into a boisterous and active youngster, Beth had struggled to contain his energy. The usual hospital quarters were small, with little if any extra space and totally inadequate for playing games when it was wet outside. The first of many footballs went through a window around that time. Her patience occasionally gave way to pleas for change, usually falling on deaf ears. She soon came to realise her husband's passion was for work and research, that he never fully understood her plight. Now, at last, those years of hardship were about to end.

'One hundred and sixty thousand dollars.' Jack handed over the cheque.

Paul Ridge inspected it, then turned to Beth. 'It's nothing more than you deserve, Mrs Hunt.' Beth smiled back. Over the weeks of searching and juggling finances, Beth and the elderly realtor had become friends. He'd learned of all the moves they'd made, listened to graphic descriptions of some of the more squalid institutional quarters. 'And I think young Danny here will settle in just fine. Around here kids walk home for lunch if they want and go to the playground after school and know it's safe.' He couldn't know how important those loud words were to his small audience. Beth glanced towards Danny, noting that the boy had had the good grace to keep his hands away from his ears.

'Most people consider this area Camelot,' Ridge continued. It was as if he was trying to soften the blow of concluding a high purchase price. 'They don't trade up if they want a bigger house. No sir, they add on. Last year there were something like one thousand permits issued for housing additions. Lot of the old stucco and brick buildings have gone this way.' The booming voice tapered off into a wistful recollection of life in the old days.

They drove to their latest investment in silence. En route they passed the modern brick and steel property they'd been on their way to inspect when they'd first spotted Joliet. It was quoted at six hundred thousand dollars and was in walk-in condition. Jack allowed his gaze to drift over its shiny newness, wondering yet again about the money they'd just spent. The roads nearby were quiet apart from a few kids on bicycles chasing one another, then someone streaked in suds as he struggled to wash his car.

'Good day to be out and about.'

Beth didn't respond, her gaze fixed firmly on the road ahead. Jack sensed a certain tension.

'Everything okay?'

Beth had stopped to turn right, indicators blinking, eyes squinting at the side mirror. 'Sure, sure.'

The car swung round the corner and along a row of red-brick houses. Ahead, Jack spotted the For Sale sign in their new front garden. He glanced at his wife, noticing her nibble on her lower lip. He put a reassuring hand on her shoulder and squeezed. As she slowed and pulled over beside Joliet, Beth gave a nervous smile. Finally, the words spilled.

'Hunt, we've never owed so much money. You're not going to spend the rest of your days regretting this, are you?'

Jack clenched his fist and punched the air. 'There's no going back, Beth. We're here to stay. Forget about the money, let's go and live our lives.'

Danny suddenly leaned across from the rear seats. 'When you two are quite ready, I'd like to go and see my room.'

They spent two hours wandering round the empty house, their footsteps echoing in its stillness. Beth had a tape measure to hand and the nursery was given special attention, measured and re-measured, each detail entered in a notebook. When his wife was busy elsewhere, Jack stole a quick look at its cover. 'Joliet' was written in thick felt-tip pen, and inside Beth had written her personal observations and decisions. *Take down old curtains and store for use when painting upstairs. Carpet to be lifted and dumped. Carpenter to restore staircase to safe condition. Master bedroom repainted and bathroom fittings replaced.* There was more on the other pages.

Danny had disappeared to his attic hideaway and his hopping about thudded on the wooden floor. Jack and Beth were below in the nursery, Beth quite dewy-eyed as she leaned against her husband's shoulder.

'Maybe we should carpet upstairs to cut down on the noise,' Jack observed.

'I guess so. I still think we'll work our way up from the first floor. Take one room at a time and do everything slowly and not in a rush.' She stood on tiptoe and kissed Jack lightly on the cheek. 'After all, we've got the rest of our lives to put it in order.'

Outside again, husband and wife linked arms and admired the lines of the house. Against the strong sun the tall, narrow roofs loomed high and the red brickwork looked warm and inviting.

'It's beautiful,' whispered Beth. 'What I've been dreaming of for years.' She wrapped both arms round her husband's waist and squeezed tightly. 'What do you think, Hunt? Happy at last?'

Jack removed his sunglasses and stared at his mortgage. 'I don't remember a finer-looking property anywhere,' he finally declared.

Whoops of delight distracted them. Danny was now on the other side of the street. He'd found an abandoned football and was chasing it along the edge of the pavement, happy as a sandboy.

'We're down to about six thousand in savings,' Jack told Beth before they finally drove off again. 'I bought the Chevy with what we'd accumulated on the new salary.'

Beth thought about this for less than ten seconds. 'Just enough,' she announced firmly, 'to start redecorating immediately.'

Only Danny's shouts stopped another argument. That and a twice-postponed appointment with Weinberg & Associates, attorneys at law.

Doctors hate lawyers. And because they know they are so despised, most lawyers hate doctors. Weinberg & Associates had offices in a mall close to the village centre. Inside their air-conditioned waiting room hung a framed clipping from the local yellow-page directory. Accompanying an obviously airbrushed photograph of Herb Weinberg (as seen on TV) ran the following text: Personal Injury and Real Estate. Hassle-free mortgages arranged. Title searches, surveys, sales contract advice, hazard insurance arrangement. And underneath the personal injuries section was the claim, 'this is a firm that truly helps victims'. That did nothing to ease Jack's nausea, which kicked in the moment he entered enemy territory. Despite Beth's looks of near despair and Danny's barely suppressed giggles, Jack continued to read. 'Winning for over thirty years; no fee unless you succeed; auto accidents . . . products liability . . . fall down damage . . . wrongful death . . . dog bites. *Se habla Español.*'

And finally Jack came across the phrase that almost pushed him over the edge: 'hospital injuries'. There is no greater bait to a medic's irrational anger than ambulance-chasing attorneys. And as Jack continued to inspect the advertisement he next learned that Weinberg & Associates had secured 'many million-dollar settlements'. That merely confirmed his worst prejudices.

The offices were brightly lit and modern with a middle-aged, blue-rinse typist hammering the hell out of a PC keyboard, the only barrier between those waiting and the great man himself. As Jack watched the low-grade activity he concluded that the partners of Weinberg & Associates existed only on paper.

'How you guys doing? Come on in.'

Herb Weinberg was a happy-looking, small and portly man squeezed into a suit so undersized it almost squealed with pain. He wore glasses which kept slipping down the bridge of his bulbous nose and had to be pushed back. Bushy eyebrows that wobbled as he spoke, purple veins on both cheeks. Small, chubby hands which he drummed along the edge of his walnut veneer desk and an accent that suggested he still hadn't shed his country strokes. A glowing PC monitor, two pens and a single legal pad were all that cluttered his desk.

They shook hands, Herb ruffling Danny's hair good-humouredly. The boy smiled back, then checked with his dad if it was okay. Jack's scowl suggested he felt betrayed.

'Moving into the area?' The lawyer leaned into his leather chair.

Beth answered. 'Yes. We've paid over our deposit on a property on Shimna.'

Herb was impressed. 'Shimna. A lot of high rollers on that street.' He turned towards Jack. 'Carter must be paying you big bucks, doc.' His grin was not returned. 'So you'd like me to handle the legal work?'

However surly Jack looked, he had to concede that Herb Weinberg showed no sign of being anti-doctor. There followed a short discussion about their needs. Beth led all the way, Jack nodding his assent only when Herb's eyes included him in the conversation. Fifteen minutes later they'd agreed fees, a time frame and initial documentation delivery.

'October eight.' Herb studied his diary. 'You take possession midday so we'd need to have everything in place early that morning. I wouldn't like to see you kicking your heels on the doorstep all that weekend.'

Beth laughed nervously, Danny giggled and Jack's scowl deepened. But by the end of the meeting Jack couldn't keep it going. Herb was no ogre. He was full of local information and advice, giving Beth tips on schools and shops, suggesting a junior league team for Danny to check out. He even gave Jack the name of his golf club. 'I could talk to a few people, move you up the waiting list.'

Jack came back with his mantra: 'I don't play golf.'

Herb looked at him as if he'd landed from the moon. 'What the hell kind of a doctor doesn't play golf? I thought they taught tee shots at med school.'

His good-natured humour won the day, and by the end of business Jack had stopped sulking and had even laughed at two of the lawyer's jokes. And as he drove against the rush-hour traffic back towards W Deming he'd loosened up enough to treat the family to dinner at a local high-class restaurant. He couldn't believe he'd been so worried and almost had to pinch himself. They finally had a house, he had a challenging job and was putting together a world-class medical division. Time to stop worrying and start living.

'You don't take kids?' he growled at the maître d'. 'We're celebrating, and you're taking this kid.'

Even Beth, always the peacemaker, stood her ground. 'Why don't you just squeeze us into that little table by the window? It's out of sight for everyone else.'

Her feminine charm won the day. That and the waiter's soft spot for blondes with brown eyes, long tanned legs and generous breasts.

19

Dr Gert Crozer was back in New York, stalking the corporation's Manhattan headquarters. From behind his large cherrywood desk Stan Danker was setting out the Cyclint marketing stall, explaining the promotional strategies now coming to fruition. His telephone networks to the world had been closed down and personal assistant Maria had been advised to hold all calls.

'Starting September twenty-nine we run a series of advertisements on nationwide television. Coast to coast, major network and cable channels. This will link in with other national broadcasting media schedules. In addition we have focused on a comprehensive consumer campaign. We've hired staff to target shopping malls and offer free heart check-ups. Promotional literature plugging Cyclint will be handed out.'

Maria came into the room, laden with coffee and sandwiches, interrupting her boss's flow. She smiled nervously at Crozer, then glanced anxiously at Danker, who nodded her away. Danker poured some coffee, added cream then selected a chicken on rye. He watched until he felt Crozer was settled before pressing a switch to his left. The office lights dimmed, automatic blinds glided along the windows. A colour transparency slipped on to a screen that had opened from behind a false oil painting.

'This is a selection of high-impact window shows and on-counter displays.'

Murmur of approval.

Click. Another transparency.

'We have interstate pharmacy educational evenings with two-hundred-dollar gift tokens for every attendee.'

'Good, this is good.'

Click.

'We're offering cash incentives to selected family medicine doctors who prescribe Cyclint. They're our biggest target group and the easiest to recruit.'

Click.

'To encourage closer liaison between prescriber and dispenser we're also offering introductory bonuses. We'll actually take a loss for the first month, but make it up in the next quarter. It forces Cyclint prominently into the marketplace at the expense of all other cardiac drugs. In addition, pharmacists will mailshot every medic in their area detailing the savings their patients could make by switching to Cyclint. It'll come across as a goodwill gesture rather than a marketing ploy.'

'This is very pleasing.'

There was a brief pause while Danker bit into his sandwich, then another click. Photograph of a young woman wearing the latest Zemdon representative uniform. Fine-cut navy blazer over white blouse over long cream-coloured linen skirt. The buttons on the blouse were open to three from the top, the skirt was slit at the side.

Click. Same girl, same uniform, different pose.

'This outfit is designed to expose flesh,' Danker explained. 'The girls can be demure or provocative. Depends on the doctor. The queers won't bite, so we play low key. Any guy with balls gets the full treatment.'

'And the women?' asked Crozer. He was totally engrossed, coffee untouched, a sandwich half eaten. 'What about women doctors?'

'Depends on our assessments. If they're young and impressionable we've got young hunks for display. The rest get whoever's on the road.'

Click. Photograph of well-known and highly regarded Boston professor of cardiology.

'There are opinion-formers we know to be vulnerable. This guy, for example, gets his rocks off with hookers.'

'Hookers?' Crozer got the word out correctly, but in the gloom his face reflected his ignorance.

'Hookers,' Danker started explaining, 'you know. Call girls . . . er, prostitutes.'

'Ah, *die Dirnen*.'

For a brief moment Stan Danker wondered about his Zurich boss. He'd never seen him overeat or drink alcohol or circulate in female company unless on business. How did he get *his* rocks off? Did he spend all day and all night peering at profit and loss statements? Or was there a chink in the armour somewhere?

'We want to compromise as many of the top guys as we can. So we've recruited rent boys and girls.'

The Brooklyn jargon may have been lost on Crozer but the general drift of the campaign was not. Danker watched him intently. He seemed pleased with what he was hearing.

Click.

'This card, attached to a bottle of wine, will be on its way to every registered doctor worldwide.'

The screen showed the front of a greeting card: large red heart with arrow striking through its upper left-hand corner.

Click. Another transparency flipped up.

'The international Web site for Cyclint will appear on 1 October. The North American site has fourteen language variations. Orders for Cyclint can be e-mailed or faxed. We've devised a three-minute online consultation form which goes to one of our qualified and registered medics. There's a one-off charge of seventy-five dollars with the drug shipped immediately the prescription is approved.'

Crozer was excited. 'This is excellent, very progressive.'

'There's more,' promised Danker smugly. This was his favourite territory. 'Drug sales in the US peaked at a hundred and two billion dollars last year with estimates of another thirty per cent increase in the following twelve months. Twenty per cent of online users are senior citizens, our most important target group. We've negotiated good-value deals with other Internet pharmacy chains and they've bought the package. I feel we can sell an extra twelve per cent volume by e-mail. And that's a lot of money.'

'Excellent, excellent.' Crozer was elated. 'This is all excellent.' He was actually smiling. Danker couldn't ever remember seeing the other man's expression range from anything but surly to hostile. 'We have exciting times ahead, Herr Danker.'

The curtains were drawn open, the screen folded away. The intercom was pressed and Maria cleared the refreshments. Danker swivelled in his chair, chin resting on splayed fingers. Finally he spoke. 'It's all coming together. Within six months Cyclint will be on every drugstore shelf in every state. Given the projections I see coming through, sales in North America alone should cover R & D costs. A year down the line and the profits will really start accumulating.'

Without the slightest warning Crozer went for the jugular. 'What's happening in Chicago?'

Danker's heart sank. He'd been dreading the question. 'Still some difficulties. Hunt isn't rising to the bait.'

'I told you to change tactics.'

Crozer moved to his favourite position in front of the floor-to-ceiling window. Below, the streets teemed with bumper-to-bumper traffic and passers-by risking life and limb to cross the road. In the far distance ferryboats ploughed the white-foamed Hudson river on their way to Ellis Island. Outside it was cool; the unseasonably high early September temperatures along the East Coast had plummeted by fifteen degrees after a cold front had swept through in the early hours.

Danker sighed. 'Dr Crozer, how many times do I have to explain this?' He sounded fractious, as if fed up lecturing some out-of-control teenager. 'We've tried every angle with this guy. He's very difficult to shift.' Crozer listened patiently but said nothing. Danker pressed on. 'There are' – he inspected a calendar on his desk – 'about thirty days until the launch of Cyclint. I'm going to give it another week and then we'll just have to call in our second choice.'

Crozer began pacing the room. 'What else are you doing?' He tapped his wire-framed glasses against his chin.

Nothing, thought Danker. I'm exhausted and fed up to the back teeth with this fucking Jack Hunt business. Why don't we just drop him and grab somebody else? Anybody. Jesus, life would be so much easier. 'I'm working through the administrator. He's as anxious as we are to pull this deal together.'

'This Steve Downes is the same administrator I was told of when we last spoke, Herr Danker. He was no use then and I believe he'll still be of no use.'

Stan Danker was taken aback by his Zurich boss's powers of recall. This guy must be dealing with every international division head, probably courting the most important cardiologists in every country, yet he's still obsessed with the Chicago situation. 'I wouldn't write him off so quickly. He's got his finger on the pulse of that hospital. He knows all the political and personality frictions, has insights on any slim chance we might get to break this stalemate. If anyone can swing this, it's him.'

Gert Crozer pushed his spectacles inside his jacket pocket. He tugged at his sleeves, then adjusted his shirt, inspecting the final result in the plate-glass reflection. 'Herr Danker, I suggest you remove Jack Hunt from the picture. Time is running out.' Without another word he left the room.

Downstairs, in the busy entrance foyer of the Manhattan highrise, Crozer clicked a cellphone into action and dialled. Within forty seconds his call was answered, and the discussion lasted no more than one minute. The Zurich director folded over the phone, made his way through the swing doors and merged with the street traffic.

20

Friday, 1 October, and the W Deming apartment looked like a disorganised storage depot. The living room, bedrooms and makeshift study were carpeted in cardboard containers. Some had been begged from the local convenience shop, others from the same liquor store from which the bottle of Dom Perignon had been bought. The rest of the boxes were larger and sturdier, supplied by a removal company.

'How many did you count?'

Danny, who'd been allowed a day off school, put on his thinking face, eyebrows furrowed, lips pursed. All that was missing was the smoke coming out of his ears. 'Twenty-two.'

'Good boy.'

Beth was excited, elated, and panic-stricken. The crates were arranged in the order she'd unpack in the new house in a week's time. The transport was hired for next Friday morning. Everything would be delivered to Wilmette later that day. Their current quarters had to be vacated and ready for the next occupants by the following Friday, 15 October. Until a few days ago she'd believed she was on top of the tight agenda. Everything was falling into place, except the weather. It hadn't stopped raining for four days in a row.

'And who's first?'

'Me.' Danny's chest puffed out with importance. 'One to twelve,' he recited as he read the labels. 'Clothes and shoes, sneakers and sweats, football outfits and boots, miscellaneous' – the word was difficult to pronounce – 'football merchandising' – even more troublesome – 'which means my photos and posters, signed balls, scarves, jerseys and shorts.'

'Now, what about boxes thirteen to seventeen?'

For the first time in weeks Beth had a chance to be alone with her boy. She'd recognised many changes in him as he progressed towards his ninth birthday in mid-November. He was taller for sure, at least up to her shoulder now. Moodier, definitely, like his father. He blushed each time there was an argument, the tip of his tongue trapped between his front teeth. Just then he looked like a ruffian with his short-trimmed dark hair, frayed denim cut-offs and grimy tee-shirt. She loved the kid with an intensity so deep it almost hurt. At last he's going to have his own room in our own house with somewhere to feel safe. For ever.

'They're for dad.'

'Correct.' Five had been set aside for Jack's meagre clothing needs: four suits (standard weight), one suit (lightweight), ten pairs of mixed-weight trousers, countless shirts and ties, six pairs of shoes, two pairs of heavy-duty boots against the Midwest snows, miscellaneous items.

'Who's last?'

'Mum.'

'Yeah. Always mum.'

Beth had claimed eighteen to twenty-two. One was kept separate for the expensive outfit she'd worn to the cardiologists dinner in July. Above the knee, plunging neckline with tiny shoulder straps, shoes and matching clutch bag, each item lovingly wrapped in soft tissue and carefully set in. Then the container was firmly secured and strengthened with strong tape. The rest of her wardrobe (most purchased low-cost at Filenes Basement) was bundled up with a lot less attention.

'Do you know,' she said, 'when we left New York everything could be squeezed into six suitcases.' She spoke to herself. Danny was now eyeing the television. *The Simpsons* were on, and outside it was drizzling so much he couldn't escape to the garden.

Beth looked around hopelessly. Apart from the ragbag of packing cases there were plastic sacks stuffed with cutlery and crockery. Lying forlornly in one corner two Australian rural-scene watercolours faced one another – wedding gifts so disliked by Jack he contrived to hang them in out-of-the-way places. Then came a collection of thick medical texts and reams of documents – Jack's research material, and considered more important than everything else. Ten months of extras had pushed the apartment space to bursting point. Something had to give. Thank God for the Carter Hospital. If I have to pack one more time after this I'll lose my sanity.

She went to stand at the front window, gazing out at the misty rain. The street was almost deserted apart from the occasional hurrying pedestrian underneath an umbrella. Big cars cruised past, their wipers swishing vigorously. The trees were now almost bare, their golden leaves a slush heap on the sidewalks.

She returned to the task at hand and began checking the total again. One, two, three . . . oh, oh . . . here it comes again. She barely made the basin in time. For the next five minutes she heaved and retched, her body drenched in sweat. As the waves of nausea passed she made her way gingerly to the bed and lay down. The room swayed in front of her eyes and she scrunched the lids tightly to shut out the light. The unmistakable theme music from *The Simpsons* drifted in as another surge of queasiness built up. How late am I? With all the changes and important decisions she'd lost track of time. What date is it today? Start of October, okay, that's . . . that's . . . oh my God, that's about seven weeks.

'Mum, are you all right?' The boy sounded concerned, but obviously not troubled enough to leave the screen.

'Yeah, just having a little rest.'

The loud voice of Homer Simpson – *'Marge, where's my dinner?'* – swamped her thoughts. But for once Beth was glad of the glowing monster in the living room. Her head sank into the pillows. I'll never fit into that dress again. Oh no, look at the time. I'm way behind. A burp, then a bitter taste as bile filled her mouth. A gust of wind shook the window frames as she closed her eyes. Thirty minutes, that's all I need.

'My contention is that specific pathogenic bacteria play at least a contributing role in early heart disease.' The professor of cardiology was presenting his research thoughts to a panel of the hospital ethics committee, his chance at last to progress the project to conclusion. 'For example, there is evidence of premature coronary artery thickening in mice deliberately exposed to *Chlamydia pneumonia*. And high-tech tests have been picking up bacterial fingerprints in patients with other chronic diseases, strengthening the case for microbial involvement.'

This board had summoned Jack to a preliminary meeting to

hear out the projected study programme. Since his module would involve so many different divisions the senior scrutinisers wanted to be sure the regime would be scrupulous and not wildly expensive. There were six listening, two women and four men, all gathered in his office on the ninth floor. Three were retired senior clinical staff, one was an independent investigator from Washington, and the last two were white-coated division heads unrelated to the disciplines involved.

Outside, Helen Bradley fielded all calls, scribbling messages on tearaway pages and ordering refreshments. She was frantic with work and the importance of the meeting. This was her boss's big day. If he could persuade this assembly then he was past the most important hurdle. After that the real work of drafting and selecting would begin. But until he had preliminary approval everything was on hold.

'The implications of this study are enormous,' Jack enthused. 'In the future we could be offering vaccination against heart disease, or treating existing conditions with anti-microbials.' Among the listeners some eyebrows arched in disbelief. 'Joseph Muhlestein of the LDS Hospital in Salt Lake City discovered that *C. pneumonia* can be found inside the blood vessel cells of people with heart disease, but not generally in healthy controls.' The arched eyebrows dropped. Muhlestein was a heavy hitter. 'This bacterium lives not on cells but inside them, much as a virus does.'

He had already handed out to his audience a three-page summary of the arguments.

'May I draw your attention to the final paragraph of the documentation?' Sheets were turned. 'I've offered this conclusion: it is possible the microbe is an innocent bystander, one that feels at home in arteries damaged by years of fat consumption and lack of exercise. However, rabbits fed high-fat diets develop arterial thickening much faster when they are deliberately infected with *C. pneumonia*, suggesting that it may actively contribute to the disease.'

There was a short pause, then Jack held up a thick ring-bound folder. 'The more detailed and referenced arguments are contained here, and Helen will distribute one to each of you on the way out. I should warn you, though, it is not light reading.' A few polite smiles broke through.

There followed an intensive ninety-minute grilling as questions were fired at Jack: How can you be sure the separate divisions will see this through? Will you need extra research staff? What personal data do you have on bacterial causes of arterial thickening? How do you propose to correlate clinical findings with laboratory results? The committee hammered home each point with ruthless determination, and by the time they'd satisfactorily completed the interrogation Jack was drained. He'd turned up in best suit and shirt, but by the end he'd shed jacket and tie and rolled up his sleeves. Sweat-streaked cotton clung to his body.

'Looks good, professor,' the chairman finally announced after time out. He was a tall, grey-haired man in a multi-coloured rollneck. The résumé put him at sixty-eight, but he looked ten years younger. 'We've got a lot to discuss, but I can tell you the initial response is extremely favourable.'

Jack gave himself a mental thumbs up. What a difference this will make to the division and to the hospital. He'd persuaded the most important doctors both inside and outside the facility to back him. After all these years of being ignored, of having his ideas ridiculed and dismissed out of hand.

Helen stood by his side while the chairman spoke. That day she had dressed in a starched, pristine white uniform with a wide red waistband, hair swept back and held in a clasp. Efficient, precise, decisive and reliable. She smiled broadly, taking great care to thank each committee member for his or her attention and time. Helen was fully behind Jack and his sweeping changes in the Heart Unit. And she'd let that be known throughout level nine. No one dared bad-mouth the chief within her earshot.

When the last of the ethics board had departed she handed over a clutch of messages for his immediate attention. 'Good news: not one call from Zemdon Pharmaceuticals.'

Jack sighed with relief. 'Thank God for that. Maybe they've finally got the message.'

He noticed Helen signalling over his shoulder. 'The bad news is that Mr Downes is waiting.'

One random drug test was acceptable. Two within a few weeks was pushing things, but Jack had bitten the bullet and complied. The third pushed him over the edge. 'For Chrissake Downes, why the hell are you hounding me?' They were in the immediate corridor outside. No good afternoons or civil exchanges, no Steve or Mr Downes. Just immediate vitriol. 'Don't you have anyone else to chase?'

The administrator remained impassive. Standing beside him was the same white-coated assistant armed with forms and glass containers. And a sour expression.

'I'm breaking my balls trying to lift this division,' Jack shouted, 'and all you do is waste my time asking me to piss into tubes.'

Helen turned away, embarrassed by the exchanges and humiliated on behalf of her boss. The outburst was doing little to reverse his hothead image.

Unusually Downes was wearing his official hospital administrator white coat, logo on breast pocket with title hand-stitched underneath. His wire-wool hair was sticking in all directions.

'Dr Hunt,' he said, words spoken evenly and slowly, as if to reinforce their importance, 'item number twenty-four of your employment contract specifically demands your cooperation with our random substance abuse testing programme.' A copy of the full agreement was waved under Jack's nose. 'Now professor, are you gonna piss or quit?'

There was an air of triumphalism about the ultimatum, and Jack grabbed the urine container from the assistant. 'In my own time,' he snapped, and made to close the office door.

Downes wedged himself between door and frame. 'In our time, if you don't mind. And our time is now.'

There was a twenty-second stand-off, both men glaring at each other before Jack relented and beckoned the assistant. 'Just don't come too close,' he warned.

Downes cut in immediately. 'My aide has been instructed to observe every action. If he's not happy then we wait until the procedure is completed satisfactorily.' He glanced at his watch. 'It's now three ten. You've got one hour.'

Helen passed Jack a glass of water. 'Drink this, it'll make things easier.'

Jack grudgingly swallowed the liquid in two gulps. Five minutes later he had his left arm bared to the elbow and was pumping his fist to make a vein stand out. He tried to force out some humour. 'You keep taking blood at this rate and I'll need a transfusion.'

'You haven't lost it, you're still looking good.'

Beth stood in front of the full-length mirror in the master

bedroom. It was coming up to six that evening and outside the downpour had blown through, leaving the apartment windows streaked and smeared.

She was in white sneakers, blue denims and a yellow cotton tee-shirt. She pushed her lower belly out. No obvious bulge. Then side-on view: no swelling. She patted her tummy, reassured by its firmness, then scanned her features. Ash-blonde hair dancing along shoulders, long dark eyelashes, high cheekbones and full lips. She pouted to inspect, then grinned like an ape to examine her teeth. A half turn and her seat was given the all clear. Tummy in, chest out, stand upright. No drooping shoulders. Five eight to the inch. You can still ring those bells, she decided. She wasn't overly vain, just careful. Ate the right foods, tried not to take too much alcohol and could control her chocolate craving, most of the time. Like all young women aware of their physical attractiveness, though, she fretted at any signs of decline. Now the eyes were scrutinised: no extra lines. Smile: some creases. At least the worry tracks had disappeared.

Over the previous few weeks Beth had felt things change for the better. The horrific events with the young thug who'd attacked Danny now seemed but a distant nightmare.

'Yar all settling along okay now?' Officer Nelson at the Lincoln Park station had telephoned. 'We're not seeing that boy in the neighbourhoods. Maybe he's off scaring folks in some other area.'

And the black Mercedes with the tinted windows was no longer around. Beth had ceased squinting out of the windows late at night, heart pounding, mouth dry, scared lest she actually did spot something suspicious. Jack was coming across as more relaxed as well, the anticipation of the move to Wilmette settling them all. And Danny was overactive with excitement. 'I'm going to have my room painted blue and I want space for my posters and pictures.' He'd even practised on the W Deming apartment.

'I think we should change the name of the house to Snowy,' he'd announced one morning, stuffing himself with Cheerios. Milk spots spattered the table.

'Don't speak with your mouth full,' his mother had admonished. Danny had straightened up in his chair and taken smaller spoonfuls. 'Snowy,' he'd offered again.

Jack had poked his nose out from behind the *Chicago Tribune*. 'Why?'

More Cheerios had disappeared. 'Because the snow stays on Shimna longer than any other street.'

'Where'd you learn that?'

'In the school library. There's a book on Chicago neighbourhoods. Wilmette has a population of over twenty-five thousand.' A list of Wilmette statistics, including snowfall, had rolled off his tongue.

Jack had grinned. 'What about Shimna? Where'd you learn about the snow lasting longer than anywhere else?'

'From Mr Ridge. The old man who shouts a lot. He told me.'

Beth had shoved a plate of pancakes and maple syrup into the middle of the table. 'I'm not so sure about that, Danny. I still like Joliet. That was its first name and maybe we should keep it for ever. Have some continuity, considering all the changes I'm planning.'

Now Beth moved from the bedroom to the living room, humming as she went. 'Danny, we're going to have a special dinner tonight. I've had enough of filling crates, let's relax a little. Dad can have that last bottle of Chianti and maybe he'll treat you to a glass.'

Danny jumped up and hugged his mother, a strong and affectionate embrace. 'Now you're talking mum. That's my kind of evening.'

Beth laughed at his adult sense of humour. She checked her watch: 6.10. Probably won't be in for an hour, still plenty of time.

For the next fifty minutes she purred and crooned her way around the chaotic kitchen. The mince was layered in pasta, sprinkled with cheese and placed in the oven. Next the dining table was cleared of cardboard and three settings were laid. From the front garden she plucked the last late-summer blooms and created a display. Then a single red candle. The Chianti was uncorked; Beth sipped it and suddenly realised how odd it tasted. She smiled to herself. It's so long since that happened.

'He's here!' Danny had been keeping vigil.

Beth had unpacked a dress, the long white one she knew Jack loved. She'd slipped into it at the last minute and sat at one end of the table, glowing with contentment.

Danny inspected her from the window. 'Mum, you look better than Britney Spears.' Beth made a mock show of surprise at her son's knowledge of sexy pop stars.

A key fumbled in the lock and Danny gave the thumbs up. Jack pushed open the door, dumped his usual collection of work materials, and looked over.

'Surprise!' Danny jumped into his father's arms and squeezed tightly.

Beth took Jack's hands and sat him down. 'We thought we'd celebrate.'

Jack looked stunned. His face was pale and drawn, forehead deeply wrinkled.

Beth kissed him lightly on the lips, then drew Danny closer. 'I haven't told either of you yet.' Danny looked up, intrigued. Beth ruffled his hair, then looked straight at her husband. 'We're going to have another baby.'

Danny leapt to his feet, then stood rock-still, mouth gaping with surprise. Finally he filled his lungs and let free a screech of delight. 'We're going to have a baby, we're going to have a baby!' He danced around the room, arms flailing, tripping over cardboard. 'I'm going to get a brother!' He stopped and gave a warning glare. 'It'd better be a brother.'

But Jack's whole body was slumped, shoulders sagging, face crumpled.

'Beth, oh Beth,' he croaked, 'oh my God, Beth.' His voice cracked with emotion. 'I've been dismissed from the hospital.'

21

'This is brilliant, fucking brilliant.'

Stan Danker sat at his office desk in Manhattan, a smile beaming from ear to ear, phone clamped to his ear.

'How did you get hold of it?' He was studying a two-page fax.

'A contact in the *Tribune* promised me the first draft as soon as it appeared on the screens.' In the grandeur of the main waiting area at Chicago's Union Station, Hend de Mart's bulk filled one of the public phone booths. He had one finger firmly jammed in his left ear against the background noises. 'Faxed it to me immediately.'

'Where?'

'To a Kinkos right here in Union Station.' De Mart had to shout to make himself heard, his Afrikaans accent absorbed in the general babble.

'Lemme go through it again.' Danker began reading. '"Top doc fired from Carter Hospital". Great headline.' He shook his head and continued:

> The Heart Unit at one of Chicago's premier hospitals was rocked today with the abrupt dismissal of its chief. Irish-born Dr Jack Hunt was dismissed after failing a random drug test. This is the second humiliation to befall the Carter cardiology division within half a year. Early in the summer the previous professor, Dr Sam Lewins, was gunned down in broad daylight along the same hallowed corridors. Lewins's killing was later linked to a child pornography ring.
>
> Hunt's dismissal, while shocking and unexpected, has been greeted with relief in some quarters. Staff claim the Irishman

> bullied his way to the top spot, then made enemies with his crusading zeal and loudly proclaimed ambitions to reform the unit. Unnamed sources today made no secret of their delight at his downfall. 'I'm very disturbed,' said one division member. 'This man rode roughshod over senior and more accomplished colleagues and upset the calm and disciplined manner in which patient care was conducted. He made such a fuss about low standards, yet now we learn he was using cocaine. I'm delighted the hospital's rid of him.'

'Where'd they get all the background?' Danker was impressed with the harsh slant of the piece.

'From me,' crowed de Mart. 'Soon as I knew he'd been sacked I rang the contact and gave him another side to the story.'

'Perfect.' Danker skimmed the closing text.

> Stung by the revelation, hospital administrator Steve Downes moved quickly to restore the Heart Unit's crumbling reputation. When contacted he confirmed he had already appointed Dr Harry Chan as acting professor of cardiology. 'Dr Chan is an experienced and highly regarded member of the Heart Unit. His good standing and mature judgement will carry it through these difficult days.' Downes is now under severe pressure to clean up the medical facility. Last January a senior ER physician was dismissed for substance abuse.

'Where else did you send this?'

'Other Chicago dailies, all the important city TV and radio networks.'

'East Coast?'

'*New York Times*, *Washington Post*, *Boston Globe*, *USA Today*. Mainly Seattle, LA and San Francisco in the west.'

'That's good, very good.' Pause. 'Same way? Through Kinkos?'

'Yah.'

'What time did they go out?'

'Seven fifteen central. It should hit the front pages tomorrow, maybe carried on the late news bulletins.'

'Did you speak with Chan?'

'First thing.'

'I'll take the next flight out. We've got to work like hell to pull this one off.'

'Got it.'

The line was disconnected.

The red candle had burned to a shapeless grease, the Chianti was untouched, the lasagne charred beyond recognition. Danny was in his bedroom. Beth had propped two pillows behind her back as she sat in the living room, listening to her husband's version of the day's events. Jack was crouched in a corner of the floor not invaded by cardboard casing. His face was drawn and pale, hands trembling with shock. It was 10.35 and they'd just caught the first report of his sacking on WLS, the ABC affiliate. It hurt so much that Beth had flicked the television off.

'They took the samples sometime after three o'clock,' said Jack. 'I had an argument with Downes, told him I was sick and tired of being targeted, especially during important division work.'

'What'd he say?'

'Nothing much. Read me the contract clause on random analysis and insisted on staying until the tests were completed.' His voice was a monotone.

'What happened then?' Beth could feel another bout of sickness building up but mentally forced it away. This was no time for interruptions.

'I went down to the intensive care unit. We had three patients admitted overnight and two were critical. They were my responsibility and I took five med students with me and used the opportunity for teaching.'

From the bedroom Danny's anguish was audible and Jack went to comfort him. The door was locked, so he knocked gently.

'Leave me alone.'

Beth cut in. 'Best let him work this one out himself. He'll come when he's hungry.' She ran a hand over her forehead wearily.

Jack sat on his hunkers again, shirt unbuttoned to the belly, dishevelled. 'I was writing up drug schedules when Helen called. Said Downes and Beck wanted me immediately.'

'Who's Beck?'

'Forde Beck. The hospital attorney. I should have known then something was wrong.'

'Why? Is Beck so important?'

'He's the one who enforces disciplinary procedures.'

When Jack arrived at his office he found both men waiting. They were grim-faced and the attorney got straight to the point. 'Dr Hunt you have failed two random substance abuse tests.' He passed over the official hospital result documentation. 'I honestly couldn't believe what was happening. My head was pounding, ears ringing. It was like the worst nightmare. Test One was positive for alcohol. Test Two was negative, but Test Three was positive for alcohol and cocaine metabolites.' Jack had started to protest but was immediately silenced. 'Dr Hunt,' Beck snapped, 'your agreement with this institution clearly states the board's obligation to terminate that contract if you are proven positive on analysis. We held back after the first result but certainly couldn't ignore number three.'

'I could hardly speak. My mouth was so dry my tongue felt like rubber.'

Beck had hit Jack hard and low. 'It is my duty to inform you that with effect from today you are no longer an employee of this hospital and you are stripped of your position as professor.' The attorney had then turned on his heels and walked away. Steve Downes had waited only long enough to usher in a security guard, a tall, heavily muscled man with a deep scar across one cheek. 'Please show Dr Hunt to the front door.' He'd turned to Jack. 'Your personal effects and paperwork can be collected at reception on street level. Apart from that I don't want to see you here again. I am obliged to notify the Illinois Medical Board of this decision. I would advise you seek legal assistance as you will face investigation and have your licence to practise medicine revoked. You will also be reported to the National Practitioner Data Bank.' Then Jack Hunt had been marched unceremoniously through the Heart Unit, past the staring and shocked eyes of the team he'd been hoping to shape into a world-class division. He'd stumbled past his secretary, Helen, who'd been weeping openly. Jack had tried to say something but the guard had grabbed his shoulder and pushed him roughly ahead. 'Shift it, buddy.' Martin Shreeve's smug expression was the last thing Jack could remember. That and Harry Chan's parting comment: 'Jack, you're leaving early. Something wrong?'

His world had collapsed.

'I don't know how I got home. I think I flagged a cab.' Jack stared at the floor, head shaking.

Beth was murmuring support, trying desperately to hold back tears. But her pain couldn't compare to Jack's anguish. He'd wanted to be a doctor since his teens, had dreamed of wearing the familiar white coat, carrying a stethoscope, being called 'doctor'. Before graduation he'd practised his title, Dr Jack Hunt, writing and rewriting it many times. After years of hardship and gruelling extra study he'd finally reached the top. Now, after one dreadful afternoon, he'd been toppled. Worse still, his reputation was in shreds. Indeed, he was unemployable. Sole possessions six thousand US dollars and a metallic silver 4×4 Chevy. Plus a deposit on a dream house in Wilmette. The family who'd chased a career trail across the world was practically destitute.

Danny didn't emerge from his bedroom, eventually crying himself to sleep. By 11.30 Beth could no longer fight the profound fatigue. 'Let's get some rest.' She hugged her husband tightly. 'We'll work out what to do in the morning.' She tossed and turned for some time, but by midnight she was fast asleep.

In the chaotic living room where cardboard ruled, Jack stared numbly at the blank television screen. He was a rational man, used to rational thinking. As a doctor he'd been trained to observe, assess and analyse. With ill patients his teachers had drilled into him the importance of listening to the story ('How did he become sick?'), then examining for extra clues ('Has he got a fever? What's the pulse? Any unusual rashes or lumps?'). Only then could appropriate lab or radiology screens be ordered to clinch that final diagnosis. It was detective work by another name, and experienced medics termed it 'clinical acumen'. Jack had always been rich in that talent.

At 1.30 he began to shiver as the October evening chill penetrated. Tiptoeing past Beth he grabbed an overcoat she hadn't yet packed. He tried the handle on Danny's door again. Locked. Using the edge of a key he turned the security bolt from the outside, waited three minutes so as not to wake the boy, then padded across the carpeted floor. Danny was snoring gently, lying on his back, mouth open. Jack tucked the duvet in where it was threatening to slip and kissed his son lightly on the forehead, careful not to disturb him. Back outside, he skirted the boxes and finally crouched, foetal-like, on the living room armchair, huddling into the coat for warmth.

His exhausted mind was in turmoil. I've lost my job. I've moved countries and continents to get the right position, dragged Beth and Danny from one miserable hospital accommodation to another while I made my career the priority. Now it's gone, but not just gone in any ordinary sense. I've been dismissed in disgrace. Humiliated. The news will spread like wildfire among the medical fraternity. Hotshot reforming cardiologist indicted like a common criminal. He felt sick at the thought of his name being dragged into the mire of a drug scandal. What'll Sinead and the family in Ireland think? For God's sake, what'll Beth's crew in Sydney say? He could almost hear their pleas. You've no home, your husband's got no job and you've got no money. Come home now Beth, while there's still time. We'll be here for you.

The scenario enraged him further, and through blind anger he tried to grasp how the dreadful mess could have happened. He knew he was innocent. And this was no mistake or mix-up: it's a set-up, no question. But why?

It didn't take long before his mind fixed on Zemdon Pharmaceuticals. The barrage of telephone calls and faxes, the holiday offer. The gorilla stalking Helen's office for days. The blatant approach by the New York executive offering all sorts of inducements. Trained nurses, state-of-the-art cardiac imagers. I'll bet that bastard knows something. And Steve Downes too. He must be in this up to his neck. *Don't fuck with me, Hunt. This deal was agreed well before Sam Lewins was shot.* He recalled the first confrontation with the administrator after his appointment. *The whole programme is in motion . . . advance advertisements, venues booked, staff lined up. This isn't something we can walk away from lightly.* And when he'd stood his ground in face of this intimidation Downes had become furious. *I'm telling you the deal's done. It's your fucking duty to see it through.* Still he hadn't relented. *It's your call, professor . . . I hope you get it right.*

The Cyclint launch. That's what this is all about.

22

On the morning of Saturday, 2 October, Jack Hunt began the offensive to clear his name.

At 7.45 he dressed in tracksuit and sneakers with a makeshift headband sweat protector. Beth and Danny were still asleep, so he scrawled a message for them. 'Gone jogging. Get dressed and meet me at Weinberg & Associates at ten. Will explain later.'

Suspicious his every move could be shadowed, he avoided the front entrance of the complex and exited through the basement fire door, then ducked along the grass verge to the back wall. It was cool, temperatures struggling to reach the mid-sixties with heavy cloud cover and persisting dampness from steady drizzle throughout the night. Most of the rear gardens along W Deming had mid-height boundaries so he was able to crawl into the adjoining patch, tearing his leggings in the process. Quick scan to make sure he wasn't being watched, then another scramble into the next plot. This continued for three more divisions until an angry-looking Dobermann confronted him. He cut his losses and diverted on to the street.

Looking neither left nor right he jogged to N Clark, then further east towards Lincoln Park, mud spats flicking at the bottom of his pants. Three minutes later he was at Columbus Hospital, dodging past hardy residents from the nearby highrises as they walked their dogs along the pavement. He skipped on to N Lake View Avenue through early traffic and headed south before zigzagging through seven different streets. Two grassy hillocks later into Lincoln Park he saw the waters of North Pond, a small reservoir where he'd once taught Danny to use a paddleboat. He circled a thick oak tree, eyes searching to see if anyone had followed. There was little activity apart from a group of cyclists bunched together and heading in the opposite direction. A skid on wet turf, then a fast sprint towards a restaurant beside the zoo. He'd been before and knew there was a public call box immediately inside the entrance. Ignoring the disapproving stares of the early-shift staff he placed a call to New York. It was 8.30 in Chicago and 9.30 on the East Coast.

'Vendine Placements, this is Ellen speaking, how can I help you?'

He heaved a deep sigh of relief. First, he wasn't certain Vendine Placements existed. Second, if they did, would their offices be open on a Saturday? He tried to calm his anxieties, speaking as casually as he could.

'Hi, could I speak with Monique Casselte?' A drop of sweat trickled along the bridge of his nose and he wiped it away.

There was a pause at the other end. 'Could you spell that name?'

Jack fumbled in his only pocket, silently groaning as he spotted pale bony knees poking through ragged rips. He'd searched in the dark for what seemed like ages that morning before finally tracking down the business card. Monique Casselte, Vendine Placements, New York – the beautiful woman who'd approached him after the cardiologists dinner with a job offer in London. Her seductive face and inviting body flashed in his mind. He called out each individual letter, slow and distinct, allowing for no confusion with his accent.

A multi-national pharmaceutical group has retained our services to make a formal approach . . . He'd spent all night going over the many contacts and inducements made since his appointment as chief. Monique's words now haunted him. *My clients will offer an attractive financial deal to include transfer of your family and short-term settlement in one of their luxury penthouses in Knightsbridge.* But who were you really representing that day, Monique? *No deal, no name . . . I am advised this company knows all about you. They are aware of your track record in research and your interests in cardiology. They've familiarised themselves with all your publications and experience in other countries.*

'I'm sorry sir, we have no one working here by that name.' The girl in New York was emphatic.

'Maybe she used to work with you? Would you be able to help with that? I'd sure like to contact her.'

‘I’ll try, sir. Give me one moment please.’

Tap, tap, tap on a faraway keyboard.

‘Yessir, we did have an employee by that name. Monique Casselte. Two-week arrangement. Commenced employment July five and left July nineteen.’

Behind him chairs and tables were being shuffled and Jack had to strain to hear clearly. ‘Any forwarding address?’

Pause, then: ‘No sir, nothing at all.’

‘Would you have any details about who contracted her for that fortnight?’ Shouts now from the kitchens to his left. He scowled in their general direction but no one was out front to notice.

‘One moment.’ More tapping. ‘Nothing showing up.’ Over the long-distance line Jack could hear other calls coming through and sensed the girl was anxious to cut.

‘Is that usual?’ he chanced.

‘I’m sorry sir, corporate information cannot be disclosed over the telephone. If you’d care to write to—’

He hung up. He’d got what he wanted. Hadn’t expected much more.

He began the long jog back to W Deming.

Herb Weinberg hadn’t risen as early as Jack. But he’d surfaced in time to struggle into another too-small suit and grab a bagel and coffee before opening his offices at ten the same morning. Herb was in a bad mood. He’d caught the first reports of his client’s dismissal the previous evening on WGN, then channel-hopped as the scandal was updated. The first editions of the *Tribune* and *Sun-Times* had headlined the story, adding in-depth analyses with photographs on inside pages. It was not pleasant reading. The explosive exposé of doctors dabbling in illicit drugs was bad enough. But the idea of a professor, one of the high chiefs in medicine, walking the corridors with a nose full of cocaine, now that was too much.

Herb hadn’t exactly warmed to Jack when they’d first met to arrange the house deal at Wilmette, considering him surly and arrogant. But he had taken a shine to Beth and Danny, wondering how they put up with such a grump. The attorney was married himself with a ten-year-old daughter who was the light of his life, and he could imagine her reaction of hurt and betrayal if he’d been involved in something similar. He leaned back in the chair behind his desk, shaking his head and tut-tutting. The *Tribune* article was merciless. This was a real tragedy. Not for the professor, but for his lovely wife and boy. And the firm had lost a good-sized property sale fee.

'Mr Weinberg, I'm sorry to burst in like this, but I've been set up.'

The words almost lifted the lawyer out of his straitjacket suit. He visibly jumped. In front of him was the man whose photograph was plastered over every major newspaper, whose downfall was being broadcast on TV and radio networks in the Midwest and beyond.

'What the hell are you doing here?' Herb was trying to be as tough as possible as he fiddled for the panic button.

Jack was unkempt. He hadn't shaved, his sweatband was ridiculously lopsided and dragged over one ear, his tracksuit was covered in dirt and grit with the knees tattered and split. His eyes were red. Forty seconds later the lawyer relaxed somewhat when Beth and Danny arrived, breathless and flustered but otherwise normal. Herb waddled to the connecting entrance and shooed his agitated secretary back outside. Then he waited for her to start torturing the PC again before pushing the door shut.

'This had better be good,' he growled.

Jack pulled a stool to the edge of the desk and spread out a folded legal pad. Beth slumped into the only other soft chair in the room, still out of breath and wondering what the hell was going on, although she had strong suspicions herself. She had dressed in a hurry: sweater inside out and hair tied back with no cosmetic camouflage. Danny sat on the floor in a chocolate-stained sweater, trousers at least an inch too short at the ankles. There was a peanut butter smear on his face.

'Someone's set me up,' Jack repeated.

Herb immediately stuck both hands in the air. 'Don't give me a line like that, doc. I never met a thug yet who said he didn't do it. Every homicidal freak was always somewhere else when the trigger was pulled.' He pushed his glasses back from the bridge of his bulbous nose. 'Don't insult my intelligence.' He was now fired up with anger, cheek veins flaring. 'If that's the best I'm gonna hear then you're wasting my time.'

Beth cut in, eager to help her distraught-looking husband. 'Hear him out, Mr Weinberg, that's all we're asking. We'll pay.' She pulled a wad of hundred-dollar bills from a money belt. 'How much?'

The attorney stared at them both, then down at the young boy squatting on the floor, eyes wide as saucers as he looked on. 'Forget the money.' He slipped off his watch and placed it on the desktop. 'I'll give you fifteen minutes and no more.'

'I don't do drugs,' Jack started.

Herb half turned, obviously unimpressed.

'I drink very little.'

The lawyer gave a cynical laugh. 'You're Irish, it's mother's milk to you guys.' He spun his swivel chair.

'But I can prove it.'

Herb stopped at a half circle. His eyes narrowed. 'How?'

Jack no longer sounded desperate; he was now on familiar territory. 'DNA testing. It's foolproof and definite. I've given several samples over the last month or so at work, and I'm convinced someone has switched them. Whatever adverse results came out of that lab were not on the urines and bloods from my body. We prove that and I'm going to sue them for wrongful dismissal and the hundred other things I know you'll come up with.'

Herb suddenly saw dollar signs all over the place. Sure there was a wrongful dismissal suit, but also loss of earnings, loss of reputation, emotional stress et cetera. Big fee claims. But he was still cautious. 'Go on.' He glanced at his watch. 'Ten minutes left.'

'Tell him what's been happening, Beth. I'm exhausted.'

So Beth opened up and told Herb all she could remember. Prompted by notes on the legal pad, Weinberg first learned about the attack on Danny at summer school and how the same assailant had vandalised their car. Then how the Lincoln Park police considered the events completely bizarre. The black Mercedes with tinted windows. Monique Casselte and her offer. Next the unusual and out-of-character responses of Harry Chan and Martin Shreeve at the Heart Unit. Everything was declared, no matter how trivial it sounded, Jack helping out with details whenever Beth looked over towards him.

'It's not enough to build a conspiracy theory,' Herb said when they'd finished. 'The way I read the *Tribune* it's much easier to accept the professor here was dabbling in coke. Maybe his dealer didn't get paid on time, maybe Danny got hit as a warning.'

'There's more,' Jack came back. 'And it really worries me.'

Stumbling to make the medical jargon more understandable, Jack elaborated on his communications with Dr Carlotta Drunker in Sacramento, of her veiled warnings about discovering a 'big brother', and finally of her suspicious death. Then he mentioned Helen's concern about his computer being moved. At this point Herb flicked the intercom and warned the typist from hell to hold all calls. He loosened the top button on his shirt and began scribbling his own notes.

'There are two issues here,' the lawyer finally summed up. 'First, and it's priority, have the blood and urine samples been switched or adulterated?'

Jack interrupted. 'The urine could have been tampered with, but not the blood. You can't force alcohol or any drug metabolites into blood.'

Herb relaxed for the first time since his office had been invaded. 'You're sounding pretty confident there, doc.'

'I'm a doctor, it's my job to know these details.' Jack tugged the sweatband away from his forehead. 'Someone wants me out of the way so much they're prepared to destroy my life and career. They don't care if my family ends up destitute. They've been very clever and ruthless, but they haven't thought of everything.' He leaned across the desk, holding the lawyer's gaze. 'I'll prove the samples were switched. Then we have to find out why.'

'Which brings me to the second issue.' Herb polished his glasses then shoved them back on his nose. 'This lady in Sacramento. Forget that for now. This is about someone doing their damnedest to get you out of that hospital or this city. That's what we have to prove.'

Jack's body slackened and he rubbed his forehead against a grimy sleeve. 'Pay the man.'

The attorney looked over. 'How much money have you guys got left?'

Beth had double-checked their financial status before leaving. 'Six thousand dollars, give or take a few hundred.'

Herb slipped off his jacket and draped it over the back of his swivel chair. 'Not a lot,' he ventured. 'And your malpractice insurance won't cover this situation.'

Beth's face fell. 'We'll go into hock, I'll wait tables, drive cabs. Anything.' Her voice cracked with the strain.

Danny butted in, eager to help. 'I'll do a paper round.'

The attorney shushed them both. 'I could cut a deal and recoup most of the ten grand deposit on the property on Shimna.'

'No,' Jack said abruptly, 'no way. That's our home and we're going to live there. I don't want that money. Beth's waited long enough, there's no turning back.' He was on his feet, fists clenched with rage. 'I'm going to find out who did this with or without you.'

Herb allowed a faint grin. 'Just testing,' he confessed. 'Wanted to see if the steel was really there.' Jack sat down. 'If you're on the level this is big and we could make a killing.' He looked straight at Jack. 'If you're lying, you're worse than dog dirt.'

'Let's go for it,' coaxed Jack. 'It's no big deal to prove it one way or another.'

The words hung in the air for a minute, then the lawyer burst into action. 'Okay, here's how we handle it.'

23

Caleb Rossi, the Carter lab tech, was small-time. He had a small-time job in a remote and small corner of the biochemistry province where he earned a small-time salary. But Caleb had ambitions. Devoid of any talent, he dabbled in whatever crooked deals came his way. Like information. Rossi had the dirt on many within the medical facility. He knew the closet queers and transsexuals; he had a diary on those prepared to pay to have a drug test faked. He remembered what pretty junior attending was seen with which much older and lecherous (and married) senior doctor. And he knew which medics crashed regularly when it came to making mistakes in the ER or ICU or other divisions. Also he had contacts, like Luther, the tough kid from the projects who'd stalked Danny and Beth.

By now Rossi had made a lot of money as Hend de Mart's hospital mole. So much that he'd tried changing his down-at-heel image. He dressed better, new duds and shoes, new hairstyle. Started growing a beard. On his skinny frame the clothes hung limply, bettering his image by a factor of zero. His recent crew-cut made him look like a day release from a correction centre while the stubble at least disguised his unpleasant facial features. But nothing could improve his mewling, squealing voice.

On the morning of Monday, 4 October, Rossi began mewling and squealing very loudly.

The story of Jack Hunt's dismissal was on all major print, TV and radio outlets. The hospital was rife with rumours, the Heart Unit in disarray despite the administrator's best efforts to restore credibility. There was much speculation as to whether the Irishman was really snorting and boozing. Those division heads he had courted for his research programme found this especially difficult to accept. They were trained doctors, experienced in detecting the edgy behaviour of an addict. Jack may have been hot-tempered but there were no other unusual features in his demeanour. As the gossip intensified, so did Rossi's unease. This was major league with big hitters and he was in it without a helmet. He felt out of his depth. And the new gear he'd so proudly flaunted now became a badge of suspicion and guilt.

'I represent Professor Jack Hunt.'

Herb Weinberg stood at the front entrance to the Carter Hospital at nine o'clock exactly. Gathered a few steps below was a cluster of journalists and TV crews, all given plenty of advance notice to be ready for a showdown. They scanned the skies nervously, collars up against the wind, watching dark clouds gather. Herb wore his best suit, a good-fit twin-breast navy with tiny blue fleck. Starched white shirt, subdued bow tie. Shoes with heels lifting his height to five six. He'd had his hair trimmed to take the pudgy look off his face and wore the one pair of spectacles that stayed on his nose without slipping. In his right hand he clutched a briefcase with enough legal clout for Death Row.

'Dr Hunt has retained the services of my firm to restore his good name to the citizens of Chicago and the world.' Herb added 'the world' at the last minute for effect. 'He denies ever using cocaine or attending hospital duties while under the influence of alcohol. My visit here today' – the lawyer looked behind and up at the large Carter Hospital Chicago sign which topped the front doors, and the cameras panned to follow his gaze – 'is to secure the so-called samples taken from Dr Hunt. They will then be independently tested for all illicit substances, including alcohol.' Herb paused while the journos scribbled down his words. He half turned to allow one TV crew to get a better close-up, then rammed home the most controversial assertion. 'We will also seek to prove that the specimens used by the hospital to force Dr Hunt's dismissal were not taken from his body.' There were a few whistles from the media pack. 'That's all I have to say at this moment.' He turned and marched through the hallowed portals, leaving behind a baying posse of frustrated reporters. Only a sudden downpour chased them to their cars and vans, where they began filing copy.

All chemical tests at the Carter, including those for drugs of abuse, were processed through a workroom at street level. Herb first waddled to the main hospital reception where he presented his credentials and was given an official one-day ID. Two minutes later he sauntered along the corridors, beaming cheerfully at patients and white-coated doctors. Monday meant the passages were crowded with the flotsam of the weekend's activities. Surgical admissions through ER were being ferried to upper levels with friends and relatives grouping anxiously to discuss progress. Orderlies hurried gurneys to different corners of the facility with drip sets and oxygen masks attached to many of the transfers.

Herb bobbed and weaved through the traffic. He was stopped once by security and flashed his identification pass. 'Weinberg & Associates, attorneys at law. I'm here on official business.' He was then accompanied directly to the lab arrival station. 'Take my card,' he said to the warden, 'never know when you might need my services.' He looked around conspiratorially. 'Especially in a place like this.'

Medical laboratories are much the same the world over. Commonly near access there is an immediate chest-high collection counter. Here a supervisor accepts the offered samples and double-checks they are correctly labelled and sealed, then enquires as to the urgency behind each test. Next the receptacles are dispatched to the appropriate sections. Some bloods go to the haematology department, others to biochemistry. Urines and sputums can be switched to microbiology for evidence of bacterial infiltration. Chemical examinations, be they for illicit drugs, regular prescription compounds or heavy-metal poisoning, are directed to a specific assay machine for analysis. Before any test can be completed a technician must first type in clinical details, then load the sample. This was Caleb Rossi's sole responsibility. Tease out the container from its transport casing, counter-check name on specimen against request form, type details into the lab PC, load the machine. He didn't have to be an Einstein, and the process was considered foolproof. However, reliability could collapse at that one point of human intervention. Which is what Jack believed and Herb Weinberg was hoping to prove.

'I represent Professor Jack Hunt.' The lawyer was beginning to sound weary with the repetition and had to shout above the background din of machinery and small talk.

At the mention of the disgraced professor's name the

department went quiet. Blue-uniformed techs with face masks and protective hair netting sitting at benches or squinting down microscopes stopped and turned to listen. The unit was open-plan, booths and desks grouped into clusters, all within walking distance of one another. They were littered with plastic bottles, glass tubes, test reagents et cetera, and the smell of chemical reagents hung everywhere. Now only the hum of equipment could be heard.

Herb produced a sheaf of documents. 'I am authorised to take possession of the blood and urine specimens used by this laboratory to process Dr Hunt's drugs investigation.' Astonished looks were exchanged. 'I understand all samples are retained here for six months,' he added. The supervisor, a young woman with hair ringlets and dressed in green fatigues, reached for a telephone. The attorney continued in his loud voice. 'These will be independently evaluated.' He recognised that was relatively uncontentious. Anyone accused of substance abuse had the right to ensure the testing had been correctly conducted and the results accurate. But then he added the punchline: 'We wish also to prove the samples processed in this division were not those taken from Dr Hunt. It is our contention someone interfered with the chain of analysis.'

A legal challenge over the results of any medical unit is controversial enough. But when that challenge suggests malicious wrongdoing, the result is explosive. So it was at that moment. The supervisor started punching buttons on the telephone and there followed a garbled and excited exchange. Behind, other techs gathered in surprised and indignant huddles. Instruments were abandoned, glass pipettes dropped as heads craned closer. Glances bounced towards one particular section. Finally the supervisor came over.

'Mr Weinberg, I cannot release any materials until this is cleared with the administrator, and he's already on his way down. Would you care to wait outside until he arrives?'

Herb grinned, relishing the discomfiture he was causing. 'If you don't mind,' he said, 'I'll sit right here.' He pulled a stool to the far edge of the counter and sat down. 'Dreadful weather, isn't it?'

There were two exits from the laboratory. One was via reception, where the lawyer now maintained a vigil, noting all movements. Then there was a fire escape to the side, frequently used by cigarette addicts to sneak out and relieve their cravings. While this contravened regulations, it was quicker and easier than walking through the main hospital and crowding at the entrance with the other tobacco pariahs.

Caleb Rossi left through the fire door.

He circled the rear buildings, dodging and ducking to avoid being seen. Overflowing waste dumpsters, steam jets from kitchens, delivery bays with spilled boxes, massive cylinders of gas and oil, various coloured doors leading to various corridors which in turn opened on to various clinical divisions. Rossi edged past them all.

Finally he was in the car lot, hunched down and squirming between wet vehicles. Five minutes later he darted along W Harrison, nervously checking to see if he had been followed. There he located a public phone booth and began dropping coins into it, nervously tugging at a lock of hair.

'I need to leave an urgent message for Mr Hend, so don't fuck me about, lady. I need to talk to him real soon.' This was the fourth communication from Rossi that hadn't been returned, and the girl on the other end was trying to convince him she had passed them all on. 'Tell him Caleb called.' Then he lost his cool completely. 'Tell him I'm in deep shit.' The receiver was slammed back on the hook.

'Mr Weinberg, why exactly are you here?'

Steve Downes stood at laboratory reception, flustered and panting. His turkey chin wobbled, wire-wool hair sticking up.

Herb, wearing a beatific smile, milked the moment. 'Nice place you got here.'

Downes seemed about to explode, but the attorney pressed on. Documentation was removed from his briefcase, one copy retained, the other passed over.

'I am instructed to secure the specimens taken from the body of Professor Jack Hunt.'

The administrator visibly relaxed. 'That's fine, Mr Weinberg. Not too many have challenged our test results before. Mainly because they're all as guilty as sin.'

There was an almost palpable tension as the lab staff listened to the exchanges. No work was being done apart from machines grinding out their load.

'Maybe so,' countered Herb, 'but we are also arranging DNA analysis. Professor Hunt contends the blood and urines tested could not possibly be from his body. He believes the samples were switched.' Herb glanced around, noticing the staring, hostile faces. 'In fact, he feels confident the swap took place right here in this laboratory.'

There was an angry babble from the benches.

'We have nothing to hide, Mr Weinberg,' offered Downes.

Herb hitched at his trousers. 'Glad to hear that. But my client thinks differently. If independent studies confirm the specimens are correct in all respects, we accept the dismissal.' The teasing was over. 'However, if that blood and urine is not from Dr Hunt's body, then you have some explaining to do.'

Confusion soon spread throughout the lab. First, Caleb Rossi could not be located. And everyone knew he was the sole tech in charge of substance abuse testing. Next, the blood and urine samples could not be found. Herb watched the flurry of activity from the safety of reception. As other specimens built up on the counter with nurses and paramedics waiting impatiently for attention, on the other side blue uniforms scurried from one cupboard to another, pulling open drawers then slamming them shut. The shaking of heads was becoming increasingly agitated.

Soon, Downes himself started searching. Storage rooms, liquid nitrogen freezers, the far reaches of the unit. Then telephone calls to other storage facilities. Finally the administrator called a huddle at the far end of the division, well out of Herb's earshot. There were furtive glances towards the lawyer, more towards the fire escape. Someone slipped over and tried the handle, finding the door ajar. Suddenly the air filled with angry shouts.

'Having trouble?'

Downes brushed past, red-faced and perspiring. He ignored the comment.

The supervisor with hair ringlets finally made her way to the desk. 'Mr Weinberg, we're having a little difficulty locating the specimens you've requested. Could you give us more time? Mr Downes has suggested you call him at one. We should have them then.'

Herb leaned across the counter and fixed a baleful eye on the woman. She visibly recoiled. 'Lady, if someone in this department has made off with Professor Hunt's test material then I'll bring the wrath of God down on all your heads.'

As the lawyer left the hospital a misty drizzle was hardening. An earlier cloudburst had petered out over Lake Michigan but the skies were still grey and depressing, the streets greasy with surface water. On W Harrison a Honda Civic had slewed on to the pavement, fire engines winching at its bumper. The TV crews and journalists had moved on to other hotspots leaving the Carter front steps free, apart from the usual passage of patients. Weinberg stood there for a few seconds and breathed in the air. His glasses misted and he pushed them into a side pocket, then walked towards the parking lot, noting the section reserved for senior staff. Mercedes, BMWs, Saabs, Volvos. Lots of expensive imports cheek by jowl with equally high-priced Fords and Chevys. The lawyer rushed for the sanctuary of his own more modest '98 Buick.

As he scanned the visitors' zone Herb suddenly noticed two DHL personnel unloading a delivery at the rear of the hospital. The shipment was labelled URGENT MEDICAL SUPPLIES: ZEMDON PHARMACEUTICALS and comprised ten individual crates. He crab-walked over and waited for an opportunity. When both couriers were distracted he ripped apart the top of one case. Inside was a carefully packed selection of premier cru red wines, each bottle with a heart-shaped calling card attached. Herb snagged one of the cards and quickly read the message.

TO REMIND YOU OF OCTOBER 8TH, THE MOST IMPORTANT LAUNCH IN CARDIOLOGY HISTORY

RED WINE IS GOOD FOR THE HEART, CYCLINT IS BETTER

ENJOY ANYWAY

WITH THE COMPLIMENTS OF THE ZEMDON CORPORATION

WORLD LEADERS IN ETHICAL PHARMACEUTICALS

These guys aren't hanging about, Herb thought. My client's only just been dismissed and already they're muscling in. This is big-time.

Rather than intimidating him, however, the discovery only hardened the lawyer's resolve. If Zemdon were caught up in this, Herb was determined there'd be one helluva showdown.

Herb had arranged lunch at Mrs Park's tavern on E Delaware. The food was good and not wildly expensive, the service efficient with lots of attitude. Herb had reserved a corner table with window, and when he arrived Jack, Beth and Danny were already toying with soft drinks. They looked up expectantly and the lawyer gave a so-so wave before sitting down. A waiter fussed, and they waited while coffee was ordered.

'They can't find the samples,' Herb said immediately, and Jack's face creased in dismay. 'You shoulda seen the panic. They were running around like headless chickens. Never seen so many stores and rooms searched. Calls made all over the hospital. Zero.'

Beth glanced at her husband for reassurance, but he remained impassive. Danny kept his head down and inspected the remains of a glass of Coke.

'What does this mean?' asked Jack.

Herb grabbed a menu. 'It means we sit tight here and have something to eat. My instructions are to call Downes at one o'clock. He reckons he'll have tracked them down by then.' He checked his watch. 'Thirty minutes. Now, what are you going to have?'

But neither Beth nor Jack had an appetite. They selected a green salad with iced water while Danny chose French fries and ketchup.

'I'm gonna have spicy tuna, then barbecued pork chop with corn bread and slaw.' Herb was feeling hungry after his efforts that morning. 'As American as apple pie,' he grinned. 'How're your new quarters working out?'

It had been Herb's idea to move the Hunt family. From the moment they'd agreed strategy in his offices on Saturday he'd insisted they temporarily desert the W Deming apartment. 'The place will be swarming with cameramen and newshounds trying to force you to say something on record. If they can't get the doc they'll target Beth. Even Danny won't be allowed to go untouched. Just lie low somewhere away from all the attention.'

First they'd needed a change of clothes; Jack especially needed to shower and shave. They'd shopped at Fox's, an outlet store on

N Clark. Just enough garments and one pair of shoes each for the immediate days ahead. Herb had reckoned the media would lay off after that and they could return to the apartment for their belongings. Then they needed somewhere to hang out for a while. After scouring the yellow pages they'd chosen the Cass Hotel on N Wabash. It wasn't much to look at, inside or out, with a simply furnished and rather small room. The TV was on a shelf and so badly angled it was almost impossible to see from a sitting position. But the rate was only sixty dollars and financial considerations were now paramount. That night Danny had slept on a foldaway couch-bed while Beth and Jack had struggled for comfort on the modest-sized divan. In the end they'd just stared at the ceiling until dawn.

At one o'clock Herb dabbed at his chin with a napkin, finished off the dregs of his coffee, then excused himself and made the all-important call.

'Whaddye mean you still can't find them?'

From the Carter Hospital, Steve Downes was passing on the bad news. 'They may have been misplaced.'

'You mean someone's taken them, don't you?'

'I'm not in a position to comment on that.'

'You've destroyed my client's reputation,' the lawyer raged, 'dismissed him from his employment and may have caused him to have his licence to practise revoked.' He stopped only to gather breath. 'And now you tell me the evidence to support your decision has gone missing.'

'That's about it, Mr Weinberg.' Downes sounded deflated.

Herb allowed a bitter chortle to escape. 'Hell, Mr Downes, I can smell dollar bills all over you.'

Back at the table, Herb explained the angry conversation.

'Lost? I don't believe it,' groaned Beth. 'How could they lose something so important?'

'They're not lost,' said Jack, 'they're stolen, probably destroyed by now.'

'Have to agree there, doc.' Herb looked most unhappy. 'And it means we have a real problem. Without those samples it's impossible to prove you were set up. We could repeat the procedure, but that would mean nothing. You could have stayed off the booze and white powder in the meantime.'

Beth's face tightened with worry. She noticed Danny's eyes well with tears and led him from the table.

When they'd gone, Herb turned to Jack. 'We can still fight this. Strong case too, what with those specimens gone missing. Probably overturn your wrongful dismissal. But it's going to take time and it'll be very costly, I've got to warn you.'

Jack didn't respond. He could feel his nightmare reaching screaming intensity. The initial flurry of activity with Herb had offered hope. But now this latest twist crushed that optimism. He had to vindicate his good name, but could see many pitfalls ahead. Especially financial ones. He wasn't fighting ordinary opposition here. Someone was using every scheming and underhand trick they could against him. And he suspected it was geared to getting him on board the Cyclint launch. When he didn't run with the pack either Downes or Zemdon had conspired against him. He appeared to be up against one of the most powerful commercial organisations in the world with billions of dollars at their disposal. And he was near broke. And now with evidence missing he'd find it impossible to prove he was innocent. It was his word against theirs, and they had stage-managed events so carefully he could look like a fool if he forced a challenge. He was a David to their Goliath, but without sling or stone.

'I can't afford it,' he said finally. 'Administration will fight this tooth and nail, they have no other option. If the lab results can be shown to be faulty the hospital will be attacked mercilessly. They'll have to defend those testing procedures and it'll be easier to support that line than cave in and admit a huge mistake.' He looked directly at his lawyer. 'They'll sacrifice me.' He clenched and unclenched his fists. 'Sure, future testing programmes will be tightened up. But they won't admit they destroyed my life and career.'

Herb shrugged, but offered nothing more. He flagged the waiter for the tab. 'Keep your chin up, doc. Things have a funny way of spinning in this game. Keep thinking, and don't let yourself get swamped with despair. There's your wife and kid to consider as well.'

Jack barely heard the comments; he was in another world. He screwed his napkin into a tight wedge, his face muscles bunched with anger.

'There has to be another way, there just has to be.'

24

Harry Chan wasted no time establishing himself as the top man at the Carter Heart Unit. While Herb Weinberg was stomping the corridors on street level the diminutive cardiologist moved into Jack's office on the ninth floor and immediately warned Helen she would be retained only until the end of that calendar month. 'After that, Ms Bradley, I feel it wiser if you sought employment elsewhere.' Shaky hands and nervous 'ahuhs' accompanied almost every other order, and Helen watched the man's unseemly excitement with loathing.

One hour later two strangers entered the professorial offices. The taller of the two introduced himself. 'Good morning, my name is Stan Danker and I'm here to see Dr Chan.' He was dressed in navy trousers and grey jacket with blue shirt and yellow bow tie. Hair gelled back, lots of teeth flashing and strong, determined-looking features.

Helen scanned the daybook but could find no entry, nor could she remember arranging such a meeting. Then again, since Jack's dismissal everything was chaotic and she was struggling with the speed of change.

'This has been agreed privately, and Dr Chan knows already.' The smooth-talking gent with the East Coast accent sounded so confident all Helen could do was offer seats and coffee. The refreshments were declined, and the strangers settled into their chairs.

Helen busied herself typing and fielding calls, one eye on her guests. The second of the duo hadn't spoken since he'd arrived. He looked older than his partner, slim and slightly stooped in a fine-cut suit and crisp white shirt with blue tie. In his right hand he held a pair of wire-framed spectacles which he repeatedly tapped against his chin. His eyes darted round the office as he waited.

At 11.15 Harry Chan hurried in, flustered and out of breath. He was in green hospital scrubs, his thick-lensed glasses slightly misted. 'Mr Danker, how nice to see you again.'

Stan Danker was on his feet. 'Harry, how are you?' He pumped the smaller man's hand. 'This is the colleague from Zurich I told you about.'

Before a name was offered, Chan ushered the two into the back suite and closed the door firmly. Thirty seconds later he poked his head out. 'Hold all calls, Ms Bradley. When Mr Downes arrives please direct him here immediately.'

The administrator joined the group three minutes later.

Inside Jack Hunt's hallowed sanctuary Stan Danker started the conversation. 'Steve, Harry. I'd like you to meet Dr Gert Crozer.' He paused while handshakes were exchanged. 'Dr Crozer is operations executive for the Zemdon Corporation and has taken a particular interest in the Chicago side of the Cyclint launch. He flew in from Zurich as soon as he felt we had the situation back under control again.' Danker then turned his attention towards Harry Chan. 'It's good to have you on board, Harry. This has been a difficult time for us and I know we'd all like to see a successful outcome.' Heads nodded in agreement. 'Mr Downes, if you can confirm Dr Chan's appointment, I can confirm that the original half-million-dollar grant still stands.'

Steve Downes nodded. His hands rested on his paunch, a button over his midriff threatened to ping. He shifted in his chair so he had Gert Crozer's full attention. 'As I'm sure you know I've had the unpleasant task of sacking our professor. His drug abuse pattern was uncovered during routine testing.' Crozer's face was impassive. 'He's already hired a lawyer to challenge the dismissal, but I can assure you that's nothing to be concerned about.' The administrator pressed ahead quickly. 'Straight after Hunt's dismissal I moved to nominate Harry Chan as the new acting chief. In time the board will ratify that decision – they certainly have no desire to go through another laborious selection procedure. Fortunately, Dr Chan agreed to my offer and commenced duties this morning. The appointment had one condition which he did not feel too onerous, and he has willingly agreed to cooperate with it.' As Downes came to the end of his piece, Crozer's gaze moved from him to the cardiologist. 'Harry will front the official launch of Cyclint this Friday. The arrangements contracted with Sam Lewins will be honoured in full.'

Downes leaned back into his seat and released the button over his midriff.

Gert Crozer spoke. 'And where is the dismissed professor? Is he still in Chicago?'

'Don't know and don't much care.'

Crozer was far from satisfied with the answer. 'But I care. Will these charges hold up? Is his reputation ruined, his career finished? Could he still be a threat?'

Downes shifted uneasily in his chair. 'Forget him, he's hung out to dry. He'll never work in this city or anywhere else again.'

Crozer made to speak but cut himself short, as if some new insight had crossed his mind. Steve Downes was immediately on his feet, pointing at his watch. 'If you'll excuse me, I've got a board conference in a few minutes.' He shook hands briefly. 'I look forward to seeing you again this Friday.'

As soon as Downes left, Stan Danker swung into overdrive. 'Harry we've got a lot of work to do to fine tune the Cyclint agenda. Why don't we break for lunch and I'll fill you in.'

Over a glass of champagne at one of Chicago's most fashionable restaurants, Harry Chan was filled in on the huge challenge that lay ahead.

The Cyclint inauguration was going to be so high-profile it would match a NASA rocket lift-off. Each national division had planned individual celebrations. Opinion-forming editors and cardiologists would be wined and dined, with no expense spared. Special luxury trains and first-class seats on flights had been laid on to take distant attendees to the main event. Lavish arrangements had been negotiated at the Hilton Head Carolina, La Jolla California, the Savoy in London, Raffles in Singapore, the Excelsior in Rome, the Ritz in Paris, the Peninsula in Hong Kong et cetera. The less important would be treated to a video promotion with a cheaper wine and cheese reception in their nearest hostelry.

At the Zurich HQ a formal ball with thirty-piece orchestra was lined up, to be followed by a fireworks display. Vintage champagne all night. But central to the evening was the planned connection to Chicago. Each centre on a reasonably close time zone would go direct to Harry Chan for a carefully scripted discussion. This would be replayed later for those enjoying the event in different time zones. Chan was being coached to announce with great conviction and no little enthusiasm that Cyclint was 'the most important and exciting breakthrough in cardiology for over a decade'. The agreed dialogue offered further extravagant praise: 'Zemdon Pharmaceuticals and their research divisions must be congratulated. I expect this wonderdrug to prevent over half a million deaths and eight hundred thousand non-fatal cardiovascular events in its first year alone.' A computer system would flip up charts and graphs to accompany each word of spoken text. Other transparencies would project the economic savings within one-, two- and then five-year treatments with Cyclint. 'We at the Carter Hospital, one of North America's cardiology centres of excellence, endorse this new product enthusiastically.' Harry would say this and nothing more. The dialogue was timed to the last second and allowed for no unrehearsed comments.

Throughout the discussion Harry Chan's mind kept drifting to his secret Swiss bank account. Half a million dollars for one hour's work. And more to come. Piece of cake.

For Jack Hunt and his family, life was most certainly not a piece of cake. That Monday evening they were still holed up in their small downtown hotel room. And fighting like alley cats.

'What the hell's this about you refusing to take on extra nursing staff?'

Beth had just channel-hopped to an early bulletin on WLS announcing Harry Chan's appointment. The news item was accompanied by a thirty-second clip of the cardiologist climbing into his car, wide smile beaming at the cameras. He looked confident and smugly self-satisfied. The anchorman finished the piece with selected quotes from a press release he was studying. 'The Carter has been fortunate to recruit four highly trained cardiology nurses which should help clear the backlog of heart surgery cases. Recently dismissed professor, Dr Jack Hunt, had blocked the hiring of this same staff quota. No reasons had ever been given, but administrator Downes today admitted this was one of many aspects of the Irishman's erratic behaviour.'

Beth was now white with anger. 'What was going on in that

hospital I don't know about?' She stood in front of her husband, chin jutting out, hands on hips.

Jack was sitting on the corner of the bed and he flicked a warning glance towards Danny. The boy was on his hunkers on the floor, wide-eyed and obviously distressed at the confrontation.

'Don't use your son as a shield,' snapped Beth. 'You've not mentioned any of this. Tell me what was going on. I deserve an explanation, Hunt. Don't you think I should know why we're here?'

Jack held his head in both hands. His legs shook as he struggled to contend with the accusation in Beth's voice. 'It's not as it seems. They were trying to bribe me. I wouldn't front their drug launch so they offered me the world.'

'And of course you wouldn't take it.' The sarcasm in Beth's voice cut Jack to the bone. 'Oh no, Mr High Principles decided it's better to drag his family into bankruptcy rather than compromise his lofty ideals.' She paced the narrow floor, hands clasping and unclasping, face overwrought.

Jack knew her words were more the result of grief and exhaustion. That and the three of them being stuck in a cramped hotel room. No one could move without bumping into something.

'Beth, we've been over all this,' he pleaded, 'don't wear yourself down.' He reached out but was angrily brushed away.

'Wear myself down?' she taunted. 'It's a bit late to start being so considerate. It's not as if Danny and I haven't been on a knife edge for the past few months. But, oh no, Mr Save the World didn't have time to listen then.' Jack flinched as if he'd been slapped. 'Now you're all over us, can't do enough since you've no work to go to.' But she couldn't keep the aggression up. Eventually her strength gave way and she slumped on to the only chair in the room and sobbed her heart out. Only Danny's frightened tears prevented more bitter exchanges.

By midnight some sense of calm descended and Beth crashed into an exhausted sleep. A few minutes later Danny's snoring confirmed he too had fallen asleep. For Jack there was no such relief, and he spent the night staring at the digital clock on the bedside table. By dawn he'd watched every minute tick past.

When Beth woke at eight o'clock she mumbled her apologies before suddenly rushing to the bathroom and being sick. As he listened to the retching, Jack's mind twisted like an emotional whirlwind.

At ten o'clock he sent Danny downstairs to prowl the lobby while he tried to plan ahead.

'When do we have to quit the apartment?'

Beth consulted her diary, fingers slowly flicking through the pages. She was physically drained from the full effects of early pregnancy, nausea kicking in each morning and progressing throughout the day. She hadn't eaten properly for forty-eight hours, nibbling on dry biscuits to try and keep her strength.

'I gave notice shortly after we paid the deposit on Joliet. We have to be out by Friday week, October fifteenth.' Her voice was hoarse from all the arguing the night before.

Jack groaned. 'That only gives us ten days.'

How the hell am I going to pull us out of disaster in that time? No job, no income, no prospects. A pregnant wife and eight-year-old son to provide for and only six thousand dollars in the bank. For a moment he wondered about three air tickets to Dublin. No, I couldn't face that. Go cap in hand like my father and ask for help? No bloody way, I'd rather die. But perhaps Beth and Dannny could go, say it was just a holiday.

He placed both hands on his wife's shoulders and held her tight, avoiding her questioning stare. 'I think you should go to Ireland for a few weeks and take Danny with you. We could work out the air fare and allow something extra for expenses.'

Beth's face tightened with shock, the blood drained from her cheeks. 'And what would you do?'

'I'll stay on here and challenge this. I can't let them ruin my life and not fight back.'

'But how would you live? Where would you stay?' Beth sounded desperate.

Jack hugged her to his chest, feeling her now frail body shudder against him. 'It's all I can think of. We haven't enough money, I can't get a job and soon we'll have no roof over our heads. What else can we do?'

Beth's sobs tortured Jack's fevered brain. By now he really believed he could think clearer and survive better without his wife and son around. Suddenly, he realised he was wishing them gone. Jesus Christ, how I fought to keep them with me, and now I'm trying to send them away. He was racked with guilt and anger, and he clasped Beth so tight he felt he might squeeze her last breath away. Then he held her at arm's length again, forcing her to look at him. The beautiful face was now pinched and drawn. The skin around her eyes was puffy and damp, the whites totally bloodshot. Mascara smears were wiped from nose to ear on both sides.

'Oh Beth, Beth. I love you so much.' He stifled his own tears. 'How did I get you into this mess?'

Jack picked up his wife, took her through to the bedroom and laid her down on the bed. He then lay down beside her and held her gingerly, as if she were made of china. 'It's okay, it's okay. I'm here. You're going to be all right.'

He quickly glanced at his watch. It was 10.40, and they had a lunchtime appointment with Herb Weinberg at one o'clock. Maybe he'll have some ideas. Please God, let something turn up.

25

Herb Weinberg knew his challenge to the Carter's lab tests would stir up trouble. He was also confident that news of Jack Hunt's counter-attack would spread like a brush fire throughout the facility. 'What we want to learn from this is the reaction in the cardiology division. Sure there's going to be surprise and astonishment. We can expect that. It's the aggressive shock I'm looking for. Who goes into a cold sweat? Who starts making sudden telephone calls? Who excuses himself for an hour unexpectedly? That's the feedback I need.' To achieve this, Jack had called his office on the Monday morning and Helen had immediately agreed to act as his lookout. She'd also agreed to front up at the Tuesday lunch meeting and report on any unusual activities. But by 2.30 she still hadn't arrived.

Herb was fretting to leave. He'd already warned Jack about the difficulties ahead. 'I've taken soundings among attorneys who've had similar cases. The word's not good. This could drag on for months. Without the original blood and urine samples the Carter could put up any number of defences as to where they've disappeared to. Maybe even make them reappear but broken and destroyed beyond use.' By then he'd delayed as long as he could. 'Gotta go, doc, the court house calls. I'll keep drip-feeding background information to all my media contacts.' He grabbed his briefcase. 'Keep your spirits up.'

Jack and Beth sat at their table in stony silence, and Danny was given another Coke to keep him pacified. Beth was more composed now, but still upset and worried.

The restaurant was near the Art Institute of Chicago, and outside shoppers laden with expensive-looking bags huddled against the wind. The lakefront was only blocks away, and biting gusts off the water whirled among the highrises. Across the road taxis and minibuses discharged their loads to nearby hotels. People looked happy and excited, flushed with money. Anxious to hit the Magnificent Mile and its abundance of high-class shops.

A quarter to three.

'Would you care to order something else?'

A Mexican waiter had the Hunts to himself, only two other tables were occupied. He had a thick droopy moustache, swarthy skin and was wearing a white apron across the midriff. Heavily accented but perfect English. He forced a smile, revealing a side tooth missing and another black stumped.

Beth looked down at her untouched plate. 'No, not yet' – she toyed with an asparagus spear – 'I'm still working through this.'

The steward's eyes rolled towards heaven. 'Take your time, lady,' he muttered, dusting crumbs away, 'I've got all day.'

It was embarrassing. They had nowhere to go and little money. Herb had cautioned against returning to the W Deming apartment at this stage and warned them not to use the new car. 'Most reporters have someone checking licence plates. They'd track you down in an hour.' So the Chevy was parked in a quiet and out-of-the-way cul-de-sac. From then on all movement was on foot, bus or train. Cabs were not allowed – too expensive.

Now they were tired and depressed. Herb's comments had crushed their spirits completely, and Helen was nearly two hours late. And Danny's patience was being stretched. At this time of year he should be at school, his mind and body occupied. Now he trailed his parents, shielded from the heavy talk and bored to distraction by the light comments.

'I wanna go home,' he finally complained.

Jack almost snapped his nerves were so on edge, and only Beth's warning glare restrained him.

Ten past three. Still no Helen. Outside, more taxis offloaded passengers.

'We'd better move,' advised Beth. She could no longer ignore the impatient glances of the restaurant staff. There are long lunches and there are delaying tactics, and they had been inspecting the same uneaten food since a quarter to one. The Mexican's looks confirmed which category he considered he'd been stuck with.

'Oh, oh,' warned Danny suddenly, 'the guy with the moustache is coming over.'

Jack went through the motions of finishing a coffee, then stood up and forced a smile. 'Time to quit. There's lots of shops to cruise.'

The waiter was beside them. 'Mr Hunt?'

'Sorry,' Jack said, 'we've been caught up in our own conversation. We haven't seen each other for years.'

Danny's eyes rolled.

'No, no.' The steward was now exasperated. 'Are you Mr Hunt? There is someone on the telephone looking for a Mr Hunt.' His eyes took in the nearly empty room. 'If it's not you then I must tell the lady so.'

'There is definitely something very odd going on.' Helen was calling from a public call box in a waiting area beside the Carter emergency room. 'I couldn't get away without creating a fuss. The division is hopping.'

She then described the previous day's meeting at the professorial suite. 'Steve Downes and two strangers, one with an East Coast accent, the other foreign. Possibly German or something like that. I only heard him talk when he was leaving. They were with Harry Chan for almost an hour. And now he's been in Downes's office since nine this morning, whatever they're plotting.'

Jack's heart raced as he listened. I was worrying about Martin Shreeve, but the real traitor was right under my nose! Shreeve's a drunk and nothing more, he hasn't enough brain cells to be involved in a scheme like this. Chan's a gambler; he'd take the risks. That's why he was so upbeat recently. I'll bet he's been waiting for this moment for some time.

'Anything else?' he prompted.

'Do you remember Trent Crilly? The health correspondent from the *Tribune* who did that big piece at the end of June?'

Jack groaned. Of course he remembered. Those so short and far-off glory days.

'He's been hounding me for an interview with you. He's already buttonholed most of the staff on the division.'

'No can do. He's well down on my list of priorities.'

'I'll tell him.'

'Any more? Doesn't matter how trivial it seems, tell me.'

Long pause. In the background Hunt could hear the noise of the ER. Shouts, crying, the general hullabaloo of a busy public treatment unit.

'Oh my God, I almost forgot.' Helen sounded frantic.

'What?'

'They took your hard disk out of the office.'

'They did what?'

'First thing this morning some guy walks in and says he'd been instructed to take your computer away. I didn't recognise him but he was in an official maintenance uniform.'

'What the hell do they want with my PC?'

'I asked but got no answer.'

Jack considered the information. He remembered Helen's comments some weeks back when she thought someone had moved the hard disk in his office. Yet no matter which way he juggled the facts nothing made sense.

'Is that it?'

'Afraid so. You stay in touch and I'll keep looking and listening. Gotta go.'

When he hung up Jack turned to find Beth staring at him hopefully. 'Nothing,' he grimaced. 'Nothing we don't know already.' His wife's face fell.

Jack spotted Danny watching the scene. As their eyes locked the boy suddenly averted his gaze, and the gesture cut straight to Jack's heart. They're desperate for me to rescue the situation, and all the time I'm hoping someone else will turn things round. We really are alone. No one's going to come out of the woodwork with startling revelations that'll clear my name overnight. This has been too well planned and executed. I'm on the ropes, and I'm the only one who can sort this out.

'Beth, you and Danny go back to the room. I'm going to the apartment. I don't give a damn if the front door's surrounded by journalists, I'm going in. I'll grab fresh clothes and meet you in an hour or so. Then we'll have to make some tough decisions.'

They counted out enough cash for a cab to the Cass Hotel on N Wabash. Then Jack hurried towards Michigan Avenue and grabbed a CTA bus to N Clark. Thirty minutes later he was striding along W Deming towards their apartment. He kept to the opposite side of the road, head down but eyes taking in the area.

As far as he could determine there were no reporters gathered at the front entrance. For good measure he walked past, checking side streets and alleyways. Nothing. They've laid off me. Harry Chan's the hot news now, I'm yesterday's man. Anger and bitterness surged, and he had to force his mind clear. Concentrate, concentrate. Recriminations are negative emotions. Keep thinking. Good. No media at least meant they could move back home.

He hurried back to the complex. Inside the downstairs hallway he leaned against the door, panting from the effort. At that hour most residents were still at work, and he knew the building would be more or less empty. Still wary, he took the steps one at a time. The stairwell was quiet and he strained not to make noise. He squinted through the rails and listened. Not a sound. Thirty seconds later he was on the first level. The floor was deserted, all the apartment doors closed. He reached into his pocket and felt for keys, selecting one for the dead bolt. For some reason he couldn't quite understand, he felt like a thief about to break and enter. The master key turned easily. Now he selected another and the Yale lock at eye level twisted. He opened the door and reached in to switch off the burglar alarm, and was surprised to find it hadn't been activated. He didn't move, trying to remember who'd been the last to leave when they'd fled. It was me. And I know I reset the system.

'Dr Hunt.'

The words almost lifted Jack out of his skin, and he spun round to find the caretaker standing behind him.

'Marty, it's you. Jesus, you scared the life out of me.'

Marty was an elderly man who turned up three times a week to check on security and maintenance. It was his job to ensure the corridors were clean and free from debris, and that the residents were complying with the development's house rules. He was a small man, barely more than five feet, with a freckled, bald head and thick grey moustache. He was in his usual denim overalls.

'Sorry to frighten you like that,' he apologised in his slow Midwest drawl. 'I was on the top floor when I heard the front door give.' He waved a hand. 'I was just checking everything was okay.' If Marty was aware of the unpleasant publicity surrounding the tenant, he didn't show it. He shuffled towards the next flight of stairs but stopped when halfway up and shouted, 'The fella from the hospital came and took away your computer.'

Jack stopped in his tracks. He couldn't believe what he'd just heard and ran out again along the corridor. 'Sorry Marty, what did you say?'

The caretaker was near the top of the steps, one hand leaning heavily on the rails, back stooped from the effort. 'Your assistant from the hospital called about an hour ago and let himself into your apartment. Had his own set of keys and switched off the alarm. When I was coming in he was at the entrance with your computer. That's where I stopped him. He showed an ID and told me he was bringing the hard disk back to the hospital. I hadn't a clue what the hell he was talking about. Hard disk or soft disk, it meant nothing to me.'

Marty turned the corner on to level two and Jack bounded after him. His heart was racing, his mouth dry. 'What'd he look like?' He fought for the right lies. 'There's quite a few working with me. I'm wondering which one it was?'

Marty's face creased in thought. 'Big fella, that's for sure.' He sized Jack up. 'Much taller than you. Maybe another three or four inches. Blond hair, well dressed.' He inspected the wall as if that might jog his memory. 'And a funny sort of an accent. Never heard it before.'

Jack grabbed the caretaker's shoulders. 'Marty, this is very important. Did he say anything else?'

Marty looked up sharply, obviously surprised by the strength of Jack's grip. 'No, not a thing. "I'm Dr Hunt's assistant and I have to take this hard disk back to the hospital." That's about as much as I can tell you. Seemed a pleasant enough fella.'

Jack was down the steps in seconds. Inside the apartment he went straight to the small study. The PC monitor was still on the desk but the mainframe was gone. Then he rushed into the living room. The cardboard containers had been ripped open, their contents strewn around. Immediately he could see the intruder had concentrated on those boxes reserved for him. Clothes and shoes and underwear lay where they'd been upended. Into the master bedroom. Every drawer had been pulled out, their contents scattered on the floor. Danny's room had been given the same treatment but with less interest, judging by the lighter mess. Back to the study. The drawers in the desk were empty, all his paperwork taken.

Jack stood in the middle of the chaos, his mind racing. What the fuck's going on? He was so stunned he couldn't think clearly. They've beaten me, and they know it. But what do they want with my computer? My *computers.* First the one out of the office, now the one from my home. What are they looking for? He rushed from room to room trying desperately to understand. Drawers upended, cartons tipped over, and it's all my stuff.

Suddenly the front door creaked and Jack ducked behind a sofa. But there was no intruder, and he stood up slowly, squinting at the outside corridor. His hands were shaking violently, sweat beading at his hairline. He slammed the door shut and turned again to face the disorder.

Marty said the guy was tall, taller than me. Blond hair, strange accent. Think, think. Big man. Who does that remind you of? Faces and body shapes flashed in his mind, but only one locked in. It's that gorilla who stalked Helen's office, the man I saw with Harry Chan in the elevator. But what did he come to steal? It can't be money, I have none. There's no ammunition here I could use to prove my dismissal was contrived. Still trying to scare me – why? Why the PCs?

Then he thought about Carlotta Drunker. Big brother. Carlotta, is that what you were trying to warn me about? The crazy messages from his late Sacramento colleague now began to take on a new and sinister meaning. What did we have in common? Our research. Was the fucking drug launch only a side issue? Why else was the persecution continuing, now that he was no longer head of the Heart Unit? His mind raced. I've got something they *really* want. Jesus Christ.

His head was in turmoil as the full implications sank in. He scrambled for the telephone and started dialling, then stopped halfway. The phone could be bugged. His eyes drifted along the room. The apartment could be bugged.

At 5.40 Jack scared the hell out of his secretary. In the early-evening gloom of the Carter Hospital staff car lot he was hunched down between her black Nissan Sentra and a brick wall. He saw the alarm lights glow twice, heard the key in the lock. Then he stood up.

'Helen, it's me. Jack.'

Helen's right hand went instinctively to her throat, her left into defensive mode. 'Oh my God, oh sweet Jesus.' She leaned her forehead against the door frame. 'Jack Hunt, what are you doing sneaking up on me like that?'

She was enraged, but Jack hushed her immediately. 'I don't have time to tell you everything right now, but you've got to trust me on this.' Helen looked straight at him, eyes full of suspicion. 'I need a very big favour.'

Now the secretary's eyes narrowed to slits of distrust. 'What exactly?'

Jack took a deep breath. 'I want you to take Beth and Danny. I need a safe house for them.' He noticed the doubting looks give way to concern. 'This is way more important than me losing my job.'

Then he started talking. Beth and Danny moved in at seven o'clock that evening.

The Bradleys lived in Chicago Lawn, a south-west suburb of different races and backgrounds clustered near one another. It was a brick-and-wood bungalow-filled locale in which people mostly minded their own business and didn't interfere too readily. Helen had two young girls, five and three years old, with plaited hair, dark brown eyes and white, white smiles. Her husband, Spencer, worked as a chef at Joe's Crab Shack on North Wells. He looked intimidating and mean, six four, broad and muscled, with a deep baritone voice. But he was a pussycat, especially with the kids. He spent an hour before his evening shift clearing a room for Beth and Danny. Then he took the mattress off his own double bed and shoved it into one corner. For Danny, he arranged a blow-up camp cot.

'Spencer,' protested Beth, 'we can't have you lying on a hard base.'

Spencer looked down. 'Mrs Hunt, if Helen says you want the mattress on the roof then you got it. She runs this house, I only dance to her tunes.'

The final space was tight, about twenty square feet. One window overlooking a small garden plot, wooden blinds for privacy. The walls were covered with Garfield, floor to ceiling. Two white chairs on which to hang clothes, creaky wooden floor. Nothing else. Both Helen and Spencer insisted Jack stay too. 'We can't have you splitting up. You're a family and you're in this together.'

That night, an exhausted Jack Hunt slept right through undisturbed.

26

'Helen, I need you to steal something for me.'

It was 7.30 in the morning on Wednesday, 6 October. The Hunt family hadn't been at their W Deming apartment since the previous Saturday, and now with their lodgings ransacked and Jack's understanding of the motive behind that there was no possibility of the situation changing. He was desperate to formulate some kind of strategy, but the tools of his trade had been stolen. At the breakfast table in his secretary's kitchen he tried to persuade her to come on board.

Two doors down the hallway Spencer was fast asleep after his night shift. Helen usually left the house around eight to allow enough time to drop the children at play school and get to work. Beth, desperate to try and help out in any way possible and repay the sudden hospitality, had made the girls breakfast and was now dressing them. Their shrieks of delight at the change in routine echoed along the corridor, followed by shushes and suppressed giggles. Danny was still snoring, despite his protests that he'd never be comfortable on a low camp cot.

'There are two diskettes in the back office. One contains my research data, the other is from the doctor in Sacramento.'

A sudden pang of guilt hit. If I'd been more tuned in to what Carlotta was trying to tell me instead of being so dismissive we probably wouldn't be in this position. But Jack hadn't time for recriminations. There was too much at stake, and he knew that whoever was after his research would be looking for him. Knowledge is power. Despite his near penury and strained circumstances, Jack felt he was the most powerful man on earth. Equally he recognised that the knowledge was entirely in his mind.

For it to be of any use it would have to be confirmed by supporting evidence, hard facts. And the most important part of the proof was two standard diskettes hidden at the Carter Hospital.

'They are inside a brown envelope no bigger than this.' He held up his right hand. 'Pull out a medical text on the second shelf of the bookcase called *Principles of Internal Medicine.* It's quite thick and has an orange cover. The envelope is behind it.'

Helen sipped on a mug of coffee, her gaze fixed on Jack. She'd showered and dressed and brushed her hair and put on a standard light cosmetic touch, mainly lip gloss and mascara. She looked good and smelled good. On the other side of the table her one-time boss was in sweat-stained vest and undershorts. Thick stubble, bare legs and feet, hair sticking up like a crazy man.

'Whatever else you do today, Jack, freshen up and get a change of clothes. If you step outside our door looking like you've escaped from the funny farm the police are gonna pull you over for sure.'

Jack blushed with embarrassment. Being lectured on personal hygiene by the same girl he'd hired only months before made him squirm. 'Okay, okay. But will you get those disks for me?'

Helen blew at the steam rising from her mug. 'The bookcase in your office?' Jack nodded. 'Big orange-covered medical text on the second shelf?'

Jack caught a glimpse of his reflection in the window and tried to smooth his hair. Helen grinned as she watched.

'*Principles of Internal Medicine*,' he reminded. 'If you pull it out fully the brown envelope is against the wall.'

Helen laid the mug on the table and glanced at the kitchen clock. 'I'd better get moving then.' She pushed back her chair, then looked over, lips pursed. 'Why did you hide them? How could you have known this would happen?'

Jack shrugged. 'It was after you told me the hard disk had been moved. I had this uneasy feeling about someone hacking into my research data. So I stored everything on disks and hid them. Along with Dr Drunker's work.'

Helen was now along the corridor. 'Kids? Kids, come on. Time to go.' There were muted protests from one room. 'Come on now, shift it. And don't wake your dad.'

Beth tugged hats and coats on to the two little girls while Jack issued last-minute instructions.

'I'll telephone every hour on the half hour from nine thirty.'

Helen started to protest but Jack pressed ahead. 'I'll ask one question: "Can we bring a critical cardiac to the Heart Unit?" If you've got the disks, say "Yes, I'll clear it through ER." If you haven't found them or can't talk, say something like "Sorry, try again in an hour and I'll see what the duty doctor says." How does that sound?' Helen was glowering, but she nodded anway. 'Whenever you can sneak away, put the envelope under the right front wheel of your car. When you're going home tonight, make sure you look to see it's gone. I'd hate you to drive over the evidence.'

The door was closed gently and Jack was left standing in the hallway.

'Hunt.' Beth was behind him. 'We need to talk before Danny wakes.'

They sat at the kitchen table, fresh coffee brewing to the side. Beth was in a blue nightdress she'd borrowed from Helen. It fitted neatly, both women around the same size. She'd dragged her hair into a clasp and was massaging the side of her head with the tips of her fingers. Jack sensed a renewed unpleasantness.

'How are you feeling?'

He reached across and brushed at a wisp of blonde hair, but Beth drew back, then faced him directly. Her eyes were sad, the sockets sunk deep from distress and loss of weight.

'This has got to stop, and I'm calling a halt.' The words were spoken in a low voice. 'I'm going home to Sydney and I'm taking Danny with me.' The coffee started bubbling, and she reached over to turn down the heat. 'I can't keep up. Five days ago we had the world at our feet. Today you're disgraced and out of a job. If our lawyer's correct there's only a slim chance of you overturning this dismissal. And as if that wasn't bad enough, now you tell me we're being chased, that it's your research they're really after and that our lives are in danger.' A stunned Jack made to interrupt, but a hand waved him silent. 'All my married life I have followed you like a good and dutiful wife. I washed your clothes, ironed your shirts and darned your socks. I looked after your son when you weren't around for him and made all sorts of excuses each time he asked why you worked so late. We moved many times and I held my tongue each time you turned down good job offers.' The unrestrained bitterness was in full flow. 'I admit I did admire your high standards and understood your drive and ambition, but sometimes it was hard not to scream "no more". But I always believed one day it would end happily ever after.' She poured herself a mug of coffee and wrapped both hands around it. 'And in this city we nearly succeeded. It was so tantalisingly close.'

Jack listened with an aching heart. Beth had never been this direct before. She reached across and gently ran a finger over her husband's cheek. Then she smiled, and Jack had never seen such a sad and defeated smile in all his life.

'I can't take any more, Hunt. I've got my son and unborn child to consider. I can't keep running, I haven't the strength.' She suddenly set the mug down on the table, one hand on her stomach, the other at her lips. 'I feel sick.' Jack moved closer but was pushed away. 'I'm going to rest for a while. When I get up I expect you'll be gone, chasing computer disks or whatever else you think these people want from you. So while you're rushing around, factor this into your calculations. A single ticket from Chicago to Amsterdam, then on to Sydney costs around two thousand dollars. Danny won't be billed full fare, but I expect it'll be fifteen hundred. I'm taking five hundred for emergencies. That leaves you with two thousand. It isn't much, and I'm sorry. You hold on to it, stay here and slay whatever dragons come your way. Or you can cut your losses and come with us.'

The door into the kitchen was pushed open and Danny was standing outside, tears streaming down his face. It was obvious the boy had heard every word, and Beth rushed to console him. The two clutched each other, the mother rocking her son gently in her arms, murmuring words of comfort.

Jack looked on, helpless and heartbroken. I've lost them, and this time it's for real. And if they do go my life is for nothing.

'It's your call, Hunt,' said Beth as she led Danny back to their bedroom.

'I want to report a burglary.'

At 9.15 Jack was in the front waiting room of the Lincoln Park PD. He'd showered and shaved and was wearing a black tracksuit borrowed from Spencer. It was at least two sizes too big, but it did make him look half respectable. At reception he'd specifically asked for Officer Nelson, but he wasn't on duty and the complaint was handled by a young female black officer.

The small area was empty, but there was a distinct sense of activity going on behind the scenes. On top of the counter was a clutter of charge reports, incident statements and evidence bags. Two telephones on the desk kept ringing without being answered, and a fax machine churned out pages.

The girl didn't look up when Jack repeated his allegation, but reached beneath the counter and handed over an official PD form. 'Read this, then fill it in. There's a carbon copy for your insurance company. You hold on to that for your claim.'

One phone started up again, and the officer lifted the receiver and set it to one side without a word.

Jack tried once more. 'Look, this is very important. It's not just about the burglary, it's about who did it and what else they're trying to do.'

Angry shouts came from within some deep recess of the building, followed by more clamour and then a scream of pain. The officer jerked her head in the direction of the fracas, then turned back. 'What was that you just said?'

Jack struggled to control his frustration. 'I'm a doctor and a major pharmaceutical company has been trying to track my research. They stole my computer . . . no . . . they stole both my computers and . . .' The blank face in front of him stopped him in his tracks, and he suddenly realised how ridiculous his words sounded. He forced a contrite smile. 'I'm sorry, I'll try and handle this myself.'

As he turned, the policewoman called out, 'You better fill in the form anyway if you want to claim insurance.'

He stood outside the grey building in the grey damp morning and tried to shake his mind clear. I'm a stranger in a very strange country.

Helen couldn't get to the professor's office.

'Ms Bradley, I'm going to be in here for most of the morning.' Harry Chan was dressed in a smart suit, shirt and tie. No work fatigues in sight. 'I'm expecting a number of visitors and I'd appreciate it if you'd show them through immediately.'

Helen's mind went into overdrive. 'Would you like me to tidy before anyone arrives?' But Chan was already closing the door. Over his shoulder Helen could just about make out the thick orange text Jack had described. Second shelf, midway along.

The first visitor arrived at 9.55, a young woman who introduced herself as Lisa Montes, an executive from Zemdon

Pharmaceuticals. She was dressed smartly in navy jacket and long grey skirt with a high slit on one side exposing lots of leg. 'I'm here to discuss the Cyclint launch with Dr Chan.'

Helen knocked politely on the connecting door and opened it. Her heart almost stopped when she saw Chan browsing the bookshelves, pulling out texts and flicking through pages. He'd already cleared most of the top row.

'There's a lady from Zemdon Pharmaceuticals to see you.'

Chan placed the book he was holding on to a pile on the desk and walked over to greet his guest. 'Come straight in.'

As she closed the door, Helen noticed the two were now head to head in conversation, Lisa producing a thick bundle of paperwork from a briefcase. Please, please, let that keep him busy.

'Can we bring a critical cardiac to the Heart Unit?'

It was half past ten exactly when Jack Hunt put in his first call. Helen was alone in her office with a mound of typing and seven messages for Harry Chan to return. Three were from the Zemdon offices in New York with another three from media sources. The last one was from the penthouse suite at the Sheraton Chicago Hotel and Towers.

'Sorry, try again in an hour and I'll see what the duty doctor says.'

Jack hung up, cursing silently. He was in a public phone booth off Michigan Avenue. One hour to kill. He counted out small change and went in search of a cheap coffee house.

As he walked the streets he mulled over the earlier exchanges with Beth. She's serious about leaving, and I'm not surprised. I've certainly had enough too, and I'm not as sick as a dog and trying to contend with Danny at the same time. I'm down on my luck in every sense, and my only hope of keeping my family together is to get those disks.

He grabbed a copy of the *Tribune* and pored over it while he tried to eke out the time. On page twelve there was a six-column profile of Harry Chan with accompanying photograph. Chan lauded for taking over the Heart Unit under such strained circumstances. Chan lauded for being a veteran of the Carter. Chan lauded for his previous publications in reputable medical journals. Jack knew they were trivia, and the exaggerated claims of his rival's superior intellect made him seethe.

*

Lisa Montes left at 10.48. Helen watched her walk along the outside corridor accompanied by Harry Chan, laughing and making light conversation. She waited until they'd rounded a corner before making her move.

Into the inner sanctum, heart pounding. The thick orange text on the second shelf almost screamed for her attention. The top shelf was nearly empty, the books moved to the desk. She stopped and listened. No footsteps. Quick as she could, Helen edged to the other side of the desk and reached out.

'What are you doing?' Harry Chan was at the door. His face was dark as thunder, his eyes narrowed and fists gripped tightly.

'I was going to clean the room for you, Dr Chan.' Even as she spoke Helen wondered where the lies came from. She forced an apologetic smile. 'I thought it looked a mess and didn't want you creating a bad impression for all your important visitors.'

Chan's features relaxed. He looked around, then nodded his head in agreement. 'You're right, but leave it 'til after lunch. I'm expecting someone at eleven.'

Helen noticed there were none of the usual nervous laughs or shaky hands. The cardiologist seemed composed for a change.

She quickly offered the phone messages to distract him. 'There's been a number of return calls for you, Dr Chan.' She'd never before heard her voice so sweet. 'Three from New York and three from journalists wanting interviews. Also one from a Dr Crozer at the Sheraton.'

At Crozer's name Chan came to attention. 'Put Dr Crozer through immediately and I'll take it in here. And no interruptions until I'm finished.'

The door was closed firmly, and Helen dialled furiously to connect and stop Chan taking down more books.

'Putting you through now, Dr Crozer.'

'Can we bring a critical cardiac to the Heart Unit?'

Half past eleven. Jack was now in a booth in the Water Tower centre. This was a massive block of brick, glass and steel with one hundred shops on seven levels, each connected by moving stairs and a constant flow of carefully ducted water. Around him people were going up and down escalators armed with expensive-looking shopping bags. Most were laughing and smiling, pointing at more shops to attack. In stark contrast, Jack Hunt was homeless, near broke and being sought by people he believed had killed his research colleague. Time was running out. If he couldn't prove his case he would lose his wife and son. And his mind.

'Sorry, try again in an hour and I'll see what the duty doctor says.'

Helen was at her desk, but Steve Downes was pacing the floor impatiently in front of her.

'When's he coming out?' Downes barked as Helen fielded another call.

'I really don't know. He's been in conference for almost thirty minutes.'

Downes snorted his disgust. 'Call me when he's free.' He stomped out of the office.

Jack went to the top of the multi-storey shopping mall, then down again. Then up and down another thirty times. He soon began to recognise the shop assistants on each level and passed the time counting the number of lights on a fast-moving central elevator.

Harry Chan's eleven o'clock meeting finished at ten minutes past twelve; yet another female Zemdon employee departed, this time clutching two bulging briefcases. He emerged from the inner suite all smiles and bonhomie.

'Ms Bradley, perhaps you'd bring some coffee.' He glanced at his watch. 'We'll have another visitor shortly.'

Helen decided to take the initiative. This could go on all day, and she was sure her nerves wouldn't hold up. 'Sorry, Dr Chan, but Mr Downes was here looking to speak with you. He seemed very put out. I said you'd go straight to his office when you were free.'

Chan frowned in annoyance. 'Why can't he come here?'

Helen put on her perplexed face. 'I don't quite know, but he was most insistent the two of you meet immediately.' It was half true, and something she could lie out of later if confronted.

Chan collected a bundle of faxes and messages and scanned them quickly. 'Okay. I'll be back in five minutes. If anyone else comes, show them straight into my office.' The paperwork was dumped and the cardiologist hurried along the corridor.

Helen made for the inner suite, then stopped halfway. She quickly considered the possibilities, then locked the main door.

Two minutes, that's all I need. The professor's room smelled of cigar smoke. Jack would never have allowed that. The desk was a total clutter of textbooks, Zemdon Pharmaceutical promotions, agreements to this and that and some serious-looking Cyclint text descriptions. Helen was in front of the bookcase with one hand on the text when both outside phones started ringing. She pushed her fingers in between the adjacent medical tomes, breaking a nail in the process. Shit, that hurt. The phones were jarring her nerves as she dragged out the orange-covered *Principles of Internal Medicine*, immediately spotting the brown envelope resting at the back. Then came an aggressive hammering at the front office door. Her heart raced, and she quickly grabbed the envelope. The book was shoved back, then adjusted so that it didn't look out of place.

'What's all the knocking for?' she snapped as she turned the key and opened the door. It was false courage, but that was all she had left.

'Why was it locked?'

Helen immediately recognised the face glowering down at her. It was the gorilla from Zemdon Pharmaceuticals.

'I had to use the goddamned washroom. Now who the hell are you to be asking me questions, and what do you want?'

Hend de Mart wasn't listening; his eyes searched the office behind. Seeming satisfied, he pushed past and sat down in one of the chairs, then scowled up at Helen. 'I've got an appointment with Dr Chan.' He picked up a magazine and began flicking angrily through the pages. 'Now get me a coffee.'

'Can we bring a critical cardiac to the Heart Unit?' Half past twelve.

Helen had one eye on Hend de Mart, knowing he was tuned in to her every word.

'Yes, I'll clear it through ER.'

She waited until Harry Chan returned, then carried two cups of fresh coffee inside. 'Dr Chan, I have to check with ER about a cardiac admission. Is it okay if I take the phones off the hook for a few minutes?'

The only reply was a dismissive wave of a hand.

Jack Hunt tracked down a computer store two blocks from City Hall where, for twenty dollars, the material on the diskettes could be printed to hard copy. Scan first for viruses, leave with the assistant, return in one hour. He walked the windy and overcast streets until impatience took over. Fortunately the disks and printouts were ready when he returned fifteen minutes early.

'Lotta pages here,' warned the helper as he added another twenty dollars to the final account.

Jack would have paid one hundred times that amount.

He made his way to the quietest corner of the Chicago Cultural Center on E Randolph. While groups of tourists admired the latest works of art on display, or plied staff with questions on where to go and what to do while they visited the city, Jack pondered the mysteries of his 'infection to heart disease' theory. He was well acquainted with his own material and it took less than ten minutes to scan those pages. But Carlotta Drunker's data was less familiar, and it was closing on four o'clock before he'd absorbed everything. By then he was starving and even more concerned.

Over three mugs of strong coffee and two salad rolls he tried to decide his next move. His mind drifted back to Carlotta's e-mails. What he'd once dismissed as rubbish was now potentially life-saving. He couldn't remember them all, but three did stick out.

JACK. RUBENSTEIN IN COLORADO HASN'T BEEN IN TOUCH WITH ME FOR SIX WEEKS NOW. DID HE EVER COMMUNICATE WITH YOU? C.

DON'T SEND ANYTHING IMPORTANT BY E-MAIL OR POST.

LEUCOCYTE TRANSMIGRATION IN DAMAGED MYOCARDIAL MUSCLE PREDICTIVE OF ULTIMATE PROGNOSTIC OUT-COME. C.

Rubenstein in Colorado hasn't been in touch for six weeks. Had they got to him as well. Was he dead? *Don't send anything important by e-mail or post*? She knew she was being watched, she knew her messages were being intercepted. So who did she trust? Me, obviously (more guilt). But was there anyone else? Then he considered the final message, which really threw him. There was just no discernible logic to it. He said 'transmigration' out loud as if that would inspire insight. But only unrelated and nonsense words rushed to the front of his brain. Transformer, transducer, transatlantic, trans-Siberian. Even transvestite.

He ordered another roll and coffee and looked for a corner. Two rooms later he was in a brightly lit nook with walls covered in garish abstract paintings. Most who looked inside withdrew without staying, frowning their disapproval. Jack stared at one particular canvas covered in splashes of green, blue and red against a black background. The work was titled *Dreamtime in a Frightened City*, and he thought it most appropriate.

Back to Carlotta's message. He decided she had concealed the real content in medical jargon. *Leucocyte transmigration* . . . White cells on the move? . . . *in damaged myocardial muscle predictive of ultimate prognostic outcome.* Damaged myocardial muscle suggested some form of heart disease. Ischemic episode? Viral destruction? Jack tried every variation of medical knowledge to make a breakthrough, but still nothing made sense. But what if she was talking about her heart? What if she meant her heart was damaged? If something tragic happens *to me*? His own pulse fluttered as the code began to break. That's it, he thought excitedly, that's what she meant. If something happens to me, Carlotta, then *predictive of ultimate prognostic outcome* might suggest a final proof, the last piece in the jigsaw. And now the first words of the sentence made perfect sense. *Leucocyte transmigration.* It's not white cells on the move, it's the evidence. She's shifted the evidence.

A cascade of emotions rushed through Jack's mind. I can do it, I can still pull this off. With Carlotta's proof and the material on the disks I can bring this corporation down. No, *we* can collapse this fucking corporation. You and me, Dr Carlotta Drunker. He punched the air with delight and relief.

Then hard reality hit home again. Where did you move the documentation? You didn't trust anyone at the hospital, that much was obvious from your communications. And you must have known your apartment was under observation. Where did you take it, Carlotta? Who has it? He feverishly considered what scant details he knew of his late colleague. Unmarried and no children. Who did you turn to in times of crisis? There was another frantic ten minutes of worry. It could be anywhere. More staring at *Dreamtime in a Frightened City*. What about your lawyer in Sacramento, the man who sent the diskettes? No, he would have mentioned something if you'd wanted me to know more. Still . . .

Jack rushed to the nearest call booth and started dialling. Helen answered.

'Can you talk?'

There was a moment's pause. 'Go ahead please, I'll take the details and pass them on to Dr Chan when he returns.'

'I need the name and number of the Sacramento lawyer who wrote to me with Carlotta Drunker's disk. I wrote a thank-you note in return. The original letter should be filed. I'll call you in twenty minutes.'

Helen's voice came back, poised and full of confidence. 'Thank you, I've got all that.'

He hung up and counted every second on his watch.

'Did you get it?' Jack's heart was racing, the back of the tracksuit soaked in sweat. The palms of his hands were wet and shaking. He had a pen poised over a scrap of paper and it trembled in his fingers.

This time Helen's voice was sharp but muted. 'He's called Tod Benson. Take this number down.'

Jack began scribbling. Then he fed a tumble of coins into the call box.

'Would it be possible to talk to Tod Benson?' He was agitated and excited all at once but managing to control himself.

'Who's speaking?' A sweet and youngish female voice. Jack tried to imagine her, relaxed and untroubled, probably polishing her nails and wondering about the weekend ahead.

'My name is Professor Jack Hunt and it's in connection with certain material Mr Benson sent to me by courier recently.'

It was a gamble, and Jack knew it. Using his formal title would get results most times. Like movie stars booking a table at a top restaurant when the floor is full. An image can impress and move things along. Equally, if his name was mud in Sacramento too he could just as easily get the brush-off.

'One moment.'

Jack stared at the wall in front of him. Someone had scrawled graffiti on it: AL CAPONE FOR MAYOR. Another fool had added his or her opinion: AL CAPONE'S DEAD, FUCKWIT. WHAT'S WRONG WITH DALY ANYWAY?

'Tod Benson here. How can I help you?' Rich, mellow tones, like an experienced newsreader.

Jack took a deep breath and explained his predicament. Everything was couched in half truths and downright lies, but he was determined not to sound like some paranoid lunatic.

'I'm not in a position to pass on details of Dr Drunker's family or close friends.'

Jack wasn't going to be put off easily. His marriage was on the rocks, he was close to Skid Row and his life was in danger. He was well past dismissive point. But he had to keep his cool.

'I appreciate that, Mr Benson, but the material you sent relates to vital medical research. I've studied it closely and I believe Carlotta wanted me to see this study through to its conclusion. However, the most important documentation is missing and I think she left it with a close friend or relative.'

There was a long pause.

'Are you still there?'

Tod Benson came back sharply. 'I'm still very much here, Professor Hunt. And right now I'm looking at a news report about your dismissal from the Carter Hospital in Chicago. Would you care to comment on that?'

It seemed then as if Jack's world would collapse. He needed that extra information and he believed Carlotta had moved it to a place of safety. But now he had some hard-nosed lawyer in Sacramento stonewalling. Jesus, give me a break.

'Mr Benson, I'm challenging that decision aggressively. My test samples were switched and I think I know why.' He took a deep breath. 'I think my sacking relates to my research. And to Carlotta Drunker's. And I think she may even have been killed for it.'

'I thought so, Professor Hunt. I had a feeling there was more to this.' Jack started to explain further but Benson continued. 'Dr Drunker has a near relative who is now in charge of her remaining assets. This lady has instructed my firm to investigate Carlotta's death more closely.'

Finally Jack got a chance to speak. 'What exactly are you hinting at?'

'I'm not at liberty to say anything else without client instruction. But what I will do is call and ask if she would be prepared to speak with you. Can you give me a number?'

Jack thought quickly. 'I'm afraid I'll be on the move for the next hour. How about I get back in, say, forty minutes?'

Rita Callard was her name. She was Carlotta Drunker's aunt and apparently a good deal older than her late niece. Jack was expecting someone younger, a cousin, perhaps, in one of the medical sciences who'd understand the complexities of cardiology. The elderly lady lived in Pacific Grove in California, about one hundred and twenty miles south of San Francisco. By 6.30 that evening Jack had her telephone number.

'Hello?' The first thing he noticed was the weak and feeble voice.

'Hi, is that Mrs Callard?'

'Yes.' Even that one small word seemed to trail off.

'My name is Dr Jack Hunt. I was speaking with a lawyer called Tod—'

Rita Callard cut in abruptly. 'I know all about you, Dr Hunt. And it didn't come from Tod Benson. Carlotta never stopped talking about you.' The voice faded again, then strengthened. 'Weren't both of you working on some research programme?'

'Yes, that's right. We swapped ideas for a few years.'

'And now you're in big trouble. Sacked from your hospital. Saw it on NBC, then read about it in the paper.'

Jack swore into his sleeve. Jesus, he could almost hear the disapproval. He wasn't ready for a lecture.

'Well, what happened to you is nothing to what they did to Carlotta.'

Jack almost crawled into the telephone receiver. 'What are you talking about?'

'I don't rightly know. Carlotta was acting peculiar for weeks before she was knocked down. I don't believe the police are telling me everything. They're asking too many strange questions.'

The conversation drifted into uncomplimentary ranting about the Sacramento PD, and Jack became more and more impatient. He was close to breaking point but strove to remain cool. He worried that Mrs Callard was slightly unbalanced, maybe hadn't got over the sudden bereavement.

'I've got a room full of her files here.' Jack nearly dropped the phone. 'I told the police but they just sent some rookie down. He tossed a few pages around, then spent the rest of the afternoon at the beach.'

'You've got them?' Jack knew he'd hit paydirt. This is *it*! Sweet Jesus, this is *it*! I can still save my marriage, my career. My life. And maybe bring this fucking chemical giant to its knees.

'Yessir. She rented a U-Haul and piled everything inside, then drove to me about two weeks before she was killed. On her own. That's a long journey – we're way below San Francisco on the map. Whatever's in there is obviously important.'

Jack took a deep breath and forced his trembling hands still. 'Now where exactly do you live, Mrs Callard?'

He made it sound like he was going to send her a picture postcard.

27 *Thursday, 7 October, 4.37 a.m., Chicago*

In the dim light of a bedside lamp Jack Hunt donned a thick sweater, denims and double socks inside heavy-duty boots bought at the Fox's outlet store on N Clark five days previously. Beth was wide awake. She was also sick, dry-retching into a plastic bag at the side of their on-floor mattress. The new baby was obviously taking a firm hold on life and its mother couldn't remember being as unwell and exhausted the first time round. Danny managed to doze through all the noises, but in the next room some scuffling confirmed the Bradley household was stirring. Face drawn with worry and pale from lack of sleep, Beth kissed her husband good-bye. Then she slumped back, images from the Garfield wallpaper spinning in her head. She willed another hour's undisturbed rest.

'Better take light clothes.' The giant Spencer was waiting outside the door, a small canvas bag held out. 'They'll be way too big again but it's all I got.' He grinned in the early gloom. 'It should be a lot warmer where you're goin'.'

Jack grasped a massive hand and shook it firmly. 'Thanks.' It was as much as he could get out. Here was a man who knew very little about him but was willing to share his house and bed and personal clothes. It was touching, and Jack swallowed hard, trying not to show his emotions.

Spencer looked down at him severely. 'Take care, ye hear?' He was trying to muffle his deep voice, but somehow it still boomed in the narrow confines. 'I don't rightly know what's goin' on but Helen is talkin' crazy about people out to get you. In this city no one uses fisticuffs. Every argument is settled at the end of a gun.'

He left the bungalow at 5.15, into a blustery and cold morning with dark skies and the smell of rain. Darting and stopping, always looking over his shoulder, he finally found the silver Chevy where he'd hidden it after the move to Chicago Lawn. If Rita Callard's calculations were correct, he was going to need its space to bring back the material stacked in her house. He gunned the engine.

The traffic was relatively light, rush hour some time away. He negotiated side streets and main roads, meeting mainly police cars and service utilities, then finally merged into a steady stream on the Tri-State Tollway. There, a snake of vehicles fought for position, dodging and weaving and overtaking, horns blaring, headlights flashing. Cars passed by vans which in turn clawed by trucks, their klaxons deafening. With the heater full on against the cold, Jack hugged the inside lane all the way to O'Hare. At one slip road he suddenly swerved off, then circled back on to the highway again. He didn't think he was being followed, but if he was he had to make some attempt to confuse them.

In the long-term parking lot he edged the Chevy between an end wall and a shiny new Lexus, then inspected the vehicle from different angles to ensure it was as tucked out of the way as possible. Ten minutes later he hunched in the corner of a people mover train on its way to the main airport buildings. Fifteen more, amid the soaring concourses and moving sidewalks of Terminal One, he checked into United and their 6.15 connection to Los Angeles, Airbus A319, flight number 129. The round trip would cost $816. He was eating into the remaining two thousand – if Beth and Danny fled to Australia. It also meant he wouldn't be going with them.

He bought himself a *Sun-Times* and saw that Herb's publicity drive was obviously working on overtime.

> Reports coming out of Chicago's Carter Hospital suggest the Heart Unit there is in turmoil. Six days ago Irish cardiology chief Jack Hunt was summarily dismissed after scoring two positives during random drug analysis. Within forty-eight hours the professor fought back, claiming his samples had been tampered. Hunt's lawyer is filing for wrongful dismissal and threatening heavier law suits unless the affair is resolved quickly. However, the administration is stonewalling. The blood and urine specimens have gone missing and rumours suggest the tech involved in the testing has also gone to ground.

I was right. The scumbag who switched the specimens has run away. He'll never be found.

A press conference scheduled for this morning has been cancelled, and calls to the administrator's office have not been returned.

On the plane, Jack set his face to the port window. A hostess interrupted and he wolfed down the offered breakfast: cold cereal, cold milk, cold croissant. At least the coffee was hot and sweet. Looking around, he noticed his fellow passengers seemed at ease: paperwork being attended to, novels being read, some dozing. He was the only one on edge.

What *has* Rita Callard got? She didn't give much away on the telephone. What if it's no more than the same data Carlotta posted on the diskette? Relax, don't torment yourself. Whatever is there won't change – it's either useful or not. And if it's not you'd better start learning how to serve tables.

He shifted in his seat and tried closing his eyes, hoping for sleep. It didn't work. He kept recalling Beth's parting words the night before when he'd told her of the latest developments. *If this is another blind alley, Hunt, I'm taking the next available flight.*

Quick glance at his watch. One hour to go. He urged the plane forward.

The Airbus touched down in Los Angeles International Airport at 8.40. Jack kicked his heels in the transfer lounge waiting for a Skywest link. Business types in light suits studied financial pages while vacationers laughed and joked, their high spirits matching their wear. Gaudy floral prints and baggy shorts seemed the agreed uniform of the day.

Soon, Jack's winter clothing became uncomfortable, and in the toilets he switched to one of Spencer's tee-shirts. It hung off him and he nipped and tucked until some sort of respectable shape became obvious. With a disposable razor, soap and lukewarm water he trimmed at his thick stubble, nicking skin and drawing blood. The end result made him look like an overaged hippie with a plague of insect bites. Fellow travellers did double-takes and avoided sitting too close. That suited nicely.

*

The flight from LAX departed as scheduled, and just after 11.30 local time he was in the arrivals hall of Monterey Peninsula airport in south-west California. With only a canvas bag as luggage he cleared quickly through to the greeting point, scanning the waiting faces. He finally spotted his name scrawled on a piece of cardboard. JACK HINT.

'You spelled it wrong.'

A pimply-faced youth in a blue uniform was holding the tatty cardboard. He inspected his handiwork, then shrugged. 'Got ya anyway, didn't it?' The kid was tall and thin with a slow drawl and unhurried movements. He looked as if he hadn't seen the sun for months.

Rick's Rent A Miser had offered the lowest car hire rates when Jack made the flight bookings, and he was beginning to see why. The valet sauntered ahead, shoulders slouched, chewing gum, indifferent to his customer. Jack followed, noting dirt and grease almost covering the logo on the blue apparel.

'Where ya heading?'

Pimpleface forced himself to make casual conversation as he led Jack past rows of cars, sunlight dancing off their roofs. The air smelled of aviation fuel, and in the near distance the revving of a jet engine swamped conversation. Jack cupped both his ears to hear better.

'Pacific Grove.'

'Nice place, great views,' the youth offered. 'Good time of the year to visit. Hardly any rain, warm days and cool evenings. It's easier to sleep that way.'

Rick of Rent A Miser fame was a disenchanted mechanic who'd once worked the coast-to-coast Rent A Wreck franchise. Convinced he could develop his own chain of low-cost car hire he bought up a small fleet of ageing, high-mileage machines. Cars, vans, trucks, sport utilities, motorbikes. Then he sat back and waited to become a millionaire. His business was five miles east of Old Monterey, south of Highway One near Del Monte lake. There, behind a rundown and graffiti-tortured mall, he stored his collection.

The office was no more than a large wooden shed with tin roof and windows so dirty they were impossible to see through. Underneath a mound of paper, trash and girlie magazines was a desk, one rickety seat front and behind. The hire agreement was so stained Jack could barely make out the print, and he left it unread. The vehicles and bikes were stored in a small lot to the side, surrounded by a chain-link fence. In one corner a hungry-looking mongrel lay in the shade of a truck with a tattered rope stretching from stud collar to a pole some twenty feet away. The dog was panting rapidly, tongue hanging out, sharp teeth exposed. An overturned water bowl rested at its front paws.

Rick was not at his desk, so the acne-scarred valet showed Jack two Jeeps, a '92 Mazda MPV and a seven-passenger Dodge Caravan. None suited. Finally they stopped beside a white '84 Ford 250 cargo van with ladder-rack shelving. It was battered on all sides and had been poorly resprayed on more than one occasion. The tyres were worn and the passenger door was tied closed with heavy-duty string, the cord threaded through a hole drilled in the side panelling. There was dirt and dust everywhere, especially on the inside dash and seats. Only one windscreen wiper worked, but the washer fluid did not.

'Musta forgot to top it up,' the kid offered. He sniffed, then looked away. 'Ya asked for a van and ya got a van. Ya want a Cadillac ya gotta pay for a Cadillac.'

Jack started to complain, then thought better of it. Time was running out. The heap of rusting metal on rubber only had to get him from A to B and back again inside twenty-four hours. Surely it wouldn't collapse in that short period?

'This runs real good,' he was told. 'Never had a breakdown.' Jack looked across, disbelief written all over his face. 'Never' was repeated, this time more emphatically. 'Here's a map of southern California and a two-day weather forecast.'

Jack studied the paperwork. The next twenty-four hours promised partial cloud with a high of seventy-five and low of fifty-six, humidity around ninety per cent. Already Spencer's tee-shirt was sticking to his skin.

'Boss says yar to pay me now.'

Jack produced a bundle of cash.

'Boss says to take credit cards only.'

Jack was uneasy about using anything traceable. He'd been forced to use his Visa for the air ticket but wanted to kill the trail dead at Monterey. He knew he was being paranoid, but he couldn't take any risks. 'I've only got cash.' He felt along a hip pocket and produced a roll of twenties. The kid's eyes widened.

'It's five hundred against damage. Refundable when you return it.'

Jack peeled off nine bills and stuck them in the kid's oil-streaked hands. He knew the money would go straight into the valet's hip pocket.

'Tell your boss any accident could only improve this wreck's delicate panelling.'

Pimpleface shielded his eyes from the glare. 'Boss won't like that.'

Jack climbed into the front seat, brushing away old crumbs and candy wrappers. 'That's his problem.'

Monterey Bay arcs in a ninety-mile semicircle across the coastline between California's northern and southern borders. Highway One cruises along the seafront, passing windswept beaches piled high with sand dunes and fields of artichoke plants on the landside. The gulf is blessed with deep green forests of gnarled, wind-twisted cypress and a vast undersea ravine, larger and deeper than the Grand Canyon.

Under different circumstances Jack might have enjoyed the journey. The town of Monterey had a well-preserved collection of adobe buildings, many still serving as government offices, restaurants and banks. Along the old waterfront was a small-scale Fisherman's Wharf with creaking docks and working fishing boats. Shops aplenty selling cups of chowder and fresh seafood to go. Right beside was a cluster of sea lions, their mournful barking entertaining tourists by day and driving nearby hoteliers to distraction at night.

But Jack had too much on his mind to appreciate the history and scenic views. Time was running out. He had a pregnant wife now being looked after by his young boy, both planning to leave the country. And he wasn't sure if he was on a wild goose chase with little to show at the end. He was stuck in an aged and battered van on worn wheels which threatened to lurch off the road. The steering was heavy, the brakes light. He'd forgotten his sunglasses and dazzle from the morning sun irritated him. His brow beaded with sweat as he fought with the air-conditioner, finally slapping his hand against the control in despair when it blew only heat.

He found Del Monte Avenue and skirted the seafront, keeping

the beach to his right. Then through Lighthouse Tunnel on to Pacific until the Ford hit Ocean View Boulevard. By his reckoning the final destination was about five miles ahead and in a different township.

Pacific Grove was a small community located on the northern-most tip of the Monterey Peninsula. It had rows of imposing turn-of-the-century mansions facing the ocean, their paint peeling with salt erosion. The town had once been a religious retreat, and that general atmosphere of rest and relaxation persisted. Locals called the area 'America's last hometown'. It was a locale where one could amble at a leisurely pace, admire the scenery, smell the sea air and relax in the warm sun.

Jack paid little attention to his surroundings, his mind focused on a specific address. Map on dash, he navigated with one hand while trying to read Rita Callard's directions. 'Along 12th Street, turn left, go for another hundred yards and turn left again.' The cab was overheating despite both windows being down and he had to tug out a corner of his tee-shirt to wipe his forehead. He was thirsty and bothered, overtired and overexcited. By his reckoning he was only a few hundred yards away from salvation or hell. He passed streets with tiny board-and-batten cottages, then prim and proper Victorian villas. Right. Left. Another turn. Right again, then Kenton. At last. Now where's 104?

He cruised slowly, looking for numbers on mailboxes. The street was quiet, single-storey ranch-style dwellings with carports. Small but manicured front lawns, their sprinkled greenness contrasting with the dry and scorched side tracts. Palm trees in abundance. Orange and yellow and red and blue flowers at boundary edges. Red spiky bottle brushes. Now flourishes of purple bougainvillea. But still little movement apart from kids on bikes, chasing one another. He sounded the horn to warn them. He spotted a shock of grey hair hunched over shrubbery, but that was 96. What a quiet road.

Suddenly, 104.

28 *Thursday, 7 October, 10.30 a.m., Chicago*

'We got another client for you.'

The office of the Chief Medical Examiner for Cook County was located on 2121 W Harrison in Chicago city. It was also the mortuary and main centre for forensic investigation with over four thousand autopsies conducted each year. The building itself was uninspiring. Set well back from the road on three levels it was a grey concrete and glass structure with straight-lined architecture, access points, exits. Functional rather than pretty, which befitted its purpose.

The front entrance led to a large and well-lit atrium. Zero furnishings. Plain walls apart from professional plaques, very basic, and squeaky-clean flooring. A single secretary behind a wide and waist-high reception desk queried all business, and unless you worked there you didn't really ever want to visit because the chances are you were coming to collect. Or be collected.

To the immediate left of this was administration, while a corridor to the right led to the main activity areas. On that side the tissue-sampling laboratories were located. Blood alcohol levels to be checked in motor fatalities. Heroin, cannabis, barbiturates, cocaine, amphetamines – mixtures and variations of these and similar drugs analysed. Brain, bone, liver, muscle microscopically inspected for clues as to cause and timing of death. Was the guy shot and then burned? Or was he still alive and burning when they started shooting? Was the girl raped and then strangled, or was she dead when the freak got excited? The pathologists and their test results revealed all.

In this zone, and past a number of carefully locked doors, was a small viewing room. Those who gave good descriptions, or had come to confirm what they already knew, were asked to inspect one body only.

That Thursday, around the same time Jack Hunt was arriving in Los Angeles, the facility received yet another delivery.

To the side of the building, and tucked well away from inquisitive eyes, was the acceptance bay. Thick frosted Perspex double flaps opened into a lobby. This antechamber was about twenty foot square, tiled floor with a stainless-steel in-ground weighing station. Beside that was a long and smooth wooden measuring stick, stored in that same position all the time for convenience. No matter what condition a corpse was in when offloaded, it had first to be weighed and measured.

About ten paces directly opposite the Perspex entrance was an outsize and extra-thick door opened by pulling firmly on a refrigerator-like handle. Within, and dimly lit by six naked light bulbs, was a large and deep chamber, maybe fifty feet long, thirty feet wide and twenty feet high. Here, up to three hundred bodies could be stored, all laid out in tiered rows. Floor to ceiling, wall to wall, head to soles of feet, and separated only by narrow passages, each corpse awaiting its turn for formal autopsy. Some still had EKG leads attached to the chest where resuscitation manoeuvres had been tried and had failed. Others were blood-stained, delivered as discovered. Stacked against the furthermost wall were pine coffins. Simple, undecorated and unpainted, these belonged to the unclaimed. Below street level, in the basement, there were six white autopsy tables anchored underneath glaring fluorescent tubes. With a packed waiting room above, the slabs were rarely empty. Priority was homicide – the cops couldn't be kept waiting. Even so, few policemen ventured downstairs to view proceedings.

'Somebody called nine-one-one.' A paramedic was explaining the circumstances. He was a small beefy black man in red fatigues. Local drawl, tinny voice. He wore protective gloves on both hands with eye shields resting on his forehead. 'Cops got there first. By the time we arrived it was just a FedEx job.' FedEx was slang for a collect-and-delivery call-out. Patient dead on arrival, transport to morgue. 'One bullet above the right ear. Eyes staring blank, like he's looking into hell.'

'That's two in twelve hours.' The receiving attendant, a tall, gaunt and pale man with plastic boots and apron, was leaning on a stainless-steel gurney. He sounded nasal, like he had a bad cold.

'No shit?' The paramedic was impressed.

'Another John Doe was hit the same way. River police fished him out near West Twenty-fifth. They reckon he was dumped from the Expressway last night.' He cocked an index finger. 'Bang, now start swimming.'

'Fucking psychos.' The paramedic loosened a button on his tunic. 'Maybe the weather will calm the war zones. Forecaster says cold and rain.'

'Any ID?' The attendant stifled a yawn.

'Nah. Just lying in a derelict house near a building site, a hundred-dollar bill sticking out of his hip pocket.' The two exchanged surprised glances. 'Nobody saw nuthin' and nobody heard nuthin'.' The words were deliberately accented. 'Nobody wanted to know anythin'.'

'Rent boy?'

'Dunno.' Thoughtful pause. 'Doubt it. His jeans were on proper.'

Next, the entry wound was examined.

'Looks like a thirty eight.'

'Yeah.' But the mortuary attendant wasn't really interested. He'd been on duty for ten hours and was feeling the effects. And he'd seen this and much worse before. He held up a stiffening and lifeless limb. 'Could be that's his name.'

The other man inspected a tattoo on the back of a waxen-like hand. 'Could be.'

The cadaver was then weighed and measured. 'Seven stone four pounds. Five foot six inches.' Immediate external identifying marks recorded. 'Three nickel rings in each ear, nickel stud outer skin left nostril.' Obvious scarring was noted. Every detail would be posted later to local police departments for help with identification.

Finally the body was lifted on to the gurney and wheeled towards the storage chamber opposite. The refrigerator handle was slowly yanked, the heavy door eased open. Thirty rows of corpses beckoned.

It was settlement day, and Luther, the kid hired to terrorise the Hunt family, was Hend de Mart's first victim.

3 p.m., Chicago

'How did you find them?'

In the penthouse apartment of the Sheraton Chicago Hotel and Towers the South African was outlining his most recent success. He sat about ten feet away from a large U-shaped mahogany table in front of a picture window with river views. That day he was in denims and open-neck shirt, his long legs crossed and his bulky frame filling the chair. The suite was fifteen hundred square feet with two doors leading off to other rooms. Lime green walls, recessed halogen spots on half power. Thick pile terracotta carpet, oil-colour paintings under wall-mounted lighting. Lounge chairs and wooden stools at a cocktail bar counter. At the far end, beside the floor-to-ceiling window, was a glass door leading to an outside veranda.

'Didn't trust Hunt's secretary,' de Mart explained. 'She had the door to her office locked when I called yesterday. The place was deserted and the phones were hopping. When she finally opened she seemed flustered.' He shifted in his chair, relishing the moment. He was the one who'd tracked down the enemy. 'I organised one of the crew to follow her.' He consulted a small notepad. 'She lives in a bungalow in a south-west suburb. The contact waited until the boy came out.' He looked up to explain. 'Hunt's son. The one that's always running around kicking a ball.' He went back to his notes. 'A minute later the blonde joined him. She was walking very slowly, holding on to the fences. Went up and down the same road twice, then called the youngster and they went back into the house.'

'And the doctor?'

'We lost him this morning.' De Mart was sifting through the notebook again. 'There's ten working on this. I put three on Harry Chan to make sure he doesn't go off the rails and five are trailing the Hunts. They work in shifts, and the early squad got confused among traffic on the Tollway.'

'That was a mistake, a serious mistake.' From the comfort of a leather high-back Zemdon executive Dr Gert Crozer watched and listened. He was in formal dress code: navy single-breast suit, crisp white shirt and company tie. He tapped at his chin with his wire-framed glasses, deep in thought. 'What about Rossi?'

'I moved him two days ago. He's in a safe house until this blows over. He'll make a few statements, give a protected interview, then melt away. When the time's right he can be squashed.' The South African put down his notebook. 'I took out the kid from the projects. Now there's no footprints connecting us to the hospital.'

The contrasting accents, Afrikaans versus guttural Swiss-German, forced both men to strain to understand.

'Does Herr Danker know any of this?'

'No, but I think he's suspicious about everything falling into place at the last minute. I don't think he'll want to dig too deep though.'

'Keep it that way.'

A sudden shower of rain drilled at the penthouse windows, its intensity forcing de Mart speak louder.

'Harry Chan's been shooting his mouth off.'

Crozer leaned forward, his hawk-like eyes narrowing. 'How?'

'Told his crony Shreeve to put his life savings into Zemdon shares.'

Crozer was livid but controlled. 'Don't do anything until after the Cyclint launch.' He dragged a white handkerchief from his pocket, dabbed his forehead and then bunched it tightly. 'When it's over, pulp him until he squeals.'

De Mart nodded. Outside, more plump raindrops plopped on to the windows. Soon the scenic view would be distorted by rivulets of water.

'I've got two watching the W Deming apartment.' The meeting had dragged on longer than the South African had expected. 'Should I pull them?'

'No, Hunt could go back there at any time.'

'If he turns up, do they move on him?'

There was no pause. 'Immediately. Take him out there and then.'

De Mart's face tensed with concentration. 'I'll move three to Chicago Lawn. That way we can cover the streets from all sides. I should have a tap on the phone' – de Mart glanced at his watch – 'within an hour.'

'How did you arrange that?'

'Bought an engineer with AT&T. Guy can hop a line in half an hour.'

Crozer stood up and began pacing the floor, firing off orders staccato-like.

'Confirm all final arrangements.'

De Mart nodded.

'Contact Zurich and let them know everything has been settled.'

'Done.'

'Tell Dr Chan I wish to dine with him alone this evening. Make sure Herr Danker is with us. I want to keep him close to me until everything has been finished.'

'Sure.'

Then Crozer turned to face de Mart directly. 'But more than anything else, find Hunt. Wherever he is.'

One hour later Helen Bradley was walking along the streets of her Chicago Lawn neighbourhood. Harry Chan had let her go early. 'Big day tomorrow, Ms Bradley. Very important pharmaceutical inauguration I'm involved in.' The cardiologist had looked over-excited again. 'Take the rest of the afternoon off. I'll need all this office space for last-minute meetings.' Helen couldn't get out of the hospital quick enough.

As she negotiated puddles and potholes she wondered how long Beth Hunt could hang in there. Helen felt sorry for her: the woman was distraught and harassed.

Fifty yards ahead she spotted Danny running in and out between parked cars, whooping with delight. She hurried to him. Then she noticed Beth about another ten yards further along, holding on to a garden wall. She was shouting and waving.

'Danny!' Helen was now beside the boy. 'You know you're not allowed on these streets. You can kick the ball in our back lot but that's as far as it goes.' She wagged a finger as she scolded, and Danny put on a hangdog look.

'I'm fed up being stuck in all day,' he complained angrily. 'Mum's too sick to do anything and there's nothing on the TV.'

By now Beth was beside them, panting and sweating despite the cold. She was still in the same blue tracksuit she'd worn for the previous five days. Grime and food stains were becoming obvious. 'Come on, Danny. That's your escape for the day. Run along back now.'

When the boy was out of listening range, Beth turned to Helen and started apologising. 'I can't keep him indoors. He's never been so confined before. Jack warned us not to leave the house, but right now I couldn't care less if half the world was following us. I don't have the strength to carry on arguing with him.'

Helen thought Beth might collapse. She linked arms and led her slowly to the house, so engrossed in the other woman's plight that she didn't see the black transit van with a plumbing company logo and sliding side panels pulling out of a side road. And she didn't hear the whirr of a camera's shutter as one of Hend de Mart's henchmen recorded their every movement.

29 *Thursday, 7 October, 1.30 p.m., Pacific Grove, California*

Rita Callard was a bird of a woman. About five feet two and probably no more than one hundred pounds, she had a weather-beaten, parchment-thin hide which sagged on her upper arms and neck. Facial wrinkles like fault lines, spindly matchstick limbs dotted with purple age spots. She had small, darting blue eyes with an ugly crusting mole above her right brow, thin grey hair held back under a bandanna. When she opened the door of 104 Kenton in Pacific Grove she was wearing a bright turquoise blouse over navy cotton shorts. Jack aged her at seventy plus.

'Yes, I'm Mrs Callard.' She inspected the wreck of a man in front of her. 'Are you the doctor from Chicago?' She seemed unimpressed by the vision. Tall, dark and handsome on a better day maybe, but at that moment Jack looked like an escaped convict. Razor nicks on neck and cheek, sweat-streaked and oversized tee-shirt. 'Feeling okay?'

Jack forced a smile. 'Yeah. I've been on the move since five this morning and I'm bunched.' He noticed his general appearance being inspected. 'Had to borrow someone else's clothes,' he explained weakly.

'Must be from a big man. If I were you I'd make sure to give them back.'

The voice was as Jack remembered on the telephone. Each sentence started off strong, then faded to a whisper. It was difficult to place the accent.

'Well come on in, and don't crowd the doorway. Neighbours'll think I've got myself a boyfriend.' Rita Callard was now grinning. 'You look as if you could do with being freshened up. How about cold tea and a home-made cookie?'

Jack had to listen carefully, but he did hear 'cold tea' and 'cookie'.
'That'd be great. Thanks.'

The property was a single-level cottage dwelling of brick and timber. To the left baskets filled with trailing red geraniums hung from a carport roof. Underneath, and skewed awkwardly to one side, was an ancient-looking Pontiac. The tyres were soft, the body low to the ground. Jack edged the Ford cargo van in behind as Rita Callard looked on. If she was dismayed at the condition of the rental, she didn't show it.

Five well-worn wooden steps led to the south-facing entrance with white support handrails on each side. The house fascia was soft yellow with white trim on window and door frames. Inside the residence smelled dusty and most of the furniture looked straight out of the fifties. Chrome stools with plastic seat and shoulder rest, chipped white veneer cupboards. In a formal dining area there was a cherrywood table and six chairs, but the room was now a mess, littered with old books, magazines and newspapers. An antique typewriter was perched in one corner, a half sheet still in place as if the communication had been suddenly interrupted. A narrow hall led to the rear of the residence with doors leading off on each side. Only one was shut. On the walls family photographs hung so crookedly they almost threatened to fall off.

The eat-in kitchen looked on to a garden where a central lawn was being irrigated by a noisy sprinkler rat-a-tat-tatting its full circle. Rainbows formed in the spray, then faded as the shower moved into shade. Shrubs and vivid cacti vied for position along one border while a black cat with white snout pawed in the air as a group of newly arrived orange and black Monarch butterflies winged past. On the other side of the allotment was a flourish of bedding plants. Purple begonias, yellow marigolds and Californian poppies of every hue. Partly shaded by the leaves of a eucalyptus tree and struggling to show its glory, a white-petal hibiscus hung limply.

Jack sat on a back step facing the grass plot and pushed his face to the sun. He felt drained, physically and emotionally, with only the adrenaline of discovery keeping him going. Somewhere in a room, perhaps only yards away, was the answer to a hundred questions. What would he uncover?

'Here you go.' Rita Callard was behind him with a tray of goodies. 'Now tell me, Dr Hunt, how did you get into such trouble?'

In between mouthfuls of crumbling biscuit, Jack told Rita his life story. Who he was and where he'd come from. Where he'd been and how he'd met his wife.

'Carlotta never married,' Rita interrupted at one point. She was sitting beside Jack, one step higher. 'Her nose was always stuck in books and she never met a man more interesting than her work.' Her shoulders slumped and there was an intense sadness all over her face. 'She was very kind to my husband. The two of us were heartbroken when he died.'

Jack had wondered if a Mr Callard existed. There had been no mention of a partner when they'd first spoken, no sign now of a man about the house. 'I'm sorry to hear that,' he mumbled.

'No need to be, young man. None of your concern.' But she told him anyway. 'His name was Richard, Rick to me and the world. Worked in air traffic control at LA before we retired here five years ago. He was troubled with blood pressure, and I'll swear it was the stress of the job. Took everything so damned serious.' She searched for a tissue in a side pocket, then gently blew her nose. 'Then, after we got to know people here, he'd help out at Monterey Peninsula when somebody called in sick.' The voice was fading again. 'Carlotta warned him about that, but he said he'd vegetate if he didn't keep his mind active.' She dropped crumbs off her plate beside a small rock in a flowerbed, then, with the tip of one bare toe she eased the stone up and seconds later a scattering of red ants emerged. 'Now he's gone.' She stopped without explaining further. 'At least I still keep in contact with some of his aircraft buddies. They're good that way, call me up to make sure I'm doing okay.'

A pained silence descended, and finally Jack decided to press ahead with his tale from marriage to the present crisis. His listener nodded and said 'oh my' at the appropriate junctures, and by the time he'd finished the biscuit crumbs had disappeared into the darkness.

'How did you meet Carlotta?'

'Never did. All our communications were by e-mail.' He coughed to hide his embarrassment. 'I don't even know what she looked like.'

Rita Callard stared at Jack with the simple astonishment of someone confused and amazed at the speed and anonymity of the world around them.

'I'll get you a photo.' As she stood up her knees cracked.

Jack stretched and wandered further into the sunlight. The brightness irritated him and he scrunched up his eyes. The smell from the blooms, the quiet, the warmth, the flourish of butterflies all contrasted starkly with the cold and gloom of the Chicago morning he'd left. He recalled Danny lying on his back, mouth open and snoring. Beth being sick into a plastic bag. He suddenly felt ashamed, wondering what they were doing at that exact moment while he basked in West Coast weather.

Rita interrupted the guilt trip. The colour photograph was quite large, about twenty by twelve inches and inside an ornate gilt-edged frame. Glass-fronted.

'Taken three years ago.' Rita gazed at the snapshot fondly before averting her eyes, as if the pain was more than she could bear. 'Just after she received another doctorate. We were so proud of her. None of our other relations quite had brains like that girl.'

Smiling at the camera was a woman in her prime, an expression of confidence and achievement. I know who I am and where I'm going. Small features like her aunt. Blue eyes, dark lashes, high forehead, jet-black hair brushed to one side with long tresses over one shoulder. Petite, pug nose and wide, happy smile showing a row of perfect teeth. Even though a narrow chin almost spoiled the final result, Carlotta was pretty.

Jack handed the frame over and there was another delay while it found its rightful place indoors.

Seeing her late niece's picture again had obviously affected Rita Callard. When she returned her expression was fixed and determined. 'What I'd like to know is this. Was Carlotta's death an accident or not?' She looked at Jack, her blue eyes drilling into his. 'She was the youngest in her family. There's two other older boys, one's a teacher in LA.' She sniffed. 'Right now the other's probably drying out for the millionth time in some hospital north of here.' The voice waxed and waned, the flow often difficult to catch. 'I have no children of my own so she was my closest kin.' They were both on the back steps again, watching the irrigation spray dazzle in arcs of rainbows. 'I don't believe it was a hit and run.'

'How can you be so sure?' Jack asked. He brushed at a fly droning near his ear.

'Detective in the Sacramento PD suggested so. But I know they're not telling me everything. Probably afraid to admit their investigation's going nowhere. That's why I hired Tod Benson. Told him to keep up the pressure.'

Jack said, 'You told me Carlotta was acting peculiar. Do you know why?'

Rita struggled to her feet, and there was more creaking of joints. She went round the side of the house and out of view, then slowly the sprinkler's strength dropped to a trickle. When she returned she stretched one leg out in front of the other, then carefully lowered herself down on to the step.

'Can't hear a damn thing with the noise of that. Now where were we? Oh yes, why was Carlotta behaving so strange? She wouldn't tell me much. Just said she was sure somebody was following her. Even paid somebody to act as a decoy the day she drove down here.'

'Why didn't she tell the police?' asked Jack.

'I told her to. When she said she was coming with a truckload of cardboard boxes I wanted to know why. Didn't mind her visiting, always delighted to see her. But with twenty cartons? That didn't make sense.'

Nothing makes sense to me either, thought Jack. Those weeks of uncertainty and suspicion. Beth squinting out of the apartment window in the middle of the night, checking for a black Mercedes. Danny's attacker. Then the deliberate and provocative vandalising of the Volvo in broad daylight. That had even perplexed Officer Nelson at the Lincoln Park PD. *This sure is the strangest carry-on I've come up against in some time.* That's how he'd described the incidents. How, then, could Carlotta have explained her worries? She was struggling on her own. If I convinced myself I was overreacting, that my imagination was running wild, how could she have handled it any better?

'What'd she say?'

'Nothing. Warned me over and over not to mention to anyone what she'd hauled here.' Then Rita took Jack's left hand and squeezed it firmly. 'I should have gone to the police then.' He saw tears welling in the old woman's eyes. 'I wanted to, but she was so severe about keeping this tight. So I did what I was told.' She dabbed at her cheeks. 'Now she's dead.'

There was a strained, painful silence, then Rita jerked her thumb backwards.

'There must be something very important in those crates.'

*

She walked in front, still in tears, frail shoulders quivering. Down along the narrow hall and past the crooked pictures and the room with the cherrywood dining suite. Finally she stopped in front of the only closed door. 'It's all in there.' She turned the handle but the lock wouldn't budge. 'Sorry.' She looked up with a rueful smile. 'Left the key in a safe place.'

Jack stared at the white wooden door. Brass turn handle and gloss paint, it was standard domestic dwelling issue, and he could have knocked it down with a few strong shoves. But at that moment it seemed like a massive rock, ten tons of solid granite separating him from some unknown beast. As he waited for Rita to return with the key, the narrow passage seemed to squeeze in, the walls to crumple tight. He suddenly felt dizzy, almost frightened, and his heart pounded so strongly it rocked his frame. He wanted to run, escape into the sunlight and the garden's sounds and smells. Don't open that room, for Christ's sake. Let's forget whatever's there. It can't be good.

'Sorry to keep you. Hid the key somewhere so safe I couldn't remember where.' The lock clicked and the door was pushed open. 'I'll leave you to it. I'm going to shift the sprinkler round. I'll be outside in case you need me.'

30 *Thursday, 7 October, 5.20 p.m., Chicago*

'California? You told me you had men everywhere. How the fuck did he get to California?'

The Sheraton penthouse was buzzing, and Hend de Mart was looking less confident than usual. He stood with his back to a river-view window, its outside glass misting with drizzle. Gert Crozer paced the floor, to and fro, to and fro. A path was beginning to show on the thick-pile terracotta carpet.

'When he left the house in Chicago Lawn this morning he was tailed all the way to the highway,' said de Mart. 'He disappeared along there.' He patted a side pocket. 'We picked this up at three twenty, and I switched a crew to comb the parking lots at O'Hare.'

Crozer moved to a leather high-back behind the mahogany desk. He rested the palms of both hands on the top, his facial muscles bunching. His wire-framed glasses were fixed firmly on his nose.

'Play the tape.'

De Mart retrieved the cassette from a zip-lined pouch and inserted it into a recorder on the desk. Next he connected a lead to a small portable speaker. It was no bigger than a cigarette pack, plastic casing, fine mesh front. 'We have four devices planted, three on the eaves at the back and another outside their bedroom. This one gave the best sound quality.' He pressed a button, adjusted the volume.

When's daddy coming back?

'That's his kid.'

He said he'd be home early tomorrow afternoon.

De Mart cut in again. 'That's his wife.'

'I know these people,' Crozer snapped. 'Stop interrupting.' He turned his head so one ear was closer to the speaker.

He promised he'd bring us something nice from the seaside. But he told me not to let you stay up late just because he won't be around to tuck you in.

Ah mum.

No ah mums, thank you. Bedtime as usual.

I can't sleep on that rotten blow-up.

Shush, Danny, Helen might hear you. They've been very good to let us stay here until your dad sorts out this mess. I can't help it if all they've got is a camp cot. It'll have to do until we get something better.

There was static, then mumbling as the subjects changed position. The conversation was too unclear to be understood.

Where's he gone?

Some place called Monterey in California.

This time Beth's voice was sharp and distinct. There was no doubting the words. De Mart snapped the off button. 'That's the first reference.' He switched the tape on again.

Why did he have to go there anyway?

He's meeting someone who's going to help him get his job back.

Who?

Crozer nearly toppled over, so far forward did he strain to hear.

He didn't tell me.

Why not?

I don't know. Your dad doesn't tell me everything that goes on at work. I'll bet there are all sorts of secrets you have at school you never let me hear when you come home.

There are not.

The tape was stopped. 'There's a lot of mush with them arguing about the kid's school reports and things. Not worth listening to.' De Mart fast-forwarded, overshot, then rewound to the number he wanted.

This lady has something your dad's been looking for.

What sort of something?

I really don't know. Maybe some papers he might find interesting. You know what he's like. Boring patient files, stuff like that.

Crozer went pale. He removed his wire-frame glasses and massaged the bridge of his nose.

He went all the way to California to get a patient's file? The voice sounded incredulous.

Listen, Danny. Your dad is working hard to get his job back.

Someone did something bad and got him fired.

Ah mum, this is like out of the movies. Danny's voice had changed to total sarcasm.

Long pause.

I wanna go outside.

You can't. You know that, so stop pestering me.

I'm bored.

So am I, but I'm trying to make the best of it. I'll get you a book to read.

I don't want to read a lousy book. I wanna go outside and kick a ball.

Well you can't and that's that.

Pause.

Why do we have to stay in this lousy room?

So Helen and Spencer and the girls have space to themselves. It's their house.

Pause.

What's so special about this file thing anyway?

I don't know, Danny. He wouldn't tell me.

Why not? He tells you everything else, doesn't he?

Most things.

So why not this?

Another long pause.

Danny, dad's real worried that the people who lied about his hospital tests will want to stop him bringing these documents back.

Static, squeaking. Crozer's fingers edged towards the recorder, but a warning glance from de Mart restrained him.

You mean they might hurt him?

Movement and rustling sounds.

Danny, you've got to take this seriously. Real seriously. Whatever it is your dad has discovered is important. Very, very important.

Long pause. Lots of static and rustling. Noises of a door being opened and shut again. Humming. Moving about. Then sobbing.

When's he coming back?

Come here, give me a hug.

Rustling.

'I didn't want to frighten you. This isn't a game, Danny, it's for real. We have to stay here until dad gets in. Then everything will be okay and we can start to lead a normal life.

Stronger sobbing.

But when will he be home? You said he'd be back tomorrow. When tomorrow?

I'd say he'll be coming through that door around six o'clock tomorrow evening.

I'm gonna be sitting at the window waiting for him.

The spindle of the tape stopped. The two men looked at the tiny package as if it had a life of its own and would suddenly start up again. Finally, Crozer spoke.

'Who else knows of this?'

'Just us in this room. The squad who record pass everything to me immediately.'

There was another strained silence. Crozer now had his swivel chair turned towards the window and only his thinning grey hair could be seen from behind the high-backed chair.

De Mart had his head down, as if he was inspecting the quality of the matting.

'I feared this day would come.' When Crozer spoke again there was an air of resignation. The chair moved slightly, his head was bent. 'I wondered when and who would it be.' There was a dismissive wave of a hand. The Zurich director was in his own world. 'I had hoped never. Maybe it all would be lost, filed away in some dark store and no one would ever open the door.' The chair slowly turned through hundred and eighty degrees.

'We can still stop him.' De Mart sounded bullish. The Cyclint inauguration was just over twenty-four hours away. All their scheming, every devious and dangerous move that had been devised to protect that wonderful occasion was for nothing if Jack Hunt got through. 'We have an army in Chicago Lawn. The minute he shows up we get the files and he's finished.'

Crozer didn't respond immediately. He twisted his chair back and forth, head bowed and resting on clenched fists.

'Send every man you have to the airport.' He was now back in control, his head up, his voice firm and commanding. 'Find the car. When he arrives, take him and the files. Then bring both to me here.' A finger jabbed towards the floor. 'But keep him alive.' He spun the high-back, stood up and gazed out of the window. 'I need to speak to him before I kill him.'

31 *Thursday, 7 October*
3.10 p.m., Pacific Grove, California

There was no beast behind the door, no raging Minotaur waiting to devour him. Indeed, what first struck Jack was the ordinariness of the setting. He was expecting a hell, a darkened closet of murder and ruin, but what he discovered was a small and neglected room spilling over with tattered, worn and musty cardboard crates.

The area was about eighteen foot square with one grime-streaked window looking on to the carport. Outside, Rita Callard's aged Pontiac blocked any view. Faded striped curtains were pulled half across, reducing the natural light even further. The walls were painted but the colour now faded. When fresh it might have been described as sky blue, but now it was spoiled by flaking and cobwebs. A single light bulb with white plastic shade hung from the centre of the ceiling, across which spiders had spun an intricate mesh. There was no furniture, and the visible edges of a threadbare carpet were scuffed and torn. An overwhelming odour of dust and mould pervaded.

The cartons were stacked from wall to wall, some of the smaller ones resting on their larger neighbours. They dominated the room to such an extent that the door would not open fully and Jack had to ease one of the bigger crates out of the way to get past. They were different sizes and shapes and in different stages of decay and condition, most frayed at the corners, coverings partly open, the original packing now mildewed. They seemed to have been bundled and pushed inside in a hurry and in no obvious order.

He counted in the gloom. There were twenty of them, but their combined mass was much greater than he'd anticipated. He could certainly squash them into the Ford cargo van but there was no way the new Chevy waiting at O'Hare would have the capacity. He tested one for weight, tilting it slightly. About one hundred and twenty pounds. Another was rocked. Same weight approximately, but this time the outer casing flaked in his hands. He squinted through a tear and convinced himself he saw paper. Sheaves of paper. Is this what Carlotta drove so many miles to hide? What she gave up her life to protect? How the hell am I going to get it to Chicago?

First a time check: 3.15 p.m. local. He'd promised to telephone Beth as soon as he had a feel for whatever he might uncover. A quick glance around and he mentally readjusted the original projection upwards. This could take hours.

He decided on the nearest container for closer inspection. It was made of thick brown cardboard, about twenty inches deep and fifteen square. Red duct tape had been stretched around its corners and flaps as protection. Possibly for the move from Sacramento, Jack decided. Slowly and carefully he edged the crate outwards, end to end, side to side, until he had it in the hallway. Out there was the only place to work, the cluttered room too tight and gloomy.

The container was scored on the side with wide green felt-tip marking. CONDY: 1947–1953. Jack doubted there were felt-tip markers in 1953; also, the lettering looked reasonably fresh. More of Carlotta's work? Probably. The top was sealed with the same red tape, and Jack broke a nail trying to tease it free.

Rita Callard came to the rescue. 'Find anything interesting?' She poked around in a drawer, looking for a knife.

Jack smiled ruefully. 'Not yet. Haven't even opened the first box.'

The woman squinted up at him. 'Better get a move on then. There's nineteen more to search.' A small blade was produced. 'I'll make some sandwiches to keep you going.'

He ran the knife along the tape, careful not to bite too deep. The flaps came away easily, disturbing dust and paper scale. Inside he could see a collection of documents, some bound together by rubber bands, others held in thick bundles by strong wire clips. More mildew, more fungus smells. Gingerly, Jack lifted the top layer, about an inch thick. There was typed lettering on parchment-thin paper with yellow discoloration on the exposed margins. He squatted on his hunkers and separated each page, laying them on the floor. With the back of his hand he quickly checked for a draught from under the front door. Nothing significant enough to disturb. Standing up, he almost dislodged one of the family portraits hanging precariously off the wall.

There were seventeen sheets in all and Jack began reading from the nearest. On its top right-hand corner was a title, Condy Institute at the State of Texas, followed by an address in Austin. Date: 03/17/49. The text was blue carbon copy and a message from a Dr Schneider, basic and simple: 'I can confirm the funds were received today'. A bead of sweat dropped on to the page, immediately spreading outwards as if on blotting paper. Jack wiped his brow.

The next document in line was inspected, again another correspondence duplicate from Dr Schneider, this time dated 10/02/49.

Dear Dr Crozer,
The programme has been discussed in detail with the Board of Governors and they are in broad agreement with our protocols. I believe we should progress with some haste as it is only a matter of time before we are forced to look elsewhere.

What the hell is this all about? Jack moved to other pages. More communications from Schneider to Crozer. All 1949 and 1950. The same drift: 'move ahead', 'advance this current strategy'.

He sat with his back to the wall in a space wide enough to stretch his legs. From the far end of the corridor he could hear his host moving around in the kitchen, humming to herself. The fly screen on the back door slammed as she went into the garden. Rat-a-tat-tat; the sprinkler was doing its circle again and he wished he could be out in the sun, enjoying the rainbow spray, smelling the flowers. But at that moment he was surrounded by decay and neglect. And mystery. He returned to the task in hand.

There was now a smudged carbon copy dated 07/19/51:

Dear Dr Crozer,
I have been in discussion with the superior of a similar settlement in Colorado. He is a very pleasant gentleman who answers only to his official religious title, Brother Sebastian. I

found him helpful and cooperative, indeed enthusiastic about the proposition. He informed me he has two hundred and twenty-four in his charge. Would that be enough? I look forward to hearing from you.

Dr Rand Schneider.

'Coffee?' Rita Callard's face peeped round the corner.

'Yeah, that'd be great.'

Jack re-read the letter, then set it aside. He delved into the carton and lifted out bundles of material. Old and outsized strong buff paper envelopes with paper records inside, each with a name in capitals on the front. In between tuna sandwiches and sips from a mug of strong brew, Jack counted eighty-nine separate folders. Names in the same handwriting, but there were numerals in different ink and script scrawled underneath.

Emilio W; 286. Anita R; 124. Samuel E; 143. Ricardo W; 181. Vladimir Z; 208. Marella R; 214. Jiuseppe N; 229.

Christian names, no surnames, Jack concluded. The numbers didn't make immediate sense. There was no sequence or pattern.

He opened one envelope, selected randomly, its gum unsticking easily. Inside were more yellowing pages, held together by old and rusting paper clips. Everything related to one person: Constantia B; 132. Date of birth: 10/02/36. Country of origin: Mexico. There was little more personal detail on Constantia B from Mexico, and Jack couldn't help wondering where she was now. By his calculation she should be sixty-three years old.

Then something caught his attention. It was the first indication of medical interest and he took the sheets outside to better light.

Rita Callard sat at her kitchen table, smoking and humming quietly. She looked up when he walked past. 'Find something?'

The only response was a dismissive wave of a hand. The doctor was deeply engrossed.

By six o'clock Jack had all the cartons open and laid side by side along the full length of the hallway. The family photographs had been cleared from the walls and only their grimy outlines remained. He'd turned the cases with a demarcated face towards the front. Not all had the green felt tip marking he'd seen on number one, so with a legal pad and pen borrowed from his host he scrawled his own IDs. Selected paperwork from each was set on the floor. He walked up and down, inspecting, double-checking.

He was beginning to get a feel for the content.

Rita Callard interrupted half an hour later, intrigued by the frenzied activity in her own home. 'Any luck?'

Jack nodded, his mind not really focused on the question. He paced the narrow passage, forcing Rita backwards as he squeezed past.

'Well, have you found anything?' she pressed, noticing for the first time the blank spaces on the walls. Her gaze finally centred on a collection of frames propped against the front door.

Jack stopped and turned. His tee-shirt was stained with sweat and dirt, his jet-black hair sticking out in all directions. That morning's poor shaving was beginning to show through as uneven shadowing. 'I'm getting there,' he offered. 'I'm definitely getting there.' He reached into yet another carton, this time producing folders of correspondence. 'It's all here. I'm just trying to get it in order.'

Rita shrugged. Her visitor was looking more and more like an escaped convict, his behaviour bizarre and edgy. 'Take a break, doc. You've been stuck at this for hours. I'll pull together something to eat.'

Jack barely acknowledged her. 'That'll be great,' he muttered.

Some more copy caught his attention, this one dated 11/30/59. The letterhead was gold embossed, a street address in Zurich, Switzerland.

Dear Dr Schneider,

Extra funds have been lodged to our account. I can arrange a wire transfer from New York should the need arise.

It might be prudent to increase remunerations immediately as this stage is close to completion.

We are very aware of the difficulties you raised at our last meeting and the company is anxious they should not become a problem. We trust your judgement in dealing with local issues; it is impossible for us to be as certain from this distance.

With the extra funding and an earlier target date I still feel confident of a successful conclusion.

I will be in New York at the beginning of February next. I

think we should meet then to resolve any remaining issues.

The weather here is bitterly cold. It has been snowing intermittently since the first of the month and many roads are blocked. I have not gone beyond my street in ten days except for essential stores. Construction at the Winterthur development has been delayed and I believe we are as much as two months behind schedule.

Consider yourself lucky in that warmer climate.

My very best wishes,

Helmut Crozer.

They dined in the kitchen on teamster-size portions of barbecue ribs and coleslaw washed down with iced water. Rita talked at length about her late husband, Richard. The work he'd done, the long hours he'd kept, the warning signs he'd ignored. 'Then wham, middle of the night he wakes up shouting about a headache. Sits upright, moaning and rocking from side to side. Minute later he just gives a grunt and goes. Local doctor was called but it was too late. Told me later it was a massive brain haemorrhage. Warned me Rick hadn't been keeping to his check-ups, wasn't taking his blood pressure tablets.'

There was a long pause and both just stared at their plates, each trying not to resurrect more pain. In the end Rita flicked on a small portable television perched in a corner and they let their eyes drift to it while the food disappeared.

'Damn me,' she suddenly complained, 'but that ad has been running on prime time for days.'

Jack turned his chair to look, careful to keep his sticky fingers away from Spencer's tee-shirt. On the screen two men were walking along a tree-lined road, deep in conversation. One was much older than the other: grey hair, wrinkled features, bifocals. He was smiling. The younger of the two was slightly taller and leaner, a good head of dark hair, strong face. It was a sunlit setting with shades of dappled green from nearby trees. In the background the gentle strains of a violin solo. Both stopped at a four-bar gate and leaned against it, staring into the distance. Cut to a lush green grassland stretching as far as the lens would allow. Then close-up of both faces.

A mature, mellow male voice spoke. 'Sixty-six-year-old Ben Travers had a heart attack last September. Thankfully he survived, and today his doctors believe he's doing fine. But Ben's still worried. Was that just the first strike, or is there another waiting round the corner?'

The two men glanced briefly at one another. They seemed contented, happy. Maybe even relieved. Both moved back along the road, heads bobbing together.

'Now Ben's doctors have prescribed Cyclint, a recently developed heart-attack preventer.'

Cut to the older man taking stronger strides than his younger companion. He outpaces him by a visible yard.

'With Cyclint, Ben Travers has a renewed strength and confidence in the future.'

Cut to the older man closing in on presumed extended family: wife, grown-up children and grandchildren, waiting in a group. There was a sudden burst of sunlight with an accompanying crescendo of violins.

'Heart-attack preventer Cyclint is now available on prescription. Cyclint is a product of the Swiss corporation Zemdon Pharmaceuticals, world leaders in ethical healthcare.'

Angry bile filled Jack's gut. World leaders in ethical healthcare? No, that should read world leaders in fraud and cheating. International specialists at destroying lives and reputations. Global thugs.

'Ever been to Switzerland?' Rita Callard asked casually.

Jack's mind re-focused. 'No.'

'Carlotta went there last year.'

He looked across. 'What for?'

'Can't honestly say. Seemed strange too. She was a girl who thought New York was as far away as the moon. And only stayed three days.' She stood up slowly, limbs creaking from the effort, then ran a hand along a shelf cluttered with mugs and glasses. Finally she retrieved a picture postcard. 'Zurich. That's the place.' The card was wiped clean, then passed across.

The front photograph was of small boats on a wide river with distant tall and narrow church spires. The city of Zurich from Utoquai, it was captioned. On the other side three sentences were scribbled. 'I came. I saw. And I found what I was looking for.'

'Damned if I understand what it means.'

Jack stared at the picture, fingers trembling with excitement.

'Rita,' he said finally. 'I saw a typewriter in that room where you keep old books, magazines and newspapers. Does it still work?'

'Sure does. I use it myself from time to time. Want me to do something?'

'Yeah, about three or four sheets.' He looked at the card again. 'First I've got a call to make.' He stood up and wiped his hands quickly. 'Then you and I have a lot of work to do.'

32 *Thursday, 7 October, 8.10 p.m., Chicago*

'We've got him.'

In the penthouse suite of the Sheraton Chicago Hotel and Towers Hend de Mart was gloating. No longer the taut and anxious face, now he was back in his confident henchman mode.

'We found his car at O'Hare. I've got four waiting for further orders. If he turns up they've been told to hold him.'

Sitting in his by now favourite leather high-back, Gert Crozer listened impassively. He had changed again, this time into a charcoal double-breast, white shirt and corporation necktie. He closed his eyes, brow now furrowed with intense concentration.

'And we tracked the rental at Monterey. According to our source Hunt has already telephoned to say he'll leave the truck in the return parking lot at Monterey airport early tomorrow morning. I'm told it's a small block, he'll be easy to pick out.'

Crozer suddenly came to attention. 'A truck?'

'A truck or a van, something like that. Big enough to carry boxes, that's what he asked for.'

Crozer stood up and slowly walked around the penthouse, deep in thought. He stopped to inspect an oil painting, then fiddled with a beer mat at the cocktail counter. Finally, he returned to the leather high-back and turned it towards the picture window. Not a word was spoken.

Five levels below, the hotel was buzzing with excitement. Preparations for the international conference allowed for two thousand five hundred guests maximum and invitation returns suggested little shortfall in that quota. Many superdocs and health journalists, medical magazine editors and media correspondents had already settled into their complimentary suites or river-view rooms and were exploring the inner recesses of the mini-bars. This was not the time to skimp on self-indulgence.

The main auditorium on the second level was being decorated with flowers while bunting in the corporation colours of red and green draped support columns and mountings. Ribbons in the same shades were threaded into floral bouquets and positioned in the middle of each dining table. At the front of the hall three giant screens were slowly being assembled while TV and audio techs arranged their equipment, checking angles and lighting and acoustics. From the podium a single microphone cable had been fed to strategically sited loudspeakers. At this focal point, carefully worded and rehearsed queries would be directed at Dr Harry Chan. They would be posed by nominated delegates in the hall and from distant centres via satellite link. The acting professor of cardiology would field them with much assurance and confidence. He knew the questions, and he certainly knew the answers. At that moment he waited impatiently in a private dining room for an important evening in the company of his hosts and selected VIPs. His wife, the redecoration and furniture removal freak, had been commanded to stay at home and study wallpaper catalogues. This was a man's event.

Along corridors and walkways Zemdon staff and senior hotel personnel huddled together discussing final business. The pre-dinner drinks, the menu, the wine list, the after-dinner brandies and champagne. How many serving crews would there be? What was their dress code? Were they regulars or contract casuals? Had they been briefed on the running order? Timing was vital to ensure exact connections with other events being staged nationally and internationally.

Tension filled the air like the crackle of an approaching electrical storm.

And not everything was going to plan. The story of Jack Hunt's challenge to the Carter testing procedures still dominated local news reports. Especially since Caleb Rossi, the biochemistry assistant who'd processed the samples, still hadn't surfaced to answer questions. Throughout the hospital people were reviewing their first judgements on the affair, rumours abounding in every division. One story claimed Jack was innocent and had been set up by begrudgers sore at being ignored when the professor's job came up for grabs. Another had it that the Irishman was as guilty as hell, that Rossi was his supplier and was in hiding in case the police investigation closed in on bigger fish. Nat Parker, the one colleague Jack trusted, had written an open letter to administration demanding an inquiry into the circumstances surrounding the dismissal. It was printed in full in the late edition of the *Chicago Tribune*.

There was now a feeding frenzy on to interview Jack, even his wife or son. But the family had gone to ground and Herb Weinberg wasn't giving anything away. 'My client will make a statement soon,' he'd announced to an impromptu gathering of journalists and camera crews outside his office in Wilmette. The lawyer basked in the publicity, convinced he had a massive law suit in the making. All interviews were held outside the facility with its Weinberg & Associates inscription prominent in the background. Herb had even gone on a crash diet in a desperate attempt to improve his TV image. It was one he'd read about in a law magazine, an Israeli army fast of grapefruit and boiled rice. It was working; he'd already lost five pounds. But it played hell with press conferences, his stomach rumbling during lulls in questioning.

'Dr Hunt is due to take possession of a fine property in this neighbourhood tomorrow. I am advised he will turn up and collect the keys as arranged. At that point he will answer all queries and explain why he has had to keep such a low profile.'

Herb was expecting to appear on most of the major local networks that evening. He also expected his law firm to be besieged by reporters the next day. Any more exposure and he'd really have to take on an associate.

Crozer was staring out of the large picture window overlooking the Chicago river. Outside, the evening gloom was deepening, the waters glinting with reflections from nearby skyscrapers. Cruise boats bobbed on choppy waves, guide ropes bouncing off their moorings. Directly across the wet divide was the Hyatt Regency on E Wacker, another monster convention hotel. There, on 14 June, a certain assassin had set out to complete a task that was still unaccomplished one hundred and fifteen days later. Had he known, he could have seen the light glowing from the exact room on the twenty-eighth floor where his hired killer had sat and planned her moves.

'I'm getting a lot of flak from Stan Danker.' De Mart was now sitting in an armchair close to the penthouse entrance.

'What do you mean?'

'He wants me in New York. Says my job's finished here, well done, but now it's time to quit. I think it's a deliberate ploy. He's asking a lot of sharp questions.'

Crozer continued to admire the enveloping nightfall. His head rocked gently from side to side, hands clasped behind his back.

'You must remain until I say your work is completed. Herr Danker's mission is the successful launch of Cyclint, and that is assured. Let him concentrate on what he does best. I have a different and more important task to finish.'

De Mart shrugged. 'What'll I tell him?'

There was short pause. 'Say I'm worried about Dr Chan, that he seems a little edgy and fractious. Say I want you to shadow him until after the inauguration.'

The South African smiled. 'That's good. Chan *is* getting nervous. He's complaining no one is paying him enough attention, that the media are still too focused on Jack Hunt. The man's looking for respect and isn't getting any.'

There was a grunt of contempt. 'He's got half a million US dollars' worth of respect in an account in Berne. Scum like him wouldn't know the difference between respect and loathing.'

There was another silence as Crozer moved from one end of the plate glass to the other.

'Where is Hunt's family?'

De Mart looked up. 'Still in the bungalow.'

'How many are keeping watch?'

'Three. And firepower.'

Crozer moved to a different view, this time overlooking a riverside path now lit up with tall lanterns. A group of joggers were struggling to fight their way through the gusts coming off Lake Michigan.

'Use them as collateral. If Hunt is not apprehended then take his wife and child.'

De Mart frowned slightly. 'Okay.' This was getting dirtier.

Crozer turned around. 'They are our bargaining tools. If the Irishman wants them to stay alive he'll hand over the files. Without the proof, any accusations are baseless.'

The Zemdon director spun the leather high-back and sat down in it, swivelling from side to side. He inspected his nails, adjusted his tie then slipped his wire-framed glasses on to his nose.

'I think you should go to California and relieve Dr Hunt of the files there.' He was squinting over the lenses. 'It might be safer.'

33 *Thursday, 7 October, 11.15 p.m., Monterey, California*

Hend de Mart passed through arrivals into darkness at the relatively small Monterey Peninsula Airport. The night sky was black with a backdrop of stars like tiny diamonds; a greeting committee of three men just as dark in their intentions awaited. One was called Silvo, an Eddie Murphy lookalike without the stupid grin, ebony skin with tight curls and thick lips. He sniffed a lot, claiming he was sensitive to smells. The other two were white: Vick was tall, lean with small eyes, a pointed nose and hair dyed bright red; Macky was small and squat with a crew-cut and squashed face.

Each had been promised a double bonus if they apprehended Jack Hunt *and* secured the documents in his possession. De Mart changed the deal immediately on arrival. From that moment their bounty applied to collecting the paperwork only. He had quietly decided to take out the Irishman himself. On the flight over he'd concluded that too much had been left to chance already, that they'd underestimated the cardiologist. Luck might have been on his side when the Denver killer targeted the wrong room and shot Sam Lewins, but since then everything they'd plotted had backfired and he was no longer prepared to consider last-minute foul-ups. Not with the massive worldwide launch of Cyclint only hours away. While he still wasn't sure why exactly Jack Hunt posed such a threat, the South African was convinced his dream retirement was on the line.

Before touchdown he'd replayed the latest tape of a telephone conversation recorded earlier that evening at Chicago Lawn.

I've got it Beth. Everything. It's all here.'

Oh thank God, I've been so worried. Will it clear your name?

It's not about clearing my name any more. These documents are dynamite. When this gets out it will rock the medical establishment.

I don't give a damn about the medical establishment. I only care about us. You and me and Danny and our unborn child. To hell with the rest. I want my life back.

That's in the bag, Beth. But now I know what's been going on all these months. Why Danny was beaten up, the apartment watched, and why I was sacked from the Carter. Carlotta Drunker didn't die in a hit-and-run accident, she was murdered. And I know who did it.

There was a strained pause before the woman's voice came back.

I don't like what I'm hearing.

De Mart had asked that his preferred handgun, a .38 calibre revolver, be made available. This was now inspected, tested on an empty chamber, then loaded. Then the group melted into the shadows.

11.37 p.m. Pacific Grove

'Is that you Herb? Jeez, I'm sorry to wake you, but I need advice.'

Jack Hunt sat at the kitchen table of 104 Kenton Avenue, phone in hand. Opposite was Rita Callard, her small frame slumped as if in pain, a tear-stained handkerchief bunched into the fist of one hand. Her eyes were red from tiredness and emotion. She too now knew every detail uncovered in the boxes spread the full length of her hallway. And she also knew that her lovely and intelligent niece had been murdered.

It was coming up to two in the morning in Chicago and at the other end of the line Jack could hear nothing but muffled curses. Nonetheless, he blurted out the bare bones of the story.

'This is worse than you'd suggested.' Weinberg sounded sufficiently awake now.

Jack went on. 'It's more than just me being dumped from the Carter, it's everything else I was worrying about too. Carlotta Drunker, another death in Colorado. The attacks on my family. For all I know there could be a lot more.'

'That's enough to be going on with, professor.' From the comfort and warmth of his bed on a wet and cold Midwest morning,

Herb was obviously struggling to keep up with the revelations.

'I'm bringing these documents back. This is my proof. I've got letters and signatures on original notepaper with exact addresses. Dates, numbers, names. Bank drafts, account ledgers.' Deep breath. 'There's so much it's almost difficult to believe. What'll I do, Herb? Come on, you're my lawyer. Help me out on this one.'

0.27 a.m., Pacific Grove

'Ready?'

Rita Callard stood at one end of the hall, clipboard and pen in hand, fired up with excitement. All the lights in the house were blazing, the passageway floodlit by a portable halogen at the end of a long cable. The front door had been edged open to allow a cool breeze to circulate.

'Sure am. Go for it.'

Jack squeezed along the space left between cardboard and walls. He was soaked in sweat, his tee-shirt now soiled almost beyond recovery. He'd run his hand through his hair so often it was sticking up crazily despite his best efforts to force it back into shape. His eyes were red-rimmed and bloodshot, his stubble itching. He was a driven man, restless, fidgety and impatient.

'Box number one,' he called out.

A finger pointed, and Rita Callard scribbled on a legal pad, tore off the page and stuck it down where directed.

'Box number two.'

Another sheet was shoved into place.

'Box number three.'

Twenty minutes passed.

'Important documents,' Jack shouted.

Rita had duct tape at the ready.

'I've packed them into six of the smaller containers.' With his right foot Jack nudged at a stack of crates laid one on top of the other. 'Seal those carefully.'

1.03 a.m.

'I'm going to miss you. I can't remember the last time there was so much excitement in this house. Things'll be real quiet when you're gone.'

The conspirators were back at the kitchen table, supping strong coffee and nibbling on heated-up pizza slices. Rita was so hunched with tiredness her frame seemed almost to have collapsed.

Jack grinned. He was now at ease, relaxed even. His legs were stretched out, he leaned back in his chair. 'I can't say this is my usual line of business. Being a doctor might be a real bore when this is over.'

The woman's eyes narrowed. 'It's not over yet, son. Not until those containers are in Chicago.' She leaned on the table and eased herself up. 'There's still that airplane journey.'

Jack yawned, then stretched. 'That I can handle. No one knows where I am.'

34 *Friday, 8 October, 6.37 a.m.*

Hend de Mart sat in the passenger seat of an open-top black VW Golf with khaki trim at the rental return lot of Monterey Peninsula Airport. The main passenger terminus was separated from the car parks by a two-lane road, one side strip for 'kiss and go' departures, then an exit with separate tracks to long- and short-term stays. The hire-car recovery allotment was sited at the end, near the outlet to Olmsted. The South African had positioned his crew so that no vehicle could discharge its load without being seen.

That morning he was in denim jeans, his large frame barely contained inside a blue on yellow striped short-sleeved shirt. Adam's apple bobbing furiously. The swept-back bleached-blond hair contrasted starkly with Silvo, sitting beside him. Silvo wore grey shorts and tee-shirt with shades as thick as the bottom of a Coca-Cola bottle. Both had handguns primed and ready, de Mart with his .38 revolver and Silvo with his preferred piece, a Glock 17. Chambered in 9mm, this was capable of five shot groups inside a two-and-a-half-inch circle at a range of twenty-five yards. He took few unnecessary chances in his line of work. His ebony fingers drummed against the VW dash, eyes checking out all pedestrian and vehicular traffic.

The other two in the squad, the tall Vick and the smaller Macky, waited nearer the entrance. Equally well prepared, they slouched in a stolen Jeep with false Nevada plates.

Resting at de Mart's feet was a fire-resistant pouch containing twenty pounds of top-grade cocaine. The plan was simple. As soon as their target was identified he would be bundled into the rear of his van and driven to a remote dirt track off Highway 68. There the vital files would be transferred while Jack was forced to snort as much white powder as they reckoned he could endure under the circumstances. Finally, de Mart would drive the rental at top speed into a tree, bailing out well before impact. The idea was to make the crash look like suicide, and to confuse forensic investigators the pack of cocaine would be left at the dead man's feet and the van torched.

'Ah love the smell of gasoline.' Silvo flared his nostrils as beyond the terminal buildings a jet revved its engines. 'Ah just love the smell of gasoline.' He spoke slowly, rolling the words along his tongue as if he was savouring a fine wine.

The rental return lot was deserted apart from a few Hertz and Thrifty and a single Avis Chrysler hatchback skewed awkwardly beside a luxury limo hire-out. In the adjoining long-term parking block spaces were filling quickly. Passengers pushing trolleys laden with baggage or carrying just single briefcases hurried to the departure end of the terminal. Recent arrivals coming in the opposite direction ambled leisurely, soaking up the early-morning glow and its promise of a fine day ahead. Sunrise was officially at 5.55, and the airport was flooding with yellow light, temperatures climbing towards a projected mid-afternoon high of seventy-five.

The previous night Rick's Rent A Miser valet, rudely rousted out of his bed, had provided much useful information. For one hundred dollars he'd confirmed that a man answering Jack's description had hired one of their wrecks. For another fifty the acne-scarred youth had offered the exact make, model and colour. He'd even owned up about the poor resprays, bad tyres and worn brake pads.

'Man told me he was going to Pacific Grove, but didn't say where.'

Silvo's crew had cruised much of Pacific Grove through the night, then given up. Their target still had to return the van, they'd nail him then. For another fifty dollars the valet had promised to pass on any calls his customer might make to change plans. All in all it had been a good night for the kid.

A DHL jet with the maroon-coloured logo on its tail fin took off, soaring northwards at a thirty-degree angle, its exhaust trailing in the air. De Mart watched as it banked about one mile out, then veered to the east, sunlight glinting off its cabin windows. He looked at his watch. It was five minutes after seven.

'You got the time right?'

Silvo had his eyes closed, head tilted upwards, sniffing the fading aircraft fumes, an expression of intense pleasure all over his face. 'Flight out through LA leaves at eight fifteen. Latest check-in is one hour before.' His eyes were still shut tight, nostrils twitching as he searched for the merest hint of gasoline. 'If this guy has a load of cargo he can't suddenly rush in at the last minute. Relax man, he's gonna turn up.'

The passenger list with Jack's return reservation to Chicago via Los Angeles had been bought for five hundred dollars.

7.10 a.m.

Against the blue skies a Boeing 757-200 of United Airlines drifted into view from the south and slowly circled the airspace, its engines screeching as it passed overhead. Ten minutes later it began its descent, giant wings tilting slightly as it closed in on the final approach.

Silvo started sniffing. 'Ah love the smell of gasoline.'

'Shut the fuck up, will you?' De Mart's head was pounding and he felt a migraine bursting through. He fumbled in his pocket for Imigran and inhaled the spray deeply.

Silvo scowled at de Mart's rebuke, then craned his neck as a Budget Mitsubishi rental pulled in close by. A middle-aged man and two young girls jumped out, followed by an equally middle-aged but harassed-looking woman. He was tall and skinny and dressed in a ridiculous floral shirt that hung out at the waist. She was small and dumpy in outsize sweats, and immediately started yelling at the kids, who stood meekly by their father's side as he unloaded the boot. Still arguing, the unhappy family made their way to the terminal.

7.25 a.m.

De Mart was becoming agitated. This was the eighth day of October, D-day in the Zemdon calendar of events. At eight o'clock that evening in Chicago, Cyclint would be officially launched to the world. The grand banquet would begin at seven exactly, proceeding at some pace for sixty minutes, then all attention would focus on a diminutive cardiologist called Harry Chan. Satellite links would immediately connect the Sheraton to similar coast-to-coast events. Dr Chan would open with some well-rehearsed introductory lines about the company and its new product. Then he would wax eloquent about the drug and its benefits to all mankind. By midnight it would all be over, Zemdon's survival assured and the South African's retirement idyll in Cape Town secure at last. And he would be a very wealthy man. When the US dollars were converted to South African rand he could live off the interest alone for many years.

The warmth of the morning reminded de Mart of his homeland. It was time to move on and start a new life. Tomorrow he would finalise his contract, say his goodbyes and leave. It was all coming together.

But where is that bastard Hunt? His flight's due out in fifty minutes.

7.35 a.m.

The Graham Airstrip was three miles from Monterey Peninsula Airport, off Highway 1 where it merges with 68 near the community hospital. It was a flight-enthusiast patch named after a retired American Airlines pilot called Bill Graham who just couldn't keep out of the skies and wouldn't pay the ground fees at the main aerodrome.

It was basic, but safe. In the middle of three acres of scrub and parched earth was a single tarmac on concrete runway, five thousand feet long and seventy-five feet wide, with landing lights. A narrow strip of track connected it with vehicle parking and a separate taxiway led to a light aircraft apron. Set well back from the taxi lane, and flapping weakly from a tall pole, was an orange wind sock. Cylindrical Avgas tanks, coloured in red against white squares, were sited about five hundred yards from the control tower. The main building, white with fading blue ID, was little more than the size of an average dwelling with an upper-level tinted glass tower offering three hundred and sixty degrees of unimpeded view. There was a chain-link perimeter fence to prevent small-animal incursions and automatic scatterguns to scare birds. The area was entered through double gates that could be bolted and locked. At that moment they were wide open, two large rocks holding them from swinging closed.

That morning there were four planes on the ground: a Piper Cherokee, two Cessna 172s and a single Cessna 340. There were also three vehicles parked at the end of the track, and one was a white '84 Ford 250 cargo van. Jack sat at its steering wheel. Behind him, and laid out in careful rows, were ten cardboard boxes, all secured with layers of tape. Some of the cartons were cut-offs from those that had been strung along Rita Callard's hallway the night before, the remainder taken from her garden potting shed, old plants and plastic containers dumped to prepare them for their new role.

From an open-topped MG roadster import clambered a bronzed, lean man wearing a tan leather flying jacket. On his left lapel was a tiny silver aeroplane badge. He reached out and grasped Jack's offered hand.

'Hi, I'm Jack Hunt. Thanks for helping me out.'

'Pat Maguire. Mrs Callard speaks very highly of you.'

Maguire looked about forty with bushy moustache and receding hairline. Lilting voice, freckled face, wide grin and inquisitive dark eyes. He was close enough to the height of his new partner as made no difference. Maybe an inch above six feet. Beneath the jacket he wore an open-necked denim shirt over black corduroy pants. He carried a bulky canvas flight bag with wings-on-cap logo imprinted on the flap. It spilled over with paperwork.

'I have to fax a flight plan before we load up. Want to come with me?'

They walked side by side, making small talk. Maguire was the son of one of Rita Callard's oldest buddies and a full-time pilot with United Airlines. He also owned a half share in a Cessna 340 and on occasional rest days he would earn a little on the side to help with the plane's running costs. He'd been hauled to the phone the night before and had spent twenty minutes listening while his father's friend offered him the bare bones of her needs. Without giving much away, Rita had explained how a visitor who was near and dear needed to transfer cargo to Chicago urgently.

'Why not FedEx or UPS?' he'd asked, not unreasonably.

The answer didn't make much sense, but as the conversation flowed Maguire realised he had a chance of making over five thousand dollars for a one-off trip which would help nicely with fuel, mechanical repairs and general maintenance. And he had the hots for a girl who worked at O'Hare. Could be an interesting trip.

The terminus waiting room was fifty foot square with low ceiling, pool table, television and dartboard. The nearby coastline was notorious for summer fog and plastic chairs cluttered around a stained wooden desk on which lay the detritus of previous wasted hours waiting for weather to clear. Empty Coke cans, snack wrappers and cigarette packs lay where they'd been dumped. The only technology was a fax machine in one corner.

That day the control tower was being manned by a part-time member of the aeroclub and Maguire communicated with him over an intercom, advising of his proposed take-off.

'We'll need three refuelling stops.' He scanned a map. 'I'd say Las Vegas' – a ruler splayed across a map of North America – 'then Denver.' More careful scrutiny. 'Probably Des Moines in Iowa before the last hop.'

7.48 a.m.

De Mart was losing his cool. He stalked the Monterey Peninsula rental and long-term parking lots, searching anxiously for a white Ford cargo van. Every car or jeep or convertible that pulled up was inspected with a venomous stare. Many of their passengers averted their eyes, uncomfortable with the intense scrutiny.

Even Silvo's earlier confidence was fast waning. He sat up on the rear seats looking into the near distance. On the floor rested his Glock 17, and he was so worked up he was itching to use it. There were vehicles coming in and out but nothing that matched the description and plates of Jack's rental.

7.52 a.m.

'Hi there. My name's Jack Hunt and I rented a white Ford cargo van yesterday.'

At Rick's Rent A Miser offices, the pimply-faced valet almost dropped the phone. 'Sure did. Thought ya would have dropped it at the airport by now.'

Jack thought the kid's voice sounded unusually animated.

Surprised maybe. 'I've had to change my arrangements.'

'Can't do that, Mr Hunt.' Almost pleading. 'Ya gotta leave that Ford at the rental lot.'

'Sorry. I'm going to stick the keys and a hundred-dollar bill under the front seat. I apologise for the inconvenience and I know Rick will be sore about this but it's the best I can do. Something cropped up at the last minute.'

The kid was now screaming into the phone. 'Ya can't fuckin' do that, ya can't!'

'I've just done it,' Jack snapped back. 'Now, do you want to know where I am? You'll need directions.'

'Hold on, hold on for fuck's sake. I gotta get a pen.'

7.55 a.m.

The Cessna 340 was twin-engine, white with blue trim and about one tenth the size of a commercial jet. Its capacity allowed for pilot and co-pilot with a passenger complement of four at a squeeze, accessed via a small retractable door in the middle of the hull. There was an ID marking, N125CJ, on the fuselage and underneath both wings. Apart from a few paint scratches and bodywork dimples the craft was in perfect condition.

As Pat Maguire walked around the plane completing his pre-flight inspection, the top of his head reached as high as the bottom edge of the cockpit windows. Tyres were kicked, tread examined. Water condensation was drained from the fuel tanks and oil levels measured with a dipstick. Finally satisfied everything was in good condition, he turned his attention to Jack Hunt's precious cargo. By now the sun was throwing long shadows along the ground and lifting temperatures to the mid-sixties. It was becoming humid.

'Two each in the wing lockers' – he was deciding how best to spread the load – 'then another two in the nose locker. The rest should fit easily inside.'

Jack started shifting cardboard. He felt good.

Earlier that morning, while he'd slept fitfully on a spare bed in 104 Kenton Avenue, Rita Callard had washed, dried and pressed his clothes. Tee-shirt, denims, socks had all been given the treatment and his attire was now back to its pristine state. Then she'd insisted he shower and shave while she rustled up some breakfast. A quick telephone call to Chicago Lawn had confirmed that Beth and Danny were well. He hadn't been able to bring himself to confess he'd spent everyone's air fare to Sydney – those explanations would have to come later. However, Helen had passed on interesting news. Harry Chan was out in the open with his ambitious plans to endorse the Cyclint release that evening at eight sharp, after a sumptuous meal in the main auditorium at the Sheraton Chicago Hotel and Towers.

7.57 a.m.

Hend de Mart could barely contain his anger. The kid from the rental offices had just made contact and babbled Jack's new arrangements. Even called the street and highway directions as he'd taken them down. Silvo gunned the VW engine and soon the car screeched out of the rental lot and along the main exit roadway. Following close behind in their stolen Jeep, Vick and Macky stared grimly ahead. Their bonuses were at risk.

8.13 a.m.

'Wait here and I'll top up the fuel tanks.'

Jack mooched around the light aircraft apron, shielding his eyes from the strong sunlight. To the north a few fluffy clouds drifted lazily against a brilliant blue background. Otherwise the skies were empty, apart from approaching or departing jets at the main airport three miles to the east. So Harry Chan is in this up to his neck, as I suspected. Mouthpiece for the Zemdon Corporation.

He suddenly looked over his shoulder. About half a mile away on a motorway horns were blaring. As he squinted he could just about make out someone leaning over a concrete division wall, apparently staring in his direction. Whoever it was then disappeared from view.

Beth and Danny are safe, that's a relief. No one has sussed out where we've gone to ground. He mentally calculated his financial status. Almost stony broke, the five-thousand-dollar airline charter draining the last of his reserves. Now none of us can flee if this goes horribly wrong. He counted out the grubby notes still stuffed in his pockets. One hundred and twenty-two dollars plus small change, the sum total of all his worldly goods.

The date square on his watch suddenly caught his eye: Friday, 8 October, the day he and Beth were supposed to take possession of their dream house in Wilmette. Here I am stuck in California when I should be at Herb Weinberg's offices, finalising paperwork, collecting keys. Jesus, what a hopeless mess.

8.20 a.m.

By de Mart's reckoning they were less than fifteen minutes from the airfield. Rush-hour traffic meant bumper-to-bumper tailbacks and short-fuse tempers. The VW Golf switched lanes and weaved across Highway 1 so erratically that many drivers had to slam on their brakes and swerve to avoid a collision. Angry fists were waved and horns were sounded.

8.25 a.m.

'Control, this is November one two five Charlie Juliet. Request taxi clearance.'

Maguire sat to the left in the Cessna's cockpit, headset on, with one hand gripping the control column while the other teased the throttle beside his right knee. The front was tight with just enough leg room, well-worn leather high-backed seats, windscreen shaped like a hornet's eye. There were rows of instrumentation on the dash; pressure and temperature gauges, altimeter, fuel and oil indicators, transponder, magnetic compass. Dials, switches, lights and buttons. Beside him, Jack listened to the crackling exchanges through his own headset.

'It's gonna feel uncomfortably warm in here for a few minutes,' warned Maguire as he checked the cabin pressure. For a split second he frowned slightly, then looked relieved as the relevant dial adjusted to normal. 'When the engines get going for a while it'll cool down.'

There was no other activity on the small airfield. Two cars and a van beside a lifeless main building, the other light craft resting silently in their allotted parking spots. Through the tinted glass of the control tower a shadowy figure could be seen moving.

'November one two five Charlie Juliet, you are clear to taxi at pilot's discretion. Runway open, QNH one zero three zero, wind is westerly at ten knots, CAV okay.'

Maguire acknowledged. 'Roger, one zero three zero Charlie Juliet.'

The engines were started and they kicked in, first the left propeller slowly spinning before gaining power, then the right. The pilot's head moved constantly as he checked everything within his visual field. There was a slight jolt as the plane inched forward.

8.30 a.m.

De Mart and Silvo had reached the perimeter gates, their wheels scorching the track and throwing up grit and dirt. Behind them their accomplices dodged the Jeep side to side to avoid the dust storm in front. They were now less than a thousand yards away from the Cessna.

8.31 a.m.

Maguire was doing an instrument check before take-off. He opened the engines to 1700 rpm, ensuring both propellers were humming and in tune. Next the magneto system and feathering device were tested. Everything was in order.

'Ready?'

Jack glanced quickly behind. Resting along the floor and strapped down with netting, was Spencer's canvas holdall and a row of duct-tape-covered cartons. Just seeing them again gave him a sense of relief.

'Yeah, I'm ready.'

8.32 a.m.

The VW Golf skidded to a halt outside the small airstrip building and de Mart jumped out. He immediately spotted the white Ford cargo van, just as the valet had described, same licence plates. He dragged open the front door and jumped inside. Ten seconds later he was out again.

'He's gone. There's nothing in there.'

The pursuing Jeep overshot the track and skewed on to scrub. Inside, Vick and Macky cursed violently. The South African now had a hand on the front bonnet of the Ford. It was warm. He looked around.

Where are you?

8.33 a.m.

'Control, this is November one two five Charlie Juliet.'

'Go ahead Charlie Juliet.'

'Take-off in two minutes.'

'Roger.'

8.34 a.m.

De Mart heard the Cessna's engines before he saw the plane. It was at the most distant point of the runway and blurred by heat haze. But he knew Jack Hunt was inside with the Zemdon files. And his future.

He vaulted into the VW Golf and grabbed his revolver. 'There, over there.'

Silvo pressed his foot to the board and burned rubber.

8.35 a.m.

Pat Maguire had seen both vehicles from the moment they'd started to speed along the outer dirt track and through the perimeter gates. The cloud they'd raised was impossible to miss. Out of the corner of one eye he followed their erratic progress closer. Whoever they are, and whatever they want, they're sure as hell not members of this air club, he decided. When he saw the VW swerve on to the far end of the runway, trailed closely by the Jeep, he made his own call.

'Control, this is November one two five Charlie Juliet. We have an illegal incursion.'

There was a moment's delay, then heavy static.

'Read you, November one two five Charlie Juliet. Suggest you abort take-off. Repeat, abort take-off.'

Jack listened to the exchanges with mounting horror. Through the windscreen he could see the vehicles as they crossed on to the flightpath. You fool, you absolute fool, they've tracked you down! That's why the Rick's valet sounded so agitated. They were waiting at the airport. They must know everything! His heart pounded so violently he felt his rib cage would explode. His mouth dried and his hands shook. He was trapped.

Maguire clutched the control column firmly, then slowly opened the throttle. The roar of engines filled the cockpit and the Cessna moved forward, gathering speed rapidly.

Crackle, static.

'Control, this is November one two five Charlie Juliet. Negative, we're going for take-off.'

8.36 a.m.

Silvo drove and de Mart tried positioning himself half upright in the passenger seat. He jammed his knees against the dash, then swung the .38 out in front, steadying it as best he could in both outstretched hands. He squeezed off two quick rounds.

8.37 a.m.

The Cessna's engines were firing at full strength, the plane now at maximum speed. The fuselage rocked, the wings bobbed from the vibration. Inside the cockpit Jack felt his body shudder. He glanced across and found Maguire white-faced, teeth exposed in a grimace of intense concentration. Over the headsets came more static and crackling.

'Pat, for Chrissake pull out!' The official flying vernacular had been abandoned, the controller now screaming. 'He's gonna hit you, pull out!'

The VW was no more than twenty feet ahead and Jack could

distinctly see Hend de Mart struggling to stay upright, both hands clasped in front of his body. Suddenly he noticed the glint of steel, and instinctively ducked.

The motor roars now peaked and Maguire pulled back steadily on the control column. 'Hold on!' he shouted against the deafening howl.

The Cessna lifted sharply, forcing Jack back into his seat. His stomach churned and he felt vomit in his throat. For a split second he shut his eyes, then the world suddenly turned blue.

The undercarriage missed de Mart's head by inches, and he tried to spin and shoot at the same time, succeeding only in toppling himself into the back seat.

Maguire continued his steep climb, not easing up on throttle or control column until his altimeter read one thousand feet. Then he gently levelled off and banked to the right, setting course for Las Vegas.

'Control, this is November one two five Charlie Juliet. We are now progressing as per flight plan. Suggest you dial nine-one-one and ask airport police to check out that hostile incursion.'

There was no reply for almost ten seconds, then: 'Read you, November one two five Charlie Juliet. Our visitors are already on their way out.'

Maguire banked the plane again so the left wing tip was forty-five degrees off central. Below, he could see tiny cars rushing along narrow roads, small houses and parched land. And to the west dust trails in the wake of two vehicles speeding away from the airstrip. He eased the Cessna level with the horizon and pointed the cone due east. The transponder was checked, the many gauges inspected, then he turned to Jack. There was no smile, no celebration of relief.

'For a heart doctor you sure keep strange company.'

35

Back in Chicago, Danny was playing on the street, no more than thirty yards from the sanctuary of the Bradley household. His mother walked slightly ahead, trying to pace herself, steadying each step by leaning on garden railings whenever she felt a wave of nausea or weakness. She couldn't eat, the queasiness overwhelming. With this lack of food and exercise and overwrought with worry, Beth was becoming more fragile by the hour, emotional and physical reserves at rock bottom. Her features were pinched from weight loss and there were dark shadows under both eyes. Her blonde tresses were dank and lifeless.

But her eight-year-old dark-haired son was still active and demanding, still unable to grasp why he had to be confined indoors if there was half a chance to run wild outside. When his nagging became unbearable Beth relented, and the two circled the block, Danny sprinting, diving, bobbing and weaving around. He made up games in his head where he was in the US World Cup soccer team, a goal down with only minutes to go. He was the star striker, but carrying a leg injury. The ball was passed from deep in defence and he trapped it despite the pain. He shimmied past two imaginary midfielders then dribbled round the central defender. There was now only the goalkeeper to beat (a fire hydrant) and in his mind he looked up to see the stadium clock move ominously closer to full time. Just seconds before the final whistle he unleashed a powerful drive that hit the inside of the goalpost, shattering the wood and causing consternation on the pitch. Did the ball cross the line or not? All eyes turned to a giant screen where a slow-motion action replay was being shown. A goal! A cheer engulfed the ground as the boy hero's team-mates ran to congratulate him. Danny's amazing run and shot had saved the day. There was no doubt he'd grab another in extra time.

So he continued, often losing the ball deliberately to prolong the distraction.

The road was wet, and there was a strong and biting wind which lowered air temperatures to the mid-fifties, a far cry from that summer's high of one hundred and five. People huddled in long coats and thick jackets, hurrying to whatever destination might provide relief from the unpleasant conditions. No one but hardy joggers or the slightly insane walked for fun that day.

The multi-coloured wood and brick bungalows along Chicago Lawn were now deserted for the most part, parents long gone to work, children at kindergarten or school. The cars that usually clung to the sidewalks had thinned out and only a black transit van with a plumbing company logo and sliding side panels remained. There was no driver at the wheel.

Above, grey clouds heavy with rain scudded across the skies and snap showers fell erratically. Sudden updraughts of cold air collected fallen leaves and mixed them with litter to produce mini tornadoes.

'Danny, you keep close.'

Beth was struggling to keep up with her lively son, his energy far outstripping her reserves. Her vigilance was ebbing as fast as her strength, and no longer was each strange face or vehicle treated with nervous suspicion. She was just too exhausted to care. Jack will be home soon. Please God, let this nightmare end.

'Come on, mum. You gotta keep up!'

Thump! The ball skidded off a fence and on to the road. Danny sprinted after it. Despite the cold and damp he was dressed lightly in blue shirt and shorts with sports sneakers.

Behind, his mother fought to maintain the pace. She too was ill prepared for the inclement weather in denim jeans and borrowed blue checked shirt under borrowed light woollen sweater. Helen had even offered a pair of walking boots which Beth gratefully accepted, even though they were a bit tight and pinched her toes.

Up in the air this time, the ball bounced on to the bonnet of the black transit van with the logo and sliding side panels.

'Hey kid, d'ye know where the Jenks live?'

Two hours and forty minutes after the eventful take-off from

Monterey, Pat Maguire guided his Cessna 340 towards Clark County McCarran International Airport in Las Vegas. He dipped and banked until he had the north–south runway 1L/19R in view. The sidelights were on and the central lines guided him to a flawless touchdown. Air traffic control directed him to a light aircraft apron where a bowser, a small truck carrying Avgas, waited.

In the heat of that desert town, Jack Hunt sweated and worried. En route he'd decided Zemdon had trailed him to Monterey hoping to grab him and the files. That they'd failed suggested they didn't know of Rita Callard's whereabouts. But they wouldn't have been in the dark about Beth and Danny. While Maguire checked his instruments and fuel lines, Jack sprinted to a small private rest facility, located a call booth and began feeding coins into it.

There was no reply from the house in Chicago Lawn. He let the tones ring out five separate times before abandoning the number. Then Herb Weinberg's secretary informed him that the attorney had left the office for the day, but that she would try and pass on his message.

Finally, he tried Rita Callard.

'Where are you now, son? I'm missing you already.'

The relief at hearing her voice was overwhelming, and Jack shouted out with joy.

'Las Vegas.'

'Keep away from the slot machines. Only time I visited I lost two hundred dollars pulling those damned mechanical arms.'

She soon lost her sense of humour when the incident at the airfield was related.

'Get out of the house for a few days until I sort this out,' Jack warned. 'Stay with friends or book yourself into a hotel. Just disappear.'

Twenty minutes later the Cessna was roaring down the runway, fuel tanks replenished, oil levels topped up. Into the harshest sun Jack had ever seen, the nose eased gently into the air. They gathered speed and banked north-east towards the Rocky Mountains.

'Did you hear the one about the Irish kamikaze pilot?'

Maguire was trying to distract his passenger. Between Monterey and Las Vegas Jack had outlined the background to the drama of which the pilot now suddenly found himself a part. As they both finally agreed, until the cargo was securely offloaded there was nothing more that could usefully be done to resolve the situation.

'Guy flew five successful missions.'

Jack tried to laugh, but the humour was wasted on him. Where are my wife and son?

36

They cruised at one hundred and fifty knots with a tail wind edging the actual pace closer to one hundred and seventy knots ground speed. Maguire kept the Cessna at a minimum safety altitude of two thousand feet above land and used VFR, visual flight rules. This allowed him to fly at low levels and also made it difficult for a hostile tracking of the flight. It also meant his flying skills were of paramount importance, with no cockpit computer to guide him. For navigation a GPS, global positioning system, checked their course.

Jack tried to pass the time listening on his headset to the crackling exchanges between crews of other planes, but he found the confined space too tight and claustrophobic, body movements restricted to the most basic. At one stage he squeezed through the gap between the front seats to double-check his cargo, but the fuselage offered little extra room in which to stretch. He had to crawl half hunched to the rear, tighten the security netting where it had dragged through seat mountings, then edge back to the front. He cooled himself in the refreshing draught of the air-conditioning system, relief indeed after the stifling heat of the turnaround at Las Vegas.

As the Cessna approached the Rockies, distant cloudbanks closed in and Maguire climbed higher to overshoot the range and gain better visibility. Through breaks in the white blanket beneath both could see snow-capped peaks and ice valleys. For Jack it was the only diversion for his tortured mind.

They touched down at Denver with less than thirty minutes' reserve in the fuel tanks. The airport buzzed with activity, large Boeing 747s, Airbus A300s and A320s and DC-10s crowding the passenger aprons. United, Virgin, American, Continental and Northwest – most of the big players in aviation had craft coming in and out of the city. Buses jammed with travellers scurried from terminal to plane while maintenance utilities, refuelling trucks and security vans beavered along side channels.

Maguire taxied the Cessna between two Learjets and a Hawker Siddeley executive, and shortly afterwards they were met by a courtesy coach, a blast of ice-cold air catching Jack's breath as he sprinted across the tarmac. The Colorado skies were totally overcast, the airport runways and connecting roads wet from a previous rainstorm. Tee-shirt weather was far behind as strong northerly winds dropped temperatures to below fifty degrees, and he was soon back in sweater, thick denims and double socks inside boots.

'There's a problem with the oxygen pressure.'

Maguire had completed a post-flight instrument inspection. He too had changed to warmer clothes using a spare kit stored underneath his cockpit seat: thermal vest under high-neck woollen, extra leggings.

'I've been able to grab an engineer to look at it but we could be here for an hour or more 'til it's sorted.' His usual wide grin had disappeared, dark eyes now full of concern. His partner's anguish was obvious. 'Why don't you break for a coffee while I try and speed things along?'

Jack gladly took up the offer and made his way straight to a call box. No reply again from Chicago Lawn, despite ten attempts this time. *Where are you?* Herb Weinberg's secretary had still not located her boss, but messages were being left all over the city. Then she put even more pressure on Jack. The lawyer acting for the vendors of the house in Wilmette had been on the telephone every hour. Was Jack going to close the sale and take possession of the property? His clients wanted an answer soon. Like the rest of the city, they knew all about the doctor's personal crisis, and while they wished a speedy resolution it wasn't their problem. Was he in or out?

'We're in,' Jack snapped angrily. 'The funds will be transferred on Monday.' He was bluffing, but felt he had to say something positive and forceful. 'You tell him I want the keys by end of business.'

He slammed down the phone then dialled Rita Callard's number. No reply. That offered some relief. He was just about to quit when a thought crossed his mind. Four minutes and one operator enquiry later his right index finger jabbed again at the number tabs.

'Sheraton Chicago Hotel and Towers, this is Melanie speaking.' Saccharine-sweet voice. 'How can I help you?'

Jack took a deep breath. 'Hi, can I speak to any of the senior Zemdon representatives?'

'One moment please.'

He was put through to a girl called Laura.

'Hi, my name is' – he glanced around and spotted a hotel sign – 'Stakis, Dr George Stakis. I was hoping to make tonight's big launch but could be delayed. I'm a medical correspondent with *American Health* and I'm planning to feature your product in our next issue.'

American Health was a coast-to-coast magazine offering readers the latest in medical breakthroughs. It was a mass-market publication courted heavily by pharmaceutical and nutritional companies who knew a single-page news spread was guaranteed to lift the profile of any product or firm. A call from one of its staff was more often than not given top priority.

'Maybe I could help you?' Laura offered. She had a hint of a Southern drawl. 'Nearly all our personnel are busy right now. But I can fax any documentation you need.'

Jack quickly decided the girl was near the bottom of the company food chain. 'No, I've got all that,' he lied, cupping his hand around the mouthpiece as a tannoy announced another airline departure. 'How about background details on management. Directors, board members, that kind of material.'

He glanced around. The terminus was crowded with passengers queuing at check-in desks, struggling with suitcases or sitting bored to death on rows of plastic seats. Nearby bins spilled over with discarded food and drink containers. Banks of TV monitors were being inspected for flight details and groups huddled together, muttering and complaining about this and that. Broadcasts about delayed arrivals, late departures and cancellations added to the general hubbub. Apart from a bunch of kids chasing one another through the snaking lines, nobody looked particularly happy.

'I could try and locate our North American director,' suggested Laura. She sounded anxious to help.

'Nah, I'll bet they're caught up pulling the programme together.'

'Sure are. And we've got the main man from Zurich breathing down our necks.'

'Oh, which one's that?' The way Jack phrased his question made it sound like he knew everyone at the Swiss HQ on a first-name basis.

'Dr Gert Crozer,' said Laura. 'He's been patrolling the corr—'

The line went dead; Jack had dropped the handset. Crozer. The very name made his blood run cold. Most of the documentation he'd sifted through the previous evening related to repeated communications from one man, Helmut Crozer. There could be no coincidence of surnames. He'd read each letter, usually hand-written on expensive paper with gold embossed letterhead. Gert Crozer, Helmut Crozer. Two men, possibly a generation or so apart, working for the same Swiss pharmaceutical. No fluke, they had to be related, maybe father and son.

And knowing what he did about Helmut Crozer, Jack now had a deep sense of foreboding.

He stared out from the main terminus viewing point as yet another storm unleashed its misery. Umbrellas and wet gear were being pressed into use by outside handling staff, truck splashes dodged. Come on Pat, let's get going.

In Chicago, Gert Crozer watched rivulets of rain track down the picture window of his penthouse apartment. Earlier, he'd pulled on an overcoat, then opened the glass door leading on to the small outside veranda and stepped into the cold. There was a break in the hail showers that had circled the city all day, and he spent the best part of an hour enjoying the river traffic, mostly covered-over tour boats offering views of the waterside architecture. He negotiated his way down a narrow metal stairway that connected to street level and inspected the inauguration auditorium from a distance. Finally satisfied, he returned along the same unsteady and circuitous route, invigorated by the frenzy of his corporation's activity.

He sat in his leather high-back behind the U-shaped mahogany desk, deep in thought. His chin rested on outstretched fingers; he rolled the chair slightly from side to side. He considered again the information that had just come to hand. We have Dr Hunt's wife and child but we do not have Dr Hunt. He has eluded me once more, and that is very distressing. He studied a transcript of the most recent telephone exchange between Jack and Beth.

I've got it Beth . . . everything, it's all here . . . these documents are dynamite . . . when this gets out it will rock the medical establishment . . . I know what's been going on all these months . . . Carlotta Drunker didn't die in a hit-and-run accident, she was murdered . . . and I know who did it.

Do you, Dr Hunt? How unfortunate. For you.

Hend de Mart made it back to Chicago by 5.30 that afternoon, local time. And he was in a violent rage. Jack Hunt had outwitted him, made him look like a fool in front of his own hand-picked crew, then damned near wiped him out with the undercarriage of a Cessna 340.

In Monterey the South African had relished the thought of finally finishing off the doctor, even fantasising about how he'd complete the act, working out the words he'd use. 'It's time to go. You put up a good fight. Even worried me a few times. But this time's for real.' Then he would drive the Ford Cargo towards some stout tree, Jack tied up in the passenger side. About twenty yards before collision a boulder would be forced against the accelerator and de Mart would bail out. Crash. Max speed impact. The boulder would be removed and the unconscious body shifted to the driver's seat. The cocaine would be dropped under the front dash, the petrol tank ignited. Then run like hell.

Except the plan had collapsed. Hunt was very much alive and somewhere in the skies with Zemdon's dark secrets. He was an even more dangerous threat than before. But de Mart now had his wife and boy. Which was of greater importance to the Irishman, keeping his family alive or being a hero? It wouldn't make any difference to the South African. He was already on his way to the cheap Southside motel where Beth and Danny were being held. He was going to resolve all unfinished business.

37

Chicago's Merrill C. Meigs Field Airport was located slightly out on Lake Michigan and immediately south of the Adler Planetarium in Grant Park. It had a single visual runway, 18/36, which was four thousand feet long and one hundred and fifty wide. All the airfield surfaces were paved in asphalt with transition taxiways to three terminal ramps. There were four helicopter pads on the south ramp and accommodation for one hundred parked aircraft using cable tie-downs.

At 6.15 on the evening of Friday, 8 October, Pat Maguire's Cessna approached the strip from the north-west. The domed roof of the planetarium was below and to the left of his visual field but partially obscured by heavy cloud. To his right the city lights glittered in the early dusk, and skyscraper roof beacons beamed their warning to passing aircraft. In front of that stretched the final destination and touchdown. From two thousand feet up the wet track looked very inviting after the long and eventful journey from Monterey. The aircraft oxygen pressure problem detected at Denver had taken less than an hour to resolve. Then there was a last pit-stop at Des Moines in Iowa, Elliott Aviation organising a quick turnaround. Tanks filled, account paid, engines started again inside twenty minutes. But the weather deteriorated all the way east, slowing progress.

Between city shoreline and airfield was an artificially created harbour where rows of pleasure boats rocked on the choppy waves. There were strong gusts coming off the lake, cutting up the waters and making the 340 jolt and sway. Maguire held the control column firmly, communicating regularly with his controller on the ground. Hail squalls had disrupted landings at

Chicago's entire airport system that day.

'Control, this is November one two five Charlie Juliet, request clearance to land.'

There was a crackling pause, then air traffic responded. 'Roger, November one two five Charlie Juliet, you are clear into the circuit, please use Shore Visual Approach. No local traffic, wind is westerly at twenty gusting thirty knots. Advise turning final.'

The Cessna was first edged due south to overshoot the runway, then banked to the left and left again until eventually it lined up with runway 36. Heavy rain from the waterside reduced visibility and the windscreen wipers fought to keep the cockpit view clear. Ahead, Jack could just about make out high-intensity lighting along the asphalt track.

'Control, this is November one two five Charlie Juliet, turning final.'

More crackling over the headsets. 'Roger, November one two five Charlie Juliet. You are clear to land, visibility good, winds gusting now to forty knots.'

The Cessna suddenly bucked and swayed, then yawed violently to the left. Jack felt himself thrown sideways and only the seatbelt prevented him crashing against the cockpit instruments. He looked across and found Maguire staring into the downpour ahead, hands gripping the control column so tightly it whitened his knuckles.

'Control, this is November one two five Charlie Juliet, I'm experiencing severe crosswinds and will overshoot.'

The roar of the engines suddenly increased and the Cessna started climbing again. To his left Jack could see the lit-up downtown highrises drift out of view, then they were out over the lake and circling. Now only the lights from an occasional cruise ship far below could be identified.

'November one two five Charlie Juliet, you are clear for a right-hand circuit and advise back on final.'

'Roger, Charlie Juliet will advise.'

Through a deep cloudbank Jack tried to make out any landmarks below. Sears Tower in the far distance, twin spires of the Hancock Observatory closer to the waterline. Tall residential condominiums near Oak Street beach. Navy Pier inching out into the lake. The Cessna banked again, slowly and gently the right wing tip moving to forty-five degrees off central, and once again the lights from runway 36 appeared ahead.

'Control, this is November one two five Charlie Juliet, turning final.'

There was static over the headphones, then a staccato response. 'Roger, November one two five Charlie Juliet, you are clear to land. Wind westerly fifteen gusting twenty.'

Out of the grey the city highrises reappeared, the small sailboats between shore and airstrip bobbing on the waters. The 340 tilted slightly as winds buffeted, but this time there were no sudden gusts. Maguire teased at the engine power and control column, steadying and correcting deviations. The nose was slightly up in the air, but the Cessna was moving in quickly on the lights. The windscreen wipers swished furiously to clear the driving rain, and suddenly the white line markings came through. Jack gripped the edges of his leather seat, expecting more turbulence, but the roar of the engines dampened and the small plane bumped and rose, then bumped again. Maguire gently applied the brakes and closed the throttle as the Cessna settled on the asphalt track.

'Control, this is November one two five Charlie Juliet. We have landed.'

6.48 p.m.

'I want to speak with Dr Gert Crozer.'

A damp and bedraggled Jack Hunt stood at a triangle of call boxes inside the Meigs Field terminal building. In the near distance doors rattled from wind squall while hail drilling at roof vents made conversation difficult. Sprinkles of raindrops hung off his hair and clothes, heavy-duty boots at least protecting his feet. Beside him were the ten precious containers of sealed cargo, laid out in a wet and soggy row. Ground staff had organised the unloading and transfer in a downpour for fifty dollars, dropping the doctor's remaining reserves perilously close to down and out.

'I'm sorry sir, Dr Crozer is unavailable to take calls.' Yet another female Zemdon small fry handling outside queries.

'He'll speak to me.' Direct and confrontational.

‘I don’t think so, sir. We have strict orders not to interrupt. He’s heavily involved in tonight’s product launch.’ The voice was straight out of elocution school via Brooklyn.

‘Say Dr Jack Hunt wants to talk with him immediately.’

‘I really can’t, I have a lis—’

Jack shouted. ‘Just do it, for Christ’s sake!’

He glanced around, noticing the disapproving stares of fellow travellers and terminal staff. There were four men in aerodrome uniform shifting scaffolding, then a clutch of passengers in raincoats and oil jackets slumped idly along a row of seating. Bags and umbrellas lay where they’d been dropped.

‘I’ll try, Dr Hunt, but I’m making no promises.’

He was put on hold and spent three minutes listening to in-house advertisements for the Sheraton Chicago Hotel and Towers.

‘Hi, can I help you?’

A male voice cut through, bursting with attitude. As in ‘don’t fuck me about buddy, I’m a busy man’. Jack’s anger deepened. The go-betweens only fired him up more, and he was already fit to kill. One call earlier he’d finally contacted Helen Bradley in Chicago Lawn. By her reckoning Beth and Danny hadn’t been in the house for most of the afternoon. And Jack knew how careful Beth was and how few chances she took in life, especially with her boy. He knew instinctively they’d been taken. And he knew who had them.

‘I want to speak with Dr Gert Crozer.’

‘And you are?’

‘Dr Jack Hunt.’

There was a rustling of pages; attitude man was presumably inspecting his paperwork. High in the building a low-pitched wail started as cold air chased along the rafters. Somewhere, a door slammed.

‘You’re not on our guest list, Dr Hunt. And I’m afraid Dr Crozer cannot take calls. Would you care to leave a message?’

Jack fought to hold his temper. While those within immediate earshot seemed engrossed in studying the ground or reading books and newspapers, he sensed they were listening to the exchanges. A doctor shooting his mouth off would sure relieve any boredom.

‘I want to be put through to Dr Crozer’ – the words were now spat with venom – 'and I want it to happen now. I can tell *you* he wants to speak with *me*. All you have to do is ask.'

The man with attitude put him on hold. More in-house advertisements.

'You want to talk to Dr Crozer, I believe.' A new deep-toned New York accent, in stark contrast to the previous representative. 'Perhaps I could deal with your query?'

'Dr Crozer is the only one I wish to speak with.'

'I apologise, but I wasn't given your name, just advised a doctor was on the line.'

Through gritted teeth. 'My name is Dr Jack Hunt.'

There was a thirty-second silence, then, 'Jack Hunt?'

'Yes.'

'Hold it right there.'

Hotel advertisements again.

'Dr Hunt, how are you? My name is Gert Crozer.' The voice was distinctly mid-European, with an ill-disguised tone of conquest. 'I've been waiting for your call.'

'Where are my wife and boy?'

The nearby hangers-on now dropped all pretence of disinterest and openly listened, exchanging surprised glances.

'They are safe and in our care. I felt they should be taken into . . . how is it phrased? Protective custody, yes that's the term. After the many dangers they've come through I thought it wiser if they were with me.'

'So help me, Crozer, if you harm them in any way I'll rip your throat out.' Jack was shouting and the listeners grouped together, openly discussing the conversation. It was getting better by the minute.

'Your anger is misdirected. Keep your threats for another day and another person.' Crozer's accent was now even more pronounced and triumphant. 'You have in your possession documents from this firm, and I want them returned.'

'I'll fucking kill you, Crozer. You hear me? Fucking kill you.'

'I hear, but I am not impressed. Bring the files to me and you can take your wife and son home.'

'I'm going to ring the police right away. I'll have you surrounded in five minutes.'

'That wouldn't be wise, Dr Hunt. If you involve any outsiders your family will meet with a terrible accident. And that would be a tragedy, wouldn't it?'

Jack slammed down the phone, cursing loudly. He punched the call box, then aimed a wild kick at his cardboard cargo.

He turned to find ten sets of eyes drilling into him.

38 *6.55 p.m.*

The Southside motel was a cheap and dingy two-storey flat-roofed complex in a district noted for its drug dealers. All doors faced to the front and there was a small side parking lot fringed with trees that helped soften the general air of neglect. The exterior paint was a flaking yellow while inside the walls were grimy white. The reception was minimalist in the extreme, with no welcoming furniture and a constant pall of tobacco haze over the front desk. Cigarette-burned and threadbare carpeting, dim lighting. The establishment was run by a paunchy, chain-smoking white Chicagoan of indeterminate years and standards who cared little about what went on inside his rooms. The punters got what they paid for, and more often than not the punters were local thugs splitting the profits from their latest crack sales, one eye on the porno channel, the other on the notes.

In unit forty-two on the second level Hend de Mart was dragging a writhing and wriggling Danny into the bathroom. It was a small, white-tiled cubicle with toilet, basin and shower. Mould and dirt along the edges, cracked mirror, one of two ceiling lights gone. The shower head dripped and the water taps looked as if they hadn't been cleaned for days. There was a strong smell of stale urine. De Mart fought to peg the boy down with blue nylon rope wrapped around and behind the toilet bowl, but Danny continued to buck and twist, trying desperately to cry out. All his efforts were in vain, and soon his mouth was blocked with wide tape, wrists and ankles bound together. The only noises were his laboured breathing as he struggled for air.

Danny's eyes burned with rage and the left side of his face showed bruising from earlier blows. His shirt and shorts were now stained with blood and tears. He looked up to find the most hate-filled eyes he'd ever seen, and instinctively believed he would never see his ninth birthday. More frantic and futile struggles.

The South African had already forced Beth into the bedroom, and she was now guarded by his local crew, the heavies in overalls who'd snatched her at Chicago Lawn. Two pillows were jammed round her head to shield her ears against the boy's grunts. She'd been too weak to offer much resistance, but Danny had given de Mart a battle, even managing to swing out a foot and catch him in the crotch. How that had infuriated him.

'See this, kid?' He drew his .38 revolver from under the belt holding up his denims. 'It's for you.'

Danny's eyes darted wildly and he tried desperately to swing out both tied feet. De Mart stepped back nimbly, grinning. He towered over the boy, white roll-neck and black windcheater covering his bulky frame. His hands were like blocks of granite compared to the puny fists of his prisoner. Making sure Danny could see every move, de Mart loaded the handgun, then admired its steel beneath the single light.

'I sent a kid called Luther after you once.' He was now hunched down, face only inches away. 'Do you remember him? A bit taller than you, head shaved, rings along both ears. One stud in the nose, as far as I recall. Real little thug. Gave you quite a hiding, didn't he?'

The Afrikaans accent made the words sound even more evil, and Danny went suddenly limp. His body slumped, his limbs ceased squirming. He looked straight at his tormentor.

De Mart cocked the .38. 'But Luther's gone to his grave now.' Danny just stared straight ahead. 'Yeah, he got taken out, just the way you're gonna go now. And I did it myself, even though I kind of liked him.'

The barrel was pressed against the skin above Danny's right ear, then twisted. Hairs got caught in the movement, and the boy winced and tried to turn away, but a large hand forced him back.

'That's nothing to what's coming.' De Mart was grinning again, Adam's apple bobbing up and down. 'And when it's all over and I'm washing your blood off these tiles, make sure to tell Luther I said hello.'

Outside, a phone started ringing.

7.45 p.m.

They met Jack at street level. There were two heavies, one tall and black in tight-fitting leathers and navy beret forced tightly down on his head, the other a small tracksuited white man. Even in the darkness both wore shades, fists bunched together at the front. The last torrential rain shower had blown through, leaving only dampness in the air and wide rippling puddles on the front concourse.

'Get the boxes,' snapped the black man.

His companion wheeled forward a porter's trolley and started stacking. It soon became obvious one carrier wouldn't be enough, and there was a five-minute delay while another was located. All the while no one spoke, eyes shifting from Jack to the crates to any immediate movement. Nervous hands hovered over a bulge under the front of the black man's jacket.

Nearby, the usual hotel traffic circulated, people scanning the skies for signs of another hail shower, flagging cabs or dragging on trenchcoats and hoisting umbrellas, weighing up whether or not it was wise to walk. Cars were being loaded or unloaded, their doors slamming and engines running.

Jack leaned against a wall, desperately trying to anticipate the moves ahead.

The black henchman led the way along dimly lit service corridors and through swing doors that had seen plenty of wear. Finally they stopped at a staff elevator and he glanced around, satisfying himself that no one was likely to interfere.

'Take the boxes ahead. I'll wait here with him.'

'You fucking will not,' growled Jack as he moved between his cargo and the inside of the lift. 'I go where they go.'

In the end the ten containers were squeezed into a corner while Jack and the short guy sped upwards. For the two-minute ride the confined space almost suffocated him: soggy cardboard, damp clothes, strained breathing and hostile stares. Jack fell out when they reached the next floor, gasping for fresh air.

'Wait here.' His minder was waving a handgun with authority.

They stood in silence until a tinkling further down the corridor announced the arrival of the guest elevator and the leather-clad thug emerged.

'Okay, shift it, friend.'

The cargo was loaded, and ten yards further along they stopped outside another lift shaft. This entrance surround was in gold leaf, the closed doors a shiny silver. There was a brass plaque to one side announcing that this was the penthouse suite. Beneath it was a security key slot. The black hoodlum slipped a hand into his jacket and produced a silencer. Slowly and deliberately, and without speaking, he screwed it on to the end of his handgun. All the time his eyes stared menacingly at Jack. Then he waved the extended barrel threateningly.

'When these lift doors open you step in and go straight to the right-hand corner and face the back.'

The white accomplice produced a plastic keycard and slid it into the groove. There was an immediate swish as the internal mechanisms shifted. Seconds later Jack was grabbed from behind and thrown roughly on to a thick-pile terracotta carpet. He stood up slowly, eyes adjusting to the light.

7.48 p.m.

The main auditorium of the Sheraton Chicago Hotel and Towers was filled with the contented buzz of people enjoying themselves at no personal expense. Two thousand and twenty-five guests plus one hundred and thirty-eight company representatives sat around two hundred circular tables in the vast hall. Promotional stands with the Cyclint logo were strategically sited throughout for maximum exposure. The banquet room was lavishly decorated with flowers and bunting in the corporation colours of red and green. White linen tablecloths, top-grade cutlery and crystal. Glasses of wine were tinkled, food relished, cigars puffed. The invitees had been called to dine at seven o'clock sharp, and there were few stragglers. The bill of fare included Beluga caviar, fresh salmon, roast beef and a special heart-shaped strawberry tartlet. There was a choice of premier wines to be followed by liqueurs and brandy. The menu was also heart-shaped, gold-embossed and inscribed with the wonderdrug CYCN emblem. It was meant to be a collector's item.

On the top table, senior Zemdon executives from all over North America – including, in pride of place, Stan Danker – relaxed. This was the culmination of a long and difficult campaign for them.

Dodgy marketing, controversial advertising, intense pressure from Zurich to get it just right in every territory. Many of them believed it the most expensive and daring product launch in which they'd ever been involved. Now, as they looked around the extravagant venue with its high-profile diners and imminent satellite links to other centres, they felt well satisfied with their efforts. Cyclint was going to be a winner, a pharmaceutical blockbuster. They puffed on their cigars and helped themselves to more wine, silently relieved that soon it would all be over.

Alongside this group sat a beaming Harry Chan dressed in smart tuxedo with bow tie carrying the Cyclint logo. Martin Shreeve was in among a bunch of similar soaks at a table on the fringes. As he struggled to get enough food and wine into him his four chins bobbled and he had to wipe at them repeatedly to keep his stubble clean.

Close to the VIP set was a small man in suit, shirt and tie with a nametag pinned on his left lapel. He had grey curly hair, bushy eyebrows and wore glasses which kept slipping down his bulbous nose. He had chubby hands, yet his face showed signs of recent weight loss. He was subdued, rarely listening in on the gossip that flowed on either side. He'd maybe smile when someone looked across, but still he seemed out of place and uneasy. A difficult man to engage in conversation.

The ID proclaimed him to be Dr Nat Parker, a Carter Heart Unit cardiologist. In fact it was Herb Weinberg, and tucked inside his jacket was a fax that had earlier clicked through from Pacific Grove, California.

While those around gorged themselves, Herb only nibbled at his food and drank iced water, keeping a close eye on his watch. At 7.50 he forced a smile and excused himself from the table.

39 *7.50 p.m.*

The first thing Jack saw was Beth and Danny. They were tied up, side by side, in separate chairs, blue nylon rope wrapped around ankles and body and wooden seat struts. Standing behind them was a tall, rugged and muscular man in denim jeans and white roll-neck under a black windcheater. In his right hand he carried a revolver, now pressed against Danny's neck. Jack recognised him immediately as the Zemdon gorilla who'd stalked Helen's office and invaded his apartment.

Beth looked distraught and haggard; tears streaming down her face, dank tresses tangled and straggling. Her denim jeans were soaked at the ankles, woollen sweater creased and streaked. Her body shook with each sob and her eyes pleaded with her husband. *Help.* Danny's clothes had dried blood caked to the front, and there was a distinct and wide pink line stretching across his mouth from ear to ear, with a torn edge of duct tape still clinging to the skin on one side. The boy's face was ridged with grime and fear, his dark hair bedraggled. Despite the restraints, his limbs shook violently and his teeth chattered.

'Dad, oh dad,' he moaned pitifully. 'Please help me.'

But Jack made no move, desperately trying to assess the situation.

That part of the penthouse he could see immediately was maybe fifteen hundred square feet with two doors leading off to other rooms. Green walls, recessed halogen spots on half power. Thick-pile carpet, oil-colour paintings under wall-mounted lighting. Lounge chairs and wooden stools at a cocktail bar counter. At the far end was a floor-to-ceiling picture window and glass door leading outside. In front of that a wide-tube television, sound off but images flickering. Then a large mahogany desk cluttered with paperwork, telephone and fax machines. At the other side, and inspecting him from the comfort of a leather seat, was a grey-haired man in a charcoal pin-striped suit, white shirt and tie.

'Good evening, Dr Hunt.' The clipped mid-European accent froze Jack. Gert Crozer. 'You have arrived just in time to enjoy our product launch.'

Crozer pressed a remote control and a different view came on to the screen, a close-up of a group in tuxedos and high-fashion dresses gathered at a circular table, heads craned in one direction. Some sipped on glasses of wine, others were still eating. A few were engaged in conversation. There was a backdrop of giant promotional props with the Cyclint name and logo boldly displayed. Red and green Zemdon colours everywhere.

Crozer said, 'You could have been an important part of tonight's celebrations.' Then he sighed, as if a sad thought had suddenly crossed his mind. 'But it is not to be, and that is your mistake.'

The tracksuit-clad heavy wheeled over a trolley full of cardboard boxes and unloaded them one by one at the desk. Crozer followed his every move.

'I see you have rescued our files.'

Three minutes later the second carrier was discharged.

'Block the lift shaft,' de Mart ordered, and an armchair was jammed into the elevator opening. 'Now lock the door and stay outside until I call you.' The only other entrance into the suite was shut and bolted.

Jack felt his rib cage heave from the thumping of his heartbeat. Crozer and the tall Zemdon thug were staring straight at him. We're trapped, and there's no way out. He struggled to stay in control. Keep them talking, keep thinking. Don't give them any space.

'Let my wife and son go, they know nothing about this.'

Crozer leaned forward slightly in his chair. 'You have been a burden to me, Dr Hunt, a great burden. I have followed your progress for almost two years and I concede you are a clever man, perhaps too clever for your own good.' He looked over at his hostages. 'And for your family.'

Beth's eyes darted wildly to her husband, and Jack sensed her thinking the same thoughts. Crozer's been tracking me for two years. This goes back much further than Chicago.

'You have even made life difficult for my employee.'

Hend de Mart grinned, then forced the gun barrel against Danny's flesh, making him squeal with pain. Jack started forward, but a warning glare stopped him dead. 'Move again and I'll blow his head off.'

Jack's hands were shaking from a mixture of suppressed rage and fear. 'I can expose you, Crozer. I know everything about you and your corrupt corporation. I've lodged papers with my lawyer. If you harm us he's been instructed to release them to the police.'

Crozer seemed unimpressed. 'You're a broken man, Dr Hunt. Totally discredited in a profession where reputation is everything.' He swung from side to side in his chair. 'Who would believe a word from your mouth now? Your ranting has already been greeted with derision. Any further utterances and you'd be considered mentally unstable.' He rested his chin on outstretched fingers. 'In many ways, if I killed you I'd be doing you a favour.'

Jack struggled to think of another angle, anything for survival, but Crozer twisted the knife deeper. 'If you disappear, Mr de Mart has arranged a scheme to convince the authorities you have taken your family and fled the country in disgrace. He has the means to create e-mail messages from you stating all this. Tickets in each of your names have been booked out of Chicago through New York and on to Ireland. We even have your passports.'

Jack's heart sank and he tried not to let it show. Defeat and death stared him in the face.

Crozer got up and stood behind his desk. 'You have no friends in this city and no one remotely worried about whether you live or die. Who do you think is going to care when you disappear? The police? Your work colleagues? To them you're a drug addict, and such trash vanish without trace all the time. No one will grieve your loss.'

'This has been planned for some time, hasn't it?' Jack was now so angry his restraint was slipping. 'And I thought it was a plot to get me out of the way so you could carry this drug launch through.'

Crozer sat back in his chair, eyes now fixed on Jack. 'Much longer than you think. The bullets that hit Professor Lewins were meant for you.'

Jack sucked in air like he was having a heart attack. Beth began screaming hysterically and de Mart slapped her across the face.

Jack started forward but suddenly found the barrel of a gun pointing straight at him.

'Give me one more excuse and I'll finish the job.'

Crozer now gestured towards the packages on the floor. 'On their own these documents mean nothing. But in the hands of an intelligent and shrewd medical investigator they become most damaging to my company. That is why you are such a threat. And that is why I had to get rid of Drunker and others you may not know about. As I must get rid of you.'

On the TV monitor the view had switched to Harry Chan standing at a podium. With the volume off it was impossible to work out what was being said, but Chan's hands were waving in the air and he was obviously shouting towards one corner of the auditorium. A close-up of the cardiologist's face showed his hair and forehead soaked in sweat, his features agitated and disturbed.

Crozer jumped to his feet, jabbing at the remote control. Now Chan's nervous and tinny voice came across clearly. 'I repeat, I know nothing of the details you're talking about.' From the floor of the hall came angry shouts.

Jack groaned inwardly. He didn't need this as well.

Hend de Mart glanced briefly at the scene, careful not to allow himself to be distracted, then back at Crozer.

'Open the boxes,' Crozer snapped. 'I want to make sure he's brought everything.' He prowled up and down behind the desk, his nails tapping on its polished surface. One eye was fixed on the monitor, the other on the containers.

Hend de Mart shuffled sideways, his handgun trained on Jack all the time. He kicked at one of the crates, but Rita Callard's tape held fast and only the soggy corners offered any immediate opening. The South African began tearing.

With the momentary distraction, Jack slowly put one foot in front of the other and inched towards Beth. She stared at him, wide-eyed and petrified with fear.

'Move again,' de Mart drawled, pointing the .38 at Danny, 'and I'll kill him.' Jack stood rock-still. 'Then,' the South African growled, ripping more wet cardboard away, 'I'll make sure your wife never sees daylight again.'

On to the TV flashed images of uproar. Many people had turned away from the lectern and were straining to look towards one area of the vast banqueting hall, some standing on chairs. Shouts and flustered replies penetrated. Crozer pulled the screen closer.

'What is going on?'

Jack was now desperate to divert attention from the television. As soon as Crozer realised his firm's secrets were being broadcast live around the world he'd order him and his family gunned down immediately.

'You're right, I am useless,' Jack shouted. 'I'm bankrupt, unemployable and totally compromised. There's no way I could damage your organisation.'

'Shut up,' Crozer snapped. He was engrossed in the scenes of chaos unfolding on the TV.

Jack calculated he was about ten fast paces from his enemy.

'Let us go and we'll disappear from your sight for ever.'

He stole one step furtively, heart racing, forehead beading with sweat. Now nine away. He caught Danny's terrified gaze and warned him to be silent with a flick of his eyes. It was then that he focused on the glass door and the flood-lit veranda outside.

More cardboard ripped, but the tape held firm, making the South African struggle.

'What is happening?'

Crozer had the sound up, hopping fretfully from one foot to the other like a madman in a confined cell. The penthouse filled with the clamour of enraged voices. The camera now panned and focused on Herb Weinberg. He was shouting and struggling to hold on to a microphone while uniformed Zemdon employees wrestled with him.

'Who is that? Who is that man?'

Jack played his final card. 'I kept one box back. It's got the most important papers.' He was begging for his family's lives. 'If you don't harm us I'll take you to them. With those your company is safe for ever.'

But Crozer wasn't listening. He was in front of the screen fiddling desperately with a zoom control.

De Mart cursed angrily. One hand alone would not free the box, so he set down his handgun to grasp both edges.

Jack had now stealthily moved forward another three paces. He was six steps from the thug with the large Adam's apple and his medical training came into sharp focus as he struggled to remember anatomy lectures. That swelling is right over his windpipe. Can I do it?

'For God's sake, let us go!' Jack was roaring to be heard above the din, clenching his fists to stop them shaking, edging ever closer.

The sound of ripping confirmed that the container had finally given way. Its contents burst forth.

'Fuck it, fuck it!' Astonished swearing. 'It's only junk. There's nothing here but old newspaper!'

De Mart looked up sharply at Crozer, and in that split second they knew they'd been duped. Crozer hurled himself across the table, baying like a caged animal. But the confusion was all Jack needed. As Hend de Mart scrambled for his handgun he swung a heavy-duty boot in a half circle, smashing it into the bulging throat. He felt soft tissue collapse and heard a winded grunt as the South African's air supply was cut off. A shot rang out, the .38 discharging in his twisting grasp. With a crack the plate-glass viewing window shattered, showering the carpet with shards.

Beth was screaming, Danny howling with terror. They fought to free themselves, Danny succeeding only in toppling his chair, and he lay on the ground, feet wriggling, head banging against the carpet.

Fists now hammered at the main door into the penthouse.

For a moment Gert Crozer just stared at Jack, face contorted with stunned rage. Then a closed fist swung in the air, catching Jack on the side of the head. He was momentarily stunned and buckled at the knees. Crozer started for the penthouse door, but Jack reached out in time to grab an ankle and the older man spun in the air and crashed heavily to the floor. He lay there motionless, barely breathing.

'Get us out of here!' screeched Beth. She rocked backwards and forwards in her chair trying to loosen the ties. Danny was sobbing uncontrollably.

Jack vaulted the U-shaped desk and kicked at the broken glass. He found a shard, sharp-edged and narrow enough to grasp.

Hend de Mart was buckled at the waist, tongue protruding, eyes bulging. Both hands clawed at his constricted windpipe, nails digging into flesh as he fought for air. Each breath was a laboured gasp. The .38 revolver lay where it had been dropped.

Jack tore off his sweater and wrapped the end of a sleeve around the piece of broken glass. First he started slicing at Danny's rope.

The thumping at the door was like drums beating in the background, and Jack looked over anxiously. The lock was holding.

Suddenly a shot rang out and wood splintered. Then another, two holes now punched through beside the bolt.

The blue nylon came apart in strands, Danny's hysterical cries only delaying Jack's fevered efforts. The disarray and clamour broadcast from the television added to the chaos. Finally the boy was free, and he rolled along the carpet, flexing and unflexing limbs with relief. He stared horror-struck as he watched his father start to slice again. Beth's twisting had only entwined her more tightly. Then the glass shard snapped in two.

Three more bullets split wood around the lock. Outside kicks were being aimed, the door shuddering with each blow. Suddenly the elevator mechanisms repeatedly jerked the silver sliding panels against the armchair. It was being pushed forward with each forced contact.

Hend de Mart had dragged himself half upright, the .38 again in his right hand. Saliva bubbled at his lips as he tried to focus. Shadowy images came into his vision: a man hunched over a chair, a boy jumping up and down beside him and shouting.

With the largest piece of the twice-broken glass Jack sawed and hacked at Beth's restraints. The rope split again in strips, each strand tearing painfully slowly. Blood dripped from his fingers where a jagged edge had cut through to skin.

A salvo of bullets then peppered the main door, dull thuds as the splintering wood was hit from another side. There was a sudden loud snap and the frame started to buckle. A black fist punched through, then fingers groped for the inside lock.

The blood-stained rope around Beth split with one final effort and Jack hauled her free from the chair. They stumbled and staggered, reaching out for their son. At that moment the elevator doors slammed closed, pushing the armchair away. The shaft mechanisms hummed the lift downwards.

It was Danny who saw de Mart taking aim. The big man was clinging to the desk for support, face disfigured and blue from lack of oxygen. He rested one elbow on the hard surface and cradled the handgun in both hands. Still gulping for air, he closed one eye and squinted along the barrel.

The boy screamed, and instinctively Jack twisted his wife around to shield her. Danny was already curled up in a ball. Four shots rang out in rapid succession.

The entrance separated from its hinges just as the elevator

reached the penthouse level again. Seconds later the two other Zemdon thugs were in the room. They found Hend de Mart in front of the U-shaped mahogany table, his lifeless eyes staring into space. Gert Crozer was half upright and clutching his rib cage, moaning in pain. Trickles of blood oozed from his nose. The picture window was shattered, shards and splinters strewn everywhere, and through the gap strong winds buffeted curtains and scattered paperwork while driving rain showered the carpeting and furniture. Two chairs were tipped over, frayed blue nylon rope trailing.

And blood-stained palm prints smeared the glass door leading to the veranda.

40

Storms buffeted Chicago for the next three days as strong northerly winds pushed whirling cloudbanks across the Midwest. There were flash floods in the plains and road closures in lowland areas. Emergency crews had to airlift one family trapped in a basin farmhouse, their cattle standing defiantly on nearby hillocks.

By Tuesday, 12 October, the gales had blown through. Now the streets were wet rather than flooded, wide puddles in every dip of tarmac and traffic splash forcing pedestrians deeper into the pavements. Service utilities struggled to clear debris carried in by the gusts and litter was bunched in tight corners or scattered along alleyways. There was a weak sun in the sky with occasional grey clouds drifting in from the west, but they didn't look troublesome. Temperatures hadn't lifted much, and Tom Skilling, chief meteorologist at WGN-TV, was forecasting a high of around fifty-eight. Winter was approaching; soon the snows would come.

At news-stands people dropped their coins and grabbed a copy of the *Tribune* or *Sun-Times*, or whatever else was available. As they hurried to work they glanced at the front page and scanned the headlines. Many stopped in their tracks or huddled in doorways to read the complete report.

In a house owned by Herb Weinberg's older and wealthier brother in the northern suburb of Lake Forest, the Hunt family was also reading the stories dominating international media attention. The property was in a wooded development in the old part of the neighbourhood, a large red-brick home with tall, narrow roofs and leaded windows. Four dogs prowled the gardens, howling at any incursion. Herb had arranged for two separate rooms to be taken over by his clients, but in the end they squeezed into one king-sized bed and slept each night holding one another like there was no tomorrow.

Much of the previous seventy-two hours had been taken up with state police and FBI interviews. Questions, questions, questions. Statements, statements, statements. Then all over again as more senior investigators became involved.

TV, radio and newsprint journalists had besieged Weinberg & Associates looking for exclusives. Chequebooks were waved and big money was on the table for the complete account as recalled by Jack Hunt. Already reporters were following up leads in California and Zurich.

At a crowded briefing the night before the FBI had issued an international arrest warrant for Gert Crozer. But it all became too much for Beth and she'd been taken into hiding and attended to by an obstetrician. The advice was rest, and lots of it. Herb had intervened, and a truce was declared. There would be no more press conferences until the family was ready.

That Tuesday morning, four days after their nightmare, Danny was curled up in bed between his mum and dad, eyes still glazed from all he'd been through. Beth was feeling better but was still weak. At least the pregnancy sickness was easing, the nausea no longer as aggressive. She'd even managed to eat a little breakfast and take some fluids. Some colour and strength was returning to her features, but psychologically she was severely traumatised. The ordeal at the hands of her tormentors and the final hair's-breadth escape had left her jittery and uneasy. She clung to her son and husband, trying to block out images of what might have happened. What if the big South African had not missed with his final wild shots? What if there hadn't been a door to the outside veranda or a metal staircase to street level? What if they hadn't fled before the other scumbags broke through? The what ifs tormented her.

Lying beside her and propped up on three pillows, Jack stared at his heavily bandaged hands. It had taken two hours of careful suturing and dressing at the Cook County ER to join together the cut and ripped flesh around his fingers. 'You'll be okay,' the surgeon had reassured him. 'There ares no tendon or blood vessel injuries. It'll all heal in time.' He eased himself down in the bed for comfort and punched at a pillow to make a nook for his head.

'Go to the beginning again,' he said.

Beth lifted the newspaper and started reading again the article headlined ORPHANS USED IN SECRET MEDICAL EXPERIMENTS:

> Zemdon Pharmaceuticals, one of the largest chemical corporations in the world, conducted secret and illegal medical experiments on children in US orphanages throughout the 1950s and early 1960s. There is documented evidence of the involvement of 362 youngsters then residing in religious institutions in two states, California and Colorado.
>
> We can exclusively reveal:
>
> - Eighty-four died as a direct result of these trials.
> - Doctors involved in the procedures falsified death certificates.
> - Nursing and religious staffs were bribed to stay silent.
> - The experiments were based on similar investigations conducted in Nazi concentration camps.

There was more on the other pages. Zemdon Pharmaceuticals had recruited a number of Second World War prison-camp doctors and used information gathered during forced experiments to explore links between genetics and disease. Then, in the late 1940s, senior company staff made frequent journeys to the US looking for suitable institutions in which to conduct their own medical trials. They made contact with Brothers in Christ, a religious order entrusted with running seven orphanages throughout North America. Two of their larger asylums were in remote and impoverished areas and chronically short of money. The Swiss company offered both direct and secret financial packages in return for full access to the children and their personal records.

The first experiments began in 1949. Three hundred and sixty-two boys and girls below the age of ten years were deliberately inoculated with different bacteria. Following the exact procedures developed in internment compounds, the researchers sought to establish how infection affected body organs and blood vessels. They also wanted to understand why some became more ill than others, why some died. Was it genetically predetermined or just bad luck? Why did a small proportion show severe damage to their blood vessels and not others? Genetics, or misfortune?

There were no ethical guidelines for such research and large sums of money changed hands to ensure total secrecy. But the results were disastrous, with deaths and severe illnesses requiring hospitalisation (more bribes paid to keep those staff on side). Many survivors were still in poor health when the homes closed in the early 1960s but with no records maintained after that there was no way of knowing the long-term outcome of these shocking trials.

'Whose idea was it to switch the boxes?' Beth asked after she'd read the full report.

They were still curled up under the duvet, Danny in the middle clutching his mother's hand tightly. On the other side his father inspected yet another ceiling as he tried to recall each detail. So much had happened.

'Herb's. After I spoke to him from Pacific Grove he called the shots. Told me to make a summary of all findings and fax them to his home. Then suggested I make up two cargoes: a bogus load to travel with me, the other directed to him by UPS. I got Rita Callard to type out the details on her rickety old Remington, then she arranged the freight company and faxed four pages through after I'd left. As soon as Herb got his shipment he went straight to the *Tribune*, then tracked down Nat Parker, and the two of them planned the confrontation at the Cyclint launch.'

His wife looked at him and shook her head in amazement. Then she tapped the front page of the newspaper. 'But what has all this to do with you? Why were they following you for so long?'

Jack dragged another pillow under his head for comfort. His hair stuck up, his stubble was grizzly. 'I've studied the link between infection and early heart disease for years. I didn't realise it, but each new ground I broke led me towards research papers owned by Zemdon supporting the data for Cyclint. And ultimately their knowledge was based on these illegal experiments. If I reached the point where I could challenge the corporation for the ultimate proof of their new compound's background it would open the trail to the orphanages. Carlotta had already gone that far.'

Danny snuggled into his mother, and for the first in a very long time began to suck his thumb for comfort.

Jack continued. 'But she had located the archives and all original documentation. Once she had the evidence, with our combined research data she became too dangerous. They made the mistake of killing her before tracing where she'd stored it.'

Beth laid the *Tribune* down and leaned back on the pillows. She was feeling drained and wanted more rest. There was so much she hadn't fully grasped yet, but she still wasn't strong enough to push for answers. That would have to wait for another day. Right now she had her son and unborn child to consider. And her marriage. Danny would never be the same again, nor would she. They had been dragged to the abyss together and had survived. But they would be emotionally scarred for ever.

She burrowed further beneath the sheets and stretched out an arm. Danny laid his head in the crook of her elbow and she cuddled him. She turned and found Jack gazing across.

'Hi. Just wanted to tell you how much I love you.'

Beth sighed and tried to smile back. 'I'd like to learn how to love you too again.' Then she closed her eyes and willed darkness to swamp her senses. 'Right now, though, I just want to sleep.'

Jack watched her limbs jerk, her body twitch. Soon a relaxed breathing took over and he felt her troubled mind was released. Danny's mouth was gaping, his eyes closed. They're still with me. But for how long? Beth has already warned me she's not raising her children in the US. Do I want to stay here without them? Is that an existence worth considering? Jack knew his faith in the system and society was crushed, his sense of fair play lost in a mire of falsified lab tests, back-stabbing colleagues and murderous corporations. The police were all over them now. But when they'd needed them they'd been no help, dismissing their complaints and looking at them as if they were crackpots. He rolled on to his side. And that bastard Crozer was right about one thing: I don't have any real friends. I've spent my adult life poring over textbooks, squinting down microscopes. There's dedication, and there's obsession. He now realised what type of a man his wife had been putting up with all these years. High principles and ambition – what are they without the human touch, without the softening of reality? Nothing.

He looked again at Beth and Danny, then edged closer to them. I spent their escape money. I took the last dollar they had for my own selfish motives. He wrapped his arms around his wife and son and held them gently.

It's your call now, Beth.

Postscript

The FBI tracked Gert Crozer from Chicago to Toronto. He'd fled the US in a private jet. Subsequently they learned he'd transferred to London by commercial flight using a false passport. The trail ran cold in England. There is still an international warrant for his arrest.

Cyclint was shunned by prescribing doctors worldwide, making it the most expensive product crash in pharmaceutical history. Six weeks after the Chicago débâcle, Zemdon Pharmaceuticals sued for bankruptcy.

Stan Danker distanced himself from the dirty tricks campaign, protesting his innocence loudly and emphatically. He hired a top New York attorney and threatened to sue anyone making unfounded allegations. He now works at senior management level with another chemical multinational.

Harry Chan and Martin Shreeve resigned their positions, and Steve Downes left the Carter soon afterwards. The administrator claimed ill health as the reason for his early retirement and denied all charges of collusion in Jack Hunt's downfall.

Caleb Rossi never surfaced. Subsequent inquiries by the FBI suggested he'd been killed and his body dumped.

Weinberg & Associates attacked the Carter Hospital with a fury. Herb didn't have any fresh evidence, but he had anger, and he wanted bigger offices in a more prestigious location. The hospital board stonewalled, desperate to frustrate a crippling law suit. After three weeks' bargaining all that Jack was offered was one month's severance pay. He took it, consoling himself with the lucrative media deals for his story.

Nat Parker eventually became the new Chief of Cardiology at the Heart Unit.

Jack Hunt left Chicago on 28 November. He, Beth and Danny flew to Amsterdam, then on to Singapore, where they rested in the sun for three days. Twelve hours later they arrived in Sydney.

Jack now works at his old hospital, Parramatta General in the North Shore district. A new position had been created at the facility, Director of Medical Research, and Jack was the first appointee. He doesn't earn as much as he would have done had he stayed and slogged it out in Chicago but that doesn't bother him. The restlessness has gone, the drive curbed somewhat.

Beth Hunt was badly damaged by her experiences. But she came out fighting, and after quite a few rocky weeks of readjustment her marriage stabilised.

For Danny, the dramatic upheavals proved difficult and he required psychological counselling. He's surfacing out of his personal hell and is starting to kick a ball again, though not with the same boyish enthusiasm as before.

Beth really only calmed down and put the past behind her when she saw the first ultrasound images of the child she was carrying. It was a girl. A new life without any emotional baggage. To her it was almost like wiping the slate clean. A fresh beginning in a safer world.